More praise for Margaret Truman and her Capital Crimes mysteries

Also by Margaret Truman

FIRST LADIES
BESS W. TRUMAN
SOUVENIR
WOMEN OF COURAGE
HARRY S TRUMAN
LETTERS FROM FATHER: THE TRUMAN FAMILY'S
 PERSONAL CORRESPONDENCES
WHERE THE BUCK STOPS
WHITE HOUSE PETS

IN THE CAPITAL CRIMES SERIES
MURDER AT THE WATERGATE
MURDER IN THE HOUSE
MURDER AT THE NATIONAL GALLERY
MURDER ON THE POTOMAC
MURDER AT THE PENTAGON
MURDER IN THE SMITHSONIAN
MURDER AT THE NATIONAL CATHEDRAL
MURDER AT THE KENNEDY CENTER
MURDER IN THE CIA
MURDER IN GEORGETOWN
MURDER AT THE FBI
MURDER ON EMBASSY ROW
MURDER IN THE SUPREME COURT
MURDER IN THE WHITE HOUSE
MURDER ON CAPITOL HILL
MURDER AT THE LIBRARY OF CONGRESS
MURDER IN FOGGY BOTTOM

MURDER
IN
HAVANA

MARGARET
TRUMAN

FAWCETT BOOKS • NEW YORK

For my son, William Wallace Daniel, who was killed tragically at the age of forty-one

This book contains an excerpt from the forthcoming edition of *Murder at Ford's Theatre* by Margaret Truman. This excerpt has been set for this edition only and may not reflect the final content of the forthcoming edition.

A Fawcett Book
Published by The Ballantine Publishing Group
Copyright © 2001 by Margaret Truman
Excerpt from *Murder at Ford's Theatre* by Margaret Truman copyright © 2002 by Margaret Truman

All rights reserved under International and Pan-American Copyright Conventions. Published in the United States by The Ballantine Publishing Group, a division of Random House, Inc., New York, and simultaneously in Canada by Random House of Canada Limited, Toronto.

Fawcett is a registered trademark and the Fawcett colophon is a trademark of Random House, Inc.

www.ballantinebooks.com

ISBN 0-449-00668-9

This edition published by arrangement with Random House, Inc.

Manufactured in the United States of America

First Fawcett Books Edition: October 2002

10 9 8 7 6 5 4 3 2 1

How did you feel when you killed him?"

"How did I *feel*?"

"Yes."

"I—I didn't especially feel anything."

"Nothing? Not a moment of doubt? Of guilt?"

"No."

"Did you know him?"

"I knew *of* him."

"Meaning?"

"I knew who he was. I knew *what* he was."

"What was his reaction?"

A bemused raised eyebrow preceded, "He didn't have time to react. It's best that way."

"I see." He added to notes he'd been making. "How do you feel now?"

"Fine."

"Trouble sleeping? Nightmares?"

"Of course not."

The sound of a window air conditioner gently bridged the lull.

"You'll be gone for two months," he said.

"I know."

"Where will you go?" he asked, knowing it was a question that would not be answered. His was not a need-to-know.

Silence.

He made another note and closed the black leather portfolio resting on his lap. "Thank you for coming in."

The opening of the door allowed the sound of office equipment to enter the room. The door's closing abruptly restored the hush. He opened the portfolio and wrote CLEARED, which reflected his psychiatric judgment, closed it, went to a safe in a corner of the austere room, opened it, placed the folio inside, closed the door, spun the wheel, checked the door, then returned to his desk and dialed a number.

"I'm leaving," he said. "See you at home."

In a moment, he would exit the building and get behind the wheel of his Cherokee. If the traffic cooperated, he'd be in time to catch the final few innings of the game.

Chapter 1

New Mexico

Max Pauling left the private airport outside Albuquerque, New Mexico, at six in the morning and flew to a small airstrip in Arizona, near the town of Maverick, on the southern rim of the White Mountains. There, his single-engine, fixed-landing-gear Cessna 182S was loaded with God knows what. The dozen pea-green canvas bags were wrapped with duct tape, low-tech security. He didn't care what was in them. He'd made the point when signing on to transport materials from Maverick that drugs were off-limits, and was assured none were involved. None, that is, if you could believe what they said, "they" being agents of his former employer, who had a reputation for many things. Consistent truth telling was not one of them.

The man who'd pulled the green pickup truck to the side of the aircraft and unloaded the bags from its bed had small lumps all over his face, some obscure disease, Pauling figured, that made him look strange but probably wouldn't kill him, though it didn't do much for Max's morale. Other than that, the man seemed average in all ways.

"Nice plane," he said.

"I like it," Pauling said.

He'd bought it used two years ago from a Maryland flying club after returning from a seven-year stint in

Moscow, ostensibly as a member of the Trade and Commerce Division of the U.S. embassy, but more accurately on assignment for the CIA. There were more up-to-date single-engine aircraft, and more expensive ones, but this one suited Pauling just fine. He'd loaded it with modern avionics; he was instrument rated, which allowed him to fly in IFR (Instrument Flight Rules) conditions, while private pilots rated VFR (Visual Flight Rules) sat on the ground until they could see where they were going. His recently earned multiengine rating turned out to be more frustrating than pleasing. He was now licensed to pilot twin-engine aircraft, but couldn't afford one. Whoever said life was fair?

The man with the knobby face told Pauling to have a nice trip and drove off, his pickup kicking up yellow dust from the dirt strip. Pauling looked around. There wasn't another person to be seen. Because Maverick did not have a refueling facility, he'd topped off the tanks back in Albuquerque. He knew there would be fuel at his next stop because he'd taken on some there on previous trips.

He did a walk-around of the plane to check for obvious external problems, climbed into the left seat, strapped the clipboard holding the aeronautical chart to the top of his right thigh, started the engine, checked gauges, ran over the preflight checklist, taxied to the downwind end of the runway, pushed down on the brakes with his toes, advanced the throttle to the firewall, waited a moment for the engine to reach maximum power, released the brakes, and bounced down the strip until pulling back on the yoke and lifting off. The lifeless, unrelieved sameness of Maverick, Arizona, fell away below.

He glanced at some of the green bags piled on the right-hand seat; the bulk of the cargo had been loaded in the back. He looked on the floor to make sure his survival kit was there, felt beneath the instrument panel where an Austrian Glock nine-millimeter semiautomatic pistol was securely strapped, and pulled a slip of paper from one of twenty-six pockets in the tan photojournalist's vest he wore, the many pockets his answer to a woman's purse. Written on the paper were instructions for crossing the Mexican border. Pauling had committed them to memory, but like any good pilot he depended upon lists to back up his brain. He was to be at precisely three thousand feet when he crossed the border two miles east of Douglas, Arizona, then bank hard right and pass over the Mexican town of Agua Prieta, set a course of 210 degrees, and fly to an airstrip just east of Hermosillo, where the mountains give way to greener lowlands.

It was important, he knew, to follow the flight plan with precision. Stray from it and you'd attract the attention of DEA pilots assigned to intercept private aircraft flying in and out of Mexico on the assumption that what they were carrying would ultimately go up somebody's nose or into someone's arm. The prescribed route he would fly this day had been worked out with the Drug Enforcement Administration, the CIA, and Mexican authorities. It was hands-off provided he stayed within the approved corridor.

He crossed the border at three thousand, turned right, and set the autopilot to a 210-degree heading. Heated thermals from the ground caused the small plane to bounce around, as expected on a sunny day in late July. The weather forecast for this area of Mexico, and for Albuquerque, was fair, no need to rush to get back home once he'd set down. He settled back and had an urge for a cigarette. Although he'd kicked the habit ten years ago, the yearning still surfaced at predictable times—at theater intermissions, over the first cup of coffee in the morning, and when cruising on autopilot. His thoughts drifted to

Jessica, the love of his life, or at least his second life. Together, they had moved to New Mexico from moonstruck Washington, D.C., more than a year ago after giving up government jobs and heading west in search of sanity, which they found in Albuquerque. He spent most of his days teaching well-heeled men and women to fly. Jessica went to work as an administrator at a local hospital during the week, and spent most weekends indulging her life's passion, bird watching, which held little interest for Max unless the bird was metal and powered by a Lycoming humming at 2,700 rpms.

Pauling began his descent into the airfield hacked out of a heavily forested area outside Hermosillo, set up for a straight-in approach, cleared trees at the east end of the strip by fifty feet, and touched down smoothly. The ruts in the ground weren't shallow, however, and he cursed as he fought to keep the Cessna straight.

The camp at Hermosillo for training anti-Castro Cuban-Americans had been established within the past year with the cooperation of Mexican authorities after media scrutiny of Florida training facilities had become nettlesome. In the time-honored spirit of all things military, the camp's leaders eschewed naming the new facility something simple like Camp Number Four, or The Mexican Camp, favoring a more mysterious and symbolic designation. It was known as Timba Candente— "Timba," the frenetic new Cuban dance music, "Candente," Spanish for red-hot. Red-hot Cuban music for red-hot anti-Castro Cuban-Americans in mottled green-and-brown uniforms, with AK-47s, mortars, grenades, and World War II flamethrowers.

A man, large in all ways—head, chest, shoulders, and arms—stood at the wing tip as Pauling scrambled down. He wore military-issue camouflage pants with ties at the ankles and ankle-high combat boots. His enormous naked torso and bald head were sunburned to leather; sweat so uniformly covered him that it was as though someone had applied it with care. He was older than he looked; a bush of white chest hair gave that away.

"Look who's here," he said in a gravelly voice that matched his physique. "Federal Express."

"Hello, Morry," Pauling said, pulling out sunglasses he'd put in a pocket after landing.

Morry grabbed a wing tip of the Cessna and moved it up and down. "What's the matter, Pauling, they don't pay you enough to buy a real plane?"

"You ever hear of austerity budgets? I fly cheap. But good. What's for lunch?"

Morry, whose last name was Popovich, barked at two young Cubans in fatigues a dozen feet away, "Unload the plane. *Pronto!*" To Pauling: "These Cubans are itching to go into Cuba and fight a war, but everything's mañana. All they think about is their *novias* back home."

"What's a *novia*?"

"Hey, Pauling, if you're going to help the dump-Castro movement, learn the language. *Novia.* Girlfriend. Sweetheart."

They walked toward a low-slung building with a tin roof and unpainted plywood walls. Two through-the-wall air conditioners powered by generators hummed like large insects. Dozens of green military tents were lined up at the western edge of the camp. Adjacent was an obstacle course dominated by a wooden tower, the top of which disappeared into palm trees.

"You convert yet?" Pauling asked as they stopped in front of a small altar of sorts, off to the side of the entrance to the headquarters building. It was a *boveda*, spirit altar of the Cuban religion Santeria. Candles, glasses of water, and small photos of deceased family members of recruits at the facility were neatly arranged on a white sheet.

Popovich snorted. "Hell, no." He patted his holstered side arm. "This is all the religion I need."

They turned as a dozen young Hispanic men in combat fatigues and carrying rifles jogged by, prodded by the shouting of a Caucasian instructor who kept step with them.

"You're wasting your time, Morry," Pauling said casually as the unit passed.

"What'a you mean?"

"Training this ragtag army to topple Castro. It's going to happen without one shot fired."

"Is that so? What the hell do you know?"

"Read the papers, Morry," Pauling said as they entered the building. "We're gradually softening up on Castro: the administration, Congress, public sentiment. Elián helped. McDonald's and Motel 8 will do the invading."

"Bull! The only way that scumbag dictator will leave is when we take him out in a box."

Pauling smiled. "And not good for your career, huh, if the diplomats and pols win the war?"

"Bull! If it isn't Castro, it'll be some other tinhorn troublemaker. Chávez in Venezuela. Gadhafi. What are you doing, Pauling, going soft?"

"No, I'm not getting soft, Morry. Getting a little older, maybe, and wiser. What's for lunch?"

A young Cuban in uniform tossed a snappy salute at Popovich and Pauling as they ducked through the door. The interior consisted of one large room with scarred dining tables and folding chairs. Two weary ceiling fans were hung low enough to decapitate tall people, slowly. At one end, more tables created a separation between the main room and a kitchen. On one wall was a large blowup of a map of Cuba; multicolored pins clustered in various locations indicated, Pauling assumed, potential targets, although he'd never bothered to ask. He'd had his fill of pins in maps when he was with the CIA and had functioned in a similar capacity with the State Department. War games. Pins. He'd outgrown them.

They went to the kitchen area where three Hispanics stirred something in large vats and turned innominate meat on a grill. A crude, handwritten sign was strung across the wall: *"Este año con valentia, disciplina y honor Cuba sera libre del tirano Castro."* It hadn't been there the last time. "What's it say?" Pauling asked.

"Cuba will be free from Castro's tyranny this year. Discipline, honor, the usual bull."

"You don't sound convinced," said Pauling.

"What's for lunch? You want to know?" Popovich said, ignoring the comment. "Cuban *cuisine*. They call it *El Campo*. Country food or something. Beans. Black beans and red beans. Rice. And always *el plátano grande*—plantains. They fry 'em, steam 'em, squash 'em, boil 'em. No American food, Pauling, because your friends back in Langley think it would be bad for morale if officers eat different from the troops."

"They're right," Pauling said with a smile. "And by the way, I don't have friends back at Langley."

"Oh, I forgot. You *retired*." Popovich had a way of making a point by stressing certain words, stretching out their pronunciation, and smirking as he did so. "You keep in touch with Hoctor?"

"No." Tom Hoctor had been Pauling's "handler" for much of his career as an operative for the CIA.

"How's retired life?" Popovich asked.

"Nice."

"Except you're playing messenger for your ex-employer. That doesn't sound like retirement to me."

"Just dabbling," Pauling said. "I like to fly."

They turned at the sound of the screen door slamming.

"Vic?" Pauling said to the tall, trim man who'd entered.

"Hello, Max," Vic Gosling said, crossing the room and shaking Pauling's hand. "I heard you were coming in today." His accent indicated he was British, or American-pretentious.

"I thought you were out of the loop," Pauling said.

"I am, most of the time. Is Morry here playing the perfect host?"

"I been teaching him Spanish," the burly Popovich said. "He's a slow learner." With that he left the building.

"Staying for lunch?" Gosling asked as he pulled out a chair and folded himself into it. He wore faded blue jeans, a white T-shirt not marred by any designer name, and white sneakers. He noted Pauling's blue air force jumpsuit with the faded outline where wings had once been sewn. "You look like you're still flying combat, Max," he said.

Pauling shrugged. Although combat missions were a thing of his past, he liked dressing like a military jet jockey even though the planes he flew these days were more often piloted by doctors in Bermuda shorts or women in flowered dresses, bored with garden clubs. He joined Gosling at the table.

"I have to admit, Vic, I'm surprised to see you here. What's it been since you left the agency, three years, four?"

"Three and a half this month."

"Writing another book?"

Gosling laughed and shook his head. "I'm a one-book author, Max. One was enough. I took a lot of heat over it."

Pauling didn't display his skepticism.

Gosling's book, published three years ago, was titled *Inside View: The CIA Exposed*. Gosling, British-born and -educated, had worked for MI-6 before marrying an American woman and moving to the States, where the CIA recruited him. He and Pauling had worked a few cases together, initially in Central America, later in Moscow.

When the book was published, Gosling allegedly resigned from the CIA under a cloud for having violated the agency's own version of the Mafia's *omertà*—code of silence. He went on radio and TV talk shows billed as the man who'd dared to let the sun shine into the intelligence organization, naming names, exposing some of its dirty tricks and tactics, and, in general, acting the traitor.

But Pauling came to the conclusion after reading Gosling's book, and hearing and seeing him on radio and TV, that he was telling tales out of school but not out of line, stories that in the end made the agency look good. Nothing he said was truly damaging to the agency or its mission; it all sounded far more revealing than it actually was. Which meant, in Pauling's experience, that the book and Gosling's subsequent promotional media appearances were, in fact, a typical CIA operation. They had one of their own out in the public soaking up information from people who believed they were talking with a fellow critic of the agency, opening up, spilling secrets or rumors they would never have divulged to anyone else. Typical agency machinations. During his career, Pauling had worked with intelligence Joes from other countries and never trusted a single one, any more than he trusted buildings painted yellow (explain that, Dr. Freud). America's intelligence community might screw up big-time, but at least its agents were—well, American. As for yellow buildings: his negative feelings about them were as irrational as his hatred of green cars and restaurants displaying color photos of food in their windows. If those were his only phobias, he could live with them, and had done so quite comfortably.

"I'm surprised to see you back in the saddle again," Gosling said after a lunch of pork, red beans, and steamed plantains that went down surprisingly well.

"I wouldn't put it that way. The deal is good. The money is good. What about you? You're—?"

"Doing what *you're* doing," Gosling said. "Yes, the money is bloody good. Just part-time. Like you."

Drop the Brit stuff, Pauling thought. *You've lived here long enough not to say "bloody" anymore.*

"I didn't know you were the military instructor type," Max said.

"I'm not. They needed a communications setup here."

When Gosling was with the agency, if he'd ever left, he was known as an electronics expert, someone who could install taps under adverse conditions and troubleshoot phones—cellular or otherwise—telephone answering machines, radios, TV sets that were really radios of a different ilk, computers, and any other electrical device. Pauling remembered an incident in Moscow when a tap Gosling had installed became disabled. He fixed it with foil from a pack of cigarettes; that they were Russian cigarettes only added to Gosling's pleasure.

"What are you doing when you're not setting up communications systems?" Pauling asked.

"Working for Cell-One."

"The private security outfit?"

"Yeah. Mr. Victor Gosling, private eye. You want to talk about good money? Their clients *throw* money at them. Fortune 500 types. Titans of industry and all that."

"Sounds like a sweet deal."

"That it is." Gosling cleaned the remaining gravy on the plate with a swipe of his bread. "You know, Max," he said, "it just occurs to me that we have a project you might be interested in."

Pauling responded with a raised eyebrow.

"Are you, ah—are you up for other assignments?"

"That depends."

"It's private sector. The client has deep pockets."

"What does it involve?"

Gosling looked around. The room was empty except for the Cuban-American cooks. "Why don't we get together another time and talk about it?"

"Fine."

"Are you flying back to Albuquerque today?"

"Yes."

"Would you like a passenger?"

"Sure. Where are you living these days?"

"California. San Jose. Splitting my time between there and London. Cell-One's headquarters is there, in the old country. Offices in California and New York, too. I was supposed to be picked up tomorrow but I'm finished here. I can catch a commercial flight home out of Albuquerque."

"Happy to have you," Pauling said.

And don't think I buy into the happenstance of meeting you here. A Mexican training base for Cuban-American freedom fighters is no place for coincidence, Pauling thought. *Like the song says, you can take the man out of the spook business, but you can't take the spook out of the man.*

That the comparison probably applied to him as well, he preferred not to contemplate.

Chapter 2

New Mexico

M—I'll be late. Staff meeting at the hospital. Cooked chicken breast in fridge, fresh tomatoes on counter, mozzarella in fridge. Should be home by 10.

Love, Me

"The domestication of Max Pauling," Gosling said, reading the note Jessica had left for Max on the kitchen table.

Pauling laughed politely. "Didn't one of our distinguished predecessors say that gentlemen don't read each other's mail? Domestication? It agrees with me. Drink?"

"Please."

"Sorry, but we don't stock Pimms at this bar."

"Good God, Max, just because I was born a Brit doesn't mean I only drink Pimms Cups. I don't enjoy bangers and mash either. Since I'm in the States, I'll have bourbon, if you have it. Neat."

"Just joking. I have bourbon. Wouldn't want to seem un-American."

Pauling poured a single-barrel whiskey over ice for Gosling, made himself a vodka and tonic. They sat at the table; Gosling offered a toast: "To friends."

Pauling nodded and they touched glasses.

"So, Max, tell me all about your idyllic life these days."

"Not much to tell. I'd had enough of the game. So had

Jess. She was with State, the Russian section. We packed it in and headed out here. Jess is working for a local hospital. I teach flying and—"

"And run munitions into Mexico in your spare time."

"Not in little green bags. As I said, the money's good. Jess isn't thrilled I'm doing it. She's afraid I'll get the itch and sign on again—long-term."

Gosling sipped, then said, "You already have the itch, Max. It never leaves you. You know that. The question is whether you'll decide to scratch it, or live with it."

"I can live with it. Sorry she's not here. I'll whip something up for dinner. You want to check flights to California?" he asked, pointing to a wall phone.

Pauling took two steaks from the freezer and went to the deck to fire up the grill.

Gosling joined him in a few moments. "Nothing tonight," he said.

"You'll stay over. I'd like you to meet Jessica anyway."

"It will be my pleasure."

They ate on the deck and continued drinking throughout dinner. It was a cool and clear night, the western sky a stunning black scrim for the light show provided by thousands of stars.

"So," Pauling said, "tell me about this project."

Gosling grimaced as he looked into the kitchen through the sliding glass doors.

Pauling smiled. "Want me to sweep the place, Vic?"

"Always a good idea," Gosling replied.

Pauling shook his head and said, "Doing what we did really screws us up, doesn't it? A tap in every phone or microwave oven, some guy in a raincoat behind every tree. Jesus! What a way to live."

"Have you?"

"Have I what?"

"Swept the place. Just because you're ex-agency

doesn't mean that they—or others—are no longer interested in you."

Pauling slapped the glass-topped table. "No, I haven't swept the place, Vic, and I don't intend to."

"I don't blame you," said Gosling, the bourbon thickening his speech just a little. "Tell you what. Let's forget the project for tonight. I'll get to meet your ladylove, sleep soundly on your couch, and tomorrow you can take me for a spin in your plane. I've always wanted to learn how to fly."

Translation: *We'll talk when we're up in the air.*

Pauling was putting glasses in the dishwasher when Jessica came through the door. She saw Gosling sitting on the deck and asked the question of Max without speaking.

"Vic Gosling," Max said, kissing her on the cheek. "A buddy from the agency days."

"The book?" she said.

"Yeah, that's him."

Gosling came into the kitchen and Max introduced them.

"I see why Max looks so happy," Gosling said.

"Does he?" Jessica asked. "Look happy?" She laughed, put her arm around Max's waist, looked into his face, and said, "That's what I like, a happy man around the house."

She didn't add that he hadn't seemed especially happy lately until he started making the runs into Mexico—which didn't make *her* especially happy. She knew men like Max Pauling only too well. She'd once been married to an FBI agent who spent most of his time working undercover, and who seemed truly happy only when he was in danger, using his wits to survive. Max was cut from that same damnable cloth, she knew, happiest when infil-

trating Russian intelligence cells or turning some Central
American bureaucrat into an informer. Danger acted like
an Adrenalin I.V., providing a burst of satisfaction, even
happiness of the sort she knew she could never provide.
No woman could.

Max poured another round of drinks for himself and
Gosling, and served Jessica a pony of brandy. They sat on
the deck and had an easy conversation—a little politics,
some background exchanged, nothing too heavy, a few
amusing stories, gentle kidding between the men about
past exploits.

"That's all history," Gosling said, "old war stories."

Pauling said, "Cold War stories. Boring."

"I'm trying to convince your man to help me out with
a project," Gosling said. "You know, Max, I was thinking of you for it before I bumped into you in Mexico.
Déjà vu, it's called."

"Or preview. If you believe in that sort of thing," Pauling said.

"What kind of project?" Jessica asked. Pauling read
the edge in her voice.

Gosling shrugged. "I'm working for a private investigation agency," he said. "No need to check your clearances,
is there?" He laughed. "Max has been telling me I'm para-
noid, which I suppose I am. Hard to shake it. Right, Max?
At any rate, I'm working for Cell-One. We have a Who's
Who of corporate America as clients, top companies. One
of them has given us an assignment that Mr. Pauling here,
with his experience, might find interesting."

Jessica silently awaited a further explanation. It wasn't
to come. Gosling yawned, stretched, and said, "Getting
close to my bedtime. Hope you don't mind, Jessica, having an unannounced overnight guest. I sleep well on
couches."

"No need for that," she said, forcing lightness back into her voice. "We have a real guest room, an office most of the time—but with a comfortable pullout."

He followed her into the room carrying his small blue canvas overnight bag. "Sleep as late as you want," she said. "I leave for work at eight." To Max: "Do you have students tomorrow?"

"Two, in the afternoon. I thought I'd give Vic a spin in the plane in the morning. He wants to learn how to fly."

"I thought you already had a spin in the plane," she said, "coming up from Mexico." Had Gosling outlined the assignment to Pauling during that flight? She didn't bother asking. *Check clearances indeed!* The games little boys play.

"That was all business," Gosling said pleasantly. "I'd enjoy a purely personal joyride. Good night. You're the perfect host and hostess."

Max and Jessica sat on the deck for another hour. She didn't ask about the project until they'd gotten into bed.

"You told me you never trusted him, Max," she whispered. "The book was a phony, you said."

"It was," he whispered in reply. "But no harm in hearing him out. It's private work. I am still employable, I think. Or I'd like to think so."

Her silence was verbose.

He kissed her on the lips. "I love you," he said.

"Me, too," she said, turning her back to him, sighing, and snuggling her head into the pillow. Max didn't know whether that meant she loved him, or herself. But as long as love was in the air. . . .

They heard the shower go on at six. When they emerged from their bedroom at six-thirty, Gosling had made coffee and was sitting on the deck, a steaming cup in front of him.

"Sleep well?" Jessica asked.

"Extremely," Gosling replied. "Hope you don't mind that I helped myself to coffee."

"Not at all," Max said. He suggested that Jessica shower. "I'll get breakfast."

As Jessica was about to leave for work, Gosling thanked her again for the hospitality. He then cocked his head, nodding in agreement with something he was thinking. "Leave it to Max Pauling to fall in love with the most beautiful woman in the State Department."

Jess didn't feign modesty. "Thank you," she said. "Please visit again." She accepted Max's kiss and was out the door.

"I meant it," Gosling said when she was gone.

"I'm sure you did," Max said. "Because you're right."

Max had met Jessica Mumford and her friends Mac and Annabel Smith a little over a year ago in the John Quincy Adams State Drawing Room at State, where a new Russian minister-counselor of trade was being fêted. Jessica was there because of her job in State's Russian section. Max had just returned to Washington from an extended stint in Moscow, operating as a State intelligence officer under embassy cover.

His attraction to her was immediate and powerful. She was tall and willowy. She wore her blond-and-silver hair short and wet. Her profile was clean and strong, cheekbones prominent, nose appropriately long and fine. He circled, planned his angle of attack, moved in, said the right things knowing she wouldn't respond to anything less—inane banter wouldn't have done it—and took her to dinner, silently relieved that Mac and Annabel couldn't join them. Things progressed urgently from that point despite his having to spend time undercover in Moscow. Eventually, he ended up saving Jessica from her ex-husband, the FBI agent, who turned out to be a snake, and a crazy one at that. Rushing to her rescue cemented the relationship. Nothing like a genuinely lovely woman to buff up an old knight's armor and make it shine again.

"Marriage on the horizon?" Gosling asked.

"Some day maybe. You never remarried, did you?"

"No. I was grotty as a husband. They deserved better."

"They?"

"I gave it a second shot. It lasted slightly longer than an hour."

Max thought of his own former wife and the two kids they'd created together, but didn't mention them. Instead, he asked, "Ready for your first flying lesson?"

"Yes, sir," Gosling said.

Pauling handed over the controls to Gosling once they were airborne, but it was obvious the "student" had little interest in piloting. He suggested Max take over. Once he had, Gosling said: "About this project, Max. Ever hear of Signal Laboratories?"

"Yeah. Big pharmaceutical company. Heavy on research. Blue chip."

"Exactly. Global. They're a client of ours, have been for a few years. Ever hear of BTK Industries?"

"Another client?"

"No. A competitor of Signal. They're both leaders in the development of anticancer drugs. Maybe that's not the right term. Too simplistic. Of course, I'm no scientist. What it boils down to is that they're in a race to develop the next generation of monoclonal antibodies, hopefully the magic bullet to cure one kind of cancer or another."

"Uh-huh." Pauling had set the autopilot and relaxed, his hands off the yoke, an urge for a cigarette coming and going. "I get it," he said. "Your client wants you to steal lab secrets from the competitor."

"Not quite."

"Isn't BTK headed by ex-senator McCullough?" Max asked.

"You're absolutely right. He chairs the board and is the major stockholder. The last of the old liberals."

"Nothing sadder, someone said."

"Hubert Humphrey, I think."

"He doesn't sound like a liberal to me. He's big business. Sounds more like a conservative Republican."

"Texas liberals are different from other liberals, Max. Lyndon Johnson did okay in business. At least Lady Bird did, with a little help from LBJ's political clout. At any rate, our client Signal Labs is convinced that BTK Industries is playing dirty pool in Cuba."

"Cuba?" Pauling's laugh was strictly involuntary. "What the hell does Cuba have to do with cancer research?"

"Aha," Gosling said. "It's always a pleasure to enlighten people about something they don't know. Cuba, my friend, that decrepit, backward banana—well, certainly not a republic—happens to have first-rate medical research, including work being done on the development of anticancer drugs. Cuba may be a Communist government headed by that bearded bastard, Fidel, and it may be on its ass economically—especially since the Soviets pulled out—but its medical research is world-class. Trust me, Max. I'm telling the truth."

"Okay," Pauling said, "so Cuba has research going. What does that have to do with Signal, your client, or McCullough's company?"

"Interested enough for me to go on?"

"You've made me curious, that's all."

"I don't want to tell you too much unless you're sincerely interested in getting involved. Need-to-know and all of that."

"How can I consider getting involved if I don't know what I'm getting involved in?"

"Where are we headed?" Gosling asked.

"Home," Pauling said. He disengaged the autopilot and put the plane in a hard left bank, virtually standing it on one wing.

"All right," Gosling said, breathing hard, once they'd leveled out. "Here's the deal."

Two hours later, after a quick lunch at Pauling's apartment, he drove Gosling to the Albuquerque airport for a flight to San Francisco.

"Glad you'll be with us," Gosling said as they stood at the security gate.

"I told you I wanted to think about it for a few days," Pauling said.

"I know," said Gosling, slapping Pauling's shoulder. "Talk it over with the little woman and all that."

"Don't ever call Jessica that to her face," Pauling said.

"Wouldn't think of it. I'll be back to you with some of the details you asked about. If nothing else, you'll be able to put that new multiengine rating to some use. Cheerio!"

Pauling watched Gosling put his little blue bag through the baggage scanner and lope down the wide hallway toward his gate. He stood there for a time, watching Gosling's disappearing figure, then went outside, got in his car, and drove home to wait for Jessica's return from work. Making the decision to sign on to Gosling's project would be easy. Placating Jessica wouldn't be.

Chapter 3

New Mexico

Pauling placed the last of his clothing in a suitcase and closed it. He consulted the packing checklist he always used before traveling and saw that he'd forgotten something, took it from the dresser, opened the suitcase, put it in, and closed it again. He turned; Jessica stood in the bedroom doorway.

"All set?" she asked.

She'd been helpful and upbeat the past few days despite the fact that he was due to leave, possibly for as long as a month. He appreciated her cooperation. Leaving under a cloud was something he'd experienced too many times before in his clandestine life. Not that it had ever stopped him from heading out, but an upbeat, loving launch was certainly preferable.

They'd made love the night before. She'd been playful: "I want to tire you out before you meet any of those sexy Cuban women," she'd said. He didn't argue, simply reveled in the silken exercise that proved satisfying to both of them.

"How long will you be in Pittsburgh?" she asked.

"Just overnight. The motel phone number is on the itinerary I gave you."

"Nervous about meeting Doris's new husband?"

"Of course not. She says he's a nice guy. An accountant."

Jessica laughed. "You won't have anything in common," she said.

"Aside from Doris."

There had been many times since becoming involved with Max that Jessica had wished he had something in common with accountants, or any other men for that matter whose livelihood was derived from more "normal" sources, and who spent their working lives traveling between office and home. Their life together since leaving Washington and settling in New Mexico had come close to achieving that goal. But she knew that it was probably only a matter of time until he again sought the brand of thrills that his previous lives with the CIA and State Department had provided. Ferrying materials into Mexico had been the first step; now this assignment to Cuba.

Although she'd never met Doris, Max's ex-wife, she felt an affinity for her. She knew what it was like to be married to a Max Pauling from her own experience of being the spouse of an undercover government agency operative. How many months would he be away this time? Two? Four? Six? Or would he come home at all, either because he'd lost his life at the hand of an enemy, or because the thought of returning to the mundane world of husband, that "normal" world, had become anathema to him?

And there were the other women. Like Max, her FBI husband was handsome and physically fit, a virile man who wore virility on his sleeve. Had there been other women in her former husband's life, or in Max's life? She assumed so, although she never questioned either of them. Max turned female heads on the street. She was flattered that he'd chosen her to be his woman. But how fleeting might that be? She sometimes wondered. It was a question she deliberately avoided because the answer might not be the one she wanted to hear.

Doris and Max had divorced years ago while he was still working for the CIA. He hadn't argued against it because he knew that she was right. He was seldom home, away on assignments for extended periods, some as long as six or eight months. But his absences weren't the biggest problem. It was when he *was* home that the friction was most intense, and it wasn't his wife's fault, he knew. He was never comfortable being home and playing the mundane role of husband and father after having lived on the edge in exotic places, dangerous places; him against the bad guys, defending democracy from those who would take it away from his wife and children. They didn't teach rationalization at The Farm, the CIA's training facility, but he didn't need tutoring in the subject; it came naturally.

Lord knows he tried to please when he was thrust into the domestic role. He spent time with his sons, Robert and Richard, playing ball with them, taking a few weekend camping trips, attending their games and other extracurricular activities at school, all the fatherly things that good dads do. He deeply loved his sons but never really enjoyed those times. As he cheered them on at an athletic event, his thoughts would abandon the moment and be replaced by memories of escaping a Russian thug by outdriving him or outthinking him, or taking part in a native ritual in Central America where he was celebrated as a great white savior, delivering illegal weaponry from the mighty country to the north, all in the name of world peace and stopping Communism dead in its tracks. Although he felt guilty when distracted from the appealing sight of his sons at play, or the quiet beauty that had attracted him to Doris, he knew that she never understood that his was not the kind of work that proceeds from nine to five, or takes time out for the weekend.

And sometimes he thought of the women with whom

he'd come in contact during his travels. There hadn't been many, which salved his conscience concerning Doris. Married men who traveled a lot and spent all their spare time chasing women were adulterous. Those like him, away from hearth and home for long periods, who fell into the occasional fling—sometimes for professional purposes—were to be excused, weren't they?

Rationalization 101. He deserved an A.

Doris had raised their two sons almost single-handedly, and when she announced she was filing for divorce, Max, sadly, breathed a sigh of relief. Acting the part of husband and father when he was home was too tough. Better to sever it clean, get on with life, and play father whenever he could. But from a distance.

"I'll miss you," Jessica said, back in the present.

"I'll miss you, too, sweetheart. Think of it this way. You'll have a month to hunt down rare birds without me around to make jokes about it. Maybe you'll run across one of those wacky roadrunners."

"I'll miss your jokes, too, Max. Take care, huh? I want you back in one piece."

"Of course I'll be back in one piece. It's not like I'm going to war. Just some snooping into a pharmaceutical company chaired by a former senator. Piece o' cake."

They embraced, kissed, hugged again, and he left the apartment. An hour later he was at seven thousand feet in the Cessna, heading for Pittsburgh for an overnight stopover to visit with his ex-wife, two sons, and their new stepfather, "the accountant." It was sure to be the most challenging part of the trip.

Chapter 4

San Francisco

R eady to go?" Ronald Goldstein asked his medical colleague Barbara Mancuso.

She pointed to the overnight bag at her feet. He grinned and glanced at his watch. If they didn't leave soon, they'd miss their flight back to Washington.

Drs. Goldstein and Mancuso were among three hundred physicians attending the four-day annual meeting of the American Society of Clinical Oncology. At the podium, the newly elected president of the organization was wrapping up the final session with words meant to inspire, but that the restless audience wasn't particularly interested in hearing. Watches were checked; bodies slipped out of their seats as surreptitiously as possible and headed for the doors.

"This has been a remarkably successful meeting," the president, an overweight oncologist from San Diego, said. "We are truly standing at the threshold of a new dawn in clinical research. The days ahead will be filled with dramatic successes, and disappointing failures. But one thing is certain. Cancer is no longer the mystery it once was. We know more about it, how it works, and how to combat it than ever before. Research into how to stop cancer cells in their tracks—dare I even say cure it?—has never been more promising. We can all go back and report to our patients that the breakthroughs they read about every day are real. There is reason to hope."

"Let's go," Goldstein whispered to Mancuso.

"I want to thank all of you for being here and contributing your knowledge and skills to the meeting. I also wish to thank you for placing your faith in me as your new president and . . ."

The closing door behind Goldstein and Mancuso silenced the speaker's words.

Traffic on the way to the airport was snarled; they arrived at the gate only minutes before their flight was closed. They settled in adjoining seats, drew deep breaths, looked at each other, and smiled.

"Ready to go to work?" Goldstein asked.

"No," she said, "but that doesn't matter."

They spent a good portion of the flight reviewing notes from the panels and sessions they'd attended by dividing up the duties and reading photocopies of the many papers that had been presented by leading researchers from around the world. The next morning they were due to brief colleagues at the National Institutes of Health on what had transpired during the four days in San Francisco.

Goldstein and Mancuso landed at Dulles Airport at one-thirty the next morning, Washington time. Later, at 9 A.M., they sat side by side in a small amphitheater at NIH, on the Rockville Pike in Bethesda, Maryland. A dozen men and women wearing white lab coats faced them from the audience. Their boss, who headed up the cancer research section of NIH, introduced them: "Ron and Barbara have just spent an informative four days in San Francisco at the American Society of Clinical Oncology's annual meeting, and, I trust, four pleasurable days in that wonderful city. I know they have interesting things to report. Barbara, Ron."

Goldstein went first; he and Mancuso alternated. They detailed the ongoing research that, in their opinion, had the best chance of advancing the state of cancer care, and cited certain individuals whose work in the field was, in their estimation, superior—Agus in California, Treon at Dana-Farber in Boston, Weber at Houston's M. D. Anderson Cancer Center, the team at Wayne State, Sloan-Kettering in New York—they went down the list as quickly as possible, summarizing what had been reported at the conference, adding their own personal evaluation of the work. But no matter how hard they tried to stay within the allotted time, a constant stream of questions interrupted their presentations and pushed the briefing session past the hour they'd been given.

Dr. Mancuso began the final report, "I know we're running long and I'll try to wrap up as quickly as possible. As many of you know, the Cuban research team presented a paper at the meeting. It's the first time this has happened, and I'm glad tensions have sufficiently thawed between us and Cuba, at least in the medical arena, to allow their researchers and physicians to take part in such meetings.

"Their team was headed by Dr. Manuel Caldoza. He's an impressive gentleman who was educated in Canada and Spain, and whose experiments with the use of vanadium to help create broad-spectrum, potent anticancer drugs has been ongoing for years. We've heard about his work, but only tangentially. The metal vanadium, as many of you know, is a soft, ductile metallic element found in several minerals, notably vanadinite and carnotite, both of which are abundant in Cuba. Dr. Caldoza and his team have developed innovative methods for purifying vanadium and are making good use of it. Of course, because Cuba is a closed society, it's difficult to ascertain the accuracy and validity of the experimental results they reported at the meeting. Also, I'm not blind to the fact that allowing him to present only a small portion of his work to us here in the States represents a tease on the part of Fidel Castro. Although his presentation isn't nearly complete, it's impressive. According to Dr. Caldoza, they've been testing more than two dozen drugs that utilize vanadium, and claim to have had positive results against eleven different laboratory cancer cell lines, as well as cells taken directly from patients."

Dr. Mancuso looked out over the sparsely populated auditorium and noticed a small, balding, nondescript man wearing round rimless glasses and a green suit. He sat far apart from the doctors. Until Mancuso had begun her report on the Cuban research team, the man seemed indifferent to what she had been saying. Now he took notes, not looking up as he transcribed Mancuso's words.

"You aren't really taking what they say seriously, are you?" an older physician asked from the first row. He had a large, square face; his jaw enjoyed more lateral movement than normal. "Pure Communist propaganda. They claim to have invented everything from the light-bulb to baseball. Now they say they're going to cure cancer?" He guffawed and shook his head, jaw in motion. The doctor next to him laughed.

Barbara Mancuso, M.D., held her tongue. She'd been reading everything that she could about medical research in Cuba for good reason; despite the island nation's impoverished society, she was impressed that Cuba's medicine and research had long been the envy of nations in the Southern Hemisphere and beyond. True, validating the results claimed by Cuba's state-owned medical research facilities was difficult. However, Mancuso's exploration of the caliber of medical research on Castro's island had convinced her that the Cuban efforts were as sophisticated as those of many independent labs and hospitals doing cancer research in the United States and other wealthier nations. She addressed the naysayer directly.

"Dr. Meadows, I understand the natural inclination to be skeptical. I was too, at first, until I made my own unofficial inquiries. The truth is—and it may be a bitter pill to swallow for the anti-Castro forces—that medicine in Cuba, and medical research in particular, especially with cancer drugs, is impressive. Sure, they're short of medicine and physicians now because of the blockade that's been ongoing for almost forty years, and cessation of financial support by the Soviets. But Castro stated early in his administration that finding a cure for cancer was to be a priority, and he's committed considerable resources to that goal."

She felt her anger rising. She knew that the older physicians in the room were thinking that aside from her impressive medical training and knowledge, she was young and wide-eyed and naïve and liberal, all the things most of them were not.

She continued.

"Before Cuba lost Soviet financial backing, UNICEF ranked the country just a few notches behind us in health care despite a Gross National Product representing one-twentieth of our own. A Cuban's average life expectancy is almost seventy-four years, the highest in Latin America. A child born today in Cuba is twice as likely to survive as a baby born in Washington, D.C."

Another physician in the audience asked, "Aren't we doing research into the use of vanadium here in the States?"

"Yes," Mancuso answered. "In Minnesota, at Parker Hughes Institute. I'm visiting there next month."

The final question from the audience was "Did you have a pleasurable four days in San Francisco?"

Goldstein answered: "If seeing it from your hotel window at night equals pleasure, we certainly did."

Mancuso's boss stood and said, "I apologize for running late, and I know you all have places to be at this hour. Let me conclude by saying to those of you who dismiss what Cuba might be doing in cancer research, there are Canadian venture capitalists pouring money into Cuban medical research, and investors tossing millions at Canadian mutual funds with interests in Canadian companies backing the Cubans." He turned to Mancuso and Goldstein and said, "Nice job."

The doctor in the front row who'd laughed off what Mancuso had said stopped her on the way out. "These Canadian mutual funds that Gil mentioned. Which are they?"

Mancuso smiled pleasantly at him. "I wouldn't know," she said. "I follow medicine, not the market."

As Mancuso left the room, she looked for the little man in the green suit. He was gone. She asked her boss who he was.

"One of our intelligence services," he said. "Whenever we have anything to report on Cuba, they send someone over to take notes." He laughed. "Even now, your words are being immortalized in a computer at Langley."

The man in the green suit had a name, Raymond Cisneros. He sat in a windowless room at CIA headquarters in Langley, Virginia, entering into a computer his notes from the briefing. He printed a hard copy and delivered it to his superior in the Cuba section of the agency. The ranking officer read it, scowled, looked up, and asked, "Who's this Dr. Mancuso?"

"An NIH physician."

"Flag her. Another apologist for Fidel. Sounds like she'd like to marry him, for Christ sake."

Pauling, Doris, their older son, Robert, and Doris's new husband, Daniel Schumer, had dinner at a local restaurant the night of Max's arrival. The younger son, Richard, opted not to join them. Max knew that the fourteen-year-old was uncomfortable being at the same table with his biological father and stepfather, and didn't blame him. Max himself wasn't crazy about breaking bread with the new man in Richard's mother's life, and bed.

It turned out to be a surprisingly pleasant evening. Schumer, "the accountant," was a good-looking, slightly overweight man with a full head of hair—mildly annoying to the thinning-haired Pauling—and an amiable table companion. He told a good story and got everyone laughing with a few tales of former clients who'd decided they could beat the tax system and ended up as guests of the federal penal system. Schumer picked up the tab, which Pauling considered appropriate.

He'd taken a taxi from the private airport to the house, and they drove to the restaurant in Schumer's white Lexus. As they stood in the parking lot waiting for an attendant to fetch the car, Schumer said, "You're leaving in the morning?"

"Yes," said Max. "An early start."

"It must be satisfying flying your own plane, avoiding those commercial flights—with commercial waiting."

"It does have advantages," Pauling said.

"I'll pick you up at your motel and drive you to the airport," Schumer offered.

"I don't want to put you out."

"I'd do it but I'm tied up with an early meeting," Doris said.

"No problem for me," Schumer said. "I have a racquetball date first thing. What time do you want to go, Max?"

"Seven too early?"

"Perfect."

They dropped Pauling at his motel, said good-bye, and left him pondering the evening over a drink at the bar. He was glad he'd made the stop. Seeing that his family was healthy and secure was important. But ambivalence reigned.

On the one hand, he was pleased that the new man in his sons' lives seemed to be okay. No, that's not fair, he told himself as the bartender indicated last call. Schumer was more than that, a decent enough fellow, kind and caring, and who seemed to have forged a good relationship with Robert and Richard. And he was obviously successful; they wouldn't be missing any meals. There were moments during the evening when he toyed with the idea of calling Gosling, bowing out of the assignment, and hanging around Pittsburgh for some extra days with the boys. But as gracious as Schumer and Doris had been, he felt very much the outsider, an intruder into a family that once had been his. Better to get on with his new life and let them get on with theirs.

He carried a drink to his room where thoughts of his family were replaced by the reason he was passing through Pittsburgh, namely, to meet Gosling in Miami and then proceed to Cuba. So far so good. Jessica hadn't been angry at his decision to take the assignment and be away for a month—at least she'd been savvy enough to not display any anger that might have existed. And he didn't have to worry about his ex-wife and sons. No wonder the CIA and other intelligence agencies preferred that their undercover operatives be unmarried, preferably without children, parents, grandparents, significant others, or friends. Having to worry about anyone other than yourself could get you killed.

Daniel Schumer was in front of the hotel precisely at seven. Pauling threw his small bag into the back and got in the front passenger seat.

"Sleep good?" Schumer asked as he pulled away.

"I always do," Pauling replied. He almost asked whether Schumer had slept peacefully next to Doris but didn't especially want to know.

Pauling gave Schumer directions, and they drove in silence until Schumer spoke. "You're flying to Miami, you said?"

"Right."

"Vacation? Business?"

"Strictly vacation," Pauling said.

"I enjoy Miami but not in the summer. Hot as hell this time of year."

"I enjoy the heat."

"Doris told me you used to be with the CIA. Hope that's okay."

"Of course it is. That was before. I'm not involved with the government anymore."

"Must have been exciting, being with the CIA, and all."

"It had its moments."

Pauling tired of the conversation and would have preferred to talk about something accounting related—

double-entry bookkeeping or even tax shelters. "I enjoyed your stories last night about clients who've ended up in jail," he said, hoping it would prompt another tale.

Schumer laughed. "People do really dumb things out of greed," he said. "My job is to keep them out of trouble but sometimes they won't listen. *They* know better. I'm also a lawyer."

"Really?"

"Tax attorney. I don't practice law but it comes in handy."

"I imagine it does."

They entered a small parking lot next to the side of a shack featuring peeling yellow paint that served as the airport's operations center. Schumer turned off the engine and turned to face Pauling. "I really enjoyed meeting you, Max," he said. "Frankly, I was a little nervous."

"No need to be," Pauling said, smiling to reassure. "You've married a hell of a good woman and inherited two fine boys."

"I know, I know. I wish my daughters could have been with us last night. They're with their mother." He pulled a wallet from his hip pocket, extracted a small color photo, and handed it to Pauling. Two teenage girls, one with braces, smiled up at him.

"They're beautiful," he said.

"I know. I'm really proud of them. They get along great with Robbie and Rich."

The use of his sons' familiar names stung Max for a second.

"I just want you to know, Max," Schumer said, returning the photograph to his wallet, "that I love Doris and the boys very much and will do everything I can to be a positive force in their lives."

It was time to leave.

"I'm sure you will, Daniel. It was great meeting you. Have a good racquetball game. And thanks for the lift."

"It was my pleasure, Max."

They shook hands. Pauling got out of the car and walked to the ops center without looking back. It took him fifteen minutes to file an IFR flight plan to Miami. When he exited the building, Schumer was still parked in the lot. Schumer waved. Pauling returned it, went to where his plane was tied down, and did his walk-around inspection of the exterior. Satisfied, he said to the line attendant, "Thanks for topping her off."

"Yes, sir. She's a nice plane."

"My baby," Pauling said, climbing up into the left seat. When he'd completed his preflight checklist, started the engine, and begun to taxi to the end of the only runway, he noticed that Schumer was still there.

What the hell is he waiting for, to see me crash? he wondered.

He didn't know that Daniel Schumer was watching him with interest and envy. Doris's new husband had been more nervous meeting Max than he'd admitted. He'd felt inferior to this steely-eyed pilot and former undercover agent for the CIA. Doris had described Max as obsessive about staying in shape, one with little patience for those who didn't.

He watched the Cessna roll down the runway and lift off. A minute later, the plane disappeared into low clouds. He touched his belly that pressed against the seat belt and grimaced. He'd better do more than play an occasional game of racquetball with other overweight professionals before Max Pauling visited again.

And as Pauling flew toward Miami with a clear mind about those in his personal life, Daniel Schumer, CPA and licensed attorney who played sports poorly, worried whether he paled in Doris's eyes in comparison to her macho ex-husband.

That afternoon he signed up with a gym just a block away from his office.

Chapter 6

Camp David

James L. Walden was known as a man *and* a politician who held his cards close to the vest, literally and figuratively. On this night, the final evening at the presidential retreat after a much-needed weekend away from Washington and the White House, he sat at the table with fellow poker players and peered down through half-glasses at the five cards in his hand. He'd drawn only two. Others looked to him for a clue as to what he held. President Walden was not known as a risk taker, although he'd bluffed skillfully enough in a previous hand to force a couple of players out of the game even though they had held stronger hands than he.

To his left sat Mackensie Smith, a law professor at George Washington University. Smith and Walden had been friends since Walden ran for governor of California as a liberal Democrat—and won. He next won the White House. Smith, who had served on a number of panels and committees at the president's behest, had become one of his closet "advisors"; read, poker buddies. Like every powerful leader, Walden needed to be surrounded with men and women who did his bidding for the most part without mounting undue challenges. Smith, along with a handful of others, fulfilled a second need. They were good company and they also spoke their minds to the president, always respectfully, of course. But their careers were not dependent upon his reactions. Their advice meant something.

"Well, Mr. President, are you seeing me or raising me?" Price McCullough asked from across the table. He'd been a five-term senator from Texas until retiring, citing the appalling lack of civility in that hallowed chamber. McCullough had gone on to pursue business interests, the largest of which was BTK Industries, a biotech company with significant investment in the development of new monoclonal antibody anticancer drugs. A few eyebrows had been raised—but only a few—when he left government to become chairman and CEO of the company that had benefited for years from his votes in Congress. BTK Industries had also realized gains from McCullough's chairmanship of the powerful Senate Appropriations Committee, plus the Subcommittee on Labor, Health and Human Services, and the Subcommittee on Education, both of which wielded considerable oversight of the pharmaceutical industry. That he went from being financially comfortable to multimillionaire status virtually overnight prompted the predictable resident cynics to cry foul, but their voices proved weak and momentary. Price McCullough's congressional colleagues congratulated him and wished him well, and some were not above hoping that such criticisms and good fortune loomed in their futures.

Walden took in the others over his glasses, exhibited a rare grin, picked up chips from a pile in front of him, and tossed them into the center of the table. "I'll see you and raise you a dollar," he said.

"Larry?" McCullough asked the governor of Massachusetts.

"Former player," Lawrence Scott said, tossing his cards facedown on the table.

"Mac?"

"I'll see you and match the raise."

The only other player, White House chief of staff Charles Larsen, had folded after drawing three useless cards and commenting on them with words containing four letters.

Mac Smith displayed his hand—a pair of kings.

The president showed a full house, aces high.

McCullough shook his head and put down his five cards, one at a time, three tens, an ace, and a jack.

"I win," Walden said, laughing and scooping up the chips from the middle of the table. "Hell, I always win. I'm the president of the United States. I'm *supposed* to win."

"Harry Truman used to say he didn't mind losing a card game," McCullough said. "Elections were another matter."

"All set for your trip to Cuba, Price?" Governor Scott asked.

"I believe so."

"Maybe you can get Castro in a card game and win the freaking island," Charlie Larsen said.

"He's a chess player," Smith offered.

"And superstitious," said Walden. "He has a favorite number, twenty-six, and makes important decisions only on that day of the month."

"He's a head case," Governor Scott said.

"A shrewd head case," Walden said. "Don't sell him short."

"Kennedy sure did," Scott said.

"Did Kennedy really buy up every Cuban cigar he could find before our embargo prohibited Cuban products from coming into the country?" Larsen asked.

Walden laughed. "He sent Pierre Salinger out to corner

the market. Salinger bought Kennedy every Petite Up-
mann in the country, thousands of them. *Then* he signed
the embargo."

There was much laughter around the table.

"Churchill smoked Cuban Romeo y Julietas," Walden
said. "Cuba gave him ten thousand as a gift during World
War Two."

"Another hand?" McCullough asked.

"Not for me," Walden said, standing and twisting his
torso against a pain in his back. "Volleyball and swim-
ming this afternoon did me in. A meeting with the attorney general didn't help."

Gentle kidding had accompanied the president's announcement after dinner that a poker game was about to
commence, men only.

"This is like a scene from a 1940s movie," Charlie
Larsen's wife had said lightly.

"Cigars and cognac for the men, a knitting competition for the women," said another wife, also uttered
lightly so as not to appear seriously offended.

"As long as you win," the president's wife, Sheila, told
him, ending the debate.

While the men wagered at the round, green, felt-
covered table, the women in their lives had retreated to
an expansive screened porch where no winners emerged
in their animated discussion of current political events,
recently published books, and other stimulating topics.
Now, with candles on tables providing the only light and
a faint breeze moderating the warm, humid evening, the
men joined them on the porch. The shadows of Secret
Service agents could be seen.

"Who won?" Sheila Walden asked.

"Who else?" Scott said. "Your husband."

"Good," she said. "We can eat for another day."

"Can *we*?" Annabel Reed-Smith, Smith's wife, asked.

"Afraid not," Smith said. "The president took every cent I have."

"That's what they say about you in Congress, Mr. President." Scott said this while settling on a white wicker love seat next to his wife.

Chief of Staff Larsen said, "That's the president's political philosophy. Take it from Congress before they take it from you."

After another ten minutes of small talk, President Walden's announcement that he and Sheila were calling it a day caused the others to stand and make similar pronouncements. Except for Mac and Annabel Smith. "I think we'll sit up a while," Smith said.

"No necking on the couch," said Walden. "You never can tell when there's somebody out there with a long lens."

"We'll try to control ourselves," Annabel said brightly.

"The hell we will," Mac mock growled.

When the others were gone, Annabel said to her husband, "What a lovely weekend."

"It's good to see the president get away if even for a few days. He's been looking exhausted lately."

"No wonder, with all the turmoil around him: a hostile Congress, the Middle East, the Far East, the fight over the Supreme Court nomination, Cuba. It never stops."

"Did you have a pleasant time with Sheila and the others?" he asked.

"While you were bonding?" She laughed. "We had a lovely time. Sheila's devotion to funding the arts in public schools is inspiring. She asked me to join the foundation."

"You will, of course."

"I will. Of course."

He took her hand and they sat in silence.

Annabel was tall—five eight—trim except where she

wasn't supposed to be. Additional advantages included a creamy complexion and a mane of copper hair. Her eyes were, of course, green as if ordained, and large. Her ears, nose, and mouth had been created with a stunning sense of proportion. She was, in Mac's eyes—which were a lighter green, the color of Granny Smith apples—at least the most beautiful woman in the world, a view shared by other men who'd pursued her. But Mac Smith was the one who'd won her hand, for which he was eternally grateful.

Smith was equally handsome by any standard, slightly taller than medium, stocky and strong, hair receding slowly and within acceptable limits, face without undue defects. When they'd taken their vows in Washington National Cathedral's Bethlehem Chapel those ten years ago, Annabel had prompted laughter when asked the question, "Will you have this man to be your husband?" She had replied in a loud, cheery voice, "Oh, yes, I certainly will."

Smith had been widowed when he met Annabel. His first wife and only child, a son, fell victim to a drunk driver on the Beltway. That vast loss created in him a whole new way of viewing life. He decided to close down his lucrative criminal law practice and took a position as professor of law at George Washington University.

When Annabel met Smith at an embassy function, she, too, had been considering a change in her life. She was a matrimonial attorney in D.C., and a good one, but years of dealing with warring couples and their inability, or unwillingness, to forge peaceful dissolutions of their marriages had worn her down. Her true personal passion had long been pre-Columbian art. With her husband's encouragement, she closed her law offices and opened a storefront gallery in Georgetown that eventually grew in size and stature.

"I envy you your trip to Cuba," she said quietly.

"In the summer? It would be worth envying if it were January."

"Speaking of heat, while you guys were male-bonding we were discussing why the president is taking so much of it these days from Congress over his Cuba policies."

"The Castro hard-liners won't let go, Annabel. They can't accept the idea that the main thing the embargo has accomplished lately is the impoverishment of the average Cuban, and the strengthening of Castro's image—him against the mighty aggressor ninety miles off his shores."

"Well, it should be an interesting trip," Annabel said.

"Should be. I was pleased when the president asked me to be part of it as one set of eyes and ears."

"How many in Price's delegation?"

"Twenty, last I heard—sixteen men and four women."

"The usual ratio." She sighed. "Cuba," she said, more to herself than to him. "I wish I'd seen it before Castro, when it was the playground of the rich and famous."

"And the infamous. Corrupt to the core," Mac said. "A gangster paradise." He chuckled. "I remember a comment by one of our ambassadors there during Batista's reign. A reporter asked him why the Mafia was so welcome in Havana. The ambassador said it was the only way to have well-run casinos that paid off. That's how corrupt Batista was."

Annabel yawned. "I'm too tired to be corrupt."

"Shame," Smith said. "Let's hit the hay anyway, Annie."

The first lady sat in bed reading a novel. Her husband hadn't changed for bed. Walden sat at a small desk in their bedroom, leaning back in his chair, feet propped up on the edge of the desk.

"It's been a lovely weekend," she said, laying the book on the bed.

"Always good to get away. Whoever invented vacations and long weekends deserves a medal. Good book?"

"If you like romance novels, which I do on occasion. Occasions like this. Makes the escape from officialdom that much more complete."

He turned at the sound of someone knocking gently on the door, went to it, and faced an aide. "The senator is waiting, Mr. President."

Walden left the room without a word to his wife. As the aide led him to a secluded wooded area a hundred yards from the house, two Secret Service agents fell in behind, maintaining a discreet distance. Former senator Price McCullough sat on a wooden bench next to a small fountain, the water flowing gently into a copper urn that spilled its contents each time it filled. Walden joined his friend on the bench.

"I caught you dealing from the bottom of the deck, Mr. President," McCullough said in his soft drawl.

Walden laughed quietly. "Sometimes you have to do that in this business, Price."

"I'm well aware of that, Mr. President. I'll be leaving first thing in the morning. I need time back home before going to Cuba. I want you to know how much I appreciate this opportunity."

Walden waved away his comment. "I never liked Ayn Rand's politics, Price, but her take on what's self-serving makes sense. We do things for selfish reasons, but that's okay because others benefit. Like the definition of a 'good deal.' If you personally benefit from your trip, that's okay because this nation will benefit, too. It's a good deal. Everyone comes out ahead."

"Any last-minute words of Walden wisdom?"

"No. Just make it work. The time is right. If we can get

them to see that there's the possibility of more open trade beyond medicine and agricultural products, a real political dialogue might follow."

"Hinting that there's the potential of lowering the embargo isn't destined to impress Castro, Mr. President," the burly, white-haired McCullough said. "It gives him his best platform to point the finger at us for all his failures with the economy. But I'll do my best."

"The time is right, Price. Castro knows he'll have to give it up one of these days. Hell, he's got three hundred million dollars stashed away in Spain, according to some intelligence estimates. His kid brother, Raúl, will never cut it as the successor, and Fidel knows it. Everything points to growing unrest since the Soviets pulled the plug on aid." He paused and rubbed his chin. "You'll be there for his birthday."

"That's right."

"Know why Castro considers twenty-six his lucky number, won't make major decisions on any other day?"

"I read the briefing papers."

Walden continued as though McCullough hadn't. "He claims he was born in 1926, although some say it was '27. At any rate, his father owned twenty-six thousand acres, and Fidel was twenty-six when he launched his revolutionary attack on Moncada on July twenty-sixth."

"Interesting," McCullough said, not wanting to remind the president he already knew all about Castro's superstitions.

"Yes, interesting. The time is right, Price. Make the most of it, in your meetings—and out of them."

Chapter 7

Washington, D.C.

"All set?" Annabel asked as he brought his suitcases from the bedroom to the foyer.

"I think so."

"Time for another cup of coffee?"

Smith checked his watch. "Sure. Car's not due for a half hour."

They sat at a small glass-topped table on the terrace of their Watergate apartment and looked down over the Potomac. Crews from George Washington University, where Smith taught, practiced their strenuous extracurricular activity on the rippling water. Two luxury yachts slowly passed the sleek sculls from upriver. It was nine in the morning. The temperature was over eighty degrees in the nation's capitol; the city's infamous humidity had already wilted the clothing, hair, and spirits of the citizens who moved along the sidewalks as though pushing medicine balls.

"Wow!" Annabel said, dabbing at her upper lip with a napkin.

"Washington," Smith said. "On days like this I think of the character E. G. Marshall played in *Twelve Angry Men*. You know, the one who never broke a sweat in that stiflingly hot jury deliberation room."

Annabel said, "If you're thinking of practicing that

feat, wait until you come back from Havana. I read the weather there this morning. A hundred."

He squinted as he looked into the sun rising across the river.

"Yes?" Annabel asked, aware that his expression meant he was thinking of something.

"The trip," he said. "The president has been talking about it conceptually for months. All of a sudden it's reality. I wonder why it had to be now."

"Window of opportunity?"

"I suppose so. That column by Broder the other day makes sense."

"That this trip is more political than trade?"

"Yeah. No doubt about it, Annabel. The president is determined to hammer out a relationship with Cuba before he leaves office, Congress be damned."

"Which wouldn't be such a bad idea." She cocked her head. "Good time to do it."

"Depends on how it's done. Charlie Larsen suggested the other night that we should not encourage a revolution or an invasion but just get into a poker game with Castro and win the island."

"Castro would cheat."

"So would the president. I'd better get downstairs."

"Yes."

She rode the elevator with him to the lobby. A black limousine was parked outside.

She hugged him and kissed him on the lips. "Oops, lipstick," she said, wiping away telltale traces of their parting. "Call."

"Soon as I settle at the hotel. Or until the hotel settles further into decay. The Ritz it ain't. Love you, Mrs. Smith."

"You'd better. Safe journey."

• • •

"Senator McCullough, you say that the purpose of your trip is to explore the possibility of one day opening further trade with Cuba beyond the current exceptions to the embargo, namely agricultural products and medical supplies. But the administration's efforts to open a political dialogue with Castro are no secret. Isn't that what's really behind your trip?"

The reporter was one of a dozen covering the departure of McCullough's delegation to Cuba. The former senator and his colleagues, including Mackensie Smith, faced the press in a room at Reagan National Airport normally reserved for grieving family members when there had been a fatal aircraft accident. McCullough, forever senatorial—venerable face, silver hair nicely arranged, custom-made gray suit, white shirt, nonpartisan tie, voice like a one-man gang—smiled and gave a little shake of his head as though to say, "There you go again," which had worked so well for the former president for whom the airport was named.

"You'd think I'd have become inured to press skepticism after thirty years in the United States Senate, but it never fails to amaze me," he said, the smile not leaving his square, tanned face. "No, there is absolutely no political motive behind this trip. We are going for precisely the purpose stated in the press handout y'all have. Cuba is a Communist nation ruled by a Communist dictator, and I'm sure there'll be no softening of this administration's posture toward Castro and his government. But as y'all know, Congress has been moving in the direction of possibly expanding trade with Cuba in the areas you mentioned. This benefits not only the average Cuban citizen, it opens up a potentially lucrative market for our pharmaceutical companies and our farmers. It seems to me that—"

"It will benefit your own company, too, won't it, Senator?" asked a reporter.

The smile disappeared. "If you're suggestin' that I would put personal gain over the needs of the American people, sir, *I* would suggest that you don't know me very well. Other questions? Time for us to get on board."

"President Walden's attempts to end the forty-year embargo against Cuba are becoming more evident every day. Are you saying his agenda isn't part of your agenda?"

"That's exactly what I'm saying," McCullough replied.

"What about Cuba's dismal record on human rights, Senator?" a young woman reporter asked. "Doesn't increased trade simply give Castro a stronger economy in which to mistreat his own citizens?"

The smile was back, more expansive this time. "How we deal with Mr. Castro and his failings in the human rights arena is up to the politicians, and I remind you I am no longer one of those. The distinguished ladies and gentlemen of this delegation represent the best of American thinking and success. They'll be meeting with their Cuban counterparts to discuss how things might open up a little with Cuba. Thank you for coming, and have yourselves a nice day."

They walked from the lounge to a chartered 727, boarded, and settled in their seats.

"First time to Havana?" Smith's seatmate asked. He was the president of a large midwestern heavy farm equipment manufacturing company.

"Yes. You?"

A hearty laugh preceded, "No. I'm older than I look. I went there in my early twenties. It was incredible, a paradise, the shows, the gambling, the women. Batista might have been a curse but at least he was no Commie. Castro and his damn revolution ruined everything, sent the island over to the Soviets, put the people in chains. Hell, all you have to do is look at how many Cubans have risked their lives on little rubber rafts to get away from that murderous bastard."

True or not, it promised to be a longer flight for Smith than estimated.

Chapter 8

Miami

Max Pauling was not flying. He had been made to cool his heels in Miami. Gosling called him from London the day he arrived: "Sorry, old boy," he'd said, "but an emergency has come up with one of our clients that will keep me here an extra day."

"What am I supposed to do?" Pauling asked, not bothering to hide his annoyance.

"Relax. Enjoy glamorous Miami Beach. Spend my money. Accommodations are to your liking?"

"They're swell, if you get off on pink concrete, neon, and plastic. Oh, and let's not forget chrome." He hadn't been to Miami in years and was surprised at the city's transformation from a purely low-lying, warm-weather tourist attraction to an international center of commerce. Skyscrapers now dominated the skyline, and ethnic neighborhoods defined the city. "When are you getting in?"

"Tomorrow. Chill, Max, as you Americans are fond of saying. I'll keep in touch."

Downtime was always the worst. Pauling occupied himself for the next twenty-four hours by walking the beach and admiring the hundreds of bronzed young women in bikinis—*Could they possibly cover less and still be considered clothed?* he wondered—reading flying magazines he picked up in a large bookstore, and having a leisurely dinner in a restaurant in Little Haiti. The following morning, the desk clerk at the Airport Regency Hotel at Miami International Airport handed him an envelope as he returned from breakfast. "For you, Mr. Pauling."

Pauling went to his room. It was compact and had a small balcony overlooking nothing worth seeing. He stood out on the balcony and opened the envelope.

Max—
Arriving this afternoon from London, Virgin Atlantic flight five, scheduled into Miami at 3:05. Meet you at the hotel.

Vic

It was nearly eleven. Pauling unpacked his small bag, put on trunks, and swam vigorous laps until a mother with three small children entered the pool and provided a lively obstacle course. He got out, dried off, and went to the small bar where he nursed a Bloody Mary, had lunch, returned to his room, and fell asleep. The ringing phone startled him into consciousness.

"Max, it's Vic. I'm in the lobby."

"Hello, Vic. Flight okay?"

He laughed. "My master believes that his employees should fly first-class. Virgin calls it upper-class. Topnotch. Even an onboard masseuse to rub out the kinks before arrival. Worth getting the kinks. Been here long?"

"Long enough to be ready to leave. Where are we meeting?"

"Come down."

"Ten minutes."

Gosling was dressed as though he'd just stepped from a boardroom, dark blue pinstripe suit, blue-and-white-striped shirt with a solid white collar, solid burgundy tie, and black wing tip shoes buffed to a mirror glaze. Pauling wore jeans, a navy T-shirt, white sneakers, and his customary multipocketed vest. Gosling frowned.

"You have a problem?" Pauling asked.

"Must be dress-down Friday, only this is Thursday."

"All the same to me. Where are we going, to a coronation?"

Gosling led them from the hotel lobby to a parked, rented tan Mercedes. "To where we can have a drink and a little chat," he said. "My superior at Cell-One will be delayed, won't be in until tomorrow. Meetings all week at the Athenaeum Hotel. I broke away to meet you. The British are as fond of meetings as you Americans. Nothing like the lure of a long conference table, some tea, and an agenda. You did bring a suit with you."

"No."

Gosling sighed. "I warned my superior that you are unconventional. How's your lady friend?"

"Jessica is fine. Where are we heading?"

"A romantic spot on the beach, given that you're so well dressed."

They drove south on Le Jeune Road to Coral Way, turned left, and drove east until reaching Biscayne Bay, then north on Biscayne Boulevard until Gosling pulled into the parking lot of a restaurant, Monty's Marketplace. Pauling followed Gosling through the building to an outdoor area on the bay where a raw bar was in operation. They sat at a varnished picnic table beneath a chikee hut, a palm-thatch structure open on all sides, affording a view of the water.

"Nice place, don't you think?" Gosling said.

"If you like this sort of thing," said Pauling. "Glad I didn't overdress."

They ordered draft beers from a waitress; Gosling ordered a half-dozen littlenecks.

After a silence, during which Gosling ate and Pauling drank: "This is all very nice, Vic, but if I wanted to suck a beer beside the water, I'd have gone to California. What are we doing? I don't like sitting around."

"You haven't changed a bit, have you, Max? The original man of action and little patience. All right. Let me fill you in. As I told you earlier, you'll be transporting medical supplies to Cuba for a company in Colombia."

"What company?"

"Cali Forwarding."

"Oh, come on, Vic. Are they still in business?"

"Ah, you remember. That's a good sign, Max. The memory generally goes before the legs. Yes, Cali Forwarding is 'still in business,' as you put it."

"And still acting as a front for The Company."

"*The Company.* I wonder who coined that as a euphemism. Nobody calls it that anymore. Not important. In this instance, the CIA isn't involved. Strictly a private undertaking on behalf of my firm's client, Signal Labs. Cali Forwarding has been acting as a middleman for quite some time now for Canadian and European pharmaceutical companies selling drugs to Cuba."

"Why do they need a middleman?" Pauling asked. "We're the only country prohibited from doing business with Cuba."

"Helms-Burton," Gosling said. "Since 1996, when the Helms-Burton Act was passed—precise name, the Cuban Liberty and Democratic Solidarity Act—signed, reluctantly I might add, by President Clinton, we've been coming down hard on our allies who continue to do business with Havana. It's made for some awkward relations with our friends. At any rate, rather than incur the wrath of Uncle Sam, some companies don't sell directly to Cuba. Let's say a Canadian company sells to a company in Colombia. That company resells to Cuba. The goods are delivered from Colombia to Cuba and everyone is happy."

Pauling sighed and rubbed his nose. "What else is Cali Forwarding reselling? There wouldn't be any pure Colombian Gold stashed with the penicillin and antacids, would there?"

Gosling shrugged and motioned for the waitress to bring another round. "I'm hurt, Max, that you would think I'd get you involved in something shady, like drugs."

"I'll want to see what's in the plane before I take off."

"Of course. Believe me, it's all on the up-and-up. You'll be taking medical supplies and medicines to needy Cuban men and women. An admirable humanitarian effort. Yes?"

"I always wanted to win a Nobel. Run the deal past me again."

"Really quite simple, Max. You know that Congress has opened up trade with Cuba allowing medical supplies and agricultural products. Only it's a bit of a sham. Your lawmakers, bless them, say your American companies can sell those goods to Cuba, but have simultaneously prohibited them from seeking financing for the deals from your banks and other financial institutions. A devious bunch, your lawmakers. They can now proclaim themselves humanitarians, concerned with the well-being of the average Cuban, but making it almost impossible for these goods to reach the sick and hungry. Other countries that aren't hamstrung in their dealings with Cuba are free to trade with Castro, provided they're willing to anger your Congress. An intriguing scenario, isn't it?" He leaned closer and grabbed Pauling's arm. "But Max," he said, a modicum of exasperation in his voice, "what you'll be doing has nothing to do with embargoes or congressional double-talk. God, I hope your short-term memory hasn't eroded. Flying supplies from Colombia is simply your *cover* for being in Cuba. You're going to Havana to see what you can dig up on BTK Industries."

"Dig up? What's the archaeology to find?"

"Whether they're playing cozy with a German pharmaceutical firm, Strauss-Lochner Resources. Whether what the Germans are doing is for their own benefit— alone. Here." He pulled an envelope from his jacket pocket and handed it to Pauling.

"What's this?"

"Your contract with Cali Forwarding to transport shipments for them. Just to make it official. The initial payment was forwarded yesterday to your bank in Albuquerque."

Pauling slowly and carefully read the one-page letter-agreement. Gosling answered questions to his satisfaction, so Pauling signed and handed it back to Gosling.

"I convinced my superiors to include a bonus for you, Max, if you get what we're looking for in less than a month."

Pauling finished his beer and pushed back from the table. "And all I have to do is dig up proof that McCullough's company, BTK Industries, is using this German firm, Strauss-Lochner, as a front for trying to buy into Cuba's cancer research?"

"There you go, Max. You've got it."

There had been times in the past when Gosling's condescending manner grated on Pauling. This was one of those.

"Where's the plane?" Max asked.

"At the airport here. We'll stop by when we leave."

"Who's my contact in Cuba?"

"Someone who'll help with your Spanish."

"I didn't ask about *that*."

"And I didn't answer your question. All in good time,

Max. Arrangements are being made as we speak. You'll be contacted at your hotel on the night you arrive in Havana."

"I don't like being contacted by strangers, Vic. This unnamed contact will pave the way for me to meet with people who might have information about what you're looking for?"

"Yes. Proof. You know, the more I think about it, the more I'm convinced we're overpaying you. This will be simpler than I imagined."

"Very funny. I'd like to see the plane. When am I supposed to leave for Colombia?"

"Tomorrow, after you meet with my superior. The meeting is just a formality, Max. You know, shake hands, let him see what he's paying for. You'll have everything you need for Colombia and Cuba: papers, flight charts, phone numbers, that sort of thing." He paused to look Pauling over like a headmaster. "Any chance of buying a suit before then?"

"No."

Gosling winced. "Come on," he said, tossing money on the table. "Let's go see your airplane. Maybe that will put a smile on your face." As they left the area, he added, "God, Max, lighten up. We have a free night in Miami, and I mean *free*."

Pauling had specified the type of twin-engine aircraft he wanted for the assignment, a vintage Piper Aztec B, the same model in which he'd received his multiengine rating back in New Mexico. It was parked in an isolated corner of Miami International along with other private aircraft. Gosling followed him around the plane as he checked it over.

"It's rented, Max, at great expense," Gosling said. "Handle with care."

Pauling ignored him, opened the left-hand door, and

peered inside. All seats had been removed except for the pilot's to make use of every available inch of space for cargo. He scanned the instrument panel; it was nicely packed with navigation equipment. "How about a spin?"

"I don't think so, Max, although I know you're itching to try it out. No, you go ahead. We'll meet up later at my hotel."

"You're not staying where I'm staying?"

"No. I'm at the Delano, on Collins Avenue. I would have put you there, too, except I had a feeling you'd prefer to be near the airport. You know, the smell of aviation fuel, the screeching of landing jets, that sort of thing. Meet me at the Delano tonight at eight. We'll do up the town."

"Don't wait for me."

"Fly safe, Max." Gosling started to walk away. He stopped, turned, and said, "Eight o'clock. Be there!"

Pauling arrived at the Delano Hotel precisely at eight. He'd substituted a blue blazer for his vest, tan slacks for his jeans, a blue button-down shirt for the T-shirt, and brown loafers for sneakers. He called Gosling's room and was told to wait in the Rose Bar, a luxe, dimly lit watering hole with hushed conversations. No rose grew there. Gosling arrived moments after Pauling had ordered.

"You look positively corporate," Gosling said as he took a bar stool next to Max. "Well, not quite, but it's certainly an improvement."

"I'm glad you approve. Fancy place."

"As I said, I work for a generous employer. Was the plane to your satisfaction?"

"It's got lots of hours on it. I hope you got a discount."

"Nice hotel, isn't it? One of those Ian Schrager creations. You know him, of Studio 54 fame. Low light everywhere. You need a cigarette lighter to read the buttons in the elevators. The singer Madonna owns the restaurant."

"I knew I wasn't hungry." Pauling had been facing the back bar. He turned to look at Gosling. "This is all very nice, Vic, but I'm not in the mood for sight-seeing. What time does your guy arrive tomorrow?"

"Same flight I took, Virgin Air, gets in about three."

"I'd like to leave before that. I've got a two-day flight to Colombia. I can't overfly Cuba. I'll refuel in Guatemala. In other words, I want to leave at the crack of dawn tomorrow."

"I understand, and I suppose Craig will, too. It's not as though he's coming here just to meet you. Other business."

"Good."

"Ironic that you can't overfly Cuba. You'll be landing there in a few days."

"Yeah. You were going to give me everything I need. I'd like it now."

"I can do that. Does your early departure rule out a bit of fun tonight?"

"I'm up for dinner. Not at Madonna's place. Nothing after that."

Gosling's sigh was deep. "Where has our fun-loving Max Pauling gone?" he asked.

"There never was a fun-loving Max Pauling, Vic. Fun-loving guys in our business—what *used* to be my business—don't last long. In fact, mind if I skip dinner? I need an early night."

"Not at all. Stay here. I'll get your paperwork from the room."

Gosling returned ten minutes later and handed Pauling a thick manila envelope. "I think you'll find everything you need in here," he said. "I trust we've supplied the right aeronautical charts."

"It doesn't matter. I'll get my own from flight ops at the airport."

Pauling prepared to leave the bar. "This contact," he said, "who'll be coming to my hotel—?"

"Last name is Sardiña. The code word is Chico."

Pauling laughed and shook his head. "Code words," he said. "Shadowy, nameless guys. Intrigue even if it's not necessary."

"Like old times, huh, Max?" Gosling said, slapping Pauling on the back. "Don't try to contact me. Sardiña will keep me informed. And Max, do a good job, huh? Remember, there's a bonus on the line, as well as my reputation with my superiors. I pushed hard for you on this assignment."

Pauling just looked at him and left. The sound of jets landing and taking off kept him awake most of the night.

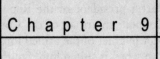

Chapter 9

Havana

". . . and so Castro was pitching in a sandlot baseball game. He walked a batter who promptly stole second base. Castro ordered him back to first and said something like, 'In the revolution, no one can steal—even in baseball.' "

Mac Smith laughed. Their plane was on final approach. Smith had changed seats during the flight, ending up next to former senator Price McCullough, who told the story.

"Not apocryphal?" Smith asked.

"Absolutely not," McCullough replied. "It was on Cuban television. Castro changes all the rules when it strikes him, micromanages everything. He decided that nurses should wear pants instead of skirts to avoid having them bend over a bed and cause heart attacks in patients behind them. His birthday's coming up while we're there."

"Yes, I know."

The approach was from the southeast, over the Caribbean Sea and the Peninsula de Zapata. As the plane descended for landing at José Martí International Airport, south of Havana, Smith looked down at the Cuban capital, home to more than two million of the island nation's almost eleven million citizens. Smith put away the papers he'd been reviewing during the flight, including a list of Fidel Castro's official titles—first secretary of the Communist Party; president of the Republic; chairman of the State Council; chairman of the Council of Ministers; commander in chief of the armed forces—and probably a few more when it suited him, Smith mused with a smile.

It took what seemed to be an inordinate amount of time for the doors of the 727 to open after it had landed and taxied to a cordoned area. During the wait, the passengers peered through the windows at preparations taking place outside. A dozen men in suits scurried about the plane, coming and going from view, their chores undefined. Farthest back stood a cadre of armed uniformed officers (military or police?), their expressions also uniform. A truck with a telescoping antenna extending high above sat near the uniformed officers twenty feet from the aircraft's exit door. A young woman got out, followed by two men, one holding a shoulder-supported camcorder, the other with a microphone mounted on a long metal pole and tethered to the camera by a cable. A sign on the side of the truck read CANAL 2: TELE REBELDE.

"The Cuban free press," Smith commented to McCullough.

"There's a second channel," said McCullough. "The Cubans love their TV, especially soap operas from Brazil."

"I heard CNN just opened a bureau here," said Smith. "Speaking of CNN . . ." A mobile crew from CNN's Havana bureau had arrived and quickly set up next to the Cuban crew.

The sudden opening of the door by a flight attendant allowed a rush of hot, steamy air into the cabin. Led by McCullough, the twenty members of his mission descended to the tarmac where they were greeted individually by two representatives of the Foreign Investment Ministry, established in 1994 to foster foreign cash infusions for the country's ailing economy. Mac Smith was surprised at their apparent youth, although he knew that Castro had initiated a program under which hundreds of bright young Cuban men and women were sent abroad to study Western marketing, advertising, and manufacturing techniques.

After handshakes, one of the greeters led McCullough to a podium where the Cuban spoke into a microphone. "It is my pleasure, on behalf of the Independent Socialist Republic of Cuba, to welcome members of this distinguished delegation to our country. I bring personal greetings from Prime Minister Castro, who wishes you a pleasant and fruitful stay in our country."

McCullough spoke next: "On behalf of my colleagues, I thank you for your gracious greeting, and we look forward to meetings that are both informative and substantive. *Gracias!*"

The entourage was led to a fleet of black Mercedes limousines, engines running, drivers standing ready beside open doors. McCullough and the others entered the vehicles. Minutes later, sandwiched between an escort of marked military vehicles equipped with flashing lights, they headed for Havana and the hotel in which they would be housed during their stay, the venerable Nacional, on Calle O, off La Rampa.

"Looks like The Breakers in Palm Beach," said one of the delegation as the limos turned into a long, palm-lined driveway. The neoclassical, twin-turreted building perched on a hill above the Malecón, Havana's sweeping six-lane seaside boulevard, protected by a seawall. The entourage entered the hotel's huge vaulted lobby with its wood-beamed ceilings, Moorish arches, and Arab-inspired mosaic tile floor. The Nacional had been Cuba's narcissistic centerpiece during the high-flying, extravagant Batista years, the playground of America's rich, famous, and infamous, whose photographs still adorned the walls of the Bar of Fame.

"Of course it does," a female advertising executive replied. "Same architect."

"I didn't know."

Check-in had been previously arranged; a dozen bellhops stood ready to lead the newly arrived guests to their rooms. Before they dispersed, however, they were led to a public room where a woman billed as their official guide introduced herself and handed them a written itinerary covering the rest of that day. In excellent English, she assured them there had been ample time built into the schedule for sight-seeing. One of the men from the Foreign Investment Ministry then introduced a representative from the U.S. "Interests Section."

"I'm sure many of you know that diplomatic relations with Cuba were severed long ago," he said in a New England accent. "The Special Interests Section was established in 1977 to function as a quasi-embassy, sans ambassador. We're limited as to assistance we can provide visitors—our mission is more political than consular. But we have registered each of you and urge you to contact us if any problems arise that indicate we might be of help. We're housed in what used to be our embassy—the Swiss have taken it over." He handed out a sheet of paper on which the Special Interests Section's address and relevant phone numbers were listed. "Enjoy your stay," he said. "And welcome to Cuba."

"Annabel. Mac."

"You're there."

"I think so. I just got to my room."

"You sound so close."

"Yeah, I'm surprised, too. They evidently brought in Italian and Mexican phone companies to improve the phone service, which used to be two tin cans connected by a string. How are you?"

"Fine. How was the flight? The hotel?"

"No problems. The room is lovely, a suite really, on a special executive floor. All the amenities. Cable TV, a safe, minibar. And obviously a telephone. Probably a wiretap. I have an ocean view."

"I didn't think you were supposed to enjoy opulent accommodations in a Communist country."

"It probably doesn't represent most of the country. What's new back home?"

"Not a lot. I spent some time at the gallery trying to straighten out the computer problems. A total failure. I'll have to bring someone in. Oh, guess who called?"

"Fidel? Looking for a date?"

"Jessica Mumford."

"That's a voice from the past. How is she?"

"She's fine. She loves New Mexico. She's working for a local hospital."

Although Jessica had moved from Washington, she and Annabel kept fairly regular phone contact.

"Is she still with the guy she moved there with? He was with State. What was his name? Max something."

"Max Pauling. She's still with him, although he's off on some assignment."

"I thought he left whichever agency he was with."

"He's not with the government any longer. Jessica says he's doing something with his plane in Miami."

"That's right. He was a pilot. Well, I'd better get unpacked. We have a briefing in an hour." He gave her the phone number of the hotel. "How's Rufus?" he asked. The Great Blue Dane was part of their family.

"Depressed. He misses you."

"Give him a kiss for me. Here's one for you, too."

"I'm not depressed—but I'll take it anyway."

Max Pauling's arrival in Havana was neither auspicious nor ceremonial. He'd hoped to fly nonstop from Colombia to Havana, but with the plane's cargo bringing it close to a maximum gross weight of forty-eight hundred pounds, he was forced to make a refueling stop in the Dominican Republic. Now he touched down at José Martí Airport shortly after midnight and was directed by ground control to one of many cargo buildings. There, his cargo was unloaded into a truck dispatched by Havana's foremost hospital, Hermanos Ameijeiras.

"I need a taxi," Pauling told a dispatcher at the facility. *"Sí, señor."*

Minutes after the dispatcher placed a call, a Russian-built Lada from Panataxi pulled up, driven by a young man wearing a New York Yankees baseball cap. Pauling told him, "Hotel Habana Riviera, *por favor.*"

The driver thanked Pauling profusely for paying in dollars instead of pesos and deposited him in front of the twenty-story hotel, a throwback to the days when Meyer Lansky and the American Mafia ran Havana. Lansky had built it as his last attempt to emulate the Las Vegas strip before being forced to flee Cuba when Castro, victorious in his revolution, announced, "We are ready not only to deport American gangsters, but to shoot them."

Next to it was the more imposing Meliá Cohiba Hotel;

well-dressed men and women, few of them Cuban, streamed through its doors.

Pauling entered and looked in on Palacio de Salsa, a nightclub, off the lobby, before going to the desk and registering, using a MasterCard issued on a Canadian bank that had been in the packet of materials given him by Vic Gosling. Cards issued by U.S. banks were forbidden in Cuba, Gosling had said. He'd also told Pauling that if he needed cash, he could use the card to obtain up to five thousand dollars at Banco Financiero Internacional, in the Hotel Habana Libre.

The room to which he was shown was large but utilitarian; some of the furniture bore scars from years of use. It was on the fourth floor. He opened a window and looked down on the Malecón. Even at a late hour it teemed with activity, hundreds of people milling about, young couples openly necking on the seawall, street merchants hawking their wares, radios blaring infectious Cuban riffs and rhythms. The music, and the heat, drifted up to him and he suddenly felt nauseous. Pauling closed the window, turned up the room's air-conditioning, and sprawled on the bed. The room was dark except for a small lamp on the desk. Even with the windows and drapes closed, the sounds from the Malecón reached him. The urge for a cigarette came and went, and returned. *Maybe a fabled Cuban cigar,* he thought; *I won't inhale.*

Then, for no known reason, as though some alien spirit had invaded his body, tears came to his eyes and he felt cold and alone.

It had been years since such a feeling had overtaken him. It had happened in Budapest while on assignment for the CIA, working through an embassy cover, handling an informer from Hungary's military bureaucracy who wanted to defect, accepting the secrets the informer brought to the safe house, feeding the man's ego along with good whiskey and food, flush with the excitement of clandestine meetings and shadowy relationships, the danger and intrigue a kind of nourishment for his own soul— until the informer was found dead one morning in a vacant lot near his modest home, discovered by his ten-year-old son.

It was that night, after the informer had failed to show up at the safe house—and after Pauling had learned the reason why—that this damnable wave of weakness and vulnerability had swept over him while lying in bed in his apartment in Budapest, hearing music and people laughing outside, and he had thought of Doris and his sons.

Now, he wondered, what was Jessica doing at this moment? Did she miss him?

He went to the small bathroom, splashed cold water on his face, but avoided looking at the mirror.

Music from the nightclub followed him across the lobby, through the front door of the hotel, and along the expansive Malecón. But after a half hour of walking, fatigue from the long flight caught up with him and he returned to the hotel. The cocktail lounge was still open. He sat at the bar and ordered Hatuey, a Cuban lager. A group of Canadian tourists, loudly proclaiming their presence, occupied a large corner table. An affectionate couple—they looked French to Pauling—held hands and kissed in another corner. To Pauling's left was a heavyset man who attempted to speak in Spanish to the bartender. On the right was an extremely attractive woman, perhaps thirty, no younger, possibly a few years older. He assumed she was Cuban; certainly of Hispanic origin. Her hair was raven black, thick and luxurious, shimmering beneath the targeted light from a recessed spotlight above her. He saw her in profile; her features were fine; good genes had prevailed. She wore a blue-and-yellow silk dress and a dozen thin gold bracelets on her left wrist.

The half-finished drink on the bar in front of her was dark, a rum concoction, he assumed. He'd noticed since arriving in Havana that Cuban women, at least those in the prime of their sexual lives, tended to be lusty and voluptuous. It wasn't so much physical assets that defined their attractiveness. It was an exuded sense that, for them, sex was to be freely and openly enjoyed, even celebrated, giving further credence to the theory that the major sexual organ is between the ears.

She'd ignored him when he sat down, never bothering to turn. Was she a prostitute? he wondered. Prostitution was rampant in Cuba, particularly with young girls, the *jineteras*, meaning literally "jockeys." Seemingly they were everywhere; he'd been propositioned twice during his short walk on the Malecón. No; too old at thirty-plus, in too good shape. If she was a whore, she was a spectacular one. He'd been told that the major hotels—was his a major hotel?—kept out prostitutes. Maybe she worked in concert with the bartender, a hefty fellow with a healthy head of salt-and-pepper hair, wearing a loose-fitting, white guayabera, the ubiquitous dress shirt of Cuban men.

Pauling motioned for the bartender and asked for the check. He was asked whether he was a guest of the hotel. "*Sí,*" he replied.

While the bartender went to the end of the bar to fetch a hotel charge slip, the woman called out softly after him, "Chico?"

The bartender did not turn. Not his name, Pauling thought. But then it registered. *Chico.* He turned and faced her. She smiled.

"You're—?" he started to ask.

The slightest shake of her head indicated that he was to be silent.

She stood, smiled at him again, and left the bar. Pauling signed the charge slip and followed. She'd gone to the street and was walking up Paseo. She moved slowly, allowing him to easily catch her.

"You're Sardiña?" he asked as they walked side by side, not looking at each other.

"Yes. And you are Max. I asked for you at the hotel desk and they said you'd left. I waited for you in the bar." Only a trace of an accent infringed on her English.

"Why did you assume I'd come into the bar?" he asked.

"I didn't. I felt like a drink. It didn't matter whether you came in or not. I would have called your room until I reached you."

Pauling chuckled.

"What's funny?"

"All this secrecy about meeting you. I didn't know you were—a woman."

"Does that bother you?"

"No, of course not."

Did she sense he was lying? That she was a woman in the general sense of it was fine. That she was a woman in whom he would be placing his professional faith was another thing. He hadn't known many female operatives in his career, and had worked with even fewer. But one experience in El Salvador had soured his view.

He'd been sent there under embassy cover to "handle" a woman from that country named Gina, who'd come over from the other side; his superiors in Langley had assured him that she could be trusted. They'd worked together to set up a sting in which she seduced a government official from El Salvador's military establishment in a hotel room rigged with a camera. It went smoothly. The official had been compromised. The photos would go to his wife and children unless he provided information from within his agency.

A meeting with the official was arranged for late one night in a secluded suburb of San Salvador. Pauling showed up at the scheduled time, but Gina did not. Nor did the government official. Waiting were a dozen armed militia members instead, intent on taking him captive and, he was certain, torturing him to death. His antennae, however, had been fully extended, he saw them before they saw him, and he made his escape, avoiding physical confrontation with the militiamen.

Later, during a debriefing at Langley, he learned that Gina had been the official's lover for more than a year. Their lovemaking had been practiced, old hat. Rather than setting up the official, she'd used the situation to target Pauling. So much for Langley's intelligence inside El Salvador. That he'd run the risk of being killed didn't keep certain colleagues from kidding him about the episode. Somehow, he didn't find it funny.

Gina's pretty face came and went when he looked at Sardiña.

Cognitively, he knew that he was supposed to view the opposite sex as equal—equal opportunity and equal pay—it was expected, and he'd tried, not wanting to be out of the mainstream of thought these days, even espousing his belief in the notion of no difference between men and women, at least in the workplace.

But there *was* a difference.

Workplace?

Going undercover to spy and putting your life on the line in the bargain hardly represented a workplace.

The smell of her perfume reached his nostrils, carrying such pragmatic thoughts into the humid Havana air.

"Where are we going?" he asked.

"An apartment."

"You live in Cuba?"

"No. It belongs to a friend of mine. She's away on business."

"Convenient."

"Very. I'll be staying there for as long as it takes you to finish your assignment."

They turned into a *solar*, a dark, narrow alley.

"The apartment's here?" Pauling asked.

"At the end."

He stopped walking, allowing her to get a few steps ahead. She stopped, too, and turned. "Are you all right?" she asked. Her voice was low for a woman, and well modulated.

"Yes, of course." His defenses were up, his senses sharpened. He didn't know this woman, yet blindly followed her into the darkness.

They reached a doorway, which she opened. A key wasn't necessary. Pauling looked up. Silhouetted against the sky was a wrought-iron balcony; clothing hung from it. A bare bulb in the tiny foyer's ceiling fixture gave scant light, as though receiving only some of the intended electricity. A set of stone steps led to upper floors. As the woman called Sardiña ascended the steps, Pauling took notice of the sway in her hips and the nicely turned calves and ankles below the dress hem. It was insufferably hot in the cramped staircase; her perfume dizzied him as he followed her to a steel door, which she also opened without a key. She reached for a wall switch and the room took shape; small, square, with two doors leading from it. The only window was open and a blessed breeze rippled white chintz curtains. There was a pullout couch, a tall, slender dresser, two red vinyl sling chairs, and a black rug that lay in the middle of the wood floor like a square on a checkerboard. She went to the tiny kitchen, light from it spilling across the floor.

"Would you like a drink?" she asked.

He came to the doorway. "Sure."

He watched her take a bottle of rum from a cabinet, and two cordial glasses, which she filled. She handed one to him, smiled, raised her glass, and said, "Salud!"

Pauling nodded and tasted.

"Habana Club," she said. "Anejo. Aged seven years."

"It's good," he said, returning to the main room and sitting on the couch. She took one of the chairs.

"You have a first name I assume," he said.

"Of course I do," she said, laughing.

"All Vic told me—you know Vic, of course—he called you Sardiña. That's all."

"I suppose he didn't want to scare you off," she said, "my being a woman. Celia. My name is Celia."

"Celia. What's your story?"

"My story?"

"Are you Cuban?"

"Born here, to the States when I was eleven."

"You, ah—you spend a lot of time here?"

"Some. I'm with the Cuban-American Health Initiative. I get to come back often, especially since the embargo allows the sale of medical supplies to Cuba."

Pauling nodded. The Cuban-American Health Initiative. Another CIA front? There were so many you couldn't tell them apart without a scorecard. What was her story?

"How did you get involved with Gosling?" he asked.

"So many questions."

"I like to know who I'm working with."

"So do I."

He grinned, pulled one of the business cards from Cali Forwarding that Gosling had given him, and handed it to her. She dropped it to the floor next to her chair.

"You're working with Celia Sardiña, who can put you in touch with the right people," she said. "Would you like another drink?"

"No. I need some sleep. Does that couch pull out?"

"For me, it does. Can you find your way back to the hotel?"

"I'll manage. When do you start putting me in touch with the right people?"

"Tomorrow."

"And what do I do, hang around the bar waiting for you?"

"Be here at four. We're having dinner with a friend."

"And what do I do for the rest of the day, send post-cards of Fidel to my friends?"

"El Comandante has had people killed for less flippancy. I suggest that if you must refer to him, you stroke your chin. The bearded one. It is the way it's done here."

"Thanks for the lesson."

"One of many I suspect you need. Please close the door on your way out."

Walter Fuentes was in his second term as the junior senator from Florida. Born to Cuban-American parents, he'd received a law degree from Vanderbilt University and had practiced in Miami until making a successful run for mayor of that city. When the senior senator, Cagney Jones, suffered a fatal heart attack, Fuentes was encouraged to run for the unexpectedly vacant seat. Photogenic and appropriately domesticated—his wife and teenage children, nicely divided between the sexes, were seldom out of camera range—Fuentes had become, by virtue of winning the senate seat, the country's leading voice for Miami's Cuban exile community.

On this day, he led two men and two women into the Oval Office where James L. Walden warmly greeted them, shaking hands and addressing each by name; his ability to remember names was well known, a useful political attribute. With the president were his national security advisor, Paul Draper, and State's assistant secretary for Cuban affairs, Kathleen James. After everyone had been seated, two white-jacketed mess attendants served coffee, brewed especially strong at the president's suggestion, and bite-sized fruit Danish. Fuentes said, "It's good of you to see us this morning, Mr. President. We know how difficult it is to make time in your busy schedule like this."

"There's always time, Senator, when the issue is important." He turned his attention to the others. "I'm not unaware," he said, "of the goals of your organization and your purpose for asking to meet. Senator Fuentes has been a committed and effective advocate for you, and for your people and their point of view. But as you know, my administration doesn't necessarily agree with some of the actions you espouse regarding Prime Minister Castro and the future of Cuba." He laughed. "But you certainly have many Republican members of Congress in your camp. Or maybe I shouldn't refer to camps at this moment."

They all chuckled. The four people with Fuentes represented the Cuban-American Freedom Alliance (CAFA). Politically implacable, well-financed, and powerful, CAFA considered itself the Cuban government in exile, an unofficial title bestowed by President Reagan when he helped establish the group during his presidency. It had been treated as such by subsequent administrations until Walden came to power. His view of CAFA was not nearly as supportive.

"Mr. President," CAFA's leader, Ramon Gomez, said, "my organization represents almost a million Cuban-born American citizens in this country, more than half of them living in the Miami area. We—"

Walden was quick to correct him. "Mr. Gomez, I am fully aware that your organization is an important voice for Cuban-Americans, but not for all of them. There are hundreds of thousands who do not share your goal of liberating Cuba through force. I met only a few weeks ago with members of Cambio Cubana, which I believe stands for Cubans for Change, and the Cuban Committee for Democracy. They share a more moderate view of how to resolve the Cuban problem, if I may call it that. With all due respect, you don't have a monopoly on Cuban policy."

"That may be true, Mr. President," Fuentes said, "but those in power never have a monopoly in a democracy. What was your margin of victory, sir, nine percent?" He smiled to soften the rebuke. "Of course, the dictator Castro *does* have a monopoly. Ruthless dictators always do."

Draper stepped in. "Surveys show, Mr. Gomez, that half of the Cuban population in the United States wish an open dialogue with Castro, not liberation by force. They want Cuba freed through diplomacy."

"But no survey is needed to show who among our people is willing to put their money behind their convictions," Gomez said.

Walden glanced at Draper; a small smile came and went. The not-so-subtle message from the Cuban leader was that CAFA had been a substantial contributor to politicians championing its cause, at least in campaign rhetoric. And that included key Democrats as well as Republicans. The numbers had been delivered to Walden before the meeting: more than $1.5 million in campaign contributions since 1981, including $125,000 to President Clinton, who tightened the trade embargo while his opponent, George Bush, withheld support for the harsh Torricelli bill that, among other things, fostered the overthrow of Castro by financing dissidents in Cuba.

Assistant Secretary James spoke up. "Mr. Gomez," she said, "our intelligence from Cuba clearly indicates that a majority of the Cuban people fear what would become of them should CAFA succeed in overthrowing Castro and become the new government in power."

"Fear us?" Gomez said mockingly. "Why would they fear us? We fight for them and their right to live in a free society."

"Their fears are well-founded," Walden said, casting a quick, surreptitious glance at a clock on the wall. He'd shoehorned them in that morning in the middle of an especially busy day, but didn't want to offend them by seeming impatient. Their constituency and its political clout was too important for that, to say nothing of their money muscle. "You've taken a stand stating you'll deal harshly with any foreign country that's done business with Cuba during the Castro years," Walden said. "The people are afraid that you'll take back all that was taken from you and grab everything the Castro government has stolen, including what they've lost over the years. They're aware that you've been a prime supporter of the embargo that not only has made the average Cuban's life difficult, it's given Castro exactly what he wants, an enemy responsible for his people's problems. He loves the embargo, Mr. Gomez. It was a gift to him. Now, I must leave shortly for another appointment. What precisely is it you want from this meeting?"

Senator Fuentes answered, "There is a growing concern, Mr. President, that you and your administration are paving the way for a so-called dialogue with Castro in the hope of establishing some form of working relationship with him. You've eroded the embargo at every opportunity."

"I've heard all this from your Republican colleagues in Congress," Walden said, "only not as pleasantly put at times. I have no intention at this juncture of advancing any further initiatives to soften the stand against Prime Minister Castro and what he stands for."

He meant it. Although he quietly harbored the desire to pave the way for a resolution of the forty-year-plus standoff with Castro, the thought of possibly having to give even the smallest concession to the Cuban leader was anathema. He was aware of all the horror stories emanating from Havana—political foes tossed into shark tanks for Fidel's pleasure, the thousands summarily executed for "crimes against the state," the beatings and other torture of Cuban citizens—and he also knew that the devil sometimes had something to offer, in this case the possibility of bringing Cuba into the sphere of democracy and free enterprise.

Walden again spoke to his guests. "Bear in mind that the embargo hasn't done a damn thing to topple Castro and turn Cuba into a democracy. Engagement is what's needed. There are nations all over the globe that aren't democracies and that have brutal regimes, but we don't put them under embargo. It's Fidel under everyone's skin, isn't it? What has he outlasted, eight, nine American presidents? I don't carry a brief for Castro, but I know that if you want Cuba restored to a democracy, the embargo is not the way to go."

"Senator McCullough's trip?" Fuentes said flatly.

"What about it?"

"Isn't he seeking even fewer restrictions on trade and travel? And with your blessing."

Walden stood and pulled his suit jacket from the back of his chair. He slipped into it, punched a button on his phone, and told someone that he was ready for the next meeting. The president turned to the five people seated in front of his desk and said, "Price McCullough is a private citizen. He went to Cuba with a number of our leading citizens to engage the Cubans in discussions on how American business might benefit from barriers to trade that have already been lowered. At the same time, he and his delegation are delivering a message stating, quite simply, that unless and until there is significant improvement on human rights in Cuba, this country will not only continue to take strong action against Cuba, it will support further restrictions. It was good seeing you. I hate to cut this short but you must excuse me. Perhaps we can soon schedule another meeting when I'm not so pressed for time."

A presidential aide led Fuentes, Gomez, and the others from the room. When they were gone, Walden said to Draper and James, "These Miami hard-liners are counterproductive to their own goals, Castro gone and Cuba free. They finance these training camps in Florida—now Mexico—what's the new one called?"

"Timba Candente," Assistant Secretary James replied. "Named after Cuban music and Spanish for hot."

"Yeah, Timba Candente," Walden repeated scornfully. "And with the CIA's blessing, if not outright support. Damn, it's like we have two governments running the country, the one in this White House and the one operating out of Langley. Next thing we know there'll be another attempt on Castro's life. How many have there been, a dozen? More? Time for another bomb in his cigar, or botulin? They *did* try botulin, didn't they?"

"Yes, sir," Draper confirmed.

"The one I enjoyed was when they managed to sprinkle a strong depilatory into his shoes and hoped his hair would fall out," James said with a chuckle. "To damage his image."

"Thallium salts," Draper said.

"What?" Walden said.

"The depilatory they put in his shoes."

"Oh."

Since taking office, Walden's relationship with the CIA had been strained, at best. He knew that the nation needed such an intelligence agency to ensure survival in an increasingly dangerous world. The problem, as Walden saw it, was that the agency's role and methods had changed dramatically since President Truman established it under the National Security Act of 1947. Truman had sought to establish an overt intelligence organization, one emphasizing the gathering and analysis of information. But the 1947 act contained special provisions exempting the CIA from certain normal congressional review processes. It methodically transformed itself from the open intelligence-gathering agency envisioned by Truman to what it had become today, a secretive organization in which furtive cells of operatives were free to function on their own with only minimal oversight by the agency's management, much less so Congress and the White House. The myriad attempts on Castro's life were justified, Walden had to admit to himself and close advisors. The man was evil; ask the hundreds of Cubans who'd been tossed to the sharks because they dared question Castro's authority and policies. Maybe if one of those CIA attempts had been successful, and not so clumsily mounted, Walden would have had a more sanguine view of the agency. Maybe if it didn't make other mistakes, miss other opportunities, and operate under such a cloak of secrecy, he would have more readily embraced its role and mission. Too many maybes where the CIA was concerned.

Participants in the next meeting were ushered into the Oval Office, and Draper and James left.

"He was convincing," Kathleen James said softly as they walked to Draper's office.

"He always is. That's why he's the president."

Across the river, in Virginia, Zachary Rasmussen, the Central Intelligence Agency's director of covert operations, sat in a room with some of his Cuban specialists. They'd run through a wide-ranging agenda. Now the final item scheduled for discussion was on the table.

"What reports do we have on the McCullough trip?" Rasmussen asked.

The person charged with keeping tabs on the delegation through contacts in Havana responded, "Nothing of interest yet. All handshakes. Their first round of meetings is scheduled for this afternoon."

Rasmussen opened a file folder. "What's this about Pauling going to Cuba?"

"He's there," another voice at the table replied.

"How long ago was he with us?" Rasmussen asked.

"Ten years." Reading from a report, he added, "He went over to State from us. Retired from State. No, correct that, no official retirement. Severed employment. Went to New Mexico with another State employee, one Jessica Mumford. Teaches flying in Albuquerque. He, not she. Signed on to ferry supplies to Timba Candente in Mexico. Another former agent, Victor Gosling, recruited him for work with Gosling's current employer, Cell-One."

"In Cuba?"

"Yes. We're cooperating with Gosling. He arranged for Pauling to use Cali Forwarding in Colombia as his cover in Cuba."

"Uh-huh. Pauling was a loose cannon as I remember."

"Correct. He once reported to Hoctor."

Rasmussen made a note on a pad to call Tom Hoctor. He asked, "What's this work he's doing in Cuba for Cell-One?"

"According to Gosling, they're trying to establish a link between Senator McCullough's pharmaceutical firm, BTK Industries, and a German pharmaceutical, Strauss-Lochner Resources. Gosling's client is Signal Labs."

Rasmussen paused and frowned before asking, "Any chance Pauling has a second reason for going to Cuba?"

"Hard to say, sir, at this juncture. He did make contact at his hotel with Celia Sardiña. She's done contract work for us in the past. Biochemistry major at Miami U, has easy access to Havana through our Cuban-American Health Initiative."

"I know her. She's now working for Gosling, too?"

"He didn't mention her, but we had a sighting of her with Pauling. They left the hotel and went to her apartment."

Rasmussen's laugh was cynical. "I'm sure they did. Show me the file on her."

"Shall do."

"And get Gosling in here. No, someplace else. Make sure he understands that because we've been cooperating with him and Cell-One doesn't mean he can get in the way of what we have going in Cuba."

"Shall do."

"Anything else?"

No one spoke.

"That's a wrap," Rasmussen said.

Alone in his office, he dialed the extension of Tom Hoctor.

"Hoctor here."

"Tom, Zach Rasmussen. Got a minute?"

"Sure."

"I want you to tell me what you know about Max Pauling."

Hoctor's sigh was long and bulging with meaning. "I'll be right up," he said.

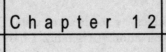

The reception was held in a large public room at the Hotel Nacional. Representatives from Cuba's governmental and industrial sectors were on hand to exchange information and views with counterparts from the American delegation. Former attorney Mac Smith sat at a small, round table with two Cuban attorneys, one civil and one criminal, and a judge from the People's Supreme Court. A waiter had served them drinks after having presented a tray overflowing with hot hors d'oeuvres. Background music provided by three colorfully costumed troubadours playing *las trovas Cubanas* tunes on their guitars lightened the mood created by so many dark suits.

"Yes, we have capital punishment, as you well know," Smith said in response to a question. "It's on a state-by-state basis, although there are federal statutes allowing for executions. They are rarely used."

"State by state," the judge, who was in fact a judicial-looking older gentleman with close-cropped white hair, smoking a long, black cigar, repeated. "Here we have only one state, although there are many provincial and municipal courts. You Americans prefer the electric chair or lethal injection as a means of ridding yourself of incorrigible criminals. We use the firing squad. It's much more efficient."

"We have a few states that still use firing squads,"

Smith said, smiling. "You're appointed to the bench, I understand."

"That is correct, by the head of state. Others are appointed by the National Assembly. I have never understood the election of judges as practiced in much of the United States. It is too political as a process."

Smith started to answer but one of the Cuban attorneys returned to the subject of capital punishment. "Your appellate process can take years."

"Yes. It often does."

"We have appeals courts, too, but our system allows for a more expeditious method."

"Which runs the risk of executing innocent people."

"We don't execute innocent people, Mr. Smith," the second lawyer said. "Our penal code accepts a defendant's confession as sufficient proof of guilt. Criminals who are executed here have confessed to their crimes."

And maybe had it beat out of them, Smith thought.

"You Americans view us as having an overly harsh legal system," said the judge, "but we are more humane than you in many ways. Here, individuals incarcerated for crimes other than political offenses are guaranteed a return to their jobs when they're released." He raised bushy eyebrows and drew on his cigar, as though to indicate that he was a clear winner in the debate.

"I'd like to see one of your courts in action," Smith said.

"I'll see if that can be arranged," the judge assured.

Price McCullough and two other members of the delegation joined them.

"Judge de Céspedes has offered to let me sit in on a court case," Smith told the ex-senator.

"Careful, Mac. You're likely to get caught up in it and start objecting."

Smith smiled. "If I do, I might end up facing a firing

squad." He checked the judge's face for signs of displeasure. There were none.

McCullough said to the table, "I've just gotten word that we might have the pleasure of meeting Prime Minister Castro himself."

"If that is the case, you are indeed fortunate," the judge said.

McCullough added, "And there's talk of inviting us to his birthday celebration."

"You'll be among many thousands," one of the attorneys said. "All of Havana will be there."

"He's still popular with the people?" Smith asked.

"Oh, yes," Judge de Céspedes said animatedly. "He did a wonderful thing for our country, ridding it of corrupt capitalism and creating a nation truly for the people. Of course, we have recently been through-difficult times since our friends, the Soviets, left us for dead. But the Cuban people's resolve and love of country would not allow that. Our economy grows every day. Under Prime Minister Castro and his policies, things are improving rapidly. A million and more tourists come each year, and the number increases." He gave Smith and McCullough a wry smile. "This number includes many Americans who consider your visitation policies toward us to be backward and unwarranted. Many of your citizens find ways around your restrictions. We now allow self-employment, and many of our state farms are being converted to private ownership. Our sugar industry is again healthy, and we now have our own mutual fund, the Beta Gran Caribe Fund." He lowered his voice as though to tell a secret. "If you wish to invest in it, it is on the Irish Stock Exchange."

His programmed defense of Castro and his accomplishments was interrupted when an aide traveling with the American delegation came to the table and whispered something in McCullough's ear, but not so quietly that Smith didn't hear: "The meeting is set for tomorrow, sir."

McCullough nodded, said nothing in return. A good-looking Cuban woman passed the table, diverting the ex-senator's attention. She smiled provocatively at him. He returned it and said something in Spanish. Smith kept his grin to himself. He'd noticed since arriving that McCullough was open in his appreciation of Cuban women. He had the politician's ability to continue speaking on a subject while his eyes took in other things.

Later, in his suite, Smith called Annabel.

"Just thought I'd check in," he said.

"I'm glad you did. How's it going?"

"Fine. I just left a reception. Had an interesting chat with a judge from the People's Supreme Court. Nice enough fellow. He said he'd try to arrange for me to sit in on a court case while I'm here."

"Sounds intriguing. Wish I were there."

"I do, too. Oh, Price told us tonight that there's a chance Castro will get involved personally in the talks. We might also get to attend his birthday party."

"An intimate affair, I'm sure."

"Just a few thousand close friends. What's new in D.C.?"

"It's hot. Senator Helms held a press conference this morning. He's calling for stiffening the Cuban embargo even more. They interviewed Jimmy Carter. He called the Helms-Burton bill the stupidest thing that's ever been passed. Helms came back and said Carter was always out of touch with the American people and still is."

"What does our current president have to say about this civilized debate?"

"Silence from the White House."

"Smart. Well, I'd better get back downstairs. Any action at the gallery?"

"Slow. Don't forget to keep your eye out for dealers looking to sell pre-Columbian artifacts."

"Getting them out of the country might be a problem. They briefed us on buying Cuban art of any kind. You need a government export license, which I understand can take days."

"Use your considerable clout."

"Or use Price McCullough's considerable clout. I get the feeling he has more than one agenda here. He's got some meeting set up for tomorrow that isn't on our official schedule. Maybe he has a date."

"A date?"

"Yeah. Our former senator has an eye for the ladies here."

"I imagine they have an eye for him, too. He's still a very handsome man, and widowed. Of course, you're a very handsome man, too, Mac, but *you're* not widowed."

"I'm well aware of that. I'd better run. Love you, Mrs. Smith."

"The feeling is entirely mutual, Mr. Smith. *Hasta luego.*"

C h a p t e r   1 3

Heidelberg

Despite having just come from Heidelberg, Kurt Grünewald did not feel like the Student Prince as he stepped from the Cubana Air DC-10 at Havana's José Martí Airport.

The new addition to his staff had barely spoken during the long flight. *An arrogant young man,* Grünewald thought as he looked at his companion sleeping in the next seat. He didn't need any help, and resented having this stranger, who wasn't even a salaried employee, being foisted on him by his superiors. *Didn't they trust him to get the job done? Evidently, they didn't. Well,* he thought as he ordered another rum and Coke from the flight attendant, *I'll put up with him as long as he stays out of my way.* He took a final glance and grimaced at the man's blond hair, cut in that ridiculous fashion popular with young people. *You look like a fool, young man,* Grünewald told him silently as he accepted the drink, one of many he'd consumed during the flight. The older man turned his back on Erich Weinert.

Grünewald had been back in Heidelberg for two days after having been summoned from Havana by his superiors at Strauss-Lochner. His recall to corporate headquarters had been last minute and blunt: "Be here as quickly as possible," he'd been told over the phone by the company's chief operating officer, Dr. Hans Miller.

The Cubana Airlines DC-10, fully booked with German tourists returning home after a holiday in Cuba, had been delayed at José Martí for four hours due to mechanical difficulty. Grünewald was glad he'd booked first-class, *clase tropical* in Cuban aviation-speak, although it was nothing like first-class on Lufthansa. The seats were narrower, the overhead bins smaller, and the food not to Grünewald's liking. He'd been in Cuba for two years but had never taken to the island's native cuisine. He'd found a few Havana restaurants that pretended to serve German food, and tended to take most of his meals at these, although business dictated joining associates in a variety of Cuban eateries. At least beer was plentiful; he bought imported Heineken by the case, and had developed a taste for Cuban rum, particularly seven-year-old Habana Club, which he had delivered to his apartment each week by Casa de Ron, located above El Floridita. This was the restaurant where the daiquiri was made popular, and where Ernest Hemingway's bronze bust looked down on his favorite bar stool that was kept unoccupied as a shrine to the bully-boy author.

Grünewald knew he drank too much. He often rationalized it to himself. What was he to do? His wife and children were back in the town of Eberbach, a suburb of Heidelberg, comfortable in their wood-beamed house on the cobblestone street, enjoying their friends and family who lived close by, enjoying being German in Germany. When he'd been asked to undertake a special assignment in Cuba two years ago, Grünewald told Dr. Miller that he needed time to think about it. But he knew what his answer would be the minute he left Miller's office. He didn't have a choice because his tenure with Strauss-Lochner Resources had become tenuous. After twenty-five years, all of them spent at corporate headquarters in the Heidelberg Technology Park, he could sense his lessened stature within the company through little things—not being invited to meetings in which he used to be routinely involved, being slighted in the routing of important memoranda, overhearing younger colleagues joke at lunch about the "dinosaurs" still with the company—little things that added up to a big reality.

Also, he was not part of the company's medical research team, the largest division and its reason for existence. Strauss-Lochner was a relatively successful developer and manufacturer of drugs developed in close cooperation with Heidelberg University and the famed Deutsche Krebsforschungszentrum Cancer Research Center, DKFZ, founded in 1964 and now an acknowledged world player in cancer treatment and research. But of late the company's fortunes had been shaky. Competition had become cutthroat in the race to develop effective anti-cancer drugs.

But Kurt Grünewald did speak Spanish. And he had achieved a reputation as an effective negotiator, particularly in past labor disputes in which the company had been embroiled. His degree from the esteemed university at Heidelberg was in international affairs, and he had gone on to earn an advanced degree in labor relations. When Miller dispatched him to Cuba, Grünewald was told that the company needed a man of his experience and knowledge to help pave the way for a deal with the Cuban government to allow Strauss-Lochner to buy a controlling interest in the state-owned cancer research institute. He was instructed to establish relationships with the appropriate Cuban officials in a position to influence Fidel Castro, with an eye toward obtaining the dictator's cooperation in the sale of the research institute to a foreign investor. He was given an almost unlimited expense account with which to wine and dine Cuban officials. Should direct payoffs be necessary, he was authorized to spend up to ten thousand dollars without having to seek permission from Heidelberg.

It wasn't until he'd been in Cuba a year that he learned through an errant "secured" communication that the money he spent so freely did not come solely from Strauss-Lochner's coffers. Much of it flowed from the treasury of the American company BTK Industries, headed by the former United States senator from Texas, one Price McCullough. Grünewald wasn't shocked, but he was concerned. His greatest midnight fear was having to go to jail. It was a more pervasive fear than death by fire or drowning. When he questioned Dr. Miller during a visit to corporate headquarters, he was told that Strauss-Lochner and BTK Industries were exploring a merger. "Nothing to concern you, Kurt. Just keep doing your job in Havana."

Which he did, of course.

Five years to the pension.

His wife's protest was vehement.

"Come with me to Cuba," he'd said.

"Nackter wilder!" she'd said, questioning his intelligence. Her affectionate name for him had always been "Boopsie," but not this day. She said many other things, all making the point that if he thought she'd leave their home, their friends, and their grown children to live in some filthy Communist country, he'd lost his mind.

And so he traveled to Havana alone, determined to make the best of however long he would be forced to stay there.

It had been two years.

Now three years to the pension.

"You must leave so soon?" his wife asked over breakfast on the last day of this most recent trip to Heidelberg.

"*Ya,*" he said, wiping his mouth with a napkin and pushing back from the kitchen table. "I would like never to go back, but it is not my choice."

After a series of meetings the previous day, Dr. Miller, Grünewald, and others had gathered for dinner at Kurfürstenstube, in the elegant Der Europäische Hof-Hotel Europa. Grünewald was relieved to be away from the sterile atmosphere of headquarters, and though he could calm himself with vodka and beer, he would have preferred to be home enjoying simpler fare with his wife. He barely ate his saddle of Limousin lamb as he tried to focus on what others at the table were saying, but it became increasingly difficult as the hours passed and the alcohol dulled his senses. Finally, after dessert—crepes flambées with bananas and maple sauce—he was free to go home and sleep.

"What do they say at the meetings, Kurt?" his wife asked at breakfast, her concern for him written on her round face. He'd put more weight on an already sizable frame, causing his shirt collar to press into the folds of his neck. His face was mottled and flushed, and damp with perspiration even on this cool morning in their home on the Neckar River from which the Oldenwald Mountains were visible on a clear day, like this one.

He shrugged, stood, and looked out the door to their garden. She'd asked that question a few times since he'd arrived from Cuba, but he'd remained true to the admonition received from Miller: their discussions were not to be revealed to anyone. Those discussions had occupied the past two days; today would be the final meeting before he boarded a plane at Frankfurt that afternoon for his return flight to Havana.

But there was another reason for not discussing the meetings with Hanna. The truth was, he'd been treated poorly at corporate headquarters, scolded, accused of dragging his feet, questioned as to his drinking habits and other personal matters that he considered out of the realm of corporate interest.

"Just meetings, Hanna," he said, turning and smiling to reassure her that all was well. "A waste of time. Miller likes to hear himself talk, jabber, jabber, jabber, full of his own importance. I will not be sorry when the next three years are gone and I can thumb my nose at them and spend the pension money. We'll have a good life, huh, Hanna? We'll take some trips, work in the garden, enjoy time together."

Her thought was that she would be relieved if he lived to enjoy retirement. Instead, she said, "I look forward to that, Kurt. But you must take care of yourself. The drinking is—"

"Please, none of that, Hanna. Not now. Do I drink a little too much? *Ya,* sometimes. But it is not a problem, not like others we know who are drunkards. It relaxes me. There is nothing else to do in Cuba."

He came up behind her chair and wrapped his arms about her, allowing his hand to brush her sizable bosom. "Don't worry about me, Hanna. Your Boopsie is just biding his time until I can tell them good-bye, and good riddance." He kissed her temple and went to the bedroom where his packed suitcase rested on the bed. For a moment, he considered calling Miller's office to announce that he was not returning to Cuba and that he was resigning, pension be damned. Then he carried the suitcase to the foyer where Hanna waited.

"When will you be home again?" she asked.

"In a few months. Once I finish the business I was sent to Havana to conduct, I am sure Miller will recall me to headquarters. Take care, Hanna. I will write as I have been doing, and call each Sunday."

They embraced. He left the house, climbed into the

BMW he'd rented at the airport, waved, and drove off, his destination the corporate headquarters of Strauss-Lochner Resources.

Had Dr. Hans Miller been born at a different time, he would have been a willing, enthusiastic Nazi, Grünewald was convinced. Slight in stature, with a narrow face and slender nose on which rested small, round, metal-rimmed eyeglasses, he seldom smiled unless it served a purpose. Miller was brilliant, Grünewald knew, and respected the man for that. But it was a narrow intelligence, as narrow as the test tubes of the labs in which Miller seemed more comfortable than with people. He greeted Grünewald with a wave of his hand and without getting up from behind an oversized desk. With him in the office were two other men, the director of research, Dr. Otto Marc, and the company's chief financial officer, Georg Hagen. Hagen had attended the previous meetings of the past two days, but this was the first appearance of Dr. Marc.

"Sit down, Kurt," said Miller. "Did you enjoy dinner last night?"

"Oh, yes, very much so. Such a fine restaurant."

"And bar, too," Miller said, raising one eyebrow.

"*Ya, ya.* Always good drinks there." Grünewald pulled a handkerchief from his jacket and dabbed at his brow and upper lip.

Miller said, "Otto will share with us this morning some of what he has learned from his recent trip to the United States. Please, Otto, the floor is yours."

The tall, gaunt research director opened a notebook on his lap, adjusted his glasses, and began to speak, using the notes as a prompt.

"I spent considerable time in Washington at the NIH, and with a most impressive young physician there, a Dr. Barbara Mancuso. She and some of her colleagues have been doing considerable investigation of what is going on in Cuba. Shortly before we met, she'd attended the annual meeting of the American Society of Clinical Oncology where our Cuban friend Dr. Caldoza presented a paper on his institute's latest research results using vanadium. As we already knew, he and his colleagues have had impressive results with some of the two dozen drugs they've been testing."

Miller interrupted. "This Dr. Mancuso, Otto. Is her interest in the Cuban research purely clinical?"

"As opposed to?"

"As opposed to a commercial interest?"

"I have no evidence of such a thing, Hans."

"NIH works closely with many American pharmaceutical companies," Miller said, "including Signal Laboratories, which, as I have pointed out numerous times, has shown a distinct interest in what the Cubans have achieved. Our sources in the States have made this abundantly clear."

"Do our sources indicate any knowledge on the part of Signal Labs of our arrangement with BTK?" the financial chief, Hagen, asked.

"That isn't clear," Miller replied. "I have been told that Signal has retained an international investigation agency, named Cell-One, to probe the matter."

Grünewald had allowed his attention to shift from what was being said in the room to his imagination, a vision of himself at work in his garden.

"What do you know of this, Kurt?" Miller asked, causing Grünewald to flinch.

"What?"

Miller's impatience was locked in his voice. "What do you know of any investigation taking place in Cuba on behalf of Signal Laboratories?" he repeated.

"Nothing. No, I have heard nothing of such a thing."

"Would you know if you did?" Miller said, more to himself than to Grünewald.

"I think I would," Grünewald said, his voice defensive, betraying nervousness. "Yes, I would have become aware of such a thing. My contacts with the Cuban ministry of health and the doctors at the research facilities are good. Very solid. Very good."

"Are you aware that Senator McCullough is in Cuba, Kurt?"

"*Former* senator," Grünewald said.

Miller sighed. "Yes, Kurt, former senator. Answer my question."

"That I knew he was in Havana? I read about it. I knew he was coming."

"Did he bring others from his company, BTK, with him?"

"I—I will certainly find out the answer to that the moment I am back."

"And you will make contact with Mr. McCullough?"

"Yes, of course, but for what purpose?"

"To assure me that things are progressing with our partner the way they were intended. I have no doubt that a man of McCullough's stature is a man of integrity and honesty. But his trip to Cuba at this time raises questions."

"I will do my best," Grünewald said, "but I am not sure what I could learn simply by meeting the senator. I have so many other obligations, other responsibilities that—"

"Yes, Kurt, I realize that you might be overburdened. I am sending someone back with you to be of help."

"Someone? Who?"

"A younger man with experience in such things."

"Do I know him? Where does he work?"

"He's not from the company, Kurt. He is an independent contractor. His name is Erich Weinert. I have instructed him to meet you at the airport. All arrangements have been made for him to accompany you on the flight, and to be at your side during the coming months."

"I—of course I am grateful for any help you see fit to give me, Hans, but this is a surprise to me, as I am sure you can understand. He will report to me?"

"He will report to *me*, Kurt."

Miller laced his fingers and extended his hands in front of him, causing knuckles to crack. The meeting was over. Miller stood, came around the desk, and perched on its edge, positioning his face only a foot from Grünewald's. "It was never my intention, Kurt, that you should know of our business arrangement with BTK Industries. The situation is extremely delicate, as I am certain you appreciate. If—*when* we gain control of the remarkable cancer research taking place in Cuba, the future of this company will be assured. You will have done a great service, and you will be appropriately rewarded. But if word should get out that we act in Cuba on behalf of the American company BTK, the future will be cloudy at best. Every step must be taken to ensure secrecy. No loose lips, no confidences extended over schnapps, or whatever they call it in Cuba. Am I understood?"

Grünewald swallowed, blinked, and nodded. "*Ya,*" he said.

Miller's sudden smile penetrated Kurt Grünewald's heart.

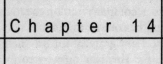

Chapter 14

Havana

Pauling was surprised at how long and soundly he'd slept. He awoke at ten and remained in bed for a few minutes to remind himself where he was, and to reflect upon his meeting with Celia Sardiña.

He'd decided after leaving her borrowed apartment and walking back to the hotel that she was as smug as she was beautiful. Smugness was, to Pauling, a weakness for anyone involved in clandestine work. Smugness equaled sloppiness, inattention to detail.

He indulged himself in a moment of introspection. Was his negative reaction to her personal? She'd placed him in a position of being her subordinate. That wouldn't do. *He* would call the shots, allow her as much leash as he thought reasonable. Was the fact that she was a woman at the heart of his attitude toward her? He assured himself it wasn't.

The bottom line, he decided as he stepped into the shower, was that he would put up with her because he needed her contacts, at least initially. If he were on assignment for his old employers, the CIA and State Department, he would veto her involvement. Those days were rife with danger. You could get killed doing what he'd done for those agencies. Friends had lost their lives.

But there was no apparent danger on this assignment. He wasn't there to subvert the Castro government, or to nurture a traitor within the Maximum Leader's ranks. El Jefe Máximo. "The Maximum Leader!" Only a man with an outsized ego would call himself that. He'd once read that Castro likened himself to Jesus, and that although he needs glasses, he never wears them in public because to do so would be a sign of weakness. *That beard probably hides a double chin*, Pauling thought as he rinsed shampoo from his hair and stepped from the shower.

When he'd gone to bed last night, he was annoyed that nothing would be happening until four the next afternoon. Now, he was glad to have a few hours to take in Havana as a tourist. Someone who'd made numerous trips to Cuba had advised him, "Eat a big breakfast. It might be the best meal you'll have all day." The hotel restaurant served a buffet, but because it was late, there were only crumbs where pastries had been, and a few slices of pineapple and papaya strewn on a platter. The only thing that hadn't disappeared was a pile of Spam.

He had coffee and juice before stepping out onto the Malecón. It presented a different picture in daylight than it had at night. Without sunlight, the three-story houses lining Havana's seafront were imposing in silhouette. But with the sun came a ruthless, unforgiving view. Once-stately homes painted in a variety of pastels—pink, yellow, orange, blue—had been battered by years of salty water crashing over the seawall, and decades of human neglect. Some were propped up by wooden scaffolding; others were simply left to sag toward the cracked limestone sidewalk once traversed by proud owners. The houses had all been turned into multiple-family dwellings. Clothing hung from the wrought-iron balconies, which themselves appeared to be clinging desperately to the crumbling façades. Caged birds and loose roosters called them home. To Pauling, the houses looked depressed and defeated. Not so the people on the Malecón. They walked with purpose, proud, as though things were good in their lives and their country. Or was it resignation leading to passivity? Men bearing huge black inner tubes with many patches on them went down to the sea and floated out into it, using the tubes as precarious boats from which to fish for that evening's supper. Could you make it to Miami in one of those things? Pauling wondered. What was that kid, Elián Gonzáles, floating on when they plucked him out of the sea? You had to be pretty desperate to take an inner tube to Florida.

He walked, enjoying the heat that loosened muscles tightened by hours in the cramped cockpit of the Piper Aztec B. Vibrancy surrounded him. The *jineteros,* male street hustlers, offered him everything from "genuine" Montecristo cigars to bootleg rum. Vintage American cars—DeSotos and Cadillacs from the 1950s—lent their out-of-tune roar and noxious exhaust to the general cacophony of the street. Their drivers offered him discount sight-seeing trips, for American dollars, of course. Teenage "virgins," the *jineteras,* promised trips to paradise.

Pauling came upon the Museo de la Revolución, housed in Batista's former palace. In front, the twisted remains of the American U-2 spy plane shot down over Cuba shortly before the missile crisis of 1962 was displayed, along with a Soviet tank used to repulse Bay of Pigs invaders. He paid the entrance fee and went inside where Castro and his revolution were immortalized, including the heavy black coat that Fidel, then in his twenties, had worn during the famous trial in which he was convicted of plotting the failed attack on the Moncada Barracks while in search of weapons for his ragtag army. Also displayed in the museum were bloodstained uniforms, old slot machines from the Mafia days, and hundreds of pictures of El Jefe Máximo, many taken when he was a young lawyer and rebel leader, sans beard. As Max was about to leave, uniformed soldiers who'd been standing guard over an eternal flame, the star-shaped monument to the Heroes of the New Fatherland, were replaced in a changing-of-the-guard ceremony. Pauling recognized the monument. He'd seen it plenty of times in Moscow, the model for Cuba's version.

He checked his watch. Three o'clock. He was hungry but decided to hold out until dinner with Celia and her friend. He consulted a map he'd taken from the hotel and found his way to the alley off which her apartment was located. Like everything else he'd seen that day, Cuba was prettier by night, he noted again. Heavy, pungent odors of cooking food wafted from the small apartments as he passed them. Spirited conversations drifted through open windows and doors. He did not pass unnoticed. Curious eyes peered at him. The alley was not listed in the guidebooks as a tourist attraction.

When he reached the door to the apartment, he paused and looked back to where he'd entered the alley. A man stood there smoking a cigarette, the same man Pauling had seen before, at the museum. He'd been standing in front when Pauling exited. Pauling had noticed him because he was not Hispanic. He had blond hair, cut to make it stand up like a spiked bush. His temples were shaved. He was extremely pale. He wore a black suit over a white T-shirt, and sandals. Pauling had thought it a strange getup for a tourist in sultry Havana, but paid no further attention.

Until now.

The man saw that Pauling had noticed him and stepped out of view. Pauling considered retracing his steps and confronting this person, but thought better of it.

Celia was showering when Pauling knocked on the upstairs door, pushed it open, and stepped inside. He called her name. She responded: "I will be ready soon."

She emerged from the small bathroom wearing a robe over her wet nakedness, and a towel wrapped about her head. "I'm sorry to be late," she said. "I had an appointment that ran late."

"That's okay," Pauling said, sitting in one of the red sling chairs.

She took clothing from the dresser and closet and disappeared into the bathroom, closing the door behind her. When she again emerged, she was dressed in tight black slacks, a teal T-shirt with tiny embroidered flowers at the neck, and sandals. Bloodred polish tipped her toes and fingers. The contour and movement of her breasts, not corralled by a bra, were lovely to behold.

"Did you enjoy your day?" she asked.

"Yes, I did. I went to the revolution museum."

She laughed. "Were you impressed?"

"No. I'm being followed."

"This is Cuba."

"It's not a Cuban. He's European, I think."

"Maybe he's a *maricón* and finds you attractive."

"Gay?"

"Yes. There are many gays in Cuba despite—" She stroked her chin. "—*his* hatred of them. Most pretend to have relationships with the opposite sex to avoid repercussions. Like Nazi Germany, yes? You'll point him out to me."

He nodded. "You have nosey neighbors," he said.

Smiling, carrying the scent of soap and perfume across the room, she leaned and whispered in his ear, "The CDRs."

He looked up at her quizzically.

She continued sotto voce: "Neighborhood spies. Comités de Defensa de la Revolución. Every block has one; there are fifteen, twenty thousand of them in Havana. You must be careful what you say. If they hear something they don't like, they'll report you to the Ministry of Interior."

"I thought that went out with Nazi Blockwarts and the Soviet Union."

She shook her head, placed her fingertips on her chin, and stroked her imaginary beard. Pauling grinned. "I get it," he said.

"Good. Ready?"

"Sure. Who is this friend of yours we're meeting for dinner?"

"His name is—" She lowered her voice again. "Nico."

"Nico what?"

"Come."

She led him down the stairs and to the alley. The blond man was nowhere to be seen. They walked to the corner where the owners of a few American cars featuring tail fins and hand-painted gaudy colors hawked rides for potential paying passengers. She opened the rear door of one of them; Pauling followed her in. In Spanish, she gave an address to the driver who floored the accelerator, pressing Pauling back against the seat.

Celia used the roar from the vehicle's porous muffler to cover her words.

"Nico works in the Ministry of Public Health. He knows a great deal about what is going on in the research laboratories."

They pulled up in front of what looked to Pauling to be a private home.

"I thought we were going out for dinner," he said.

"We are. It's a *paladar,* a restaurant in someone's

home. The best food in Cuba, better than the hotels." She looked at Pauling and said, "Pay him. In dollars."

He paid the driver the amount that Celia suggested, and they stood in front of the modest house. It was painted purple and had white shutters. When they entered, a stout Cuban woman enthusiastically greeted Celia. Obviously, she was a regular customer. Celia introduced Pauling, who received a long, animated welcome in Spanish from the *paladar*'s owner and cook.

"Nico?" Celia asked.

Pauling caught enough of the answer to know that her friend hadn't yet arrived.

They were led to a tiny garden at the rear of the house where four tables, shaded by colorful umbrellas, had been placed among trees and other plantings. They were the only customers in the garden. The owner gestured to a table beneath a silver *yagruma* tree. Shimmering in a breeze that had kicked up, the tree appeared to be frosted. Pregnant white blooms of the lily family hung above the table like paper party lights.

Pauling took in his surroundings. "There are a lot of these home restaurants?" he asked.

"Not as many as there were before the government started charging licensing fees to put them out of business." She stroked her chin. "He won't eat in them because *he* says they make the owners rich. Not very Communistic. The fees put many out of business, but they have gone underground again. Like this one."

The owner came to the table carrying bottled water and handwritten menus.

"You want beer or wine?" Celia asked.

"Beer."

She ordered two bottles of Cristal.

Pauling read the menu. The most expensive meal was six American dollars.

"Is the food any good?" he asked.

She chuckled. "I told you *paladares* have the best food in Cuba. Eat in a few state-owned restaurants and you'll see what I mean."

She looked up, smiled, stood, and greeted a handsome young man with slicked-back black hair. He wore a white guayabera and chino pants. They embraced before joining Pauling at the table. He introduced himself only as Nico. Nico whatever-his-last-name-was spoke good English. After some mandatory badinage, Pauling asked about the restaurant. "Celia tells me these places aren't exactly legal, Nico. You work for the government, right?"

The Cuban broke into a wide grin. "A man has to eat, huh? The food is good and the prices are right." He asked Celia in a stage whisper, "Lobster?"

"Lobster?" Pauling said, not attempting to lower his voice. "I didn't see that on the menu."

Celia and Nico put their index fingers to their lips. "Lobster is illegal for the illegal *paladares* to sell," Celia said. "Shrimp and beef, too. The state has a monopoly on them. But the rule is broken now and then."

Pauling sat back and sipped his beer while Celia and Nico chatted in Spanish. Typical, he thought. Pass a stupid law and the people will find a way around it. Like Prohibition. The two people at the table with him were obviously comfortable breaking the law here. None of those CDRs she'd spoken about were in this garden unless they were up in the trees.

They drank more beer and ate at a leisurely pace. Pauling began to wonder when they would get to the topic of interest to him, but was reluctant to broach the subject. Nico was Celia's contact. Let her take the lead, at least in this situation. She finally did, over dessert of coconut pudding and heavy, sweet coffee served in tiny cups.

"Tell us what is new in the Health Ministry, Nico."

He knew what she meant. After a glance about the empty garden, he looked directly at Pauling and said, "You are interested in the cancer research."

"Yes."

"Do you know how advanced we are in such research?"

"I've been told you're doing good things."

"Better than that. Our cancer researchers are the best in the world, like many of our doctors. Are you aware that we have been doing heart transplants since 1985, and heart-lung transplants since 1987?"

"No," Pauling said, trying to mask the annoyance he was feeling. He wasn't in the mood for a pep talk on the wonders of Cuban medicine.

Nico pressed on. "Our center for nervous system transplants and regeneration is the world's best for treating Parkinson's disease. We transplant fetal brain tissue with wonderful results."

"About your cancer research," Pauling said.

"Very advanced," Nico replied. "El Presidente promised when he took power that our people would have the finest health care in the world, and that we would find a cure for cancer. We have made great strides, but the Special Period, after the Soviets pulled out, has set us back. It did not hinder our research, but our hospitals are short of supplies now. We have suffered, and the American embargo has been very detrimental to us."

"So I understand. Your cancer research labs are all state owned, right?"

"Yes, of course."

"But I understand there are foreign companies wanting a piece of the action."

"Piece of the action? Oh, yes, of course. I have heard that, too."

Pauling looked at Celia, who appeared to have removed herself from the conversation. *This guy has "heard it," too?* Pauling's expression said. *Big help!*

She said nothing.

"Do you know about a German company, Strauss-Lochner Resources, Nico?"

"Yes. The Germans are very active in Cuba. They bring a lot of money to our economy."

"Are they interested in buying your cancer research labs?"

He frowned in thought and ran his tongue over his lips. "It is my understanding that they have expressed an interest," he said.

"Okay," Pauling said, "what about an American company, BTK Industries? It's headed up by a former U.S. senator, Price McCullough, who, by the way, is in Cuba as we speak."

"I know that. What about the American company?"

"Have you heard anything about the German company acting as a front for BTK Industries?"

"A 'front'?"

Pauling nodded. "A cover story, a disguise, a—well, beard."

"No, I have not heard that. I could make inquiries, if you would like."

"I would like that, Nico. Quiet inquiries. I would be very appreciative. How soon can you find out something about it for me?"

He shrugged and fell silent.

Pauling thought for a moment. "How much?"

Nico waved a hand over the table, and shook his head. "Let's not talk about money now. This has been a pleasant evening. Money will make it unpleasant. I will see what I can find out and contact Celia. I will tell you this, Mr. Pauling. Strauss-Lochner has a representative in Havana named Grünewald. Mr. Kurt Grünewald."

"What's his job?"

"He is the liaison with our government's Health Ministry. I have met him a few times. He is a nice man. He enjoys his rum. I must go. Thank you for a lovely dinner, Mr. Pauling. I will be in touch with Celia."

He and Celia embraced as they'd done upon his arrival, and he left the garden.

"Paying him's not a problem," Pauling said after he and Celia were alone at the table. "Just a matter of how much."

"Let's see what he comes up with first," she said.

Spoken like a true operative, Pauling thought. *Make an informer show his or her hand before committing to an amount. Let them know that the better the information provided, the higher the payoff. You show me yours, then I'll show you mine.*

The restaurant's owner delivered the check. The three lobster dinners, including side dishes and the beers, came to thirty dollars. He paid. They found a taxi on the street.

"I'll drop you at your hotel," she said.

"I thought I'd buy you a drink," he said.

"I have someplace I must be."

"A date?"

She didn't answer his question, although a small smile on her red lips said that was probably the case.

A stitch of jealousy came and went.

As they approached the hotel, the blond man in the black suit was standing in front of the Meliá Cohiba, next to Pauling's hotel.

"That's him," Pauling said, pointing. "Ever see him before?"

"No."

As Pauling stepped from the taxi, the man disappeared. Pauling pulled out his wallet to pay the driver.

"I'll take care of it," Celia said.

"When do I see you again?" Pauling asked.

"Tomorrow," she replied. "I'll call you at noon at the hotel. Be there." She smiled, stroked her imaginary beard, and told the driver to leave.

Chapter 15

Havana

Senator McCullough and his assemblage were taken on an hour-long bus tour of Havana before arriving at Plaza de la Revolución, dominated by a huge granite and marble monument to José Martí, the martyred intellectual author of Cuba's freedom from Spain at the end of the nineteenth century, and Fidel Castro's acknowledged inspiration. Multiple antennas appeared to sprout from its top, the highest point in Havana, the vultures perched on them providing a grim metaphor for Cuba in the desperate post-Soviet days. Members of the group recognized the place as the backdrop for the many political rallies at which Castro delivered his famous eight-hour grandiloquent harangues.

"We have arranged for you to go to the top of the monument following the meeting," the group's official escort announced on the bus, "and to tour the museum, which I know you will find inspiring."

Mac Smith stepped off the bus and took in the sprawling plaza, Havana's largest. It had the same monolithic grayness of plazas he'd visited in Eastern European countries. The government buildings defining its perimeter were constructed of thick concrete, the windows recessed as though to make it more difficult for light to penetrate the murky offices behind them. The Ministry of Interior building, in which Cuba's most secretive and sinister

agency was located, featured a huge mural of Che Guevara, Castro's partner in revolution.

They were led behind the Martí monument to the former Justice Ministry, now home of the Central Committee of the Communist Party, where Castro and his senior
ministers conducted the nation's business.

"Please, do not attempt to take photographs of the
building," the escort warned. "It is forbidden."

Smith shook his head as he moved with the others into
the labyrinthine Palacio de la Revolución, its façade the
color of early-stage jaundice. He looked up at an enormous ceramic tile mosaic of flowers, trees, animals, and
birds, and noticed that at the top, the depictions were cut
short. He turned to one of the accompanying Cubans and
mentioned it. The young man whispered, "The artist did
his work before the building was completed. The ceiling
is lower than planned."

Smith smiled, said, "We have a few of those gaffes
back in the States."

"Gaffes?"

"Mistakes."

The young man, obviously sorry he'd admitted such an
error to a foreigner, nodded glumly and walked away.

The meeting room was on the second floor, a large
space containing a long, scarred wooden table with
dozens of chairs around it. The McCullough delegation
was seated and asked to await the arrival of the minister
who would lead the discussions. A large color photograph of El Jefe Máximo, also known as *el barbudo,* the
bearded one, in his familiar military fatigues, looked
down on them.

They passed the time with small talk until a door
beneath Castro's photograph opened and three men
entered. They wore the usual dark suits and even darker
expressions. They took chairs that had been left empty at

the head of the table. The one in the middle opened a file folder, placed half-glasses on the tip of his nose, frowned as he perused whatever papers were in the folder, looked up, removed his glasses, and smiled. "Well," he said in good English, "you are here, and I welcome you on behalf of our leader, Prime Minister Castro. You are distinguished ladies and gentlemen in your professions. I have had many favorable comments from those of us who have had the pleasure of speaking personally with you."

He looked to McCullough for a response.

"We feel honored to be here, sir," the former senator said, smiling broadly. "You've been most gracious in your welcome since our arrival, and I speak for everyone at the table in expressing our gratitude."

Smith smiled. This sort of posturing had been going on since their arrival, and he found it amusing. He reminded himself, of course, that flattery and circumspection were at the heart of diplomacy, unless you were rattling sabers across a conference table at a peace negotiation between warring parties. He was never especially comfortable with the niceties of negotiation. His reputation when practicing criminal law was that of a no-nonsense, mordant advocate who did not suffer fools, and who cut through salving blather to get to the point. He knew he was not destined to be appointed ambassador to any country, even the smallest of them.

The platitudes continued back and forth for fifteen minutes. McCullough cut through when he said, "I think the minister knows that those of us who've come here do so in the interest of exploring richer trade opportunities between Cuba and the United States."

The minister closed his eyes and sat back. The Americans wondered whether he'd suddenly fallen asleep. When he came forward and again looked at McCullough, he said, "Talk of trade between our two countries is always of interest, Senator, but of little practical value. As long as your laws prohibit your companies from doing business with us, it is nothing more than an academic exercise."

"That's changed, hasn't it?" a member of the delegation offered. "We can now sell medical supplies and agricultural products."

"On paper, yes," the minister said. "But your laws continue to prohibit the financing of such transactions through any U.S. bank or other financial institution. It is like your laws against Americans traveling to Cuba. You do not prohibit it, but any American tourist coming here must not spend any money. Your laws regarding us are hypocritical."

McCullough stepped in. "As you know, Minister, I am no longer involved in government. I am a former United States senator, and happy to be. But it has always seemed to me that we have a compelling mutual interest. We would like to open Cuba as a lucrative market for our businesses, and you and your people would benefit greatly with what we can sell. And, of course, we represent a huge market for your goods."

The minister spoke: "That may be true," he said, "but you have many former colleagues in Congress who not only resist increased trade with us, they would like to choke us into submission."

"That's unlikely to happen to you," the ad executive said. She added, "You engage in extensive trade with many nations, European, Asian, Canada."

The minister nodded. "Our economy is on its way to health once again, thanks to our trading partners."

"But the United States could be your most important partner," McCullough said.

"The United States has far more to gain from us than we have to gain from you."

"Perhaps if there were an improvement in your human rights record, Mr. Minister," said McCullough, "your enemies in Congress would begin to soften."

Mac checked for an angry reaction from the Cuban. If McCullough's comment had angered him, he didn't show it. He said in a level voice, "There is no room for bending on our part, Senator. We are at war with you and the brutal capitalistic society you represent. As our prime minister has said, 'My sling is the sling of David.' "

Smith winced and wondered whether their trip to Cuba was about to be cut short. He was surprised when the minister added, "These questions, and so many others, have been debated for decades, and will continue to be, I am certain. In the meantime, let us not allow them to interfere with the pleasure of your visit to Cuba. We will continue to discuss trade issues even though there will be little fruit born of our conversations. I am pleased to tell you that Prime Minister Castro himself wishes to join in our discussions, and will do so at a later time." Now he became almost gleeful. "I am pleased to issue each of you a personal invitation to his seventy-fifth birthday party in a few days. To be asked to celebrate with him and the Cuban people is an honor not casually bestowed upon visitors."

After touring the Martí monument, they were driven back to the hotel where they gathered in small groups at the bar.

"I really admired the way you laid the cards on the table, Price, about human rights," McCullough was told.

"I thought we might as well get it out in the open right up front," the affable former senator said, downing a Bacardi cocktail.

"I was afraid he'd take offense," someone else said.

"I didn't care if he did. The truth is—and they know

it—as long as they ignore basic human rights, Congress will keep the screws on tight."

"Despite President Walden."

"Yes, despite the president. Excuse me, ladies and gentlemen, there's someone I must see."

Smith watched as McCullough left the bar. He turned to the president of a regional airline whom he'd befriended during the trip and said, "The minister was right. This is all very pleasant, but there's really nothing that can be accomplished unless Congress eases up on the embargo."

"We might accomplish something, Mac," he said. "The more times Castro gets the message about human rights, the more likely he'll come to understand it."

"And change? Won't happen."

"I've heard he has three hundred million dollars stashed in Spain for when he bows out," the airline president said. "Maybe he'll decide it's time to give it up and live out the rest of his life in luxury, learning to dance the flamenco and play the guitar."

The figure cited by the airline president jibed with what President Walden had confided in Smith during their weekend together at Camp David. Obviously, Spanish banks didn't have the secrecy standards of the Swiss.

Smith laughed. "I don't think Mr. Castro is close to packing it in," he said. "Castro said about giving up his revolution, I'm paraphrasing, 'If I'm told I'm the only one left who believes in my revolution, I'll continue to fight.' I think he means it."

"He's a madman."

"A committed one. Have to run. I want to check in with my wife."

"Annie, it's Mac."

"Hello, stranger. How's everything going?"

"Fine. We had a meeting with some of Castro's ministers. Interesting. Price McCullough brought up the human rights question. The minister didn't bat an eye, or acknowledge it. Castro says he intends to personally take part in our meetings, and, oh yes, we've been invited to his birthday party."

"You devil," she said. "I'd love to meet him."

"I'll invite him to the apartment for one of your chicken pot pies." He stopped. "You know, I had a funny feeling at the meeting, something I don't think the others felt."

"What's that?"

"I had the feeling that Price's little speech about human rights was scripted. As though he said it on cue."

"What do you mean?"

"It was as if the Cubans expected it, and Price knew it wouldn't mean anything to them."

"I'm sure it doesn't—mean anything to them. They must be used to hearing it by now."

"You're right, of course, and I'm probably off base."

"Any Cuban señoritas giving you the eye, Smith?"

"Hundreds. I've had to hire a bodyguard to fend them off."

"Have him send me the bill. I'll be happy to pay it."

She filled Mac in on the happenings at home, at the gallery, and in a variety of charitable organizations with which she was actively involved. She chaired the city's humane society, raised money for the Washington Opera and for Ford's Theatre, and devoted a half day a week to a battered women's shelter. He loved her industry as well as her natural physical beauty.

"I'll call again," he said. "Love you."

"Love you, too, Mac. Take care."

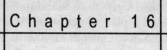

C h a p t e r 1 6

Havana

Pauling didn't sleep late.

A series of blackouts during the night had rendered the air-conditioning unit useless. He got out of his soggy bed at six, exercised—stretches, sit-ups, followed by push-ups—despite the heat and humidity, showered, dressed, and walked into the hotel dining room at seven-fifteen. Before coming down he'd gone through the Havana telephone directory in search of a listing. Favorite sayings by Fidel Castro were printed at the bottom of many of the directory's pages, in case you forgot who was in charge.

He found Strauss-Lochner listed at an address in the Miramar section of Havana, and wrote the street number and phone exchange on a slip of paper, which he put in one of the many pockets in his photojournalist's vest. The buffet was more bountiful at this earlier hour. He filled his plate and carried it to a table in a far corner from which he had an unrestricted view of the door.

His shadow of the previous day was very much on his mind as he ate. The man probably posed no danger, at least for the moment, but Pauling knew that when someone was following you, for whatever reason, that could change. If the man were Cuban, Pauling wouldn't have been concerned. Just a case of Communist paranoia. But this wasn't some PNR—Policía Nacional Revolucionaria—cop assigned to keep tabs on a foreigner. This guy was a Caucasian who looked German or Scandinavian.

He formulated a plan of action while at the table. He wasn't interested in a confrontation with Blondie, but he did want to know why he was being followed, and more important, who was interested enough in him to order it.

Pauling didn't have to continue contemplating the man because he walked through the door to the restaurant, looked in Pauling's direction, then chose a table at the opposite end of the room. He placed a newspaper on the table and went to the buffet table where he chose nothing but fruit, a mound of it.

Interesting, Pauling thought. *The guy knows I've spotted him, yet he strolls in here where I can see him and has breakfast. He's either inept or he has a purpose in being visible.*

Pauling signed the check and wrote his room number on it. His intention was to take a stroll and see what happened next. But his tail beat him to it. He laid down money on the table and left the restaurant. Pauling waited a beat before doing the same. He surveyed the lobby; no sign of him. He stepped out onto the sidewalk and looked left and right. The blond man in the black suit was nowhere to be found.

Pauling walked up the street, pausing occasionally to pretend to look into a store window but using the moment to look behind. Nothing. He stopped at a busy intersection to consult the small map of Havana that he carried, pinpointed the location of Strauss-Lochner, decided it was too far to walk, and hailed a taxi, a '50s DeSoto.

Back at the hotel, Erich Weinert, concealed in an alcove behind the registration desk, handed the Cuban clerk ten dollars in American money. *"Muchas gracias, señor,*" the small, older man said repeatedly as he handed over the key to Pauling's room.

Pauling didn't have any purpose in seeking Strauss-Lochner's Havana offices, except to go to the source. You never could tell. That the German company had a listed address and phone number in Havana wasn't surprising. Foreign companies doing business in Cuba were there legally—everyone except American companies. He could have whiled away the morning playing tourist again until noon, when Celia was to call. But that represented the sort of inaction that set him on edge. He'd done enough sight-seeing the previous day. Also, he wasn't anxious to extend his stay in Cuba any longer than necessary. He'd been told that he was to return to Colombia in a week to pick up more medical supplies to give credence to his alleged reason for being in Cuba. With any luck, he'd come up with the proof Gosling was looking for—evidence that Price McCullough's American company, BTK Industries, was using Strauss-Lochner as a front—and do it before the week was up.

There was something unsettling about Cuba.

On the one hand, there was a pulsating spirit of life among the people on the streets that had been absent in the old Soviet Union during his assignments there. Commuters, after waving down flatbed trucks to hitch a ride, shouted greetings to fair-skinned tourists as they passed. Old men leaning with their ancient bicycles against walls did the same. Children no older than ten sold shaved ice cones streaked with fruit syrup; other women only slightly older offered sweets of a different sort. Salsa bands performed on street corners for coins tossed into a straw hat on the ground. The women were openly flirtatious, and the Cuban men were as overtly sensuous to the women. Horse-drawn carriages plied the streets of the city, and bicycles were everywhere, a million of them imported from China: "Expanding the use of the bicycle is an indicator of cultural advancement," Castro had said after ordering his people to start pedaling to ease the perpetual fuel shortage.

No doubt about it, a fun-loving group.

But there was another side of Cuba and its forty-year experiment with Castro and his brand of Communism. Uniformed PNRs were everywhere, watching, frowning, their eyes locking on every passerby. And there were those thousands of the CDRs Celia had spoken of, neighbors spying on neighbors and reporting to authorities what they considered inappropriate words and deeds. Castro's face was ubiquitous, his picture on lampposts and on the sides of buildings. Signs proclaiming SOCIAL-ISMO O MUERTE—Socialism or Death—hung side by side with the Big Beard's likeness glaring from billboards across the city. On the opposite side of the street from the U.S. Interests Section, on Calle L, was Havana's most photographed site, a huge, colorful billboard showing a crazed Uncle Sam glowering menacingly at a Cuban soldier, who is shouting, *"Señores imperialistas: No les tenemos absolutamente ningún miedo!"* "Mister imperialists: You don't scare us at all!"

Not exactly all fun and games, Pauling thought. Good people, bad government. What else was new?

His driver took him to Miramar via the Malecón, which led into a tunnel beneath the Almendares River. When they emerged on the Miramar side, they were on Quinta Avenida, Cuba's Fifth Avenue, a wide boulevard lined with fig trees, the center of Cuba's economic life.

Strauss-Lochner's Cuban offices were located in a four-story building on Quinta Avenida. The building, once a mansion for the rich during pre-Revolution days, was in need of a face-lift, like most of Havana's buildings. Its architecture reflected the late-eighteenth-century baroque style that had arrived in Cuba, its more sophisticated design melding with what had gone before, the *mudéjar* school of architecture that fused Spanish, Christian, and Muslim traditions. Attempts to cover crumbling exteriors only exacerbated the deterioration. A curved, colored-glass panel above the door, in greens and blues, was the only hint of the grandeur that once existed before terminal neglect had set in.

He walked up and down the busy boulevard to gain bearings. Miramar was certainly different from downtown Havana, he thought. It had become the commercial center for foreign companies that had chosen to defy the U.S. ban and invest in Cuba. There were neon signs atop some of the buildings—Benetton, Castrol, Bayer, and Philips. Pauling passed other former mansions now housing embassies. The imposing former Soviet embassy, now virtually deserted, towered over everything.

There were no signs on the front of the building in which Strauss-Lochner was situated. Pauling opened the door and stepped into a dusty foyer with cracked white and yellow tiles on the floor. A photograph of Castro was the only wall decoration. Pauling leaned close to a building directory, the glass almost opaque with grime, and read the names. Strauss was on the third floor.

Pauling slowly climbed the stairs. As he reached the second-floor landing he was face-to-face with an old woman holding a broom and wearing a floor-length gray housecoat.

"*Buenos días,*" he said.

She returned his greeting with a toothless smile.

A CDR?

She watched him placidly as he continued up to the third floor. There were two offices there; the door to one of them was open. He looked into the reception area and saw a sign above a desk: STRAUSS-LOCHNER RESOURCES. He went to the door and surveyed the small space. Empty. He considered entering. As he pondered that, a stout man suddenly appeared from an inner office. He wore a white shirt, red tie, and red suspenders. Pauling's presence startled him. "May I help you?" he asked. The accent was guttural.

"No, thank you. I must be in the wrong building."

"It happens. So confusing, Havana. Who are you looking for?"

"An export firm. They gave me this number on San Rafael but were obviously wrong. Sorry to have bothered you."

"No bother." To Pauling's surprise, the man extended his hand and said, "I am Grünewald. Kurt Grünewald."

"Oh. A pleasure meeting you, Mr. Grünewald."

"American?"

"Yes."

"It's always good to see someone who isn't Cuban. You do business in Havana?"

"No. I'm—ah, visiting a friend. How long have you been in Havana?"

"Two years." He wiped his brow with a handkerchief. "Like it?"

Grünewald shrugged and grimaced. "The food is not to my liking. I have a sensitive stomach, ya? The heat, too, is difficult. But we do what we must."

"That's the spirit. What sort of company is Strauss-Lochner?"

"Pharmaceuticals," he said proudly. "Research into many diseases. Cancer mostly these days. Here." He handed Pauling his business card on which both his office number and home number were listed.

"Thanks," Pauling said. "It was nice meeting you.

Name's Pauling. Max Pauling. Maybe we'll run into each other again."

"*Ya*, I hope so. I enjoy talking to Americans. Maybe a drink some night, dinner, a show? Have you seen the show at the Tropicana?" His round face broke into a satisfied grin. "A wonderful show, but so expensive. The best seats are fifty dollars American. The women—" He touched his fingertips to his head. "Beautiful women."

"Sounds great," Pauling said.

"*Ya*. Well, if you want, we could go together. I have been many times. There is so little to do here in Cuba at night, *ya*?"

"Maybe so," Pauling said. They shook hands again and Pauling left.

The cleaning lady was on the second-floor landing as he descended the stairs. He reached the street. It had been overcast when he left the hotel that morning, but the sun had broken through. It was like a steam bath, making breathing difficult, his eyes feeling as if they were being parboiled.

It was ten o'clock, two hours until Celia's call. He returned to the hotel and asked the desk clerk whether he had any messages.

"No, señor, no messages."

Pauling took a look around the lobby in search of his blond shadow, and checked the restaurant. No sign of him. He rode the elevator to the fourth floor and approached his door. It was closed. Nothing unusual—except for the heavy smell of cheap cologne hanging in the air outside his door. Something was wrong. He'd learned over the years to trust his instincts even though they often were unfounded. But when they were right—

He stood outside the door and pressed his ear to it. The AC was working, the only sound coming from inside.

He looked back up the hallway. He had it to himself.

He pulled the Austrian Glock nine-millimeter semi-automatic from the largest pocket in his vest, placed his other hand on the doorknob, and carefully, slowly opened the door, the weapon held pointing up, next to his ear. His eyes swept the room. No sign of a person. But he saw the open drawers in the dresser, and clothes on the floor.

He checked every corner of the room, the bathroom, behind the shower curtain, the closet, under the bed. Feeling secure, he closed and locked the door and sat on the bed.

Because he traveled light, there had been very little in the drawers or the closet. There had been no need for Blondie to have tossed things on the floor. He'd done it so that Pauling would know he'd been there. A warning. A message that his presence in Havana had not gone unnoticed.

He picked up the few items of clothing from the floor and returned them to the dresser. He opened the drapes and stood in front of the air-conditioning unit, reveling in the cold air that bathed his face. Four floors below, Havana was on the move.

Not a wasted morning. He'd met the German, Grünewald, who'd been mentioned by Nico. As for the blond Nordic or Aryan guy with the strange haircut, if he wanted to play a game, Pauling was willing to compete. He smiled. Maybe this was going to turn out to be better sport than he'd anticipated.

Victor Gosling chose to meet Tom Hoctor at Les Halles, on Pennsylvania Avenue, because of its upstairs cigar lounge where he could retire after lunch to enjoy a Cuban Cohiba, a dozen of which were sent to him on a regular basis by a friend in Prague.

Gosling and Hoctor were as different in their lifestyles as they were physically. Gosling towered over the diminutive Hoctor, although both were slender men. Gosling had a full head of hair. Hoctor was bald. Gosling wore expensive English suits custom-made on Savile Row, originally from the venerable Gieves & Hawkes, more recently from the trendy upstart Ozwald Boateng. Hoctor bought off the rack, and only when there was a sale. Gosling smoked cigars, enjoyed whiskey, and ate heavy food. Hoctor neither drank nor smoked; his appetite approached vegetarian.

After lunch downstairs in the popular French bistro, Hoctor reluctantly followed Gosling to the cigar lounge where the Brit, his CIA colleague from earlier days, lit up, and sipped from a snifter one of the elite alembic cognacs. Hoctor was content with a cup of tea. They were alone.

Gosling directed a stream of blue smoke away from Hoctor and leaned closer to him across a tiny table. "I'm telling you, Tom," he said pianissimo, "there's no reason for anyone at the Company to give a second thought to my using Max Pauling in Cuba. Hell, I shared with you his assignment, and I shouldn't have done that. It's strictly private, none of your business back in Langley. I told you about the assignment only because we go back a long way together, and I knew I could trust you."

Hoctor tasted his tea. After placing the cup back in the saucer, he rubbed his right eye, which tended to droop, more so when he was tired or under pressure. He thought for a moment before saying, "Zach Rasmussen wants to know about Pauling because—" He leaned forward. "Because there are ongoing projects that are particularly sensitive. Zach doesn't want there to be any chance—*any* chance—that what Max is doing could cause a problem."

Gosling dragged on his Cohiba and finished his cognac. He again leaned forward. "Not to worry," he said.

"Celia Sardiña," Hoctor said in a voice so soft it was lost in the room.

But Gosling heard it. He cocked his head and smiled. "What about her?"

"You have her involved, too, in this private assignment for your client."

"So?"

Another rub of his eye before speaking in a tone meant to chastise, "You know damn well why I bring her up. She has other business, Vic. Important business. For us. Sensitive business."

"The last time I heard, Tom, she was an independent contractor, available to the highest bidder."

Hoctor was angry at having his concerns so casually dismissed. In all his years with the Central Intelligence Agency, he'd never grown comfortable handling independent contractors, men and women who sold their services to the agency for a period of time or specific operation, for a fee. They were necessary, he knew, but he preferred dealing with agency employees, like himself, who were accountable to a higher authority in the chain of command. The freelancers were harder to control. As far as they were concerned, they had a specific job to do—"turn" an informer in a foreign country whose language they spoke, take surveillance photos from a mile away, seduce a government official and record the pillow talk, bug a phone or room, launder money, cut a deal with drug runners in return for information, assassinate someone deemed worthy of a bloody "wet job"—and the hell with the bureaucracy.

Most part-time contract employees had once been agency employees, like Victor Gosling. Hoctor had always found Gosling to be atypical of the usual electronics expert. Generally, these were introspective men, narrow in focus and consumed with specific knowledge and its applications. Gosling was gregarious, even flamboyant. It was the flamboyance that had caused him to be chosen as author of that book, helped by an agency-approved ghostwriter, purportedly critical of the intelligence community, yet containing only that which had already been written about, certainly nothing damaging. Gosling's early departure from the agency, and its pension system, was quietly handled behind the scenes. With the lump sum he'd been paid, and the notoriety achieved through the book, he was quickly recruited by Cell-One and offered a compensation package only a fool would have turned down. Victor Gosling was no fool. He considered money the most worthy of motivational factors, and tended to live that philosophy.

Hoctor had handled both Gosling and Max Pauling during their agency days, providing their only contact with Langley when the men were off on covert assignments in other countries. Gosling had been a team player. Pauling was another story. He acted more the part of independent contractor than employee, bucking superiors, deviating from the playbook, improvising, and criticizing his bosses. But he'd never failed an assignment; Hoctor had to give him that. Yet of all the undercover operatives he'd handled over his long career, Pauling was the most anxiety provoking. Hoctor sometimes joked that he wondered whether Pauling had stock in Tums, considering how many he'd prompted Hoctor to take.

The little bald man finished the tea and primly dabbed his mouth with a napkin.

"I want Celia Sardiña off your case," he said in his pinched voice that lacked overtones.

"I can't do that, Tom. I still fail to see why—"

"Do it, Victor."

"Why?"

Hoctor stared at him, one eye slightly lower than the other, mouth set in a straight line, a vein pulsating in his temple. Gosling had seen that expression on Hoctor before, most notably during a hurried, clandestine meeting between them in Budapest. That night Hoctor had instructed Gosling to kill a Hungarian informer with whom he'd become close. The Hungarian had been a valuable source of inside military information, and was scheduled to be rewarded with a new life in the States.

"Why?" Gosling had asked.

"To be sure," Hoctor had replied.

"Sure of *what*?" Gosling dared to ask. "I'd bet my life on his loyalty."

Hoctor's reply was to exhibit what passed for a smile, and to walk away from where they'd met in a park. The Hungarian's dream of a better life in the democracy known as the United States ended two nights later.

Like at that meeting in Budapest, Gosling was left without any tangible reason for dropping Celia Sardiña from the Cell-One project. He did know, however, that

Hoctor, the consummate Company man, was reflecting an order from higher-ups at Langley.

"I'll have to make arrangements to replace her, Tom."

"Just do it quickly. Thank you for lunch. I'll have to have this suit cleaned. Martha hates the smell of cigars and so do I."

Chapter 18

Havana

Twenty minutes after Pauling received Celia's call at the hotel, she arrived in an aging black Russian-made Gaz jeep driven by a Cuban teenager.

"This thing runs?" Pauling said.

"Most of the time," Celia said from the front passenger seat. "When they aren't stealing parts out of it." In the back was a narrow wooden bench with a couple of ripped, faded cushions. "Get in," she said. "We're going for a ride."

Pauling hung on to the back of Celia's seat as the driver headed west, the self-destruct system working well, every bump in the road magnified into a rib-rattling jolt.

"Where are we going?" Pauling asked over the Gaz's mufflerless roar.

"An island. Cayo Levisa. Very pretty."

"I'm sure it is, but why are we going there?"

She glanced over at the driver who sat ramrod straight, eyes straight ahead.

Pauling got the message and stopped asking questions. They rode in silence as the driver negotiated a relatively smooth coastal road until reaching the town of Mariel. There, he jogged left, turning on to a rugged, ragged two-lane road paralleling the northern coast. It was slow going at times. Large, unwieldy ox-drawn carts brought traffic to a crawl before turning off onto narrow dirt paths leading to *vegas,* the lush, verdant tobacco fields for which the Pinar del Río province was noted. The road was lined with palm-thatched cottages, and hordes of hitchhikers who looked at them, eyes pleading, as they passed.

After stopping for gas, for which Pauling paid in dollars, they pulled into Palma Rubia, a small fishing village. A ferry was loading passengers for the forty-minute trip to Cayo Levisa. Celia instructed the driver to wait for them, and led Pauling to the ferry where they found an open space in which to stand at the ship's bow. The sun was hot, reddening faces. A variety of birds could be seen in the mangrove-lined marshes along the shore—white egrets, blue herons, and sea ospreys. Black frigate birds spread their long, scimitar wings as they glided above in search of fish dropped by other birds. Pauling thought of Jessica and her love of bird watching. She would have appreciated the scene more than he.

"You like being out on the water, Max?" Celia asked as the ferry left shore. The breeze rippled her hair. Her eyes were shut tight; her full, red lips were set in a contented smile.

Pauling ignored the question. He noted that no one was within hearing distance. "Mind telling me why we're here?"

"To relax," she said.

"I'm not getting paid to relax."

"You should learn. Cuba is a wonderful place to relax."

He was about to say that he didn't need lessons from her on how to live life when someone suddenly interrupted the conversation. Pauling turned to face Nico.

"Hello," Pauling said.

"Hola, Señor Pauling. Cómo está?"

"I'm fine."

Nico grinned and accepted Celia's kiss on the lips.

Pauling stepped back and leaned against the railing while Celia and Nico chatted away like reunited lovers, laughing at obvious inside jokes spoken in rapid Spanish. They were thoroughly enjoying themselves. Pauling soon found the scene mildly annoying. Celia's cloying ways were getting to him. She treated him like a schoolboy who had to be led by the hand to the bathroom, in *this* case to someone who might provide the proof Vic Gosling needed for his client.

"I hate to break this up," Pauling said.

Celia and Nico turned to look at him. Pauling smiled and cocked his head as though to ask, What the hell am I doing on this ferry?

Celia came to where Max stood at the railing. "Nico has some information to give you. I didn't want us to meet in the city. Too many eyes and ears. It's better out here. Not as many CDRs. Still, too many people."

Pauling said nothing.

"Nico places himself in a dangerous situation," Celia said. "I would think you would respect that."

"Oh, I do, Celia."

"When we get to the island, we will be able to speak more freely. Until then, Max, enjoy the sun and water and blue sky. They're free."

Forty minutes later, the ferry bumped hard into the makeshift dock. The timbers were rotted, and Pauling wondered how many more assaults by the ferry it could withstand before collapsing into the sea. What appeared to be a resort was not too distant. Stretching out to the left and right was a white sandy beach dotted with thatched-roofed huts in which men and women, mostly Caucasian, sipped drinks and ate at the resort's tables beneath royal palms and majestic ceiba trees.

Pauling and Nico followed Celia down a rickety set of

stairs to the dock and they walked toward the resort. Celia chose a vacant beach hut and led them inside to a table and four chairs. Moments later, a young Cuban wearing a starched white waist-length jacket appeared and asked what they would like to eat and drink.

"They have wonderful lobster and shrimp here," Celia announced. "It is the advantage of eating where the fishermen are." She ordered a platter and asked Nico and Pauling what they wished to drink. Pauling opted for beer. Nico and Celia ordered daiquiris.

When the waiter was gone, Pauling asked, "How do you know *he's* not a CDR?"

"I can see in his eyes that he is not." She smiled. "The CDRs have a look about them that is unmistakable. There is fear as well as guilt in the way they look at you, fear that they, too, might be turned in, and guilt at doing it to their neighbors. No, we are safe here. We can talk."

They covered inconsequential topics until the waiter had delivered a sizzling metal platter heaped with lobster meat and shrimp. He put down a basket of bread and their drinks. When he was gone, Pauling turned to Nico. "What is this information you have for me?"

"It is not so much information I have as wanting to speak with you about what I must do to get it, and to . . ." He stopped in midsentence.

"And what?" Pauling asked. "To find out how much you'll be paid?"

Pauling's directness seemed to offend Nico.

"Do you find it strange that he would want to know what his reward will be if he delivers?" Celia asked.

"No," Pauling replied, "not at all." To Nico: "Go ahead. What is it you want?"

Nico looked at Pauling with his big, round, black, doe-like eyes for what seemed an eternity. Finally, he leaned closer and said slowly and deliberately, a long pause between each word, "I want to come to the United States with you."

Pauling held Nico's stare. He wasn't sure what to say, so he did what people generally do in that situation. "You want to come to the States with me?"

Nico was unblinking. "Yes," he said. "I want to come to the United States. Celia tells me you are a pilot and flew here, and that you will fly away when your assignment is finished. If I get for you the proof you need, I want you to take me back to the States in your plane."

Celia said, "It is a good bargain, Max. Nico has a degree in biochemistry from our best university. He will have an opportunity to put his education to better use in the States."

"Is that how you know each other? School together? Both biochemists?"

"No," she said, "but we share that interest. Will you do it?"

"I'll have to think about it. I'm not sure I'm free to. Besides, I haven't seen anything from you yet, Nico."

Nico glanced out the open door. "I have sources within the Health Ministry who can help me get for you the proof you need. The American company BTK is using the German company to buy into our cancer research. The government is beginning to put many projects and programs in private hands, but so much of the money does not come back to the government or the people. It goes into the pockets of the bureaucrats and—"

"Just business as usual," Pauling said.

Nico swallowed hard. "Such an arrangement cannot be made without the personal approval of Prime Minister Castro."

"Which means we know where most of the money is going. Into his IRA," Pauling said, stating the obvious.

"What?" Nico asked. Pauling waved him on. Nico added, "There are those in the government who feel that Castro is planning to step down and go to Spain. If that is true, he will want to take as much money with him as possible. If he approves the sale of our research results to a private company, the amount of money that will exchange hands is millions."

"If your cancer research is as successful as you say it is—and I've heard it is from many sources—"

Nico interrupted with enthusiasm. "It is very advanced. I am not a scientist. I am a bureaucrat. But I hear from the scientists about their work. You are familiar with monoclonal antibodies?"

"I'm no scientist either," Pauling said.

Nico thought for a moment. "The use of monoclonal antibodies is the most effective treatment for many cancers today. These antibodies target certain cancer cells, without destroying the healthy ones. What our laboratories have managed to do is to make these antibodies four, five, even six times better. To be able to do that is very important."

"Millions?" Pauling said. "It'll be worth mega, mucho millions to whatever private company gets the goods."

Nico looked to Celia to see whether he should continue. She nodded.

"I don't know whether you will believe this, Mr. Pauling, but there is more to my helping you than being able to go to the United States. I am Cuban. I love my country and my people. When Fidel Castro took power after the Revolution, he promised to do many things, including devoting whatever resources are necessary to cure cancer. I want that cure to come from the Cuban people, from *our* doctors and researchers, not from an American or German company. If the information I give you will help ensure that, I will feel as though I have made a contribution to my people."

Pauling tended to be skeptical about patriotism as a motive for spying and leaking information to the enemy. It had been his experience that money was the most compelling reason for deciding to become a turncoat. But he had dealt with men and women during his career whose patriotic fervor was legitimate, individuals whose sense of right overrode other considerations. The jury was out on Nico. Pauling simply didn't know him well enough to pass judgment.

Obviously, Nico had just as many questions about Pauling. He asked, "What will you do with the information I give you?"

"Use it to expose how an American company is planning to gobble up your cancer research," Pauling replied.

"You will do this?"

"Me? Personally? No. I'm working for another American company that doesn't want to see it happen."

"Why? So that it can do the same thing, 'gobble up' our medical research?"

Nico had a point, Pauling knew, but what Gosling and Cell-One did with the proof that BTK Industries was using the German company as a front wasn't his concern.

"I don't know," Pauling answered truthfully.

"This Cell-One," Nico pressed. "It is part of the CIA?"

"CIA?" Pauling guffawed with too much vigor to be believed. "Of course not."

"I do not wish to offend you, but Celia has told me you once worked for the CIA."

"Past tense, Nico. A long time ago. No, I'm not with the CIA. This is strictly a private assignment. Now, are you finished asking questions? I'm getting annoyed. Either we trust each other, or we don't. Your call."

Nico looked at Celia, whose expression was noncommittal. "All right," he said. "We will trust each other."

"Good. When can you get me the proof?" Pauling asked.

"Soon. There are documents that are secured, locked from sight, but there are ways for me to get to them. It will cost money."

"For whom?"

"Those I will have to pay to allow me to photograph the documents."

"Nothing for you, of course."

"Yes, there will be something for me."

"How much?"

"Ten thousand, American."

And a one-way ticket to Disney World, Max thought. *A bargain. Ten thousand dollars to derail a multimillion-dollar deal.* "Ten grand for you, Nico. How much for these other people you'll have to pay off?"

Nico shrugged. "Maybe ten thousand more. There is one man, the doctor in charge of all cancer research in Cuba. His name is Dr. Manuel Caldoza, a fine man and a brilliant researcher."

"Are you saying he'll sell out?" asked Pauling.

"Perhaps, but not for money. He works for the state, of course, as we all do. But his loyalties are not to Castro and the government. I believe he is aware that there are plans to sell the work of his laboratories and his staff to foreign interests."

"Are you saying that he doesn't want that to happen?"

"Yes. Like me. He is very proud of what his team has been able to accomplish in cancer research. He recently was in the States to give a paper at a medical convention. His work is respected all over the world. But the government restricts his travel, like that of our athletes and performers."

"How far do you think this Dr. Caldoza would go to keep Strauss-Lochner and BTK Industries out?"

Nico shrugged. "I can try to find out."

"Quietly."

"Yes, I will be careful."

Pauling drained his glass. He ate some shrimp and lobster. He tore off a piece of bread and started chewing, his facial muscles reflecting difficulty.

Celia laughed. "Che Guevara once asked why the Cubans can't make decent bread."

Pauling pulled the remainder from his mouth and put it on his plate. "What's the answer?"

"Rice," she said. "We prefer rice."

"Oh," he said. "What's next?"

Nico said, "I mentioned to you a man who works for the German company Strauss-Lochner. His name is Grünewald. I can introduce you to him."

"I've already met him," Pauling said.

"You have?" Ceila said.

"Then I suggest you talk to him," Nico said. "He is an unhappy man alone in Cuba. I have had drinks with him. He drinks too much. When he does, he says things he shouldn't about his company."

"About fronting for BTK Industries?"

"Almost." Nico grinned. "He would say things to you, Celia. I think he appreciates a pretty woman."

"Maybe I'll go back and see him," Pauling said. "Even if I'm not pretty."

"Maybe I would be more successful than you," Celia said playfully.

Pauling asked Nico, "Have you met a young guy who looks as though he might be German? Blond hair cut like a bush on top, wears a black suit and sandals. I figured he might work for Grünewald."

"No," Nico said.

"You've seen him again?" Celia asked.

"This morning, at the hotel. He paid my room a visit,

tossed things around, didn't take anything. Not that there was anything to take."

"I don't know of such a person," Nico said.

"If you find out anything about him, let me know."

"We have a deal?" Nico asked.

Pauling took the last piece of lobster from the platter and savored it. "Delicious," he said, with genuine appreciation. "Do we have a deal? Yeah, we have a deal—provided you produce what I need. And, Nico, do it fast. I too am a man alone in Cuba."

Nico extended his hand. Pauling took it, let go, and stood. "All right, kids, picnic's over. Work to do. Life can't be all picnics and rice."

The courier from Washington arrived at the U.S. Interests Section in downtown Havana at noon. He handed over the diplomatic pouch he'd carried from Washington to a clerk in the secured message room. The clerk signed for it and took it to her superior, who opened it and sorted the contents for delivery to appropriate people within the building.

Chief of section Bobby Jo Brown received his batch of documents, sat back, and started to read, yawning as he did. Most were on State Department stationery and were marked CONFIDENTIAL. Some bore the red stamp TOP SECRET. Few called for immediate action; they were concerned more with administrative matters and all-points directives that bore little resemblance to the reality of operating the Interests Section in Cuba. State tended to impose a one-size-fits-all approach to its stations around the world, whether what they demanded of them was practical, or even doable.

But one piece of paper captured his attention. He picked up the phone and called an extension within the building. The call was answered on the floor below by Gene Nichols, a seventeen-year CIA veteran who'd spent the last eight of them in Havana. A few minutes later he walked into Brown's office and closed the door.

Brown handed Nichols the document he'd just received from Washington.

Nichols handed it back after reading it. "There's nothing to report," he told Brown, who'd been posted to Cuba a little less than a year ago. "He's being watched. We had a little problem this morning."

"What problem?"

"He was picked up at his hotel by Celia Sardiña. She was in a car, a jeep actually, driven by a Cuban male, identity unknown. They headed west out of the city. We had someone on them but he got stuck behind a couple of those damn ox-drawn tobacco carts and lost them."

"No idea where they went?"

"No."

"None of our CDRs reported on them?"

"Negative again."

Nichols's alleged assignment to the Interests Section was as consular officer handling the hundreds of visa applications filed each day by Cubans seeking entry to the United States. There were always throngs of them outside the concrete building with its tinted glass that prevented anyone from peering inside. Dozens waiting to be interviewed slept for days in their cars, or on the ground in a tiny nearby park at Calzada and K. But like more than half the staff, Nichols had other duties, primarily recruiting Cuban CDRs to share their information with him and his employer back in Langley, as well as with Fidel Castro's government. He had hundreds of them on the payroll, in Havana and across the country.

It didn't take much to "turn" a Cuban during these days of the Special Period. The economic hardships that had begun in June 1992, when the last Soviet oil tanker left Havana, made things desperate for most Cuban people. The *buzos* reappeared, literally "divers" in Spanish,

Cuban slang—for those who eat from garbage cans. The government mandated long blackouts to conserve fuel. Crops rotted in the fields, and everything was rationed—staples, food, toiletries, cigarettes, four ounces of coffee a month from state-run grocery stores, six pounds of rice, four ounces of lard, if those items were even available.

Things had improved only marginally by 1995, and Nichols continued to have easy success turning CDRs into eyes and ears. The U.S. Interests Section had many concerns in Cuba, and not all were solely for America but for the Cubans, too.

"You'll pick up Pauling's trail again when he comes back to the city?" Brown said.

"Of course," Nichols replied.

"What's with the McCullough group?" Brown asked.

"Nothing. One of their guides is ours. She reports in through my contact in San Antonio de los Baños."

"The filmmaker?"

"They're lovers."

"There's an awful lot of interest in Pauling back at Langley," Brown said reflectively. "Why?"

Nichols shrugged. "I think they just want to make sure he doesn't get in the way."

"Why would he?"

"Because he has a history of getting in the way. He's an improviser, Bobby—gets things done but hates the rule book."

"But he's here on a private assignment for Gosling's group, Cell-One."

"According to Gosling. I've never trusted Old Vic. He's a little too slick for my blood."

Brown laughed. "I know what you mean, all the fancy suits and the fancy way of talking. What about our Miss Sardiña?"

"Gosling recruited her, too, for Pauling's gig. She was

supposed to have come back here on standby, cool it, and wait for orders from Langley. Looks like she's killing time moonlighting for Gosling."

"Well," Brown said, "let's stay on all of them. Put somebody who doesn't get lost in traffic on Pauling. I don't want any surprises and have to hear it first from Langley."

Pauling and Celia were dropped at the head of the alley. They walked past open doors and windows, went up the stairs, and she opened the door. It looked to Pauling like everything was precisely as he'd remembered it in the small living room, except for a little vase of white, fragrant flowers on the coffee table. But Celia went immediately to the window where the white curtains hung limply, unrestrained by flimsy white tiebacks. She tied the curtains open, turned to Pauling, and said, "I must leave."

"Why?"

"To meet someone."

He went to the curtains, fingered them, and looked at her quizzically.

She nodded. "They were tied back when I left this morning."

Pauling pointed to a phone on a small desk.

She shook her head. "I'll drop you at the hotel," she said. "We'll meet up later—if I'm free."

"Am I supposed to wait around until Nico comes up with something?"

"He will get what you need."

"And what if he doesn't?"

"He will, he will. Excuse me."

She disappeared into the bathroom and shut the door. Pauling glanced at the oversized handbag she carried, woven from reeds from the *malanbueta* plant, and opened it. The contents were normal except for a classic Colt .45 automatic handgun. Her sudden emergence from the bathroom startled him.

"Find what you're looking for?" she asked.

He pulled the Colt from the handbag. "Nice fire-power," he said.

"Yes, it is. It's *his* favorite." She stroked her chin.

"That's good to know," said Pauling, returning the weapon to the handbag.

"What do you carry in the many pockets of your vest?" she asked.

"*My* favorite."

"I have to go. Can I reach you at the hotel if I am free?"

"Give it a try."

"I have another life, you know," she said, "other than this job. I have separate responsibilities."

"Yeah, I'm sure you do. Let's go. I have one or two re-sponsibilities of my own to take care of."

She took one of the white blooms from the vase and af-fixed it to her hair.

"So the person you're meeting will recognize you?"

"No," she said. "It is mariposa, butterfly jasmine, the national flower. Cuban women wear it to demonstrate patriotism and purity."

"You're both?"

"When I need to be. Come."

Blondie wasn't anywhere to be seen when Pauling got out of the taxi in front of Hotel Habana Riviera. He went to his room and stretched out on the bed for a few min-utes before pulling out the business card. He dialed.

"Mr. Grünewald, this is Max Pauling. We met this morning when I wandered into your office by mistake."

"Ah, yes, of course. How are you?"

"Just fine. Thanks for asking. I was thinking about

your offer to show me around, perhaps the Tropicana show. I'd be more comfortable going with someone who knows the ropes."

"The ropes?"

"Knows where to go. Are you free tonight?"

There was a pause from Grünewald before he said, "I believe tonight would be good for me. Usually I am busy with business meetings at night, but this night happens to be free. *Ya,* tonight is good."

Pauling smiled. Of course he was free that night.

"That's good," Pauling said. "Where shall we meet?"

"At the Hotel Comodoro. It is on Avenida One and Calle Eighty-Four, in Miramar. It is close to my office."

"I'm sure I'll find it."

"It has a very good bar and discothèque."

Of course it does, thought Pauling.

"The show at the Tropicana starts at nine-thirty. We will meet for drinks and something to eat at seven. The Tropicana is not very far from the hotel."

"Seven it is," Pauling said. "I'll be on time. And, by the way, it's my treat."

"I couldn't let you do that."

The hell you couldn't, Max thought. "No argument, Mr. Grünewald. I'll be very appreciative having someone with your knowledge take me by the hand."

"If you insist."

"I do. See you at seven."

This is Lolita Perez reporting from Cuba. Meetings between the U.S. trade delegation, led by former senator Price McCullough, and Cuban Trade Ministry officials are going smoothly, according to sources familiar with the sessions. Cuban trade officials are urging McCullough and his group to pressure the administration to ease the embargo on trade with Cuba that has been in effect for more than forty years. McCullough, it's reported, has consistently raised the issue of Cuba's record on human rights. Although nothing tangible is expected from the talks, U.S. president Walden commented today during a press conference that opening greater avenues of dialogue between the American government and Cuba is in the best interests of both parties.

"I've also been told that the entire McCullough delegation has been invited to attend Fidel Castro's birthday party two days from now. If past birthday celebrations are any indication, they'll be among hundreds of thousands of Cubans who'll turn out to pay tribute to the Cuban leader.

"Lolita Perez, CNN, Havana."

Annabel Lee-Smith turned down the television in the Watergate apartment to answer the ringing phone.

"Annabel, it's Jessica Mumford."

"Hello there. How are you?"

"Fine. You?"

"Good, except I miss Mac. He's in Cuba."

"I just saw a report from there on CNN."

"So did I. I'm not sure paying tribute to the Cuban leader is what Price McCullough and his group have in mind, but that's the way CNN sees it. Is Max still in Miami?"

"Last I heard. He's not good about keeping in touch when he's traveling."

"You'll have to train him better."

Jessica laughed. "He's not trainable. Actually, he's in Cuba, too."

"He is?"

"I'm probably not supposed to tell people that, but maybe he and Mac will cross paths."

"That would be wonderful. Where is he staying? I'll tell Mac when he calls."

"I, ah—I'm really not sure."

Their conversation was interrupted when call waiting told Annabel someone else was trying to reach her. It was Mac.

"Hello, stranger," she said after telling Jessica she had to beg off.

"*Buenos días,* as they say in Havana."

"I was just on the phone with Jessica Mumford."

"Want me to call back?"

"No. We finished. I just saw a CNN report from Cuba. Make sure they photograph your good side."

"I didn't know I had a bad one. Things are going smoothly so far. I'm pretty much an innocent bystander, like the others in the group. Price does most of the talking. I have met some interesting Cuban attorneys. The system is different, of course, but I get a sense that there's been a gradual softening in the Cuban view of us capitalists. There are changes taking place here. I'm scheduled to sit in on a trial tomorrow."

"That'll be interesting."

"I'm sure it will be. I'm thinking of working material on the Cuban legal system into one of my classes, maybe arrange for some of the Cuban attorneys I've met to come and lecture—if they're free to travel."

"Great idea. Oh, Jessica mentioned that her boyfriend, Max, is in Cuba."

"Is that so? Doing what?"

"She didn't say, and I didn't press. Sounds as though he's on some sort of assignment. She obviously didn't want to get into it."

"I'll say hello if I run across him. Where's he staying?"

"No idea. Would you even recognize him?"

"I think so. Anyway, just wanted to check in."

"Rufus had his checkup this morning at the vet. The beast is hale and hearty."

"Speaking of beasts, I'd better get on my horse. We had a meeting scheduled in an hour but Price isn't free, some conflicting commitment. We're touring a hospital instead. Love you, sweetheart. Best to Jessica if you speak with her again."

The men in McCullough's entourage had each been offered female companionship by members of the Cuban delegation. If any of them had taken their hosts up on the offer, they were discreet enough, and mature enough, not to mention it to others.

That was the case with Price McCullough.

The female escort provided the ex-senator was no *jinetera*. No teenager, she was a mature woman, a nurse who provided company to important visitors to supplement her meager income at the hospital. She and others like her offered their services through the Ministry of Interior, the ominous agency responsible for all security in Cuba. Aside from being paid for their services, they received extra for reporting back anything of use to the ministry, slips of the tongue, pillow or drunk talk. McCullough's escort disappointed her employer; the former American senator had said nothing to her beyond the usual terms of endearment, flowery expressions, appreciation of her beauty, ample figure, and skills as a courtesan.

She'd given her phone number to him when she left his suite in the morning, and he promised to call her before leaving. Now, a few hours later, showered and shaved and dressed in a freshly pressed suit, he prepared for an encounter decidedly less lascivious.

He paced the room until the knock on his door. He opened it. Two men in dark suits, one wearing large sunglasses, the other severely pockmarked, stood in the hallway. McCullough nodded, took a final glance about the suite, and followed them to a service elevator at the rear of the floor. They stood in silence, waiting for the elevator to arrive. When it did, they stepped inside and rode down to a subbasement. A short distance from the elevator was a heavy metal door leading to a small parking space shielded from view of the curious. A black Mercedes sedan was parked within feet of the door, its engine running, the rear door on the passenger side open. One of the men accompanying McCullough got in first, followed by the former senator, then the other escort. The door was slammed shut and the driver, separated from the rear compartment by a heavily tinted Plexiglas panel, slowly maneuvered the vehicle from the area and up a ramp to an alley behind the hotel. Waiting there were two other black Mercedes sedans. One led the way, the other fell in behind, and the three-car motorcade navigated the narrow streets of Old Havana at imprudent speed, scattering pedestrians like chickens as it went.

They slowed as they turned into an alley barely wide enough to accommodate the vehicles. People who'd been in the alley had been brusquely cleared out by uniformed PNR, along with plainclothes members of the Ministry of Interior's secret police. The alley ended in a circular courtyard in front of a two-story baroque mansion that stood out because of its size and enhanced state. It had been recently painted a subtle, pale blue. A pair of massive, burnished mahogany doors dominated the building's façade. Windows on both levels were covered with ornamented *antepechos,* wrought-iron grills flush with the front wall.

The driver came around and opened one of the car's rear doors. McCullough followed the man wearing sunglasses and stepped onto the cobblestone drive. He looked back down the alley. It had been closed off by a marked PNR vehicle parked across its entrance. Dozens of police had taken up positions along the alley's walls.

The door to the building opened and four uniformed security men carrying automatic weapons exited and took up positions on either side of it. Others followed and formed a gauntlet between McCullough and the building. At the door was a heavyset man wearing a tan suit and Panama straw hat. He motioned for McCullough and his two escorts to follow.

There were still more security personnel inside, lining a hallway leading to the rear of the house. McCullough could see a courtyard through French doors at the end. He followed the man with the hat down the corridor to a set of doors on the left. The man knocked.

"Entrar!"

The door was opened and McCullough stepped into the room. Seated at a table were three men. The one in the middle waved his hand to indicate McCullough was to sit in the only other chair in the room, directly across from him. McCullough came around the chair, smiled, and complied. He was greeted in English by one man, and asked by another whether he wished something cold to drink, an offer he declined.

Then Fidel Castro, his signature beard now totally gray, and wearing his familiar combat fatigues and hat, fixed McCullough with tired eyes. Although he was fluent in English, he spoke in Spanish, which was translated by the man to his left: "Go on. I am listening."

Victor Gosling sipped one of seventy single-malt scotches offered by the Athenaeum Hotel's Whisky Bar. He was a frequent guest; the hotel functioned as his home when he was in London to meet with colleagues from Cell-One. He was commenting to the barman about the splendid run of weather London was experiencing when the concierge came to tell him he had a telephone call.

"I'll take it in my room," Gosling said, gulping down what was left in his glass and heading for the elevators. He entered his suite on the ninth floor and picked up the phone from the desk. "Gosling here."

"Hello, Victor."

"Ah, Celia, dear. You got my message."

"Yes."

"I was enjoying a scotch in the bar when you called."

"Should I apologize for interrupting you?"

He chuckled. "Just trying to inflict some guilt upon you. How are things going?"

"All right."

"You and my friend have met?"

"Yes."

"What do you think of him?"

"As what? A potential husband?"

"Good God, no, but I did think you'd find him attractive."

"A matter of taste. Actually, he's pleasant, for the most part. A little snappish, impatient for action. We're enjoying our time together."

"Good. Then you're making progress in your . . . mission."

"Yes. Good progress."

"Did he say how long he'd be staying?"

"A week, I believe."

"I'm afraid I'm going to have to interfere with your budding romance, Celia."

"Oh?"

"Another of your ardent suitors wants you back."

"I'm flattered. Which one?"

"Your favorite. He misses you and wants you to toss over this latest beau and be available exclusively for him."

"Do I have a say in it?"

"Oh, you know him, Celia, he's very demanding, always gets what he wants. Besides, he's rich. The man I sent to meet you isn't. Go for the money, Celia. Always go for the money. Have I ever steered you wrong?"

"Frequently."

"I'm hurt. Actually, my dear, let my friend down easily. No need to break it off abruptly. I'm not sure his ego can withstand sudden bad news."

"All right."

"Everything else going well with you?"

"Yes. You?"

"Couldn't be better. Thanks for ringing me up. Stay in touch. I'll be here in London for another two days. By the way, severing your relationship with my friend won't cost you. Full payment guaranteed."

Gosling hung up and placed a call to Washington where he reached Tom Hoctor.

"I passed along your message to our friend Celia."

"Good," Hoctor said.

"Just thought I'd let you know I'm still the good soldier."

"Good."

"And never received the recognition I deserved."

"Thank you for calling, Victor."

The click in his ear said the conversation was over.

He returned to the bar. "Another of the usual," he told the barman. "No, a double."

Celia Sardiña thanked her friend and left the art gallery on Calle Obispo, one of Havana's most famous streets, lined with shops and galleries, many of which were the rooms of private homes rented for business purposes by the artists themselves. She'd placed her call to London from the state-owned gallery's back room where the manager, a failed middle-aged artist, maintained a satellite telephone system for use by Celia and others in their network. Because he represented only art and artists approved by the Castro government, he was above suspicion, a true Fidelista, a son of the Revolution. Privately, he supported the anti-Castro movement in Cuba, and shared the desire of Miami-based Cuban-Americans to see Castro toppled by force. Maintaining the communications system was his contribution—and an important one it was—to the effort.

She returned to the apartment, poured herself a glass of mineral water, and sat by the open window. The city was in the midst of another blackout. Without air-conditioning, the small room was oppressively hot and humid.

Gosling's message was plain enough. He'd been instructed by someone in the Central Intelligence Agency to pull her off the assignment. The question was why. She could only surmise.

She'd been sent to Cuba by her handler at Langley a short time before and told to remain there until receiving further instructions. When Gosling first contacted her and suggested she might like to do something for him and one of his clients, she declined. Her allegiance, at least at that moment, was to the agency for which she'd undertaken freelance assignments before. But then Gosling explained that another former CIA operative, a man named Pauling, would be involved, and that the agency was aware of the project.

She considered running it past her handler at Langley but decided against that. What she did in her spare time was her business, she reasoned. Besides, she'd begun to sour on her role as an independent contractor.

Her involvement had begun two years earlier when she was approached by a friend, a member of the Miami-based anti-Castro Cuban-American National Foundation. He suggested that because of Celia's easy entry into Cuba as part of the Cuban-American Health Initiative, she could help the cause by carrying messages, and sometimes money, to the group's Havana counterparts. Celia eagerly agreed. It wasn't the extra money that appealed. Rather, it was doing something tangible to help a movement in which she strongly believed. It meant really being a part of something, not just a freelance come-and-go artist, without any long-lived involvement and commitment.

She had made a few runs on behalf of her friend, delivering envelopes to the art gallery on Calle Obispo. It was there that she first met Victor Gosling, who was in Cuba as a guest of Fidel Castro himself. The Cuban leader had praised Gosling's book and its criticism of the

American intelligence agency, including some of the failed attempts on his life. That those few incidents, each a comedy of errors, had already been made public in newspapers and magazines, went unnoticed by El Presidente, blinded by his hatred for the CIA. Gosling, the *former* agent, now a published turncoat, was treated like a hero in Cuba. For the most part, his movements were relatively unrestricted. The leash was long, giving him opportunities to make contact with anti-Castro forces within the country.

This most recent trip to Havana would be, Celia had decided, her last. She'd been asked to do things in the past that had challenged who she was and what she stood for. She'd met those tests, but not easily, by falling back on the strength of the powerful metaphor of patriotism, of commitment to justice and human rights and the God-given right of people to live in freedom. She would take on this final assignment, do her best, and sever the relationship. In the meantime, what could be wrong in helping Gosling on behalf of his client? The twenty thousand dollars she was being paid would be a welcome addition to her bank account, as well as—some of it—to the coffers of her Miami friends engaged in bringing down Castro. It wouldn't interfere with what she might eventually be called upon to do by Langley. According to Gosling, Pauling's assignment promised to be a quick one, a week at the most, and she certainly had time to kill until hearing from Langley. Also, it was a private matter, for a private client, nothing political about it.

For those reasons, and a dozen others, she'd said yes to Gosling.

Now Langley wanted her off the pharmaceutical case. Why? It could mean only one thing: the CIA had some operation that was about to be put into action.

Should she tell Pauling right away? Or at all? Gosling's

comment about not severing the relationship too abruptly said to her that she didn't have to disengage immediately. If Nico came up with something real in a day or two, it would be over anyway.

She placed a call to Pauling's hotel. There was no answer in his room. Just as well. She needed a night alone. She opened that day's copy of *Granma*, the official publication of the Communist Party, named after the wooden luxury yacht Castro used in his December 1956 invasion of Batista's Cuba, the beginning of the Revolution. She checked the movie listings for Havana's more than 170 theaters, sat through a dubbed version of *My Fair Lady*, returned to the apartment, and went to bed early.

   She barely slept.

Chapter 22

Havana

As Celia Sardiña sat in the darkened Cine Charles Chaplin Theater, listening to a male singer perform "With a Little Bit of Luck" in Spanish, Max Pauling was getting out of a taxi in front of the Hotel Comodoro, on Avenida One. It was an ugly, function-over-form '60s-style building, a Spanish-Cuban joint venture that had succeeded despite its uninviting appearance, popular with German and Greek tour groups. He found Grünewald at the bar in the hotel's disco, an intensely brown, almost black, serious-looking drink in front of him. Because it was early, there were few people in the disco. The music was canned, and loud.

"Ah, Mr. Pauling," the affable Grünewald said, hitting the glass with the back of his beefy hand as he stood, causing some of the drink to slosh over the rim. Although the air-conditioning was cranked up to its coldest setting—power had been restored to the city an hour earlier—he was sweating profusely.

"Mr. Grünewald," Pauling said, shaking hands and taking an adjacent bar stool. "I see you have a head start on me."

"*Ya.* For once, I was able to leave the office early. You found it easily?"

"No problem."

"Jesús, a drink for my American friend," Grünewald told the bartender.

"Rum on the rocks," Pauling said.

"Habana Club for my friend," Grünewald said. "The seven-year-old." To Pauling: "It is what I drink. Very good rum."

Pauling held up his glass in a toast. "To meeting you," he said.

"*Ya,* I will drink to that."

Pauling took in the room. A few young couples danced to the incessant beat of the music coming from large speakers in each corner.

"They have rhythm, *ya?*" Grünewald said, smiling and draining his most recent drink. "These Cubans, most come from Africa, you know—the slaves the Spaniards brought—they like a good time, hah! Almost as much as the Germans."

Pauling wasn't sure that comparing Afro-Cubans with Germans made sense but he nodded anyway and watched Grünewald finish off his drink and motion for another.

"I get the feeling you like being in Cuba," Pauling said.

Grünewald's face suddenly turned serious. "Like being here? No, I do not like being here. My family is home in Heidelberg. Have you ever been there?"

"Can't say that I have."

"A beautiful place, Heidelberg. Nothing like here. I have many friends."

"I'm sure you do. Your company is headquartered there, isn't it?"

"*Ya.* You know that?"

"Yeah. You told me when we met."

"I did? Ah, the mind goes as we grow older, *ya?* You are right. Heidelberg is the center of medical research in Germany. Many of the best scientists in the world are there."

"What does your company do?"

"Research. Medical. Cancer research mostly. We are developing powerful new drugs to cure cancer. What a terrible thing cancer is, *ya*?"

"I wouldn't want to have it."

He laughed. "You speak plainly, like all Americans. I would not want to have it, either. Are you hungry? The food here is not so bad. Not like at home what my wife makes, but not so bad."

"I am hungry," Pauling said.

"They have many restaurants in the hotel, but I have my favorite. More European food than Cuban. I do not like Cuban food. Do you?"

"It's not so bad once you get used to it."

"And I have never gotten used to it. Two years here and I am not used to it." In a moment, he ordered another round. Pauling paid and they carried the drinks to the restaurant, where they were seated at a corner table partly hidden by potted palms from the rest of the room. Outside the window was a sprawling terrace edged by almond trees. The hotel's small private beach was in the distance.

Pauling led back into the conversation they'd been having at the bar.

"I have this family member back home in the States, Mr. Grünewald. She—"

"Kurt. It is Kurt."

"Right, Kurt, and I'm Max."

"It sounds like a good German name."

"Well, there's a little German somewhere in my background. Anyway, my aunt has cancer and she's always searching for a cure, anything, herbs, witch doctors, anything."

"In hope of a miracle."

"Right. She was telling me before I left for Cuba that

they're doing incredible research into cancer right here. Is that true?"

Grünewald nodded. The waiter came to the table and the German ordered another drink. He was quite drunk by now.

"Is that true?" Pauling repeated.

"What?"

"Cancer research in Cuba. I understand it's very advanced."

Dimly recognizing the state he'd reached, Grünewald drew a series of deep breaths and mopped his brow with a handkerchief. His grin was wide and sappy. "Too much of the rum," he said. "Perhaps we should order dinner. Chicken. The chicken is good. The steaks are not good."

During dinner, Grünewald seemed to sober up somewhat. Pauling avoided revisiting the subject until the dessert the German had ordered, *tatianoff,* chocolate cake smothered with cream, arrived. Grünewald ate with the same gusto as he drank.

"Oh, yes, we were talking about medical research," Pauling said.

"Yes, we were. It is hard to believe, isn't it, that in such a backward country they could do such sophisticated work? Very advanced. Yes, very advanced indeed."

"Who owns the research, the government?"

"*Ya.* It owns everything here. It is a Communist country after all."

"I wonder if they'd be interested in having a private investor."

Grünewald's forkful of cake and cream stopped halfway to his mouth. "Private investor?" he said.

"Yes," Pauling said. "That's what I do back in the States. I'm a venture capitalist. I came to Cuba looking for investment possibilities for some of my clients."

"It is the government that owns everything," he said, completing the fork's journey.

"I know, I know, but I've heard that Castro is in the process of privatizing some things here in Cuba. Have you ever thought of trying to buy into the research, grab a piece of the pie?" Pauling displayed his widest smile.

"No, I—that is an interesting idea, Max, but—well, I mean, it has been considered by my company but . . . How much would your clients be willing to pay for such a thing?"

"Plenty. Millions. You know, Kurt, running into you might have been the best thing that's happened to me in a long time. You must know the right people in the government to approach about something like this."

"Yes, of course." The waiter brought another rum, a beer for Pauling, the previous one largely untouched. "I am well connected here in Havana with very high-ups in the government. It is my job to make those contacts on behalf of my company. But I am not sure that—"

"That you can trust me?"

"No, no, that's not what I meant."

"I wouldn't blame you, Kurt. We've just met. And I'm just throwing out an idea. Probably a silly one at that."

Grünewald turned from Pauling and stared into his empty dessert plate. "Not so silly," he said in a low voice.

"Huh?"

"Not so silly," he said, again looking at Pauling. "But too late."

"How so?"

"Nothing," he replied, waving away the comment.

"I'm surprised your company hasn't been after it."

"My company is—well, no one knows what will happen. We never know, do we, what will happen in our lives?"

The rum had now reached whatever area of the brain

that turns happy drunks into morose ones. Grünewald looked sad.

Pauling glanced at his watch. "Are we going to the Tropicana?"

"Ah, yes, of course. I get into a conversation and forget about time."

As Pauling waited for the check—Grünewald never made a move toward his wallet—Pauling asked, "How many people work for you here in Cuba?"

"Just one, my secretary. A Cuban woman. Very intelligent."

"That's it, huh, just her?"

"And the new one."

"A new employee?" Pauling said, placing American dollars on the check. "What does she do?"

"*He*—" Grünewald mumbled what Pauling assumed were German four-letter words. "They sent me an assistant from Heidelberg. He flew back with me the last time I was there, not so long ago. *Blöder Trottel!*"

Pauling forced a laugh. "What's that mean?" he asked.

"Useless imbecile. They send him to work for me but he talks only to those back in Germany. He does nothing, is almost never there. When he is, he sits in a small extra room and broods."

"Sounds like a charming young fella. Is he young?"

"*Ya.* Young, dumb. He wears a silly haircut, like a blond bush on the top, nothing on the sides."

Pauling had been right. Blondie was German.

"Does he have a job title?" Pauling asked as they moved to leave the hotel and in a moment climbed into a taxi.

"Vice president, huh?" Grünewald said after instructing the driver where to take them. "Vice president of stupidity. I don't even want to think about him. We go to the Tropicana, have a few more drinks, and enjoy the beautiful Cuban women on the stage. I will say that Cuban women are beautiful, better than the food. A shame I am a happily married man. Otherwise . . ."

Pauling had been alert while in the disco and restaurant for anyone demonstrating undue interest in them. He saw no one. But that didn't mean his meeting with Grünewald had gone unnoticed.

A middle-aged Cuban man who'd dined alone at the opposite side of the restaurant left immediately after their departure and hailed another taxi: "Follow that one," the passenger told the driver.

And across the street from the hotel, in an outdoor café, Erich Weinert rose from the small table and walked in the opposite direction than the taxis had taken. "Keep an eye on him" he'd been told by Dr. Miller when Miller had hired him to accompany the overweight Grünewald to Havana. "He drinks too much, talks too much. Do what you must to keep him from blabbering to the wrong people."

Fifteen minutes later he let himself into Kurt Grünewald's apartment with a duplicate key made shortly after arriving in Havana. He poured himself a glass of Habana Club from the stock in the small kitchen, turned off the lights, pulled a chair up to an open living room window, and waited.

Gene Nichols, CIA operative assigned to the U.S. Interests Section in Havana, took the call at home.

"Pauling went to the Hotel Comodoro," he was told. "He had drinks and dinner there with the German, Kurt Grünewald."

"Any idea what they talked about?" Nichols asked.

"The waiter—he is one of us—told me that they said something about cancer research, he thinks, in Cuba."

"Specifics?"

"None. Grünewald also spoke of the beautiful Cuban women at the Tropicana."

"What was their mood?"

"Grünewald was drunk. They went from the hotel to the Tropicana. The German fell asleep at the table."

"Who paid?"

"The American, Pauling."

"Where did they go after that?"

"A taxi to Grünewald's apartment building. It is only a few streets from his office. Pauling helped him to the front door, got back in the taxi, and left Grünewald standing alone. He fumbled for his key and dropped it a few times."

"Then?"

"I followed Pauling. He returned to his hotel."

"And?"

"He went to his room. I waited an hour. No further sign of him. I went back to the Comodoro and spoke with the waiter."

"Thank you for the information."

"Of course."

Pauling had returned to his room to sleep. But once there he knew that alcohol would cause sleep to elude him and didn't even try. He considered phoning Celia but thought better of it. She was not the sort of woman who would take kindly to a 3 A.M. call to say hello.

He replayed the evening as he paced the room, stopping occasionally to peer out the window at the street scene below. *Don't they ever stop the music in Havana?*

He had, in fact, enjoyed the show at the Tropicana. Grünewald was right; the women, their dark bodies and minuscule costumes, were indeed shapely and lovely. Grünewald was in no shape to appreciate anything and distinctly unlovely. He'd nodded off during the orchestra's overture, his head resting on the table between his glass and a bottle of rum he'd ordered. They'd had to wade through dozens of *jinteras* on their way into the massive outdoor theater that seated fifteen hundred people. One young woman was especially aggressive, white-blond hair, dusky skin, fresh-faced with large, round blue eyes and a melting smile. She said she was a dance student who aspired to join the show at the Tropicana but didn't have the admission charge. Would they take her in with them? Grünewald happily agreed, saying she reminded him of his dear, sweet youngest daughter back in Heidelberg. But Pauling dismissed her with finality, rudely perhaps, but necessary. He didn't need a fifteen-year-old Cuban hooker growing old prematurely becoming part of his time with Grünewald.

Grünewald!

The German hadn't confirmed absolutely that his company was involved in buying into Cuba's cancer research, but his few comments convinced Pauling. But was the German company doing it as a front for Price McCullough's BTK Industries, as Vic Gosling claimed, or for itself? There was nothing untoward if Strauss-Lochner was operating on its own, for its own gain. But if McCullough's company was using it to get around U.S. embargo restrictions. . . . Well, that's what he was there to find out.

He felt sorry for the German. *He is obviously a fairly decent man, nearing the end of his career, whose drinking undoubtedly didn't go without notice back at headquarters in Germany. Was that why they'd sent the dumb-looking punk to Havana, to keep tabs on him?*

Or on me?

What was Blondie all about?

Obviously, Grünewald isn't the one who sicced him on me, Pauling reasoned. *It had to have been his superiors back in Heidelberg. But how did the Heidelberg crowd even know I was in Havana? Since it was obvious that they did, they must also know why I'm here.*

Who could have told them?

Celia? Gosling? Gosling's client at Signal Labs? Jessica? . . . Pauling was annoyed at the number of people who were aware of where he was, and what he was doing. *Tell one person, you tell the world.*

He thought of Grünewald at home, uneasily sleeping off his drunkenness. His apartment had been only a few blocks from Strauss-Lochner's offices on Quinta Avenida. The office would be unoccupied. The Cuban secretary was probably home in bed with her hubby. As for the blond thug, it was unlikely that he slept in the office.

Pauling had taken note of a back entrance to his hotel, and there was a staircase at the rear. He checked the pockets of his vest. He had everything he needed—the Glock, a Swiss Army knife with enough folding appendages to open a fort, a small flashlight, money, and some business cards he'd been given identifying him as a pilot for Cali Forwarding.

Pauling opened the door and stepped into the hallway. He was alone. He made his way to the rear stairs and tried the door. It was unlocked. He went slowly down the four flights, pausing at each landing to detect sounds from the other side of the doors. Nothing.

The door at the lobby level opened into a utility room in which kitchen supplies were stored. A rat scurried beneath shelving. The small space was thick with the odor of spices.

The rear exit was across a short hall from the storeroom. It led to a narrow street only slightly wider than an alley. Like every street in the city, there were people, listening to music from boom boxes, necking, tossing dice against a cement wall, and whooping it up when someone won the throw. Pauling nodded at those who noticed him and walked to a busy intersection where the usual assortment of geriatric American cars waited for paying passengers. He climbed into one and gave the driver the address.

Unlike central Havana, the wide boulevards of the Miramar district were relatively quiet. A few prostitutes wearing Spandex tights and low-cut blouses tried to sell their wares to drivers stopped at traffic lights; one succeeded and got into a vehicle as Pauling passed. The world's shortest ride, with a few seconds of paradise promised.

He stood across the street from the office building and sized things up. The building was unlit. So were the buildings flanking it. He waited until there was no foot traffic, then crossed the street and ducked into the alcove by the front door. He tried the door. Locked. He took out his knife, chose a blade, and was inside within seconds. He paused to see whether anyone had noticed him and was coming to check. It didn't happen.

The stairwell was black, but he took the steps two at a time until reaching the third floor. To his surprise, the door to Strauss-Lochner was unlocked. Grünewald had probably forgotten to lock up in his haste to get to the hotel bar. Pauling took out the penlight, flashed it quickly about the room, and extinguished it. Draperies on the windows facing the street were drawn back. He pulled them shut before turning on the flashlight again.

The suite consisted of three rooms: the reception area, Grünewald's office, and the small storage room where Blondie probably did his brooding, according to Grünewald. He looked for file cabinets. There was a four-drawer cabinet in the reception area, and two two-drawer ones in the office.

He went behind Grünewald's desk and tried the drawers. All were unlocked. He rummaged through them. Not much there: personal items, medications, pens and pencils, a Strauss-Lochner employee handbook, a couple of wrinkled ties that should stay in a drawer, water glasses, and two bottles of Habana Club. No surprises.

He swiveled in the chair and trained the flashlight on the file cabinet, rolled to it, and opened the top drawer. Folders were neatly labeled, titled by projects. Nothing of interest there. He tried the bottom drawer. Locked. Because sensitive documents were housed there? Better to bury such materials with unimportant documents than to make the point of their value by putting them under lock and key. It was like putting a sign on the drawer: LOOK HERE. He'd been taught during his early CIA days that it was more secure to send such things by regular mail, the innocuous way diamond merchants often sent their precious gems, than to plaster an envelope with stickers proclaiming the importance of its contents.

His knife blade opened the bottom drawer in a second. One file tab immediately jumped out at him: BTK.

He pulled the thin folder from the drawer and examined its contents. It contained only two pieces of paper, both memos, one from Grünewald to a Dr. Hans Miller, CEO at corporate headquarters in Heidelberg, and Miller's reply. That's the extent of what Pauling could understand. The memos were in German. He had no idea what they related.

He took the file to the reception area where a photocopying machine sat next to the receptionist's desk. He fired it up, copied the two pages, folded them, and placed them in one of his vest's hidden interior pockets, turned off the machine, returned the file to the drawer in Grünewald's office, made sure things were left as they had been, closed the door, and went down the stairs to the street. He had to walk a few blocks before coming upon an available taxi.

At his hotel, he stayed outside on the street for a few minutes and looked around. No sign of the blond one, or anyone else. There was a marked PNR car parked in front of the hotel, and he could see a couple of officers in the lobby. Cubans bragged that their crime rate was among the lowest in the Western Hemisphere, but that didn't mean there weren't criminal types preying on oblivious tourists.

He stepped into the lobby. His thought at that moment was that he needed to find someone to translate the memos. Maybe Celia could help. She seemed to know lots of people. He hoped she could help; he wasn't about to stop some tourist who looked like he belonged in an oompah band and ask a favor.

He was halfway across the lobby when he heard the

desk clerk shout something in Spanish. He stopped walking and turned. The clerk was pointing at him, and two PNR cops headed across the lobby in his direction. That wouldn't have been quite so upsetting if they didn't have their weapons drawn and pointed at his belly. They yelled commands in Spanish, punctuating them with thrusts of their weapons. Pauling raised his hands and tried to think of something conciliatory to say. He came up blank. One of the officers pulled a radio from his belt and spoke into it. That quickly brought more uniformed police, and a detective dressed in a suit and tie, into the hotel. To Pauling's relief, the detective spoke English: "Do not move, señor. Do not do anything foolish."

"Okay," Pauling said, his hands still in the air, "but what's this about? I think you've got the wrong person."

The detective's reply was to order one of the officers to put cuffs on Pauling.

"Hey, wait a minute," Pauling protested. "I'm an American citizen. I'm here because I delivered medical supplies to your hospital and—"

His arms were jerked up high behind his back and the cuffs were affixed.

"You will come with us now," the detective said.

"Why? For what?"

"To be questioned, señor."

"Questioned about what?" Pauling asked as he was ushered past a dozen curious onlookers to the street. He figured it was for breaking and entering, or whatever the phrase for simple burglary was in Spanish.

"About murder, señor. Murder."

Chapter 24

Havana

Price McCullough's meeting with Castro had lasted a half hour. Because the deal had already been worked out with high-ranking types from the Health Ministry, there was no discussion of specifics as to how BTK Industries would take control, in stages, of the crucial findings from myriad clinical trials of Cuba's cancer research and the drugs it produced. It would ostensibly be accomplished through Strauss-Lochner Resources, which would distribute $60 million of BTK Industry's money to selected members of Castro's cabinet. In return, Strauss-Lochner would receive 20 percent of BTK's profits from the marketing of the new drugs in the United States where BTK was big and Strauss-Lochner nonexistent.

Castro used the occasion of meeting with the former U.S. senator to pontificate on the superiority of the Cuban medical establishment and its scientists. McCullough listened patiently, feigning intense interest as Castro became more splenetic in a diatribe hailing all that his Communist regime had done for the people of Cuba and lambasting the corruptions of capitalist America. Of course, the hypocrisy of his adamant anticapitalist stance wasn't lost on McCullough, who was about to hand over $60 million, most of which, he was certain, would go directly to a Castro account, unnamed but numbered, somewhere in Spain or Africa.

The meeting ended when Castro stood without as much as a good-bye and left the room, followed by his translator and his minister of health. McCullough continued to sit alone in the room, unsure what to do. Maybe Fidel had temporarily run out of words and had departed to get a fresh supply. Or maybe a man just had to wait. His dilemma was solved when the stooge in the straw hat and tan suit appeared and motioned for him to follow. He was taken to the Mercedes that had delivered him to the mansion, and driven back to Hotel Nacional. There, others in McCullough's delegation took note of his ebullient spirit. One would think he was campaigning for elected office once again, given the way he slapped backs and flashed what had always been a winning smile.

Castro, too, was in good spirits as he entered his office in the Central Committee of the Communist Party building. His sudden, often inexplicable shifts in mood were familiar to those who worked closely with him. He'd been combative during the meeting with McCullough, and retained some of that seeming anger during the short ride back to Plaza de la Revolución. But once there, he was in a playful frame of mind, even joking with aides and a visitor, a high-ranking official from Algeria where many of Cuba's famed "Flying Doctors" had been providing medical services since 1963. In fact, thousands of Cuban doctors were currently serving in twenty-two Third World countries. The Algerian was among many government leaders who'd come to Cuba to celebrate Castro's birthday.

"I am asked," Castro told his Algerian visitor, "what was lost and gained in the Revolution. I tell them that the Cuban people gained better education, health care, and sports. What was lost? Breakfast, lunch, and dinner."

He laughed at his own joke, and so did the Algerian.

Castro's aides knew it was one of their leader's favorite jokes. They also knew that only he was allowed to tell it.

Others were not as full of joy as the ex-senator and the Maximum Leader.

In the back room of the art gallery on Calle Obispo, where the anti-Castro forces in Cuba maintained their satellite telephone system, the gallery owner sat with three others, one of whom, a young man, had just arrived with a cassette tape. They huddled around a small table as the tape began to play in a battery-powered recorder.

Castro: "I made a pledge when the Revolution was successful that I would cure cancer. I keep my word. Our scientists are the best in the world. We are on the verge of eradicating cancer as we did with malaria and polio and diphtheria and measles. We have one doctor for every two hundred citizens, twice as many per capita as your country."

McCullough: "Your system of health care is the envy of every nation in Latin America."

Castro: "Of every nation in the world. Medical care is available to every citizen free of charge. My people are healthy and happy because they do not need to worry about paying for health, unlike the situation in your country where millions of the poor do not have care. We have managed this despite your embargo that is hateful and cruel."

McCullough: (Unintelligible)

Castro: "I will tell you and the American hatemongers again—"

He continued to berate the United States without a word of protest from McCullough. Then:

Castro: "You will give credit to Cuba and our scientists for discovering these cancer cures."

McCullough: "Of course, Mr. Prime Minister. That's

part of the agreement, when we can market the results of your research in the U.S., buying it ostensibly from our German colleagues."

Castro: "And your friend President Walden, he will be encouraged to change your Congress and the embargo against my people."

McCullough: "I've agreed to that, too, Mr. Prime Minister. The embargo has been a mistake from the beginning. I believe I have enough influence on the president, as well as with certain members of Congress, to bring about a change."

A series of quick thoughts had come and gone in McCullough's mind as he had given these assurances to the dictator. One man couldn't do it all. But it wouldn't take any influence on Walden to get him to alter his posture on Cuba. It would add to his already sizable legacy if relations could be profitably established with Castro and Cuba during his administration. McCullough also thought of what Walden had confided to him at Camp David. As they sat in the secluded wooded area, late at night, he'd whispered, "Castro's getting ready to pack it in, Price. Our intelligence tells us that he's close to relinquishing power to his brother and getting out while the getting's good."

That Castro was now calling privately for an end to the embargo, not in the usual public display meant to show his tough stance against the yanqui Imperialists, but in real terms, was telling. Everyone knew that the embargo was the best thing that had happened to Castro. It gave him a scapegoat to blame for all that was wrong within his country. Improve relations? He *was* getting ready to leave.

The tape went silent until the sound of a chair moving, and a door being closed, were heard.

The gallery owner stopped the tape and looked to the young man who'd brought it.

"This meeting was today?" the gallery owner asked.

"*Si.*"

"Who taped it?"

"I would not like to say. A friend. In the government."
He stroked his chin, then ran his index finger across his
throat.

"Yes, of course."

"So, the rumors must be true," a shopkeeper said. "He
will sell everything he can, take the money for himself,
and flee."

"What do we do with this information?" the one
woman in the room asked.

"There are people who must be informed," replied the
gallery owner. "Now!"

Pauling had been taken to an unmarked building on the Prado, officially known as Paseo de Martí. Inside, it had the usual trappings—a desk and desk sergeant, scarred benches, grungy walls, unpleasant, unidentifiable odors. After being photographed and fingerprinted, he was led to the quintessential interrogation room complete with a table, two wooden chairs, stone floor, and no windows. There was a yellow legal pad and a dirty ashtray. He was asked for his wallet and passport, which he handed over. The plainclothes detective who'd taken him from the hotel instructed one of the uniformed officers to remove the cuffs from one hand; the free end was then attached to one of the table's legs. The detective removed his suit jacket, carefully hung it on a peg protruding from the wall, pulled out a pack of Populares, lighted up, and offered one to Pauling, who shook his head. The detective took a sheet of paper from his jacket and laid it on the table.

Mr. Pauling at Hotel Comodoro at 7:30. Staying Hotel Habana Riviera. Tropicana after dinner.

"What's this?" Pauling asked.

"That is for you to tell me, Señor Pauling. Before that, I should introduce myself." He handed Pauling his card.

"I am Senior Detective Francisco Muñoz, Policía Nacional Revolucionaria." He spoke textbook English, with a trace of British accent.

"I'd say it's a pleasure to meet you," Pauling said, "but it isn't. Why have I been arrested?"

Muñoz nodded at the handwritten note.

"It says someone was meeting me tonight. So what?"

"That someone was?"

"Not that it's any of your business, but his name was Grünewald. A German. We had a few drinks and dinner, then went to see the show at the Tropicana."

"Did you enjoy the show?"

"Yes. Now, about this note. What's it mean to me? Or to you?"

"It was found in Mr. Grünewald's apartment."

"Is there some Cuban law against having dinner with a friend and catching a show?"

"No, of course not."

"You said you wanted to talk to me about murder. What murder? Whose murder?"

"Señor Grünewald."

"Jesus," Pauling muttered, and exhaled.

Muñoz sat silently.

Pauling absorbed the shock, then looked up. "You don't think I had anything to do with it, do you?"

The detective shrugged and lit another cigarette.

"Look," Pauling said, coming forward and pushing the note with his free hand toward Muñoz, "I barely knew Grünewald, and I sure as hell didn't have any reason to kill him."

"I thought you said you were friends."

"In a manner of speaking. We were just a couple of bored guys out on the town."

"What are you doing in Havana?"

"I'm a pilot. I delivered some medical supplies here

from an export company in Colombia, Cali Forwarding." He fished in his pockets and came up with the business card, which the detective looked at for a moment, then dropped to the table.

"You say Grünewald has been murdered? Where?"

"His apartment. You went there with him?"

"No. We shared a taxi back from the Tropicana. I dropped him off in front of his apartment building."

"He was drunk?"

"Very. He dropped his keys a few times."

"And you didn't stay with him until he entered the building?"

"No, I didn't. I figured he'd eventually make it inside and sleep it off."

"I see." Muñoz picked up a pencil and twirled it between his fingers. "How did you meet Señor Grünewald?"

"An accident. I was looking for an address and wandered into Grünewald's building by mistake. He gave me his business card and I called him later in the day. He suggested dinner and the show."

"That was the extent of your relationship?"

"That's right. How was he killed?"

Muñoz ignored Pauling's question. "You say you flew medical supplies to Havana. Why did you not leave Cuba after that?"

"My employer, Cali Forwarding, arranged for me to make weekly flights. I have a week off between flights."

"You are an American."

"Right."

"Working for a Colombian company."

"I'm an independent contractor and a private pilot. I work for many different companies. Could I see that note again?"

The detective slid it in front of Pauling.

"Grünewald didn't write this note," Pauling said.

"Why do you say that?"

"You said it was found in his apartment?"

"That is correct."

"In the first place, Grünewald went directly from his office to the hotel. He told me that. He couldn't wait to get to the bar. He didn't stop home. He had one hell of a drinking problem. Or maybe it was a loneliness problem."

"Go on."

"The note says we were meeting at seven-thirty. We met at seven. Why would he write seven-thirty?"

"I don't know."

"He was drunk when I got there at seven. He'd obviously arrived earlier than I did. Look, Detective Muñoz, I know you've got a job to do, a murder to investigate. How was he killed?"

"It appears he was strangled. An autopsy will be performed."

"You're sure he was murdered? He was a heart attack waiting to happen."

"There were signs of foul play."

Another detective entered the room, handed Muñoz a piece of paper, and left.

"I'm telling you," Pauling said, "I had nothing to do with Grünewald's death. I'm sorry it happened. He said he had family back in Germany. Heidelberg. I know he had a daughter because he mentioned her. And his wife's alive. At least he spoke about her as though she was."

"He worked for a German pharmaceutical company," the detective said.

"That's right. Strauss something or other."

"Strauss-Lochner Resources. Did you and he discuss his business?"

"No. He did say that there were two other people who

worked for him, a Cuban woman, his secretary, and a young blond guy who'd recently accompanied him back from Heidelberg."

"Blond? Why would he specify blond hair?"

"He laughed about this guy's funny haircut. That's when he mentioned he was blond."

"His name?"

Pauling shrugged and fought an urge to join the chain-smoking detective.

Muñoz sighed and smiled at Pauling. He held up the paper he'd been handed and gave it a shake. "We contacted your Interests Section, Señor Pauling. Because we do not have full diplomatic relations with your country, the people there have little—I believe the word is 'clout'—with us. But we are a nation of laws, and do what we can to assist visitors in the situation you find yourself in."

For the first time, Pauling expressed anger. He leaned across the table and fairly growled, " 'The situation I find myself in'? There is no situation. I didn't have anything to do with Grünewald's murder, if it was murder. I want a lawyer."

"That won't be necessary."

He went to the door and summoned a uniformed officer with keys to Pauling's handcuffs, who unlocked them and left the room. Pauling rubbed his wrist, stood, and stretched against a pain in his lower back. He looked at Muñoz. "I'm free to go?"

"Yes. Your wallet and passport are at the desk."

"Just like that?"

The detective chuckled. "Just like that," he said. "I do ask that you not leave Havana until we have had a chance to investigate further. When did you plan to leave for Colombia to pick up your next delivery?"

"A few days."

"That may have to be delayed."

"That's all right. I assume the Interests Section said the right things."

"I am not free to discuss conversations we might have had with them. Thank you for your cooperation, Señor Pauling. We will be in touch again."

Pauling walked from the room and went to the desk where he was handed his wallet and passport. They hadn't frisked him; his Glock semiautomatic hadn't been touched, nor had the photocopies of the pages from Grünewald's office. Strange procedure, he mused as he stepped out onto the street. Trusting, these Cuban cops, nothing like he'd been led to believe about their brutal tactics. Muñoz had been courteous to a fault. Of course, Pauling reasoned, he hadn't been detained for a political crime. Maybe murder, especially of a foreigner, was considered a misdemeanor compared to crimes against Castro and the state.

He got his bearings and walked in the direction of his hotel. While a guest in the interrogation room, he hadn't spent much time thinking about the dead Kurt Grünewald. As he told the detective, he barely knew him. Now he visualized the corpulent, drunken German lying dead on his apartment floor, eyes bulging, tongue hanging out if he had, as Muñoz claimed, been strangled. It was a disturbing picture. But then the movie screen in his head added another person, Blondie, who had been thrust upon Grünewald by his superiors. Had he been Grünewald's executioner—on orders from Heidelberg? Or had it been a Cuban with a grudge? Maybe Grünewald wasn't the straight arrow he claimed to be. Maybe he'd gotten involved with a Cuban woman whose macho husband wasn't happy about it. Or maybe Kurt had flashed too many pesos in front of the wrong person.

Or . . .

My money's on the blond one, Pauling decided as he approached Hotel Habana Riviera. As he prepared to cross the street, an unmarked PNR car containing two men, one in uniform, slowly passed. Its occupants' attention was openly on him.

Great, he thought. *They may have let me go easily, but they'll be watching me every minute. So will Peroxide, unless he killed Grünewald and is on the next plane to Deutschland. The big German looked physically strong, but as a tail he's been a flop. A big, dumb palooka with schnitzel for brains. And a killer?*

He went to his room and decided to call Celia. If she woke up like a beast, so be it. He wasn't in an especially good mood, either. She answered groggily.

"Sorry to wake you, but I have to see you."

"What time is it?"

"It doesn't make any difference. Where can we meet?"

There was no sound on the other end.

"Celia?"

"Give me an hour. The Hotel Habana Libre, in the Vedado District, across from the Coppelia Ice Cream Park. There's a bar on the twenty-fifth floor."

"Ice cream park?"

"Wear a jacket."

"It's open this late?"

"This is Havana. An hour."

Chapter 26

Havana

The Hotel Habana Libre was another ugly Havana building, built by the Hilton crowd during the final few months of the Batista regime. After the Revolution, Castro, who took over multiple floors and governed from there during the earliest days of his reign, made a habit of shooting the breeze with kitchen staff late at night. He ended that cheerful nightly habit when a cyanide capsule, which was supposed to have been slipped into one of his favorite chocolate milk shakes, was discovered broken in the freezer. Castro stopped eating there.

Pauling went through the surprisingly dismal lobby where a few tired-looking *jinteras* tried to salvage the night, and took the elevator to the twenty-fifth floor. A burly Cuban collected an entrance fee at the door, in dollars only. *The view had better be worth it,* Pauling thought as he paid. It turned out not to be a value. Celia was already at the bar. Her sour expression shouted that she wasn't happy. A bluesy tune played by a young Cuban pianist confirmed her mood.

"Hi," he said, sliding onto a bar stool next to her.

"Why did you have to see me?" she asked.

"Strictly lust."

She turned angrily from him and drew her drink through a straw. She'd removed the tiny paper parasol from the cocktail and laid it on the bar.

"I just spent a pleasant hour in handcuffs at one of your local police stations."

She slowly turned. "Why?" she asked.

"A little mix-up. I spent the evening with the German from Strauss-Lochner, Kurt Grünewald. We had dinner and took in the show at the Tropicana."

"Why?"

"Is that the only question you can ask?"

She resumed drinking.

"After I left Herr Grünewald, somebody strangled him in his apartment. They think I might have done it."

"Why?"

He laughed. The bartender approached, and Pauling ordered a Cuba Libre, more for the Coke than the rum.

"Why did they think I killed him? Because whoever did wrote a dumb note, supposedly by Grünewald, indicating I was with him. Even the cop who questioned me saw through it."

"And they let you go."

"I'm sitting here. Somebody at the Interests Section must have said the magic word. What do you hear from Nico?"

"Nothing yet. You'll have to continue without me."

"Why?"

Now it was her turn to smile. "Is that the only question you can ask?"

"Why can't you continue? Because I was arrested? Can't be seen with an alleged murderer?"

"I was told."

"Told what?"

"That I am not to help you anymore."

"Who?"

"Easier to answer than *why*."

"Gosling?"

She nodded.

"Great," Pauling muttered. "How am I supposed to wrap this up without help? Nico's your boy."

"It doesn't have to be right away, Max. I can give it a few more days. Hopefully, by then, you'll have what you need."

" 'Hopefully' is a word I've never put much faith in. Can you reach Nico?"

"Yes."

"Then do it."

"All right. Why did you go to dinner with the German?"

"To see what I could find out from him about the deal between his company and McCullough's. He drinks. Or did."

"Were you successful?"

"More than he was. I'm alive. I need help with this." He pulled the photocopies of the pages he'd discovered in Grünewald's office from his jacket and handed them to her.

"What's this?" she asked, squinting at them in the bar's dim lighting.

"That's what I want to find out. They're copies of pages I found in a file in his office. It was labeled BTK Industries. They might say something that implicates McCullough in using Strauss-Lochner as a front. I don't speak or read German. Do you?"

"A little, not very much. I can ask Mehta."

"Who's that?"

"A friend. She works at the German embassy here."

"Can you trust her? For all I know, the whole damn German government is involved in this."

"That's silly."

"The hell it is. Grabbing this so-called breakthrough Cuban research wouldn't hurt anybody, including the government."

"I can trust her."

"I'll take your word for it. I don't have much choice. How fast can you get it translated?"

"Today, if I can make contact with her. I haven't seen her in a while. I hope she isn't on holiday back home."

"Do what you can."

Pauling shook off the bartender's offer to refill his drink. He said to Celia, "Gosling didn't tell you why he wanted you off this assignment?"

"No."

"Dance with me," he said abruptly.

"Dance with you?"

"Yeah."

Pauling left the bar and went to the piano where the musician was lighting a cigarette between tunes. "Do you know 'As Time Goes By'?" Max asked.

"I know it."

"Good." Pauling placed an American dollar bill on the upright. "Play it for me, nice and slow."

He returned to where Celia sat, took her hand, and pulled her off the stool.

"I don't want to dance," she said as he pulled her close and started to lead.

"Sure you do. Like this song?"

She'd been rigid in his arms. Now she relaxed, her sudden suppleness allowing her body to conform to his. They moved together slowly, the only people on the dance floor, saying nothing until Pauling sang a line of lyrics into her ear.

"*Woman needs man and man must have his mate, that no one can deny.*"

"You dance better than you sing," she said, mirth in her voice.

"I don't do either well, and you know it. *The world will always welcome lovers, as time goes by.*"

He'd maneuvered them to the piano as the song ended. Max pulled another dollar from his pocket and tossed it on the piano. "Play it again, Sam," he said in what passed for a Bogart impression.

"How do you know his name?" Celia asked as they began dancing again.

"I don't. It's a line from an old movie. *Casablanca*. You never saw it?"

"I saw it. I don't memorize lines from movies."

He pulled her as close as possible and exaggerated his movements as the pianist neared the end of his second version of the Herman Hupfeld classic.

"We seem to have developed hard feelings between us," she said, stepping away from him. He followed her to the bar where she drew the remains of her drink through the tiny straw and checked her hair in the mirror behind the bar.

"I must go," she said.

"The night's young," he said. "This is Havana, remember?"

"I'll call you at the hotel. Noon?"

"Sure. I'll be there. Celia, I—"

He didn't want to see her go, but she did—with purpose.

He lingered at the bar for a few minutes. The piano player came to him and asked if he had any more requests.

"No, thanks. You play good."

"*Gracias.* She's a beautiful woman."

"Oh, her? Yeah, she's okay, I guess. Thanks again."

Had he been truthful, Pauling would have admitted to the pianist that at that moment—at that late hour—Celia Sardiña was the most beautiful woman in the world.

The Cuban section had been established at the Central Intelligence Agency shortly before Castro's Revolution succeeded in 1959. The Eisenhower administration had been pumping in arms and money to prop up Batista while Castro and his ragtag army continued its assaults on government bases and arms depots. At the same time, perhaps with Eisenhower's knowledge and approval, maybe not—the general-turned-president never acknowledged it—the CIA was channeling illegal funds into Castro's coffers. Covering all bets? The proverbial left hand not knowing what the right hand was doing? Different agendas within the U.S. government?

No matter. For more than four decades, Cuba and its enigmatic, charismatic dictator had commanded the attention of a considerable number of people at the CIA's headquarters in laconic Langley, Virginia, and plenty of intelligence dollars. He'd outlasted nine U.S. presidents and was the world's longest-ruling political leader. And on this day, interest at Langley in the Communist island ninety miles off the coast of Florida was ratcheting up.

Joe Pitura had been with the section for twenty-four years, its chief of operations the past eleven. He'd joined the agency after three highly decorated tours in Vietnam where he was known as a specialist in organizing

Vietnam's Montagnards into effective guerrilla groups. He was known throughout the agency as a no-nonsense, straight-shooting, hard-nosed hawk who'd been advocating a full-scale armed invasion of Cuba ever since arriving at Langley. But because that option had been scotched by a succession of presidents, he contented himself with conjuring covert activities against Castro. It was a favorite exercise; he'd spend hours at a time with trusted aides coming up with ways to strike at Castro, most of them outlandish and totally unworkable, some potentially doable, an occasional idea causing Pitura's broad, creased face to light up, and sending him up the chain of command in the hope of seeing it put into action.

During his Vietnam days, he'd been an imposing physical specimen, barrel-chested, with powerful arms. But rheumatoid arthritis had wracked his body. His fingers were gnarled, his wrists misshapen. His feet had broken down under his weight; despite orthopedic shoes, he walked with a painful waddle. During meetings, he would occasionally yelp when a sharp pain stabbed a joint. His people were used to it and ignored it, which is what he preferred.

"I've got nothing against Fidel Castro," he was fond of saying. "But I wish I did—cold steel against that murdering bastard's neck."

On most days, Pitura went about his duties with a sense of impotence verging on boredom. Watching successive administrations fumble in their relations with Castro and Cuba was perpetually frustrating. He considered the embargo to be a weak substitute for direct military intervention. In his judgment, the Helms-Burton Act and Torricelli Cuban Democracy Act represented only political showboating.

On this morning, however, Pitura appeared to colleagues like a man with a purpose.

He'd been in his office all night, catching only a couple of twenty-minute catnaps in his chair. Most of his staff had spent the night there, too, poring over reports arriving with regularity over secure lines of communication from operatives in Havana, and from Cuban-Americans in Miami who served as conduits between Pitura's Cuban section and friends and family in Havana. At seven, he gathered in his office those of his staff with need-to-know security clearance.

"Okay, let's go over those reports again, in order," he said, blowing his nose in his trademark red-and-white railroad handkerchief. The lights were dimmed.

"First, there are these reports on Fidel's birthday celebration," a staffer said, using an overhead projector to display transcripts on a collapsible movie screen.

"If I had my way," Pitura said, "he wouldn't be celebrating another birthday. Any surprises?"

Another transcript appeared on the screen. "None that we can see, Joe. The usual excuse for Castro to give a four- or five-hour speech, although he has been keeping them a little shorter lately. Heads of state have been arriving. McCullough and his group are invited guests, VIP status. The word is out, as usual, that everybody in Havana is expected to show up and shout their praises for El Jefe Máximo."

Pitura snickered. "If you don't shout loud enough, you get shot. Is everything in place on our end?"

The answer was affirmative and unanimous.

"Okay, let's get to the meat," Pitura said, turning to his senior staff analyst. "You haven't actually heard the tape. Correct?"

"Correct. They rushed through a verbal report on it, came up with a fast synopsis."

"Let me see it again."

A different sheet of paper was slid into the overhead

projector. It was typewritten, short sentences separated by dashes or dots.

"Can you believe this?" Pitura said, more to himself than to the others. He'd said it a half-dozen times since first being handed it during the night. "Price McCullough going into partnership with the devil. What a world."

"I never did like McCullough," someone said.

"Our esteemed president does," said Pitura. "Turn up the lights." He sat back and rubbed bloodshot eyes. "Christ, McCullough is helping fund Fidel's retirement package."

"Not the only benefactor," the senior analyst said. "Fidel's cutting deals with all sorts of foreign businesses, selling off a piece of Cuba here, a piece there."

"For the good of his people, of course," Pitura growled.

"The question is whether the president knows about the deal."

"Of course he does," Pitura said. "Clinton shook hands with Castro. Walden wants to climb in bed with him, bring Cuba back into the fold, have plenty of Cuban cigars in the humidor. I had a phone briefing a half hour ago from Zach Rasmussen. Tom Hoctor's been keeping him up-to-date on what Max Pauling is doing in Havana."

"And?"

"He got himself arrested."

"Arrested?"

"Yeah. I'll get back to that. This report on the meeting between McCullough and Castro raises an interesting question."

They waited for him to continue.

"Rasmussen wants us to hold off until we see what Pauling comes up with for Vic Gosling and his client. I suppose I can't really argue with his position. The way he

sees it, if Pauling comes out of Cuba with proof that Mc-
Cullough's company is cutting a deal with Castro, we
could leak that to whip up sentiment against Fidel in
Cuba, and with the Miami crowd. Not that our foaming-
at-the-mouth Cuban-American friends need more
prompting. If Castro seems like a traitor about to skip
with three-quarters of his country's resources, it would
help us foment a strong uprising against him by his own
people. Gosling agreed to give us everything Pauling
comes up with. He's as much a whore as McCullough.
But Pauling's job is to link McCullough's company to the
German outfit, prove it's using the Germans as a front to
get around the embargo. All that accomplishes for us is
to paint the esteemed former senator as a lawbreaker, and
I guarantee you McCullough and his pal in the White
House will spin the hell out of that." Pitura laughed.
"Want to hear something funny?" he asked.

"Castro's been photographed with choirboys?"

"I should only hope."

"Pauling was arrested for being with choirboys?"

"No—for murder. The German Strauss-Lochner rep in
Havana got himself killed, and the Cuban cops questioned Pauling about it. Seems they enjoyed a night on
the town together just before he got it."

"Pauling's off the hook?"

"Yeah. Bobby Jo in Havana at Special Interests reported it."

"Maybe Pauling will get out of Cuba fast," it was suggested.

"Chances are he'll keep looking for what Gosling
wants. As a spook, Pauling was never easily spooked."

Pitura stood and looked out of a window at the
parklike setting surrounding the building in which assas-
sinations were planned and occasionally carried out successfully. Things were coming to a head; he had decisions

to make, and had to make them fast. Plans had been in the works for months leading up to Castro's annual birthday bash. Everyone had been put on alert—Cuban exile groups in Miami, paramilitary training camps in Florida and Mexico, Cuban operatives inside Havana. The McCullough meeting with Castro hadn't been anticipated, nor had Max Pauling's assignment to Cuba. But those unexpected twists were manageable. Pitura's feet might be a wreck, but he could still think on them.

He was glad Tom Hoctor had ordered Gosling to sever Celia Sardiña's relationship with Pauling. What was she thinking of when she agreed to become involved? He'd sent her to Havana too early, he knew, giving her too much time on her hands. Operatives like her needed to be kept busy, occupied, like little kids with too much idle time. That was always the trouble with using independents for sensitive assignments, especially the hotheaded Cubans. They tended to go off on their own unless the leash was short and maintained by a firm grip. But sometimes you needed them, like now.

He turned and faced his staff.

"All set?" he asked, taking in each person at the table. Nods all around.

"No hitches?"

"None, Joe."

"Then it's a go," he said, and left the room.

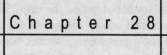

After Celia had left the hotel, Pauling lingered at the twenty-fifth-floor bar before going downstairs and out to the street. The Vedado section of Havana had a different feel from bustling, decrepit central Havana. The boulevards were wide and lined with royal palms. There were many hotels patterned after those in Miami Beach; the majestic Hotel Nacional looked down from its perch above the Malecón as though to proclaim its superiority over lesser ones below.

Pauling looked across the street to the Coppelia Ice Cream Park that Celia had mentioned. Prior to the Revolution, this trendy part of the city had been the scene of numerous ice cream parlors catering to Havana's well-heeled citizens. Blacks and poor *mestizo* Cubans weren't welcome. But in 1966, Castro ordered the sprawling, lush park be built to include the ultimate democratic ice cream parlor, the world's biggest, serving dozens of flavors to as many as forty thousand customers a day. The park had been closed for repairs for two years in the late '90s; cynical Cubans believed the true reason was that the government could no longer import the necessary ingredients for the ice cream. But it had reopened six months prior to Pauling's arrival and was busy despite the early morning hour.

As he crossed the street, he noticed a PNR car with two

men inside parked just beyond the park's entrance. He
was tempted to wave but stifled the urge. He entered the
park and went to its center where the ice cream parlor,
which looked like a giant flying saucer, was located. Regardless of the hour, and what had happened to him during the night—or because of it—he was wide awake,
charged, wired, and throbbing with nervous energy. He
found a vacant bench beneath a tree, sat, and tried to put
a finger on what to do next. He was certain of one thing.
Get out of Cuba as quickly as possible, ideally with the
information he'd been sent to collect. With any luck,
Nico would come up with some credible documentation
of BTK's deal with Strauss-Lochner Resources before the
end of the day. Also, the papers taken from Grünewald's
office, once translated, might provide additional proof.

A pretty young Cuban woman dressed in a red tartan
miniskirt approached and asked if he wished to order ice
cream. "Only vanilla," she said apologetically. Pauling
shook his head and she walked away.

Another young woman, a teenager, came up to him
and offered a paper flute of peanuts coated in sugar from
a makeshift cardboard rack she carried. "Yeah, okay," he
said. "*Sí.*"

He munched on the peanuts as he left the park and
walked in the direction of his hotel, mind still racing. He
was acutely aware of his surroundings, a natural instinct
for Pauling, made more so as he thought of the young
blond German he was convinced had killed Kurt
Grünewald. He hadn't known Grünewald well, had no
connection to him aside from being aware that he
worked for Strauss-Lochner, and having spent an evening
with him. Still, the man's murder was more upsetting
than he'd realized. He'd liked the fat German; felt sorry
for him was more like it. A plain guy in a difficult situa-

tion, going for the pension, he'd said at dinner, a family
back in Heidelberg waiting for him to come home and
putter in his garden and pinch his grandchildren's cheeks.
Anger rose as he thought about Grünewald and the end
he'd suffered. The German was right in labeling the
blond aide foisted on him "Vice President of Stupidity."
Maybe his mistake was in not adding "VP of Bloody
Wetwork" to his titles.

As he approached Hotel Habana Riviera, Pauling realized that Blondie had now become a cause with him. It
was a personal weakness, he knew, one he'd suffered before. Once, in Vienna, he'd been part of a team that had
identified the source of leaks from the U.S. embassy that
had gotten a CIA colleague killed. Pauling's mission had
been successful. The informer, an Austrian civilian employee of the embassy, had been fingered, his fate placed
in the hands of others. But rather than leave when scheduled, Pauling had stayed in the city and physically attacked the source of the leaks one night in a secluded
park. He'd been called on the carpet by Hoctor for that
breach of orders. He couldn't justify to his superior why
he'd done it—except that *he had to*. The slain agent had
been Pauling's friend.

"You jeopardized the mission," Hoctor had said when
they met at Langley. "Your stupid attack might have
served as a tip that we were on to him."

"Nonsense," Pauling had replied. "As far as the creep
knew, he was mugged by an Austrian. That's why I
cleaned out his wallet before I left." He held up his hand
against what Hoctor was about to say next. "No, Tom, I
didn't pocket the money. It went down a sewer, where he
should have gone."

Pauling didn't bother trying to provide Hoctor further
justification for his actions. The truth was, the agency

might have let the informer walk, might have even paid him off to get lost somewhere in South America. He'd witnessed that resolution before.

"Your file's getting thick, Max," Pauling had been warned as the Langley meeting came to a conclusion, referring to official reprimands that had been inserted in Max's file over the years.

"You should be happy about that, Tom," he'd said when leaving. "Your job is safe. No threat from me."

Despite Pauling's cocky justification for having roughed up the Austrian, he was well aware that carrying a vendetta against an individual wasn't smart, unless that person posed a distinct threat to your personal health. He didn't view Blondie in that context. Still, there was a score to settle. Grünewald didn't deserve to die that way. He wouldn't jeopardize the assignment to make a statement to the big German. But if an opportunity happened to present itself—well, that he'd deal with if it did.

The police car continued to follow at a snail's pace, stopping each time Pauling stopped, in order to confirm it was still with him. The throngs of people who had been on the streets earlier in the evening had thinned somewhat; even Cubans have to sleep sometime.

He entered the hotel. The wizened Cuban desk clerk nodded sleepily as Pauling passed him and went to the waiting elevator. He got in and pushed the button for the fourth floor. The doors slowly jerked closed, as though unsure they wanted to. The trip up was equally as halting, the elevator's groans loud. Would it make it? It came to a stuttering halt. Pauling waited until the doors were fully open before taking a step toward the hallway. He knew immediately that it was a step he shouldn't have taken. Too late. He hadn't seen the hulking Cuban standing just to the left of the elevator, but sensed he was there, and then could smell his breath, feel his heat.

The man was one of those weight lifters whose body bulked up so much that it made his shaved head seem unnaturally small. He wore a tight black T-shirt, jeans, and sneakers. His face was expressionless as he brought his right forearm down on Pauling's left shoulder and neck, sending him across the hallway and to his knees. The Cuban was on him in an instant, bringing his right arm around Pauling's neck and jerking his head back while his left fist pressed hard into Pauling's back. Pauling managed to twist to his right and fire his hand sharply up into the Cuban's groin, bringing forth a noise and loosening of the grip. Pauling lunged backward, moving the man into the middle of the hall. With more room to maneuver, he drove his elbow into the Cuban's chest. Now free, he spun around on his knees and went straight for his face, thumbs finding the attacker's eyes. The pained scream reverberated through the hallway. Pauling stood, reached for a head of hair that wasn't there, abandoned *that* move, grabbed the front of the T-shirt, and jerked the Cuban to his feet. He drove for the groin again, this time with his knee. The Cuban slumped to the floor, his hands desperately trying to find the pain and make it go away. For a second, Pauling stood over him, chest heaving, perspiration stinging his eyes. The Cuban lunged suddenly for Pauling's ankles but it was a feeble attempt. Pauling laced his fingers together and brought both hands down on the Cuban's neck, sending him face first into the carpet.

Pauling stepped away, leaned against the wall, and pulled the Glock from his vest pocket. He wanted to shoot to make sure the bastard stayed harmless, but told himself not to go overboard. He wasn't anxious to end up in a Cuban police station again, this time for shooting a Cuban citizen.

He decided to leave him lying there and get down to

the lobby. But as he replaced the Glock in his pocket, movement to the right caught his attention. Someone had been hiding by the door leading to the back stairway.

"Hey!" he called out.

There was the sound of the door closing. Pauling sprinted in that direction and yanked open the door. He heard running footsteps on the stairs. For a moment, he wasn't sure in which direction they were going, up or down. Up. He again pulled out the gun and headed up the stairs, pausing before entering each landing to be sure he wasn't about to be ambushed. He continued his climb until reaching the top floor, directly below the roof. Again, the sound of a door opening and slamming shut. He went more slowly now, weapon at the ready, every sense amplified, prepared for anything. He paused at the closed door and pressed his ear to it. The coolness of the metal felt good against his ear and cheek. Was someone waiting on the other side? Was he armed?

Slowly, he turned the knob, wondering as he did whether the person on the other side was watching it turn. He pushed the door open, inches at first, then more fully until able to see where he was. A nearly full moon provided good but intermittent illumination; low, fast-moving clouds turned it on and off like a light switch.

He checked to his left before pushing the door fully open so that it went flat against a wall. If anyone was behind it, he'd used up his food ration books a long time ago. He held his breath to muffle the sound of his own breathing while he advanced, his eyes taking in the rooftop. The only sound came from far below on the street, Afro-Cuban *yambú* and *guanguancó* and *columbia* music drifting up from boom boxes still being played. *Don't they ever stop?*

His ability to see the entire sweep of the roof was hindered by huge containers in which the hotel's air-conditioning and other electrical equipment was housed. Was there a way down other than the stairs? He wondered if there was a fire escape or other sort of ladder. A dozen feet to his right sat one of the containers, good cover. He darted there, pressed his back against it, listened, then peered around a corner. Nothing. The next container was farther away, twenty feet, one of two in the center of the roof. If whoever was up there with him was armed, he'd pose a tempting target trying to span that distance. He weighed his options. He could simply go back down the stairs and leave whoever was on the roof up there. But that person had been on the fourth floor. He was part of the attack by the muscle-bound Cuban. Let him walk away, and Max would be setting himself up for another attack at another time, maybe a more successful one.

He considered calling out in the hope of prompting him to respond. His location, he knew, was no secret to the person he'd followed up the stairs. He wouldn't be giving anything away. Still, there was safety in silence, at least for the moment. He'd simply wait for his target to make a move, a sound, cast a shadow, cough, decide to attack. He was in no rush, although his neck and shoulders ached. Visions of a massage, or whirlpool, quickly came and went. "Come on, come on," he whispered to himself. "Let's get it over with."

It seemed a long time before things happened, but it was actually less than a minute. What came was the sound of something, someone, bumping up against a solid thing, maybe an elbow, or a head against a low-hanging object. The twin containers in the roof's center. Pauling peeked around the corner again but saw no one. But he knew where his prey was. Pauling was now calm, his breathing regular, his heartbeat slow and steady, but loud. He waited until a cloud moved across the moon, casting darkness over the roof—and then he made his move, crouched low, Glock held with both hands out in front, eyes glued to his destination. He reached the twin boxes safely and switched on his senses again. Was it breathing he heard? That damnable music from the street and the moan of air-conditioning units made it impossible to know.

He drew a breath, held the gun up next to his ear, and made a move to see what was around the corner. He never made it. The body came down on him from the top of the container, dead weight, a hand desperately grasping the wrist of his right hand, in which he held the Glock, another hand grabbing his hair. The force of the body jumping from eight feet above slammed Pauling to the roof and pushed his forehead into gritty tar. He'd heard people who'd suffered sudden pain say they saw stars, but he'd never experienced it himself—until now. The pain shot through his head; his brain felt as though it had been dislodged from its moorings. At the same time, the reality that he was about to be killed echoed inside his head.

A voice shouted in Spanish: "Who is here? What is going on?"

Pauling's attacker scrambled off him, got to his feet, and ran to the open door where two hotel security men stood, flashlights trained on Pauling and his fleeing assailant. Pauling just had time to raise his head and see the blond head push past the unarmed guards and disappear through the door. He slowly, painfully pushed himself up so that he was on all fours, and tried to shake the fog from his brain. The guards came to him and spoke in Spanish: "Who are you? What happened? What are you doing up here?"

Pauling got to his feet and gently touched his cheek

with fingertips. Blood came off on them. He still held the Glock in his right hand and slipped it into a vest pocket. The guards turned at the arrival of another man, the hotel's manager, who spoke good English.

"Why are you up here on the roof?" he asked.

"It's a long story," Pauling said.

"Are you a guest of the hotel?"

"Yes. I was attacked in the hallway outside my room."

"Attacked? Who attacked you?"

"I don't know his name, but I know what he looks like. He's a Cuban with big muscles and a shaved head."

The manager looked at the security guards.

"Another man was here," one of the guards said. "He ran past us."

The manager said to Pauling, "This other man. He was up here with you?"

"That's right. He was with my attacker. He jumped me."

"Do you know who he is?"

Pauling hesitated before saying, "No, I don't."

"I will call the police," the manager said, turning to leave.

"No, don't do that," Pauling said. "It was just a misunderstanding. Actually, I think I know who they are. We had an argument in a bar earlier this evening and they were angry at something I said. You know, about a señorita." He managed a pained smile. "Just forget about it."

"I don't know," said the manager.

"No, it's okay," Pauling said, walking to the door. "Thanks for your concern. I just need to get cleaned up and grab some sleep. Thanks again. *Muchas gracias!* No problem. Good night."

He descended the stairs, wincing at each step he took

as pain radiated throughout his body. As far as he could tell, nothing was broken, but everything had been bent. He hesitated before stepping into the fourth-floor hallway. The Cuban who'd jumped him was gone.

He carefully entered his room, closed the door, turned on the lights, and made sure he was alone. The AC had been shut off by the housekeeper; the room was like a steam bath. He switched it on and went into the bathroom to examine the damage to his face. The left side was scraped and bleeding slightly, black particles from the roof embedded in it. His lip was cut, too, and a purple ring had begun to develop around his left eye. He cleaned up as best he could, changed shirts, sat on the bed, and decided what to do next. Sleep was at the top of the list but somehow he didn't think he'd relax enough for that to happen. He turned on the TV. A special program about Castro's birthday party later that day was running on Canal 2: Tele Rebelde. Pauling had watched Plaza de la Revolución being transformed earlier into a venue for a celebration. Huge posters of Castro had been hung on every available surface in the spacious square. A podium had been set up, and a large roped-off area near the podium had been established for VIPs, Pauling presumed. The reporter, a striking Cuban woman, spoke rapid Spanish to accompany the video footage taped hours before. Pauling understood some of what she said, but not enough to continue listening. He turned off the set, reached for the phone, and was put through to an international operator who, after five minutes, connected him with New Mexico.

"Max?" a groggy Jessica said.

"Yeah. Can you hear me okay?"

"Yes, you're clear. How are you? Is something wrong?"

"No, I'm fine. Sorry to wake you."

"What time is it there?"

"I don't know. Early."

"You've been partying?"

His laugh was rueful. "No, no parties, Jess. I've had a busy night. Been arrested for murder, and got jumped by a Cuban orangutan."

She sounded more awake now. "Good God, Max," she said, "you said it would be easy. What's—?"

"I don't want to get into it on the phone. I called because I miss you."

"I miss you, too. Are you sure you're all right?"

"I'm fine, a little bruised, that's all. Look, I expect to wrap this up in a couple of days."

"That's good."

"Yeah, I want out of here as soon as possible. How are you? Seen any strange birds lately?"

She chuckled. "Just a few doctors at the hospital. Max, please take care."

"You know me, Jess, *my* neck gets saved before anyone else's."

His words did not comfort, but she didn't pursue it. Instead, she said, "I spoke with Annabel Lee-Smith."

"Yeah? How is she?"

"She's fine. Her husband, Mac, is in Cuba, too."

"Is that so?"

"I thought maybe you'd run across him."

"Cuba's a big place, Jess. Where's he staying?"

"He's with the Price McCullough delegation. I saw on TV that they're staying at the Hotel Nacional."

"Fancy place. Maybe I should give him a ring."

"That would be nice."

"I have to go."

"Go to bed," she said.

"Yes, boss. See you soon."

Her "I love you, Max," was lost as he replaced the receiver in its cradle, already asleep.

Chapter 29

Havana

Pauling was stretched out on the bed, the Glock semi-automatic at his side. The brief conversation with Jessica had calmed him. He'd felt sleepy and allowed himself to drift off. Now, two hours later, he awoke as sunlight streaming through the window played over his eyes. He struggled to his feet, groaning as he did. Every muscle ached, his face stung, his head throbbed. He stripped off his clothes and stepped into the shower; a prayer for hot water was answered.

Celia had said she'd contact him at his hotel room at noon. It was seven. He didn't want to wait that long. Talking even briefly with Jessica had crystallized his need to get out of Cuba. Things were falling apart. He'd been hauled in because he was with Grünewald just before Grünewald was murdered, and now he'd damn near been killed by another German, the blond thug sent to keep tabs on Grünewald, and ultimately to kill him—at least that was the assumption.

He made a decision while dressing that he would leave Cuba no later than the next day, whether he had Nico's documentation for Gosling or not. Celia intended to take the papers from Grünewald's office to her German friend that morning, and attempt to contact Nico. Would she follow through? he wondered. She'd been told to back off from Pauling's assignment, and although she'd said she didn't have to disengage immediately, he didn't trust her enough to take her at her word. She could have left the bar and decided to wash her hands of him. She was pulled off the assignment because someone higher up, probably at Langley, had given the order. Such an order would take priority, and he understood that.

His thoughts then went to Celia's connection with the CIA. What was it specifically? She'd been instructed to come to Cuba and wait for further orders. What were those orders? To try to develop an informer within the Castro government? Aid in a planned unauthorized exodus of Cubans to Miami? Or . . . ?

He was thinking too much about her, he knew. Being sexually attracted to her was one thing, just a normal male reaction to female beauty and sensuality—he was years from Viagra.

What *was* of concern was that he wanted to know her other than sexually, wanted to spend time with her, talk, find out all about her, who she was and what she'd been, her childhood, experiences with other men, learn what philosophies drove her, delve into her values and beliefs and . . .

Get off it, Max, he told himself. *Rein it in before you know more than what's good for you.*

After taking a final look at himself in the bathroom mirror and grimacing at what he saw, he left the room and went down the back stairs to the street. He assumed the police shadows would have both front and rear entrances to the hotel covered, but he saw no one who looked like a tail. He was ravenous and stopped to buy a churro, a deep-fried sugared donut stick, and a cup of thick, sweet coffee from a street stall. The stall owner looked at Pauling's bruised, scraped face and frowned.

Pauling smiled, made a fist, and directed it at his face. The stall owner laughed and uttered a string of words that Pauling didn't understand.

He carried the churro and coffee to a shady spot beneath a balcony, ate, and watched the street scene that was in full swing. Celia had told him in passing that despite Cuba's dire economic straits, the people were fastidious about their personal hygiene. She'd stroked the imaginary beard on her chin and said, "He can take away food and rum and cigars, but take away soap and the regime collapses." Now, as he stood on the streets of Havana, he took note of the men, women, and children who passed him, and she was right. Even those wearing frayed clothing were clean and well groomed. A group of schoolchildren, eight or nine years old, wearing green-and-white uniforms, with teachers at the front and end of the line, crossed the street in front of him. A uniformed PNR cop stopped traffic. The scrubbed faces and laughter reminded him of when his sons were that age, oblivious to governments and international conflict, unaware of corporations competing to reward their stockholders at any price, monetary or ethical, immersed only in their own young world of fantasy and dreams. A few of the kids noticed him and his face; they pointed and giggled and spoke to each other. He kept from laughing because it hurt when he did.

He crossed behind the children and walked in the direction of Celia's apartment, stopping occasionally at government kiosks, on which the latest edition of *Granma* was posted, to see whether he was being followed. There were many PNR officers on the streets, but none seemed to pay particular attention to him. As he walked, he imagined turning a corner and finding himself face-to-face with Blondie. That contemplation kept his adrenaline flowing and his sensors extended.

It didn't happen. Instead, it was like a fiesta. There was a palpable air of excitement in Havana that morning, and the signs promoting Castro's birthday celebration that had been hung on buildings overnight explained why. Other signs in shop windows announced the closing of the shops at three in order for their owners and staff to attend the party.

He reached the entrance to the narrow *solar* and looked down its length. People from the apartments were out in the alley. Despite the time of day, two Cubans had set up barbecues and were cooking what smelled like pork. Not his idea of breakfast, Pauling thought. An itinerant troubadour played and sang romantic urban folk music, *nueva trova,* which sounded like a combination of pop and Spanish classical music. Women sat in straight-back chairs in front of their apartments while four men sat at a folding card table playing dominoes. Recently laundered clothing flapped in the breeze from upper-story wrought-iron balconies. Had he still smoked, Pauling would have had a cigarette. Without that prop, he entered the alley and walked slowly to the apartment. Men nodded at him; a few said a greeting. The guitarist paused in the middle of the song but continued where he'd left off, nodding toward a straw hat at his feet. Pauling fished in his pocket and came up with two quarters that he tossed into the hat. Two children, who should have been in school, came up to him and asked for "Dollars, yanqui dollars!" Pauling ignored them and kept walking. The women, most of them older, did not demonstrate the same friendliness as their men. Dark eyes bored holes in him as he reached the door to Celia's apartment, pushed it open, and went up the stairs. There was no response to his knocking. He tried the door and it opened.

His eyes went immediately to the white curtains. They were tied back in their usual, no-message-intended way.

"Celia?" he called. She didn't respond. He closed the door behind him and went to the bathroom, where everything was neat and clean. He ran his hand over the inside of the plastic shower curtain. It was wet. It hadn't been too long since she'd taken a shower. He wandered through the rest of the apartment, not much of a trip considering its small size. Everything was in the order he remembered, nothing out of place. The kitchen was clean, the sink empty except for a single glass.

He returned to the living room where a pile of papers sat on a small table just inside the door. Pauling picked up the top piece. It was a full-page article torn from the most recent edition of *Granma* about Castro's birthday celebration, to be held later that afternoon in Plaza de la Revolución. Included in the piece was the schedule of events, notices of when the speeches would be given and when various bands and other entertainment would perform. Castro would deliver his speech at five. Judging from the Cuban leader's past verbosity, it could last into the evening. Could Celia be planning to attend? he wondered.

He folded the article, put it in a vest pocket, and pulled one of the red vinyl sling-chairs to the window. It promised to be yet another brutally hot day in Havana, and he thought of the cool mountains of New Mexico. He and Jessica enjoyed making a picnic lunch and hiking up into the foothills, sitting against a tree next to a fast-flowing mountain stream, reveling in the pristine air. Sometimes they took fly-casting equipment with them and fished the streams for trout, occasionally catching one on a hook whose barb had been removed, and easily returning it to the cold, clear water, wishing it bon voyage and suggesting that it be a little smarter next time.

After reflection, he put the chair back where it had been and left. As he moved along the alley gauntlet again, he tried to figure out which were CDRs, ears and eyes looking for scraps of information about their neighbors to report back to their Communist contacts at "Minint," the (Jacobinical) Ministry of Interior. Had to be the women mostly, he decided. Their eyes had that look Celia had described, fear mixed with guilt. Besides, they were there more often than the men, with better opportunities to snoop.

He reached the end of the alley and decided what to do next. He'd considered waiting in the apartment for her, but there was no assurance she would return. If she followed through on her promise to call him at noon, it didn't mean she would do it from the apartment.

A Cadillac of '50s vintage, hand-painted green, pulled up and the driver asked if Pauling wanted a tour of Cuba, very cheap, all the best places, dollars only. He got in and said he wasn't interested in a tour, but gave the driver the address of the Strauss-Lochner Resources office in Miramar.

Mac Smith was up early and worked out at the Hotel Nacional's gym. It promised to be a busy day of meetings and receptions, capped by the big birthday celebration. Breakfast was to be with the Council of Ministers, Cuba's highest-ranking executive body. The delegation was to then take a tour of the Central School of Cuban Communist Party from which all government leaders must graduate after having been educated in Marxist theory. Next came lunch hosted by the Federation of Cuban Women; another tour, this of the Museo de la Revolución for a reminder of how unjust and unsuccessful the United States had been in attempting to overthrow Castro and his government, and testimony to the miracle of Castro's triumph over this evil; and finally the birthday bash in Plaza de la Revolución.

Mac intended to call Annabel but decided to wait until that night when he'd have more time to talk. He fought to sustain interest through breakfast and its numbing succession of translated speeches by the ministers, but perked up while touring the Marxist university and compared it to the buildings of his George Washington University. He said silent thanks for having been born an American, teaching in a free society where government policy and philosophy didn't constitute the core curriculum, unless you opted for such courses.

By the time they returned to the hotel for the luncheon, he was ready to pass up the rest of the official proceedings, take a nap in his room, and spend a few hours as an unofficial tourist, perhaps buy something to take back to Annabel. As gracious and welcoming as their Cuban hosts had been, he'd had enough of political posturing and prescribed protocol. Perhaps if he'd seen some tangible sign of progress in the talks, he'd have felt more enthusiastic. As it was, the meetings had been nothing more than platforms for hollow minispeeches, a few polite admonitions meant to sound tough, and a lot of eating and drinking, handshaking and assurances that all would meet again. What had Adlai Stevenson once said? "A diplomat's life is made up of three ingredients, protocol, Geritol, and alcohol."

But Smith again reminded himself that diplomacy usually took such a route, tactful flagstones laid one by one without a specific destination in the hope that they would one day lead to something real, preferably peace and understanding.

After going to his room to wash up, he entered the dining room where most of the McCullough delegation had already assembled, and was greeted by a line of Cuban women. Most were in their late twenties and early thirties, although there were a few older women and four teenagers. They shook his hand and greeted him in English as he navigated the receiving line. At its end, a waiter stood with a tray of champagne. Mac took a flute and joined colleagues at a buffet table laden with hors d'oeuvres.

"What did the college professor think of the Communist university?" Smith was asked.

"Very focused," Mac replied, sipping champagne. "Some of our own elected officials could benefit from taking a few civics courses."

"A few *civility* courses," someone said, laughing.

"That, too," Smith said, surveying the room. The women in the receiving line had dispersed to mingle with members of the delegation.

"Hello," Smith said to one female "greeter" who came to where he stood with the others. She introduced herself in good English as Yvette.

"What do you do here in Cuba, Yvette?" he said.

"I am with Cubapetróleo," she answered, smiling brightly. All the females in the room, young and old, were attractive and personable, handpicked for the occasion, Smith was sure.

"Your national oil company?" Smith said.

"Yes."

"You've been exploring for oil with a number of foreign companies," said one of the delegates, who managed an oil industry service business in Texas.

"That is true," Yvette answered. "We are finding oil with companies from Sweden, Canada, Brazil, Mexico, Germany, so many others. We are partners."

The oilman said to Mac, "They're drilling in at least twenty fields."

"Twenty-five," the woman said pleasantly. "In two years we will have enough oil to take care of all of Cuba without having to import."

Mac decided to find another conversation. He wandered off to a vacant corner of the room, leaned against a pillar, and surveyed the room. Everyone seemed in good spirits, especially Price McCullough, who stood by the bar, a tall drink in his hand, attention focused on an extremely attractive woman wearing a black linen suit with a thigh-length skirt, the top buttons of the jacket undone to reveal the beginnings of a handsome bosom.

Another member of the delegation joined Mac and nodded in McCullough's direction. "He's an old fox, isn't he?" the man said, laughing. "As smooth with the ladies as he was with the voters."

"He's foxy, all right," Mac said. "So is she. Hard to tell who's the hunter." He didn't add that he hoped the former senator had the good sense to not pursue women too young, or goals too ambitious. "Looks like lunch is about to be served."

Max Pauling made one stop and arrived back at his hotel precisely at noon to receive Celia's call. He got looks as he crossed the lobby from the desk clerk, and the manager, who happened to be standing near the elevators.

"Feeling just fine," Pauling said to the manager, gesturing toward his bruised face. "Just fine." He pushed the button for the elevator and waited, aware that the manager, who'd moved a few feet away, continued to stare at him. Pauling stepped into the elevator, turned, gave forth a literally pained smile, waved, and watched the doors slide closed.

He called the desk from his room. Two minutes past two. "No messages for me?"

"No, señor."

He'd picked up a small bottle of rum on his way back to the hotel—no sense in paying room-service prices—

poured a small amount into a glass taken from the bathroom, pulled a chair up to the desk, and waited.

Pauling had the cabdriver drop him a block away from the Strauss-Lochner office. He went to a small bodega with two outside tables, sat at one, and ordered a coffee. He could see the entrance to the building, as well as the window to Kurt Grünewald's third-floor office. He wanted to return to the office and continue his search. But he observed movement in the office, figures moving back and forth, two of them, he decided, identities unknown.

He was on his second cup of coffee when the men emerged from the building. The blond was one of them. The other gentleman was short and slender, with a pinched face and nose. He wore round, metal-rimmed eyeglasses. Blondie was in his usual black suit, white T-shirt, and sandals. The other man wore a gray suit, white shirt, and tie. *Didn't they know it was already over ninety degrees, with a hundred percent humidity?* The skinny man carried a satchel that appeared to be stuffed to capacity and handed it to Blondie. Who was this? Somebody from corporate headquarters back in Heidelberg who'd come to Cuba to clean out the files? Who had informed Grünewald's wife that her hubby was dead? Did they say he'd been murdered, or did they tell her he'd died of natural causes? If Blondie had strangled Grünewald, was the guy with him the one who'd issued the order? The answers to those questions shouldn't matter, Pauling told himself. His responsibility was to find proof of the deal between the pharmaceutical companies.

Just seeing Blondie started his motor.

The two men walked away from the building. Pauling paid for his coffee and tracked them from across the street. A few blocks later they turned a corner. Pauling navigated traffic and crossed. He lingered at the corner and saw them enter the apartment building where he'd dropped off the drunken Grünewald after their night on the town. He looked for any sign of the police for crime scene activity. There was none. The murder of a foreigner evidently wasn't important enough to prolong any investigation, or the PNR cops were too busy rehearsing "Happy Birthday."

With no outdoor café in which to wait, he stood beneath a tamarind tree, the heavy pods hanging low enough to shield his face from view. After a half hour, he felt the need for a bathroom but knew he couldn't leave. He became edgy and impatient. What were they doing up there? "Come on, come on," he muttered, shifting from leg to leg, brushing insects away from his face. He wondered whether he was being observed. He checked his watch; they'd been in the apartment for forty-five minutes. He'd been on surveillance details earlier in his career with the CIA and State Department and had hated every minute. It was like waiting for water to boil.

The men suddenly left the apartment building and headed in his direction, Blondie now carrying two cases. Pauling quickly turned the corner and ducked into a doorway. The two passed within three feet of him. He waited a few beats before looking out from his refuge and saw them cross the boulevard and go down a narrow street. Pauling moved, careful to remain far enough behind to be able to use cover in the event they turned. They walked four blocks until they entered a run-down, four-story building. Pauling slowly approached. When directly across the street from it, he saw a small, crude sign that said HOTEL.

Again, he waited until he thought they'd probably

cleared the lobby and gone to a guest room—if one of them was staying there. Maybe they had to go to the bathroom, too, and stopped for that purpose. He might have exercised caution and not gone into the building, but he went up the three front steps and walked into a small, air-conditioned lobby no larger than his room at the Habana Riviera.

"El baño, por favor?" Pauling asked a woman dozing behind the desk. "Ah, *lavabo?"*

She pointed toward the rear of the room. Pauling thanked her and found a unisex bathroom with the standard chain-flush toilet. When he was finished, he carefully opened the door and looked to the lobby. It was empty except for the woman, who was now dusting the desk.

"Señora," he said, "I am a friend of someone staying in this hotel. He is my amigo." What was the Spanish word for German? "Oh, right, *alemán. Alemánia."* He made a gesture over his head. *"Blanco* hair, huh?"

She grinned. *"Sí,"* she said. *"Señor Erich Weinert, habitación cinco."*

"Room five. *Gracias."*

He left the hotel and went to the corner. He couldn't linger much longer, not if he meant to be back at his hotel in time to take Celia's call. He didn't have to loiter. Blondie and the other man came to the street and approached a waiting taxi. The gray suit placed the two cases in the front passenger seat, along with a small overnight bag, got in the back, and the cab drove off.

Pauling considered confronting the German, but he had disappeared back inside the hotel. Pauling checked his watch; time to get back. He hailed a cab, got in, and smiled.

He knew where the punk was staying. The shadow had

shadowed the shadow. The tables were about to be turned.

"Max, it's Celia."

"You're late. I was about to give up on you."

"I was detained. I have the translation."

"Good. When will I see you?"

"Tonight, perhaps. Mehta is going to drop it off at my apartment within the hour. She'll put it under the mattress on the pullout couch."

"What about Nico?"

"I don't know any Nico. Our young friend says he needs until tomorrow to get what you want. The birthday gets in the way of everything. He'll have it for you tomorrow night."

"Okay, no names. I was planning on leaving tomorrow morning."

"Do what you want, Max."

"What do the translated pages say?"

"I don't know. I didn't ask."

"I want to see you."

"I'll call tonight after—"

"After what?"

"I must go. Pick up the pages."

He heard the click in his ear.

Celia stepped from the phone booth at the Hotel Nacional, looked over her hair in a mirror on the wall, adjusted her skirt and jacket, and returned to the dining room where former senator Price McCullough was still talking with the managing director of the Cuban-American Health Initiative, who'd introduced Celia to McCullough at her request. The director drifted away, leaving McCullough and Celia alone.

"Make your call?" the ex-senator asked.

"Yes."

"Like I told you, you could have made it from my suite."

"Thank you. Perhaps another time—if I have another call to make."

Her smile was dazzling.

"Are you busy tonight?" he asked.

She shrugged. "I have no special plans."

"How about showing me the Havana I haven't seen?"

She smiled demurely.

He leaned toward her ear and breathed in her perfume. "Is that a yes?" he asked.

She nodded.

"Good. I've got some things to take care of this afternoon, meetings and Mr. Castro's birthday party. Are you going?"

"Of course," she said. "All loyal Cubans will be there."

"I hope you're not too loyal a Cuban."

"Like most Cubans, I am loyal enough to stay out of trouble."

He laughed. "I like that," he said. "Come to my suite after the party. We can have a relaxed drink there and then—"

"I will be there."

"Good. You have yourself a good afternoon. I'm looking forward to spending some time with you."

"And so am I."

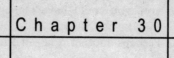

The Duchess of Windsor allegedly once said, "Living well is the best revenge." Whether that prickly bit of philosophy was valid or not, its underlying sentiment appealed to Pauling at that moment. The last meal he'd had was a sugar-covered donut and black coffee, after a dinner of peanuts. The best revenge would be a left to Blondie's jaw, but he wasn't up to it at the moment. Celia had said her friend Mehta would deliver the transcribed pages to the apartment "within the hour." No sense getting there before they arrived. And Mehta might not want to be seen with him.

For some unexplained reason, he had a sudden craving for Chinese food. Were there any Chinese restaurants in Havana?

He left the hotel and stepped into the sunlight. Two suited men in a PNR car parked across the street showed a distinct interest in him. He ignored them and walked toward central Havana. He'd gone a few blocks when he noticed a group of Asian tourists gathered on a corner, consulting a map.

"Excuse me," Pauling said to a man in the group. "I'm looking for a Chinese restaurant."

"Which one?" the man responded in clean, British-tinged English.

"A good one."

"A good one?" The man chuckled. "This is Cuba. Go to Barrio Chino. That's what they call Chinatown here. It isn't far, only a few blocks. We had dinner there last night in a restaurant called Pacifico. A favorite of Hemingway and Castro himself, we're told."

"They have egg foo yung?"

The man looked at him. "They have Chinese food that tastes like Cuban food," he said. "Enjoy your meal."

The Pacifico was state owned, which meant it could serve lobster and other dishes forbidden to the privately owned *paladares*. Pauling, frustrated by inactivity, gorged on lobster and rice. Feeling better, he ventured out onto the street and went to Celia's apartment. The translated memos from Grünewald's office, paper clipped to the originals, were where Celia said they would be, beneath the mattress on the pullout. He hauled a chair close to the window and read.

The first was a communication from Grünewald to his boss in Heidelberg, Dr. Hans Miller. He'd handwritten across the top of the page TOP SECRET, as though that would ensure privacy.

Dear Dr. Miller,

I write you not to complain, but as a loyal employee of Strauss-Lochner. I am sure you will agree that in my more than twenty years of service to the Company, I have performed my duties with efficiency and honor. It has always been a source of great pride to me to work for the greater good of the Company without concern for my personal needs. As you know, being posted to Havana represented a great hardship for me and my family. Although such a posting to this wretched, impoverished island was not how I envisioned spending the final years of my service to you and the Company, I put aside those feelings and rose to the occasion, again in the interest of serving the Company's greater good.

I feel as though a stake has been rammed into my heart. I have functioned here in good faith on the assumption that my efforts in paving the way for Strauss-Lochner to benefit from the Cuban cancer research was for the Company's exclusive benefit. How proud I would be if my efforts under difficult circumstances resulted in our ability to become a world leader in finding a cure for this dreaded disease.

But now I learn through a mistaken communication that it will be another company that will benefit most from my work, the American company BTK Industries. Do you have such little faith in me that you would choose to not inform me of my true role here in Cuba? I can take nothing else from having been excluded from your confidence. It is so hurtful, Dr. Miller, to be placed in that position.

Please do not misunderstand. I continue to be the same loyal, enthusiastic employee of the Company. Strauss-Lochner has been my life and will always be. But I felt I must communicate to you my true feelings, knowing you are a sensitive and caring leader who will know that what I say is from the heart.

Faithfully,

Kurt Grünewald

Pathetic, Pauling thought. *Poor naïve, whining, drunken Grünewald. What did all his loyalty get him? A broken neck. Loyalty was supposed to be a two-way street.* In Pauling's years with the CIA and then with State, he was loyal to two things, his country and the person signing his checks. Do the job as long as they're paying you, but if you no longer wish to do the job, walk away, as he had done, and stop taking the checks. Had he been in a position to counsel Grünewald, he would have told him to write the memo, let it sit on his desk overnight, and tear it into small pieces in the morning. He thought the fat German had been like some government employees back in Washington, in it for the pension, nothing else, no psychological payoff for a job well done, no glory, no satisfaction from standing up for what you knew was right. Keep your mouth shut, do your job, and spend weekends looking for a retirement cottage in a low-rent area.

Miller's response to Grünewald's letter was both threatening and patronizing. The head of Strauss-Lochner was shrewd. There was no mention of a deal with Price McCullough and BTK Industries, nor was there any indication how the communiqué had been delivered.

Dear Kurt,

I am in receipt of your memorandum and wished to respond with all possible speed. You do not need to remind me of the outstanding job you have done for Strauss-Lochner. Not only do I view you as a friend, you are one of our most valued employees, a man of integrity and principle who has been a role model for so many of your colleagues.

It is always difficult for someone in my position of leadership to determine who in the chain of command must know of certain sensitive projects being undertaken. It is a matter of judgment, nothing else. I will say to you, Kurt, that it is the health of the Company that must be my uppermost priority. Strauss-Lochner's success is not only necessary to reward the fine men and women who strive to find medical solutions, it is necessary to the millions of men, women, and children around the globe whose very health and life depend upon how successful we are. In that sense, anyone who jeopardizes the mission of the Company must be considered expendable.

One day soon, you will leave the Company and enjoy a well-deserved retirement with your fine wife and family. Treasure the contemplation of that, Kurt, keep up the fine work, and rest assured I take personal interest in your life and work.

> Sincerely,
> Hans Miller, Ph.D., Chairman and CEO

If Kurt Grünewald had been a drinker before, receiving that thinly veiled threat from his boss must have really sent him on a toot. Pauling knew all about threats. He'd been on the receiving end of them from his handlers at the CIA and the State Department's covert intelligence unit more than once, particularly from Tom Hoctor who'd managed his overseas assignments from spook HQ. His relationship with the little bald man with the drooping right eye had been one of love and hate. He admired Hoctor for his professionalism; when push came to shove, Hoctor made decisions that ensured the job got done. At the same time, Pauling never really trusted his handler, never viewed him as the sort of person you wanted at your back in a parking lot when Hell's Angels were coming at you with knives and chains.

He put aside his personal responses to the communiqués and reread the first one, the memo to Miller from Grünewald. Although Miller hadn't confirmed what Grünewald had said in it—"But now, I learn through a mistaken communication that it will be another company that will benefit from my work, the American company BTK Industries."—the memo would have value for

Gosling and his Cell-One client Signal Laboratories in putting together a case against McCullough and BTK. It wouldn't be enough proof on its own; Grünewald's statement could be interpreted in more than one way, depending upon who was doing the interpretation and the agenda. He'd need more. Ideally, Nico would come up with it.

Where was Nico? Some agent.

Where was Celia? Some interpreter.

Pauling folded the papers and put them in a vest pocket. He pulled out the tear sheet from *Granma* and reviewed the schedule for Castro's celebration. Was Celia attending? Should he go to Plaza de la Revolución to see if he could spot her in what was sure to be a huge crowd? Might as well, he thought. How often would he have the opportunity to wish Fidel a happy birthday? He'd rather wish him a happy retirement. But dictators don't retire—unless shove came to push. Besides, he had nothing else to do until she again contacted him and set up a meet with Nico.

He hated being in the position of having to depend on someone else. The career gurus preach that the ability to delegate authority is an important attribute for business leaders. If that was true, Pauling knew he'd be a dismal failure in business, had always known it, which was one of the reasons he'd gravitated to the sort of work he'd ended up doing, for better or worse.

Two hours until the celebration. He decided to pass some of the time in Celia's apartment on the chance she would stop in or call. He removed his vest, hung it over a chair, and stretched out on the couch, like an animal conserving energy for when it might be needed.

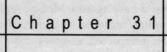
D r. Manuel Caldoza, Cuba's most renowned medical researcher and head of the Health Ministry's cancer research institute, sat at his desk. The lights flickered; another brownout or blackout? Bad timing, he thought. Fidel would not be happy to have the lights go out at his party.

The flickering stopped and the single bulb in his desk lamp glowed steadily. Caldoza had closed the draperies tightly and turned off the overhead lights. His door was closed. The AC hummed. He wore a deep blue shirt, maroon tie, and white physician's lab coat. All was quiet on his floor. The faint sounds of crowds gathering forced their way through the draperies' heavy material. A military brass band played a familiar march, which didn't deter the young people with their battery-powered boom boxes from competing with the uniformed musicians. They would be ordered to turn them off once the official festivities began. Until then, it would be every man for himself, a battle of the loudspeakers.

How many of the thousands of people who would gather in Plaza de la Revolución that afternoon truly wanted to be there? he thought. *How many of them who did come would bestow a heartfelt tribute to their leader?* The PNR, and the Minint secret police, would have rounded up every stray, sane man, woman, and child and

ordered them to be present to cheer and sing, at the top
of their lungs, the Cuban national anthem:

> *Al combate corran Bayameses*
> *Que la patria os contempla orgullosa*
> *No temáis una muerte gloriosa*
> *Que morir por la patria es vivar*

> To the battle, run, Bayamases
> Let the fatherland proudly observe you
> Do not fear a glorious death
> To die for the Fatherland is to live

Caldoza rubbed his eyes and sighed. *So much promise
unfulfilled,* he thought. In the beginning, he had embraced Fidel and his revolution, as had many around the
world. The Batista regime had corrupted Cuba and its
people to an obscene extent, had turned the lush tropical
island into a brothel, a gambling den and hangout for the
most vicious of American mobsters, chiefly for Batista's
personal gain. Castro's triumphant battle against superior Batista forces had filled Caldoza's heart with pride
and hope. Cuba's new leader had promised many things
under his Socialist leadership, including the eradication
of cancer in his lifetime, and he'd put his money behind
his words, devoting a stunning percentage of the yearly
budget to cancer research and health care in general. His
emphasis on medical research and providing quality
health care for every Cuban citizen had inspired Caldoza
to throw himself into his work, toiling day and night in
search of that elusive deeper understanding of the way
the body works, how certain cells cease functioning in a
normal way and create malignancies, going mad in a
sense, ravaging the body until it no longer can withstand
the relentless attack. He knew there was an answer to it,

and reveled in the vast sums the government provided to find the answers. Funds had doubled once Fidel embraced the Soviets. His Communist partners began funneling billions to the island, providing oil and food and unlimited money for an assortment of programs, including medical supplies, physician training, and laboratory essentials.

But even when the Soviet Union itself collapsed and the plug was pulled, the research, already far along, continued. A breakthrough was around the corner, Caldoza was convinced, and it would involve the use of the metal vanadium. Results had been more than encouraging. Clinical trials had brought about dramatic remissions in a variety of patients with different cancers, particularly those in the lymphoma and myeloma families, cancers of the blood. By combining the drugs with monoclonal antibodies, the cancerous cells could be induced to "commit suicide," to die off and allow normal cells to proliferate.

So close.

But now the tape.

They'd come to him last night at home, three of them, colleagues at the research institute. It was not unusual for them to visit his home in the Vedado section. Maria Caldoza ran what amounted to an open house for her husband's friends from the hospital and labs. They came and went, young and old, seasoned physicians and researchers, medical students and their friends. All were always offered drinks and meals created by Maria, an acknowledged superior cook. Her *ajiaco,* meats and vegetables spiced with judicious amounts of onion, oregano, cumin, and sour oranges, was a particular favorite, especially in these days of food shortages, when her creativity at substituting ingredients never failed to please.

Because his was a prestigious position within Cuban society, Dr. Caldoza and his wife enjoyed a quality of life unavailable to the majority of Cubans. Their house was of Spanish colonial design built around a courtyard in which Maria had created a colorful display of plantings—African golden trumpet, fragrant mariposa, begonia, oleander, flame-of-the-woods, and bright pink morning glory. It was to this multihued setting that Dr. Caldoza and his three visitors repaired after dinner. They lit up cigars—they may have been doctors but this was, after all, Cuba—and sat around a green wrought-iron table, small cups of strong coffee in front of them, drawing on their Upmanns and Cohibas, watching the blue smoke drift up into the still, humid Havana night.

Caldoza spoke first: "So, it will happen," he said, his flat voice not reflecting the inner turmoil.

The three visitors murmured agreement.

"This tape," Caldoza said. "Tell me about it again."

One of the men at the table recounted the conversation between Fidel Castro and former U.S. senator Price Mc-Cullough.

"Who recorded the conversation?" Caldoza asked.

"Someone close to El Presidente, obviously not a loyalist."

"Obviously," said Caldoza, drawing on his cigar, deep in thought. He said as though speaking to a royal palm swaying above, "This is a startling development. The rumors have been alive for a year, sí? Many rumblings about Strauss-Lochner negotiating with the government for our team's research. There have been countless meetings with Grünewald, their liaison here. Those so-called secret meetings have not been so secret. I have been kept abreast of what has been discussed in them, and while the thought of seeing our work end up in the hands of others would be heartbreaking, it has been my evaluation that such a betrayal could not happen. Strauss-Lochner is almost no longer a viable company. Its laboratories are decaying, suffering from too little cash to invest in costly research. It has been my opinion that it would not be able to raise sufficient money to buy its way into our work. As you know, there have been other pharmaceutical companies, particularly Canadian, that have made such inquiries, but they have not been taken seriously, according to my sources. But now this. BTK Industries is a very successful company, as you know. It has virtually cornered the market on many proprietary drugs and has the advantage of being led by a distinguished former United States senator."

"It must be stopped!" said the man seated across from Caldoza.

"An excellent suggestion, Felix," Caldoza said, smiling. "I am sure you have a foolproof plan to achieve this."

Felix cleared his throat. "There is an American in Cuba who was sent here to uncover proof that BTK Industries is behind Strauss-Lochner's bid for our research."

Caldoza placed his cigar in an oversized ashtray and leaned forward. "How do you know this?" he asked.

"Through one of the people who brought news of the tape to me."

"One of that group?"

"Yes. She is—"

"She?"

"Yes. She is part of that group. This American was sent here by Signal Laboratories."

"BTK's competitor."

"Exactly. Cell-One—that is a private investigation agency with headquarters in London—represents Signal in this matter. The person chosen to come here once worked for the American CIA. He reports to someone else who once worked for that agency."

"Your source," Caldoza said. "This woman. How does she know this?"

"She was recruited by Cell-One's representative to help this agent here in Havana find the proof. His name is Pauling. Max Pauling."

"That is interesting," Caldoza said, "but of what value to us?"

"If this American is successful, the information he uncovers can be used to discredit BTK Industries—"

"And—" someone added, stroking a beard that wasn't there.

Caldoza again drew on his cigar and said, "Is this woman you mention willing to share with us what she and this American come up with?"

"Yes, she will."

"How soon before—?"

"Before she and the American are successful?"

"Yes."

"Days, she tells me. A matter of days."

"And where will they get this proof? Surely not from us. We do not have, as far as I know, any documentation that would help. All negotiations must have taken place in the highest echelons of the ministry."

No one had an immediate answer.

"There are those in that higher echelon who might be persuaded to release such information for the right price," it was suggested.

"Have we become that corrupted?" Caldoza mused.

"The mere act of accepting money to reveal traitorous secrets is not necessarily synonymous with corruption," his question was answered, "not if those secrets bring about needed change and benefit our people. It would be a tragedy, a true tragedy, for an American company to profit from all the good research that has been conducted here in Cuba, by Cubans."

They fell into silence until Caldoza said, "It appears the rumors may be true about El Presidente planning to leave."

"I do not believe that will happen," said a female visitor, Casandra. "I remember his words as clearly as if it was yesterday. 'If I am told that ninety-eight percent of the people no longer believe in the Revolution, I'll continue to fight. If I'm told I am the only one who believes in it, I will continue.' No, he will only leave office in a pine box."

"We shall see," Caldoza offered. "In the meantime, I would like to be kept informed about this American—Pauling, is it?—and his efforts."

"Of course."

"You will continue to be in touch with this woman?"

"Definitely."

"Good."

Caldoza stood, prompting the others to follow.

"Dinner was wonderful, as usual," one said.

"Tell Maria," said Caldoza. "If we can be as successful in the laboratory as she is in the kitchen, cancer will be but a memory. Thank you for coming. It is always a pleasure having you."

Now, alone in his office, Dr. Caldoza reflected on the conversation of the previous evening. Most of the research institute's staff had left to attend the Castro birthday celebration. He knew their motives in doing so were mixed. There were those who, like himself, had believed in the Revolution and saw it as a new, cleansing dawn for Cuba and its eleven million people. It certainly wasn't a matter of personally profiting from the new Socialist regime of Fidel Castro. Everything, including the medical establishment, became state-owned and -operated. Salaries were cut dramatically; Caldoza was paid only a tenth of what he would have earned under the open Batista government. But there were the sudden infusions of money into his research budget, and Castro's pledge to mitigate personal loss.

He ran his fingertips through tufts of white hair at his temples and turned to look at a photograph on his desk. It had been taken ten years ago during a family vacation on the Peninsula de Ancón, a beautiful stretch of beach on the southern coast, two hundred miles from Havana. Caldoza and his wife and two sons stayed at the tourist resort Playa Ancón, where they'd snorkeled together at Cayo Blanco, enjoying the white, powdery sand beach and clear, warm water. Caldoza had asked a tourist to take a family portrait with his camera, and they posed at the base of a palm tree, his sons clowning a little, his wife beaming, he sucking in his stomach at the time the shutter was released. Both boys had gone on to Cuban medical schools but eventually left Cuba for Canada where they practiced medicine and started their own families. They'd tried to convince their mother and father to leave Cuba, too, but Manuel Caldoza wouldn't then consider it. His work at the labs was going well, the results providing a level of psychic satisfaction that was like a daily shot of Adrenalin. And it was his home. Leave Cuba? Inconceivable.

He removed his lab coat, put on the jacket to his suit, and left. As he walked to the elevators, he passed a young lab assistant who looked up from her worktable and smiled. "Going to the birthday celebration, Dr. Caldoza?" she asked.

"Yes," he said. "You?"

"I would like to but I cannot leave in the middle of this experiment."

Caldoza returned the smile and patted her on the shoulder. "What you are doing is more important than attending," he said. "Besides, there will be thousands there. You will not be missed."

He rode down the elevator and went to the parking lot where he got into his car, started the engine, waved to the security guard at the gate, and prepared to pull onto the street. Plaza de la Revolución was to his left, the route to his home to his right. He never hesitated. He turned the wheel to the right and headed for Vedado and his house where the phone call would come from the States.

After his guests had left the night before, Caldoza had placed a call to the home number of Dr. Barbara Mancuso in Silver Spring, Maryland, a number she'd given him during his presentation to the American Society of Clinical Oncology. Their conversation was brief. At its conclusion, she said she would have to consult others at the National Institutes of Health for answers, and said she would call the next day.

"At your office?" she'd asked.

"No," he replied, "at my home." He gave her his number. "Anytime," he added.

Pauling stayed at Celia's apartment until a few minutes past four. The phone had rung once, but when he answered, the caller hung up.

The alley was comparatively empty when he came down the stairs. An old woman watched him from inside her apartment as he walked by. He gave her a small nod but her stern expression never changed. A CDR if he ever saw one. Or if ever one saw him.

The children were gone, evidently off to serenade El Jefe. Pauling could hear the faint roar of a crowd, and dissonant march music coming from Plaza de la Revolución. He walked in that direction, aware that the streets most distant from the plaza were virtually empty. The music, and the crowd, became increasingly louder as he approached. Now the narrow side streets that fed into the vast plaza were clogged and he had to squeeze through in order to reach a point where he could see the raised platform and podium. There were staging areas for the bands, other speakers, and VIP guests. The rooftops were chockablock with spectators, like birds on a wire. Smoke from barbecues on the street and roofs stung the eyes while tickling the nostrils. He kept looking for Celia in the sea of celebrants.

As he moved into the plaza itself, he began to feel the party atmosphere. If the thousands of Cuban citizens were there only because it was the prudent thing to do, their exuberance didn't reflect it. People danced to music being played by a festively costumed band, the incessant beat infectious. He continued to inch closer to the stage. He could see the people on it now, dozens of government bureaucrats and Castro cronies surrounding the podium, chatting, laughing, and slapping each other on the back. Directly in front of it was a large, roped-off VIP area. Uniformed PNR officers were stationed every six feet along the ropes, their eyes trained on those special guests.

Pauling was aware of other men in the crowd who looked as though they might be plainclothes detectives, or Minint's secret police. Positioned along the edge of the Ministerio del Interior and Ministerio del Justice roofs were armed members of the military. Looming witnesses to the event were the huge, black metal mural of Che Guevara dominating the front of the Interior building and the imposing Monumento José Martí. Fidel was everywhere, his face and piercing dark eyes on dozens of blowups of his image.

Although Pauling was not the only Caucasian foreigner among the thousands of spectators, he felt that he was. Armed Cuban officers scattered throughout the crowd seemed to take particular interest in him, and he wondered whether he might be stopped and searched, detained, taken off the streets in the interest of national security. He knew the bruises on his face didn't help him avoid scrutiny. *Who was this gringo wearing a vest with dozens of pockets in which, Dios knows what, something destructive, might be concealed—a grenade, a knife—and looking as though he'd just survived a train wreck?*

He continued to keep an eye out for Celia, the blond one, and anyone else of recent acquaintance. He remembered that Jessica had told him Mac Smith was in Havana with the Price McCullough delegation, and strained to see him among the VIPs gathered in front of the podium. He had a vague recollection of what Smith looked like, although he wouldn't swear he could pick him out of a police lineup with certainty. It didn't matter. He was still a little too far away to distinguish individual faces in the VIP section.

When it seemed that the noise level in the plaza couldn't become any louder, it did, a different sort of noise, one filled with expectation and excitement. A deafening cheer went up as Fidel Castro, dressed in his signature combat fatigues and wearing his green fatigue hat, appeared from nowhere and stepped to the podium. He held his hands high above him and uttered a rapid-fire greeting in Spanish. Pauling noted the security officers in his area, and thought they'd never cut it in the U.S. Secret Service. Their attention had turned from watching for potential assassins to their leader, who'd transformed Cuba from a hedonistic playground for the rich into a Communist state ninety miles off the shore of the mighty United States, and done it with arrogance and bravado that had perplexed president after president and generated heated public discourse for more than four decades.

Pauling tried to translate what Castro was saying. *What does this guy possess to have pulled it off and kept it going for so many years?* Colleagues at the CIA and State had offered many explanations in the past. "He's the best TV actor in the world," was one. "He's a dictator," was another. "He gave his people hope," a more sanguine colleague offered. "He's smart, knows what buttons to push and when," said another. Castro's close friend, the Nobel Prize–winning Colombian author, Gabriel García Márquez, explained Castro's success this way: "His rarest virtue is the ability to foresee the evolution of an event to the farthest reaching consequences. He is a masterly chess player."

One thing was certain, Pauling knew. The man could talk—and talk, and talk. An ancient entertainment. The people in the plaza seemed spellbound as their leader went on, stopping only to allow a chorus of schoolchildren to sing to him, their sweet voices bringing smiles to everyone. When the children were finished, a chant went up: "Fidel! Fidel! Fidel!" And he picked up where he'd left off, to the crowd's seeming delight.

Although Pauling understood little of what Castro was saying, he found himself drawn into the forceful, passionate delivery, fascinated by the man's presence even at that distance. He maneuvered through the crowd to get closer, a moth drawn to a summer candle. "*Perdón,*" he said as he squeezed by people. "Sorry. Excuse me." He reached the rope separating the VIP section from the main crowd. A burly Cuban officer glared at him. Pauling smiled and nodded to indicate his approval of what Castro was saying. He slid to his right, away from the guard, stopped, and looked up at the podium where Castro was making what was obviously an important point, his voice rising and falling in passion, a finger jabbing at the air.

Pauling now took in the assembled dignitaries behind the ropes, but saw only their backs, their attention turned to the speaker. One man moved for a moment; Annabel Lee-Smith's husband? Pauling couldn't be sure, but he did recognize Price McCullough. He looked closely at Castro. No matter how the assignment turned out, he'd gotten within twenty feet of the man. He felt like a groupie, a fan club member trying to catch a glimpse of a pop idol. As that unflattering thought ran through his mind, he realized again how dangerous someone like Fidel Castro was, able to whip a nation into patriotic frenzy through the power of his words and ferocity of his delivery.

People to his left and right began to sway in rhythm to

Castro's vocal cadence, bumping into Pauling. He decided it was time to leave. He'd had enough. He peered over heads on his left, in search of Celia, then tried the right. As he did so, the man pressing next to him drew his attention. He was middle-aged and considerably shorter than Pauling. His eyes seemed to be glazed, his face expressionless, unlike the smiling, humming people under Castro's verbal spell. Celia had told Pauling that in advance of the celebration, the police would sweep the streets of suspicious types and corral them somewhere until Castro was safely offstage. Pauling wondered why *he* hadn't been included in that group; this guy certainly should have been.

Pauling turned to begin the tortuous route back through the crowd and out of the plaza, but something unstated caused him to look again at the man with the crazed expression. He was reaching slowly beneath his white guayabera and pulling a handgun from his belt. Pauling froze for the second it took for the man to raise the weapon in Castro's direction and to shout "Murderer!" Pauling lunged, his hand hitting the weapon and turning it from its target. It discharged once, then again. Other people pounced on the shooter and immediately began punching and kicking him. Castro had been flung to the stage floor by bodyguards. VIPs within the roped area hit the ground, too. Pandemonium broke out in the plaza. The cheers and chants changed to screams and wailing, a swelling chorus of curses and questions and accusations. A nervous soldier on the rooftop of the Minint building opened fire into the crowd. People tried to run from the square and soon were knocking each other down, stepping on and over the fallen, panic as thick in the air as the aroma of food and the density of the speech had been.

A security guard, who'd seen what had happened,

began speaking loudly and quickly with a fellow officer, pointing at Pauling. Mac Smith, who'd gone to the ground at the sound of the first shot, stood and looked in Pauling's direction. He was certain it was Jessica's boyfriend. He shouted the name "Pauling," but his words were drowned by the din in the plaza.

Others who'd been standing close to Pauling and the gunman when it happened started yelling things at Pauling that he didn't understand, but they sounded angry. *Did they think* he'd *been with the shooter? That he was part of the plot?* He didn't wait around to find out. He pushed past them, sending an older man to the ground, found some open room, and began to run, dodging knots of people, searching for other breaks in the crowd, trying to move away from security forces who seemed as confused as the rest of the people. Then he reached a narrow *solar* and ducked into it, his breath coming hard, his sides aching. Soon, he reached the opposite end, thankful it wasn't a dead end, crossed a wider street, and entered a small park. He found an iron bench nestled in a thick clump of trees and bushes and sat down. The sound of police sirens reached him in this temporary haven. He drew deep breaths and shook his head in an attempt to clear it. The last few minutes had been a blur. Now things returned to focus.

An attempt had been made on Fidel Castro's life, and he, Pauling, had been there to thwart it. It probably wouldn't have made any difference whether he'd knocked the gun away or not. The shooter was unlikely to have hit his target from where he was standing. The gun looked like a cap pistol. Not a very creative approach to taking out the Cuban leader, but Pauling's former agency's high- *and* low-tech attempts at the same target hadn't been effective either.

Pauling tried to think. Who was the guy with the cap pistol? *Jesus!* He had shouted, "Murderer!" A nut looking to make a name for himself? Was the failed assassin on his own, or was he part of a larger conspiracy? If it had happened in the States, he'd soon be branded a lone assassin with no ties to anyone, no matter how illogical that might be. *Governments don't like conspiracy theories; "the people" can't handle it, they rationalize.*

Who was the guy? Was he still alive?

Pauling stood and looked through the bushes at the street. Sirens continued to wail, and there was the sound of people shouting from outside the park. He tried to get his bearings. Once he had them, a decision had to be made where to go next, Celia's apartment or his hotel? His first inclination was to rule out the latter. But he decided there was no reason not to go there. He hadn't done anything to make anybody mad, unless saving Castro's life was sufficient. Hell, they ought to give him a medal and a year's supply of free *mojitos.*

He made his decision based upon which place would more likely put him in touch with Celia. Had she been in the plaza? If so, he reasoned, she'd probably go back to her friend's apartment.

As he made his way carefully, staying off major streets in favor of smaller, less populated ones, Celia Sardiña got out of a taxi in front of the art gallery on Calle Obispo. The blinds on the windows were tightly shut, and a sign in the window said CLOSED. She rang the bell and waited. A minute later the gallery owner peeked through the slats and unlocked the door. She followed him to the back room.

"It failed," the owner said.

"Of course it did," she replied. "Did you think sending someone with a pistol would succeed?"

"The message had to be sent that all Cubans are not happy with Castro. The world will know."

"The world will know we are inept when trying to rid ourselves of him."

The owner hung his head. "I must report to Miami," he said, looking up. "The tape? McCullough? What is new with that?"

"That is not a problem," she said. "I am taking care of it."

He looked at her quizzically.

"I must go. Roberto is in custody?"

"*Sí*. They beat him, I am told. An American hit him, pushed his gun away."

"An American?"

"*Sí*. You were not there?"

"I had things to do."

"You can stay for dinner?"

"No, *gracias*. I have other plans." She checked her watch. Ex-senator McCullough would be back at his suite by now. "I will be leaving Havana shortly."

He nodded.

"This is a crucial period for us," she said. "Huge changes are about to take place. We must be ready for them."

"I will do what I can."

She embraced him, left the gallery, and told the taxi driver to take her to Hotel Nacional.

This is Lolita Perez reporting from Cuba. An attempt was made today on the life of Fidel Castro as he spoke during his annual birthday celebration. The attempt by a lone gunman, who fired two shots at President Castro, failed, and the assailant was taken into custody by the police."

Footage taken at Plaza de la Revolución during the celebration aired, with the correspondent talking over it. When it was finished, her face again filled the screen.

"I'm at Havana's famed Hotel Nacional where former senator Price McCullough and a trade delegation he's led to Cuba are staying. The senator and his delegation were at the birthday celebration when the assassination attempt took place."

The shot widened to include McCullough standing next to the reporter.

"Senator McCullough, what happened today during President Castro's speech? What did you see?"

"What I saw, Ms. Perez, was a crazed gunman try to take the life of President Castro. Fortunately, he missed. I understand a member of the security forces was hit by one of the bullets, but wasn't seriously injured."

"Were you and your delegation in danger?"

McCullough laughed gently and patted her shoulder. "No, young lady, we weren't in danger. I'm just glad that aside from a few minor injuries in the crowd—and my goodness, it was some crowd to wish President Castro a happy birthday, wasn't it?—I'm glad that a tragedy of international proportions didn't occur here today."

Annabel Lee-Smith had been watching CNN while making a key lime pie. When the report of the attempt to kill Castro came on, she dropped the pie plate to the counter and stood close to the TV set. Behind the reporter and Price McCullough stood members of the trade delegation, including, thank God, her husband, Mackensie.

The report ended and CNN went on to other stories. Annabel tried to place a call to Havana, but all circuits were busy. "Damn," she muttered, returning to the pie. She'd try the call again in a few minutes.

At CIA headquarters in Langley, Virginia, Zachary Rasmussen, the agency's director of covert ops, watched it on a TV in his office.

"That's the best they could do?" Rasmussen said, slowly shaking his head.

"They had something better planned, Zach," Tom Hoctor said, "but it got derailed at the last minute. At least that's what we get from Miami."

"Who's the guy they sent to do the job?"

"I don't know. A sacrificial lamb, I suppose. They wanted to take a shot at Fidel during his birthday bash to make a statement. If by some chance they actually hit him, that would have been a bonus."

"We told them it would be a wasted effort," said Rasmussen.

Hoctor shrugged and rubbed his right eye. He'd come to Rasmussen's office carrying a sheaf of papers and now handed one to him. Rasmussen frowned and chewed his cheek as he read. He handed it back to Hoctor and said, "*He* saved Fidel's life?"

"According to Bobby Jo Brown at the Interests Section, they lost touch with Pauling for a period of time. Then he shows up at Fidel's party. According to Brown, Pauling was standing next to the shooter and took a swipe at his gun hand."

"And?"

"Brown's tail lost him. Gene Nichols. He's one of us. Pauling ran."

"Where?"

"Brown doesn't know. He's disappeared."

"What's this about Pauling looking like he's been beaten up?"

"That's what Nichols reported. Bruises on his face, a black eye. No idea how it happened." Hoctor displayed one of his small, wry smiles. "Pauling always did have a penchant for putting his face where it shouldn't be."

"Have you heard from Gosling?"

"Yesterday. He was leaving London and said he'd check in with me tonight."

"Progress on *his* project?"

"He says it goes well."

"He's in touch with Pauling, I assume."

"Negative on that. Celia Sardiña is his only contact."

"I thought you pulled her off that project."

"I did. At least I told Gosling to do it, and he assured me he had. I'll lean on him again tonight."

"Everything else is set, Tom?"

"I believe it is."

"Good. Let's not have another amateur night."

The attempt on Castro's life changed things in Havana, as would be expected.

After giving his interview to CNN, Price McCullough and his group were marshaled into a room off the hotel's lobby. The schedule had called for a night free of official gatherings, although a performance of the Cuban National Ballet Company at Teatro Nacional had been arranged for those wishing to attend. Half the group had elected to take in the performance, including Mac Smith. McCullough was among those who'd declined.

"What's the purpose of this?" McCullough asked the senior Cuban government official who'd instructed the delegates to gather in the room.

"What happened today, Senator McCullough, has serious ramifications. We feel it is necessary that you and your people receive instructions as to how to respond to questions that might be asked of you."

"That's not necessary," the ex-senator said in stentorian tones. "Hell, we didn't see anything that anybody else would want to know about. We were all down on the ground once a shot was fired."

"I know, sir, but I ask that you respect our needs in this matter. You will not be detained long, I assure you."

"We're not used to being told what to say or not to say, sir."

"That may be true in your country, Senator. But we are in Cuba, our country. Excuse me."

As the official walked away, McCullough looked past him through open doors to the lobby where he saw Celia Sardiña talking with one of the desk clerks. He crossed the room, stopping briefly to deflect questions about why they were being detained, and went to her. Her expression said she wasn't happy.

"We have a problem here?" McCullough asked.

"I told them you had invited me to your suite, but they refuse to give me the key." Her pout was exaggerated.

"Just bein' prudent, I suppose." He said to the clerk, "It's all right. The lady has official business with me."

Celia's face softened.

The clerk handed McCullough a key and he held it out for Celia. "I'll be tied up here for a while, but not too long, I'm told. You go on up, make yourself a drink—it's all there in the bar. I'll join you as soon as I can."

"No," she said.

"I thought—"

"Can we go outside?" she said.

McCullough looked around to see whether their exchange was being noted. The only interest in them seemed to come from a few of his fellow delegates who were watching from inside the staging room, and the Cuban official who did nothing to stop the ex-senator.

"Senator," she said when they were outside, "I am uncomfortable being with you in this hotel. There are so many people who will see that we are together. It would not be good for me or for you."

"What do you suggest?" he asked.

"I have an apartment. It belongs to a friend of mine who is away. We can be alone there, relax, and after that—"

His was an understanding smile tinted with lechery.

"After *that,* I will take you to a wonderful Cuban restaurant, one of the best in all Havana. I promise you will not be disappointed with the food or with—"

"With you? I'm sure I won't be. Where is this apartment?"

She handed him a slip of paper on which she'd already written the address. "I will go directly there," she said, "and wait for you."

Pauling reached the apartment, went to the kitchen, pulled the bottle of Habana Club *anejo* from the cupboard, and took down a clean glass. The lone cordial glass that had been in the sink was still there.

He was sitting by the window, sipping, when Celia came through the door. Her usual unflappable demeanor changed momentarily at the sight of him. She stiffened, but managed a smile. "What are you doing here?"

"So glad you're happy to see me."

"It isn't that," she said. "I see you've helped yourself."

"I didn't think you'd mind," he said. "Did you enjoy the birthday party?"

"I wasn't there. I heard what happened." She went to the kitchen and poured herself a drink, saying over her shoulder, "You have to leave."

He came to the kitchen door. "Why?" he asked.

"I have a visitor coming in a few minutes."

"Anybody I know?"

She placed her glass on the counter, turned, and said angrily, "I'm not in the mood to discuss my life with you, Max. God, you look terrible. Now please leave."

"I'm still looking for answers, Celia."

"I'm not working with you anymore."

"You said you didn't have to bail out right away. Where's Nico?"

"I spoke with him today. He says he will have the

material you need by tomorrow night. What did the translations of the German's memos say?"

"Not a lot, although if combined with more tangible proof, it'll all help. Where are we meeting Nico tomorrow night?"

"I don't know. He will call me when he's ready." She smiled, came to him, and placed her nicely manicured right hand on his chest. "Max, please, you must leave. Trust me. The person who is coming here can be helpful to you."

"Really? How?"

Her anger surfaced again. "Leave!" she said. "I will call you at your hotel tonight. Late."

"After you and this person are through doing whatever you'll be doing?" he said, the sexual inference not lost on her, or on him. Incredibly, he knew that he was jealous, and he wasn't happy about it.

He put his glass down on the counter and asked, "What time will you call me?"

She sighed with impatience. "Ten. Eleven."

"Which is it?"

"Ten-thirty."

"I'll be in my room, Celia." He walked from the kitchen, turned, and asked, "Did Nico tell you what he's come up with?"

"No, only that you will be pleased."

"Good."

Another few steps toward the door, then turning and saying, "By the way, I saved Fidel's life today."

"*What?*"

"Yeah. I was the one who knocked the shooter's gun away. Not that it made any difference. He wasn't about to hit anybody. Strictly an amateur. Know anything about him? Was he there on his own, or part of a conspiracy?"

"I have . . . no idea."

"Just thought I'd ask. I'll look forward to your call."

He went down the stairs and made another trek past the ever-curious Cubans in the alley, aware that his bruised face evoked interest, but more concerned about what they were thinking of him in light of the attempt on their leader's life. They couldn't know he'd been the one to deflect the weapon; they sure weren't viewing him as a hero. But maybe, because he was a foreigner—and a big, bad American to boot—they wondered whether he was grieving over the failure to blow Fidel away, which he wasn't. Fidel would one day be gone because he died, or decided to leave. Trying to assassinate him was folly.

The CIA had its hard-core hawks who saw assassination as the only answer to ridding the world of every undesirable leader who didn't embrace the American way. They spent part of their careers conjuring exotic means of murder and developing what they thought were ingenious devices to carry out the fantasies. He knew, of course, that the world would be a better place if certain leaders were eliminated (nice bureaucratic word for *killed*) by CIA-sponsored wet jobs; Saddam, Stalin, and Idi Amin came readily to mind. And, of course, less notable troublemakers in virtually every part of the world, particularly the Middle East, plus Central and South America.

He lingered near the end of the alley in the hope of catching a glimpse of Celia's visitor. Whoever it was, she'd said he could be of help. Had she said "He"? Could it be a woman perhaps, her friend Mehta, who'd translated Grünewald's memos? He doubted whether the person scheduled to arrive could, or would, be of help, but he found Celia's need to explain away her visitor an interesting vulnerability.

He felt a distinct lack of pride standing there. Who she entertained and slept with was none of his business, nor did he cognitively wish it to be. But over the course of the time he'd been involved with her, he'd found himself having more than one carnal thought, the most recent five minutes ago. Celia Sardiña was a hands-down, irrefutable beauty who exuded sensuality without having to try, always the best kind. Of course he was attracted to her. TO JESSICA: *I'm like President Jimmy, honey, I only lusted in my heart.*

But as he thought about having developed these feelings, he realized that how she lived her life was as much an aphrodisiac as her ample, nicely turned body, full red lips, brilliant white teeth, large, dark oval eyes, and luxurious black hair. She was like him, he realized, drawing energy from danger, regularly replenishing her supply. Behind her external female warmth and softness were ice and steel, which he found at once unsettling and appealing. He'd seen this dichotomy in female agents before. They had an advantage over male operatives in many instances because their femininity was a perfect disguise for what lurked behind it—strong nerves, unshakable resolve, and a steady hand when holding a lethal weapon. Men who knew they were targets kept their guard up when confronted by a male agent. When it was a woman holding the weapon, those same targets never knew what hit them.

He left the corner and walked slowly toward his hotel. It was seven-thirty. Night would soon engulf Havana, masking physical flaws and bringing out beauty, drama, and a licentious soul.

The music! It was time for the music to start.

He had three hours before Celia would call. Was she lying when she said Nico would come up with the goods by the following evening? *Whether he does or not, I'm leaving,* he thought as he continued to walk. He was ambivalent about how to spend the next three hours. Should he go into hiding because of what had occurred in the plaza? He decided that wasn't necessary. The identity of the would-be assassin was obvious. Those in close proximity had apprehended the gunman. The only reason the cops might want to find him would be because Fidel was summoning the gringo with the busted-up face and the vest to his palace for an awards ceremony. Not likely.

He wasn't hungry. There was some appeal in stretching out on the bed in his hotel and watching TV, viewing the party line on the Castro attack. He had a craving for ice cream, and smiled. First Chinese food in Havana, then ice cream. Could he be pregnant?

He hadn't made up his mind what to do until he turned a corner and was in Plaza de Armas, the city's oldest square. It was bustling already, the dozen or so outdoor cafés filled with men and women enjoying the balmy early evening, music coming from an orchestra performing at the square's far end. He stopped in front of one café with a few vacant tables, sat at one, and ordered a *mojito*. He sat back, stretched his legs, and took a sip. The rum and citrus dropped a veil of well-being over him. He thought about bringing Jessica here one day after Castro was gone and Communism with him. Meanwhile, the parade of men and women entertained, as such processions always do when enjoyed from a table in a friendly outdoor café. A few women, walking with deliberate slowness, openly flirted with him, which he enjoyed, raising his glass and smiling, but having to wave away two who mistook his toast as an invitation.

The drink, coupled with the events of the past twenty-four hours, made him drowsy. He decided to leave. He paid the check and was poised to stand when his attention was drawn to the opposite side of the street. He narrowed his eyes and leaned forward. Erich Weinert stood in front of a café. With him was a skinny young Cuban girl, no older than sixteen, who came up to his chest, and whose hair was black with blond streaks. The big German wore his black suit and wraparound sunglasses. Pauling watched as they took a table that had just been vacated. Weinert had a big smile on his square face, a smug, contented smile; an Arnold Schwarzenegger wannabe. The girl was openly, professionally affectionate, nuzzling his neck and running her fingertips over his chest.

"Señor, you want something else?" the waiter asked Pauling.

"What? No. No, *gracias.*" He waited for the German to turn and kiss the girl before he stood, left the table, and ducked inside the café. Rest rooms and a door were at the rear. Pauling exited into an alley wedged behind the row of buildings that housed the cafés and shops. He ran until coming back to the boulevard, which he crossed, and approached the café where Weinert sat with the girl. Pauling stopped behind a tree to observe the couple. He had no idea what he intended to do, nor was organizing a plan important to him at that moment. He just knew that he owed Blondie something, not only for being jumped by him on the roof of the hotel, but because of Grünewald. But he didn't suffer any delusions about achieving justice for Kurt Grünewald, unless he killed Weinert, which he wasn't about to do. It was tempting.

What were the couple's plans? An ice cream cone at the park? Take in a Walt Disney movie? German lessons for her? If Pauling was going to be able to do anything, he knew, it would have to be when they weren't in a crowd. He didn't need to be arrested again.

After fifteen minutes, he decided to give it up and head for his hotel. Blondie had been downing beers while the girl continued to fawn and paw over him. But then Weinert suddenly pushed her away, hard enough to send her off the chair and to the concrete. Customers at adjacent tables yelled at him as the girl got to her feet and started screaming at him in Spanish, not terms of endearment. Weinert stood and answered the girl and his detractors in loud German. He was drunk and almost tipped over his table as he pushed her to the ground again, lurching to the sidewalk, knocking into people as he went. The girl continued to scream Spanish obscenities but Weinert ignored her and strode up the street in Pauling's direction.

Pauling turned toward the tree; the man passed without noticing him. The German's gait was unsteady but arrogant, a swagger more than a walk. He was muttering in German, oblivious to the fading shouts from the girl and customers in the café. Pauling fell in behind and followed him for two blocks until the German suddenly crossed the street and entered a pocket park. Pauling stopped at the park's entrance and observed Weinert going to a bench and sitting heavily on it, legs extended in front of him, arms on the bench's backrest. He pulled off his sunglasses and dropped them on the bench. They slid off, but he didn't bother to retrieve them. Pauling thought of Kurt Grünewald's drunkenness and how different it was from Weinert's. Grünewald was an alcoholic, pure and simple. Weinert probably wasn't, just an oaf who guzzled too many beers on occasion, particularly when out on the town with a girl on his arm. What had caused him to physically reject her in the café? It didn't matter. Pauling didn't dwell on those questions. Act now, he told himself, or forget about it.

He approached the bench, which was only a dozen feet inside the park. They were the only two people there, although recorded Cuban music coming from behind bushes indicated someone else in the vicinity. Weinert's eyes were closed; his head flopped against the backrest.

Pauling slipped the Glock from his vest, sat silently on the bench, and slid over. The German sensed a presence, opened his eyes, and turned in Pauling's direction to find himself looking directly into the semiautomatic's barrel that Pauling held a few inches from his head.

Weinert straightened and said something in German.

"One bad move, Nazi, and you're dead," Pauling said, coming around in front of him and grabbing him by the lapels with his left hand, the right continuing to hold the weapon inches from the German's face. He saw fear and confusion in Weinert's eyes, as well as anger.

"What do you want?" Weinert asked in English.

Pauling's answer was to raise the Glock in his right hand to bring it down across Weinert's nose. But before Pauling could reverse its arc, Weinert brought up one of his hands with surprising speed, grasped Pauling's right hand, and twisted it. Simultaneously, despite his sitting position, he brought a leg up into Pauling's groin, literally lifting him an inch off the ground. Pauling grunted but hung on to Weinert's jacket. He managed to pull him off the bench to his knees on the dirt path, and pulled his own right knee up under Weinert's chin, snapping his head back and loosening his grip. Pauling kneed him again, this time in the face, wrenched his right hand free, and brought it and the Glock down on Weinert's neck. The big German slumped to the ground at Pauling's feet. Pauling didn't take any chances. He struck the back of Weinert's neck again and heard all the air come out of him. He was unconscious.

Panting, Pauling pondered his next move. He went to where he'd entered the park through a break in the bushes, intending to leave Blondie out cold on the ground. But the sight of a *cacharro,* a 1950s vintage Hudson parked at the curb, its driver smoking, triggered a thought. The driver, who was leaning against the vehicle's right front fender, asked in English whether Pauling needed a taxi.

"You have any rope or tape?" Pauling asked.

The driver didn't comprehend, so Pauling demonstrated, then spotted a small section of the Hudson's right front fender that had been patched with gray duct tape. He touched it. The driver's face lit up and he produced a roll from the front passenger seat. Pauling pulled out a twenty-dollar bill, handed it to the driver, and said, *"Uno momento, señor."* He disappeared back into the park where Weinert was now sitting up, a hand to his head.

"Sorry," Pauling said, hitting him on the right cheek with his fist, sending him to the ground again. He worked quickly, binding his ankles with tape, doing the same with his wrists behind the back. A protest from Weinert was muffled by tape across his mouth.

Pauling yanked Weinert to his knees and dragged him through the bushes to the Hudson, whose driver was now behind the wheel, the motor running. As Pauling shoved Weinert into the spacious, leather-covered rear seat, raised eyebrows were the driver's only sign of curiosity or concern. Twenty dollars bought a lot of tact and cooperation.

Pauling got in and slammed the door. Weinert moved against the tape that bound him, but Pauling pressed the Glock against his temple, and he stopped. Pauling dug through pockets in his vest until he found the business card given him by Policía Nacional Revolucionaria senior detective Francisco Muñoz. He handed the card to the driver. "Take me to that address," Pauling said.

"Policía?" the driver said, his voice full of concern.

Pauling reached over the back of the driver's seat and handed him another twenty.

"*Sí, señor,*" the driver said, slipping the gearshift into DRIVE and pulling away.

Pauling took a small pad and a pen from his vest and wrote: "This man killed Kurt Grünewald of Strauss-Lochner Resources." He shoved it into the breast pocket of Weinert's suit jacket, making sure enough of the paper showed.

When they'd reached the street on which the police station was located, he instructed the driver to pass it and go around the corner. He told him to stop and make a U-turn. "I want you to drive past the police station again, and go fast. *Comprende?*"

"I understand."

"And then just keep going. Don't worry about what I'm doing. Just keep driving and take me to the Hotel Habana Riviera. Okay?"

"Okay," replied the driver.

Pauling pushed Weinert up into a sitting position, reached past him, and put his hand on the door handle. The driver made the U-turn, rounded the corner again, and accelerated. When they were twenty feet from the front door of the police station, Pauling pushed open the door and shoved Weinert through it, wincing as he watched the German leave the car and tumble head over heels, coming to a bloody rest at the foot of the steps leading up to the station.

At the Hotel Habana Riviera, he paid the driver an extra ten dollars, told him to forget what he'd just seen, and entered the hotel.

"Any messages for me?" he asked the desk clerk.

"No, señor."

"Good," Pauling said. He looked at the clock behind the desk: 10:15. "I'm expecting an important call in a few minutes. I'll be in my room."

The call came at precisely ten-thirty.

"Max, it's Celia. Can you come here now?"

"The apartment?"

"Yes."

"What are we doing? Is Nico there?"

"No, but I can fill you in when you arrive."

"Celia, I want this over. I've got to get out of Cuba."

"You make it sound as though I'm keeping you."

"You're not helping."

"What would you have me do, Max, break into the Health Ministry myself? I've put you in touch with the right person. He'll come through. Now, are you coming or not?"

"I'm on my way."

Chapter 35

Washington, D.C.

was so relieved when I saw you, knew you were all right," Annabel Lee-Smith said to Mac when he called. "Wasn't that lucky?" she added, relief still in her voice. They'd had a very brief conversation between the time the McCullough delegation was released, and dinner and the ballet, just long enough to assure her he was okay. Now there was time to talk without feeling rushed.

"I'm glad everyone's all right, Annie. It was a tense couple of minutes in that plaza."

"Did you see the gunman?"

"Yeah, but only for a second. A scruffy-looking guy, lots of hair, wearing one of those white shirts everyone seems to like here. I was thinking of buying one."

"CNN aired some footage of the attack, although they never showed the gunman. What happened after they took him into custody?"

"With me?"

"Yes, you and Price and the others."

"They herded us into a room here at the hotel and gave us a lecture on how to respond to any questions that might be asked of us."

"What did they tell you to say?"

"To say nothing, basically, except to express concern, and gratitude that Castro wasn't harmed."

"In other words, speak from the heart."

He chuckled. "Something like that."

"Price came off well on TV."

"No surprise. You don't win five terms in the Senate without being good in front of a camera."

"Is he still eyeing all the pretty señoritas?"

"As a matter of fact, he is. And some are eyeing back. Speaking of señoritas, spectacularly lovely ones, how are things there with you?"

"Fine, but I miss you."

"Home in two days."

"Did you ever hear from Max Pauling, Jessica's fellow?"

"No. But I think I saw him in the plaza, at the party."

"Really? Sure?"

"No."

"Tell me about the ballet. I didn't think you liked ballet."

"I'm not sure I do, but since our gracious hosts arranged for us to attend—it was the Cuban national troupe—I thought it was a good opportunity to broaden my cultural base."

"That's nice," she said. "Putting it that way. Well, don't let your base get too broad or you'll have to go on a diet. I can't wait for you to get home."

"The feeling is entirely mutual."

Senior Detective Francisco Muñoz stood in a treatment bay at Havana's Hermanos Amerijeiras Hospital. Two nurses and a physician had just completed their initial evaluation of E. Weinert, who was draped in a sheet and lying on an examination table. The man's face was a mess, raw and red; the skin on one side had been shredded. There were gashes in his head; the doctor suspected

multiple broken bones and wanted the patient to have
X rays immediately. His knuckles were bruised; he had
done some hitting, too, though with less effect.

"Just a few minutes with him?" the detective asked.

"Just a few."

Muñoz moved to the side of the table and looked
down. "I am Senior Detective Muñoz," he said, "Policía
Nacional Revolucionaria."

Weinert mumbled something through puffy, split lips.

"Who did this to you?"

Weinert said something unintelligible. Muñoz put his
ear close to the patient's lips and heard what he thought
was "pulling."

"Pulling?"

Weinert shook his head, groaning at the pain it caused.
"Pauling!"

Muñoz straightened and said under his breath, "Max
Pauling." He came close again and held up the piece of
paper found stuffed in Weinert's jacket pocket. "What
does this mean?" he asked. "Pauling wrote this?"

A painful nod.

"Is it true?" Muñoz asked.

The doctor tapped the detective on the shoulder. "This
will have to be continued at another time, Detective," he
said. "There may be internal injuries. I want him in X ray
now!"

"Of course," Muñoz said.

He left the small treatment room and went to the ER's
admitting desk where two uniformed officers waited for
their boss. The two had accompanied Muñoz and Weinert to the hospital after finding the German sprawled on
their doorstep. "I will instruct the staff here that he is a
suspect in a murder case and is not to be released without my permission," Muñoz told them. "I want you here

around the clock to make sure that order is followed. Keep me informed at all times."

He returned to police headquarters and instructed another officer to put out an all points bulletin on the American named Maxwell Pauling.

He didn't waste any time getting to Celia's apartment. Pauling took a taxi from his hotel to the *solar* and made his way down the alley. It had started to rain in the past twenty minutes, not hard, more a mist, but enough to have sent the alley dwellers indoors. He opened the ground-floor door and looked up the stairs. Celia's door was closed, but a small shaft of light squeezed beneath it and spilled onto the landing.

He climbed the steps, paused, and knocked. By now, he knew she always left the door unlocked, but was reluctant to simply walk in. She said there would be someone with her—or had she? She originally said she was preparing to receive a visitor, someone she claimed could help him. But when she'd called him at the hotel, she hadn't mentioned anyone.

He knocked again. Still no response. He raised his hand for another try but dropped it to the doorknob and turned it. As expected, the door was unlocked and opened easily.

"Celia?" he called through the opening. "It's Max."

He pushed the door open a little farther, stopped, and cocked his head. There was no sound coming from inside the apartment. He opened the door to its fullest extension and surveyed what he could see of the main room from where he stood on the landing. He saw that lights were on in the kitchen and bathroom, although he couldn't see into the rooms themselves.

He called her name one more time before stepping through the doorway. He looked at the white curtains; they were tied back. He approached the partly opened door to the bathroom and felt a solid presence behind it. Whoever was in there had chosen not to respond.

He placed his fingertips against the door, and pushed it fully open. What he saw hit him with the force of a physical blow to his stomach. The toilet lid was down. Slumped on it was Price McCullough. His white dress shirt was mostly unbuttoned. A tie hung over the chain-pull toilet tank. He wore trousers but his shoes were lined up just outside the shower. His feet were bare. His wide-open eyes testified to the incredulity of the last thing they'd seen, someone with a weapon who had sent a single bullet into his chest. The front of his shirt was stained red, and blood had pooled on his lap.

Pauling stood frozen. He made a tentative move to close the gap between his position and the body but restrained himself. Instead, he backed into the living room and turned in a slow, three-hundred-and-sixty-degree circle, looking for an answer, a reason for what he'd seen in the bathroom, and maybe its author. He went to the clothes closet. It was empty. So were the dresser drawers. The counter in the kitchen was clear of objects; only the cordial glass remained in the sink.

He returned to the living room and saw that the pile of papers on the small table just inside the door was gone. Everything was gone. It was as though no one had lived there.

The ringing phone startled him. He went to the small desk and picked up the receiver. "Hello."

"Celia? Is Celia there?"

Pauling recognized the voice. "Nico?"

"Yes."

"It's me, your pilot."

"Oh, hello, Max."

"Celia isn't here," Max said.

"When will she be back?"

"Ah—not for a while. She told me to be here for your call. Are we all set?"

"Yes. Tomorrow night. I have the documents you need."

"Good. Where will we meet up?"

"Cojímar. It is a fishing village sixteen kilometers from Havana. There is a small motel by the sea, Casa de Mar y Sol."

"What time?"

"Midnight."

"I'll be there."

"You will have the money for me?"

"Of course."

"And we will leave together."

"That's the deal."

"Celia will be with you?"

"I don't know. Yes, I'm sure she will."

"Good. Until tomorrow."

"Right. Until tomorrow."

He hung up and took another look at McCullough, who now listed sideways, his head resting on the wall immediately next to the toilet. Pauling considered wiping his prints but they'd be everywhere—no time. He left the apartment, closing the door behind him, went down the stairs to the alley, and headed in the direction of the larger street at its open end. He was within six feet of it when he heard the police sirens, then saw two marked PNR cruisers come around the corner at breakneck speed. Pauling pressed himself into a doorway. The vehicles slid to a stop across the entrance to the alley and uniformed and plainclothes cops spilled through the doors and ran down the alley, guns drawn, orders shouted.

Everyone from the cars had headed down the alley, leaving no one to observe Pauling as he stepped from the shadowy cover of the doorway and went to the street. He took one final look back to see them pouring through the downstairs door leading to the apartment where McCullough's body waited for them. The reality was blatantly obvious. Someone had tipped them to the murder of a former senator. That someone had to be . . .

That unpleasant certainty flipped Pauling's stomach as he walked away. But what really brought bile to his throat and mouth was the additional reality that she'd called the police to coincide with his arrival at the apartment.

She'd set him up.

F rancisco Muñoz sat in his office at the precinct. A
subordinate who'd been with the initial contingent at
the apartment, and who had recognized the murder victim as the United States senator, had summoned the senior detective. Once there, Muñoz took over the
investigation, including a thorough search of the apartment. McCullough's wallet, which seemed to be intact,
confirmed his identity, prompting Muñoz to call a superior at the Ministry of Interior, who put into motion the
necessary notifications to other government officials, including Fidel Castro. Bobby Jo Brown, chief of section at
the U.S. Interests Section in Havana, had been awakened
at his apartment. He contacted his supervisor at Langley,
Virginia, who phoned President Walden's national security advisor, who informed the president.

Muñoz looked down at items on his desk taken from
the apartment. An officer had found a business card beneath a chair: MAXWELL PAULING, PILOT, CALI FORWARDING,
CALI, COLOMBIA. The only other potential piece of seized
evidence was the cordial glass found in the kitchen sink.
It had been dusted for prints, as had numerous surfaces
in the apartment—the phone, doorknobs, kitchen
counter surfaces, the bathroom mirror, and the metal
toothbrush holder. Muñoz leaned closer to the glass to
better see the brown whorls indicating where fingers had

touched it. PNR's budget had been drastically cut after the Special Period began. Expensive imported fingerprint powder had been replaced with the less sensitive brown powder produced locally from charred palm fronds.

"Pauling," he muttered. How convenient that he'd left his calling card at the scene.

He opened a file folder bearing Pauling's name. It had been started when he'd landed at the airport and unloaded the medical supplies from Colombia. The dispatcher there, after handling Pauling's paperwork and calling a taxi for him, had made the call expected of him to the official at Minint responsible for collecting information on airport arrivals other than passengers on scheduled airlines.

An officer had been assigned to keep tabs on Pauling's movements while the American was in Havana, although it was not a priority. The man's credentials were in order, his reason for being there an acceptable one. There had been few notes in the file until the death of the German, Grünewald, and the questioning of Pauling regarding that death. There had been no reason to hold Pauling. Muñoz could have detained him, or even ordered him out of the country, but he'd declined to take either action. There were others in his position who took every opportunity, grabbed every excuse to harass foreigners, drill them with Cuban Communist doctrine, and embarrass them by booting them out of the country. Muñoz knew those colleagues acted out of frustration at the situation in which Cuba had found itself under the Special Period. He also knew that many of them were not happy with Castro's Communist government. Nor was he. But you did what you had to do to keep your job and avoid censure. Surviving in Communist Cuba was the ultimate test of pragmatism.

"Pauling."

Muñoz would have forgotten about him if the bound and gagged German, Weinert, hadn't been delivered like an unwanted baby at his front door, and confirmed that it was Pauling who'd made the delivery. That was sufficient reason to put out an all-points on him. He wanted to question him about the accusation that the German was the one who'd killed Kurt Grünewald. Weinert wasn't unknown to Muñoz. Minint had tracked him since his arrival from Heidelberg and had taken note of his behavior while in Havana. He'd been fingered as a prime suspect in the Grünewald killing because of his professional relationship to the victim and his general demeanor. Pauling was probably right, Muñoz thought.

But now this—a highly visible American visitor, a former United States senator, close friend and confidant of the American president, and leading businessman found murdered in cold blood—with Pauling implicated again.

Another detective poked his head into Muñoz's office. "The apartment, Francisco, it is owned by an *escoria,* scum," he said, using Castro's favorite term to describe Cubans who had defected to Miami.

"It has been empty?"

"We are questioning everyone in the area now. There are three CDRs who live in the alley. Hopefully, we will learn who has been using the apartment."

"The picture of Pauling. Where is it?"

"I have it." He handed his boss the mug shots taken when Pauling was brought in for questioning in the Grünewald murder.

"See that every officer has this by morning."

"The call," Muñoz said. "It came from a woman?"

"Yes. She did not identify herself. She said a man had been murdered at the address."

"She did not say who the victim was?"

"No, sir."

The other detective left when Muñoz's phone rang. He picked it up and heard the voice of the second-ranking official with the Ministry of Interior. There was no preliminary conversation. The minister said, "We are preparing a statement to give to the Americans regarding the senator's death. You are, I assume, making good progress in your investigation."

"Well, sir, it is very soon after the death and—"

"El Presidente wants the statement to indicate we are close to apprehending the killer. That is true, is it not?"

Muñoz held the phone away from his mouth as he sighed, then said, "Yes, sir, we are close to identifying the killer."

"Who was it? A Cuban?"

"No, sir. It was an American."

"American? What American?"

"His name is Pauling. Maxwell Pauling. We found evidence linking him to the crime, and have issued an all points bulletin."

"What is his business in Cuba?"

"He is a pilot. He flew here from Colombia to deliver medical supplies. He was a suspect in the murder of the German, Grünewald."

"I want a full report on my desk within the hour. Do you have a picture of this Pauling?"

"Yes, sir."

"Include it in the report. CNN wants a statement. That the assailant was American like the victim is indeed fortunate. Within the hour."

"Yes, sir."

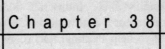

Pauling put a few blocks between him and the alley before ducking into a restaurant and bar where he took a table as far from the front door as possible. The initial discovery of Price McCullough's body had been shocking, but the actions he'd taken, including the phone call from Nico, had focused his thinking while still in the apartment. Now, with a glass of rum in front of him, and salsa music by the popular Cuban group La Banda pouring from a jukebox, the full impact of the past half hour hit him hard. His hand shook as he raised the drink to his lips, and he kept closing and opening his eyes as though he could squeeze clarity into his thinking.

Although it was anathema to him, the reality that Celia had caused him to be at the apartment when the police arrived was too compelling to shake off. His anger about this truth was intense, but the question of *why* she'd done it was even more prevailing. As hard as he tried, he couldn't make sense of it, couldn't come up with a rational reason as he sat there. He assumed that she'd shot McCullough. That raised another *why*. And how had she enticed McCullough to the apartment? A sexual come-on? Had she promised him a romp under the covers as a ruse to get him alone and vulnerable?

Why McCullough? As far as Pauling knew, the ex-senator had meant nothing to Celia—until Vic Gosling had paired her up with Pauling to try to uncover proof that McCullough's BTK Industries had been using Strauss-Lochner to cut a deal with the Castro regime. She was being paid to help Pauling; had there been a bigger payoff for murdering the former senator? Had this been part of Gosling's plan from the beginning? If so, what was the motivation? Had his client Signal Labs felt so threatened that it ordered Gosling's employer, Cell-One, to eliminate BTK's chairman? It was true, Pauling knew, that gaining control of Cuba's impressive advances in cancer treatment could potentially be worth billions. But assassinate an ex-pol in order to win? He had to accept it as a possibility. People were killed every day for a lot less: for pocket change, a leather jacket, a look perceived as disrespectful.

He forced himself to push these questions to the back of his mind and concentrate on his situation at that moment. His first belief was that although he'd been at the apartment and had come across McCullough's body, no one else knew he'd been there. Celia's setup had failed. Her timing had been off. If he'd lingered another few minutes, things would have worked out differently, and he'd be in custody instead of sipping rum in a down-and-dirty Havana bar. But there was no one to link him to the apartment that night. Even if someone living in one of the apartments in the alley, one of the CDRs, had seen him, they'd have no way of knowing his identity, could provide only a description. While that might be sufficient for the police, particularly Detective Muñoz, the I.D. would take a while, most likely time enough for him to go back to the hotel, gather up the few things he had there, and leave the city. He'd head for the fishing village where he was to meet Nico the following night. After that, providing he still hadn't been linked to the apartment and the body, he could get to his plane and fly out of Cuba to

Miami, deliver to Gosling whatever Nico came up with, and head home to Albuquerque. He'd like to leave Mc-Cullough, Grünewald, Muñoz, Fidel, Weinert, and the rest of the characters in this sordid play as another set of memories.

He left money—Cuban—for the drink and went to the café's door, now acutely aware that he had to move fast, and with stealth. His rationalizations while sitting at the table had been just that, manufactured reasons to feel secure. He'd been away from danger too long, he reminded himself. Let down your guard for a minute, and that would be the minute that the third-act curtain came down.

He headed in the direction of the hotel, using narrow, less populated streets and alleyways. It meant a longer, less direct route but a prudent one. He paused in shadows or doorways at each intersection, scanning the area for police or anyone else who might take an interest in him. He stopped at a sidewalk vendor and bought a hat, the largest *malanbueta* the vendor had, and a flowing white guayabera shirt that he slipped on over his vest.

"*Queso y jamon?*" the scraggly, doe-eyed salesman asked. "*Caramelos?*" The mention of ham and cheese and sweets caused Pauling's stomach to rumble. He handed over more Cuban money for a small bag of candy of unidentified origin and was about to walk away when the vendor grabbed his sleeve. "*Collares,*" he said, holding a beaded necklace in front of Pauling. "Very good luck, señor. Blessed by Yoruba saints."

Pauling pulled another dollar from his pocket. Good luck! He didn't believe in luck, had always been convinced that people who seemed to experience it had worked hard to bring it about. But he stuffed the necklace in a vest pocket, smiled briefly at the vendor, and walked away.

He reached the hotel's street and stood behind a kiosk from which he could observe the entrance. There didn't appear to be any unusual activity at the hotel from his vantage point, and he stepped forward, about to cross the street, when the sudden blare of a siren virtually pushed him back into the safe haven of the kiosk. The police vehicle was headed straight for him. Pauling backed into the park beyond and crouched behind shrubbery as the car came to a screeching stop next to the small structure.

A uniformed policeman jumped out of the vehicle, secured a large sheet of paper to the kiosk with thumbtacks, got back in the car, and sped away. Pauling waited until the cruiser had disappeared around a corner before leaving the park and approaching the kiosk. He couldn't believe what he saw.

Staring back at him was his own likeness, the police mug shot taken when he'd been hauled in for questioning in the Grünewald murder. Aside from the mention of his name, he understood from the writing beneath the photo that he was being branded a murderer. He was also fingered as armed and dangerous and, most remarkably, an enemy of the Independent Socialist Republic of Cuba. Christ! It was like an old cowboy movie. He was wanted dead or alive.

He tore the photo from the kiosk, crumpled it into a ball, tossed it in the gutter, retreated into the park again, sat on the damp ground, and tried to put his thoughts in order.

Priority Number One was evident: *Get out of Havana.* Hopefully, it would take the authorities more time to spread the word and his picture to outlying areas. If it were the United States, Great Britain, or Germany, that could be accomplished almost immediately. But this was Cuba. They may have highly developed means of treating cancer, he mulled, but their expertise obviously didn't extend to the communications system.

How to get out of the city?

He couldn't trust just taking the next taxi that came along. The police would have made a special effort to distribute his photo to the city's cabdrivers. *Rent a car?* His face was probably hanging next to every car rental agency's list of rates.

He could adopt the old saying originally about Rome—When in Cuba, do as the Cubans do, and hitchhike. Out of the question. The same with hopping a bus. Celia had pointed out to him what she called *los amarillos*, a division of Policía Nacional Revolucionaria, men in yellow uniforms stationed at bus stops to supervise the crowds hoping to board a bus, or to be shoehorned into a passing truck.

There was, of course, the appealing notion of making his way to the airport, climbing aboard the twin-engine aircraft he'd flown from Colombia, revving up the engines, and heading west. That would mean, of course, leaving Nico and his documentation waiting in some seaside motel, but at this juncture, neither the young Cuban, nor the proof for Gosling, seemed terribly important. But the Cubans knew he was a pilot who'd flown into Cuba. By this time, his plane had probably been impounded, chained, maybe even partly dismantled.

A powerful fatigue swept over him as he wrapped his arms about himself. He hadn't murdered McCullough. Maybe the best thing would be simply to turn himself in and hope that reason would prevail. But that, he knew, was the worst idea of all. Throughout his career, he'd learned that when you ended up in a position such as the one he faced at the moment, there was only one person you could depend on, not local police or government

officials, and not your own government, especially either
of the agencies he'd worked for. He was on his own. That
realization, rather than depressing him, provided a spark
of comfort and renewed resolve. There was no one in the
world he trusted more.

"I can't believe it. Price murdered?"

"It's like a bad dream. Have they said who killed
him?"

"Must be a madman."

These comments, and dozens of others, flew around the
room to which the McCullough delegation had been relegated by its Cuban hosts. Their patience was running
thin. They'd been herded into the room more than an
hour before without any explanation as to why they were
being detained—again. They weren't all present. A few of
the men had ventured out to taste Havana's nightlife and
still weren't accounted for.

With Price McCullough no longer alive, the group had
anointed Mac Smith as spokesman because of his friendship with McCullough and the president, and because he
was an attorney of note, or had been. In this new role, he
attempted to get further information about the tragedy of
McCullough's death, and an indication of what lay in
store for the delegation until it left for home. When the
senior Cuban official finally arrived, Smith approached
him and asked for a private conversation.

"Of course," the official said, leading Smith to a
smaller room off the main one.

"As you can imagine, sir," Smith said, "there's a
great deal of confusion out there. We've been told that Senator McCullough has been killed, murdered, but that's all
we've been told. We're being kept in isolation and given no
further information. In addition to that, we're—"

The Cuban held up his hand and smiled. "Señor

Smith," he said, "I understand your frustration. But you must also understand that what has happened to your leader, Senator McCullough, has placed us in a most sensitive position. You and your delegation came here on a trade mission, a peaceful mission. Now it has turned into a violent one for your distinguished leader. There are considerable political ramifications. And, I might add, there is the safety of you and your people to be considered." The Cuban official was a heavyset man with deep acne scars and a voice made husky from the cigarette that seemed always to be in his hand.

"Can you tell me anything more about the circumstances of Senator McCullough's death?" Smith asked. "His murder. Is there a suspect? It was murder, wasn't it? An assassination?"

"Murder, assassination ... the words have specific meaning, Señor Smith, and I hesitate to use them. Yes, there is a suspect. He is being pursued aggressively."

"I'm glad to hear that," Smith said. "Do you know of a motive?"

"No, I do not."

"Where was he killed? There's a rumor among the delegation that it happened in an apartment here in Havana."

The Cuban nodded.

"Whose apartment?"

"I do not know."

"Who's the suspect?" Smith asked. "Are there political overtones, or was it a single deranged individual?"

"Again, I cannot say because we do not have that information. I will say that the suspected murderer is not a Cuban."

"Is not."

"That is correct."

"I imagine that gives you a modicum of comfort."

"It gives us pause to be grateful for small blessings, señor."

"Am I out of place asking you to tell me who the suspect is? Is he European, from a Central American country, from—?"

"You hesitate asking whether he might be an American."

"I—is he?"

"Yes."

"No small blessings for *us* today," Smith said, shaking his head. "Who is he?"

"May we keep this in confidence, Señor Smith? Between us?"

"I'm always uncomfortable being asked to keep a secret, sir. I'm sure that by morning, it won't be a secret any longer, and not because I've passed it on. Who is it?"

"He is a former employee of your Central Intelligence Agency."

Smith let out a whoosh of air and rubbed his eyes.

As though to comfort him, the Cuban said, "We are not saying he killed Senator McCullough upon orders from that agency."

Not yet, Smith thought. "But that's a possibility?"

"Everything is a possibility at this stage."

Smith hesitated before asking, "A name? Does this American have a name?"

"Yes, he does. His name is Pauling. Maxwell Pauling. He has been in trouble with our authorities before."

"Pauling?" The weakness in Smith's voice revealed his shock.

"Yes. We are looking for him now."

Smith almost said that he knew Maxwell Pauling, but held himself in check. That would accomplish nothing. He said, "I appreciate your candor. When will we be allowed to leave the room? We have loved ones back in Washington who will want to hear from us."

"In a short time. Have I answered your questions?"

"Yes, you have, sir, and I appreciate it."

"We need not be enemies," the Cuban said. "It is time there was understanding between our two countries."

Smith said, "Hopefully, an understanding will develop one day."

"You are a personal friend of President Walden."

"Yes."

"He seems to lean toward dialogue with us beyond trade issues."

"That's true, although I don't have any special knowledge of his feelings. We're personal friends. I'm not a political confidant. We enjoy playing poker together."

The Cuban laughed, coughed, and lit another cigarette. "I enjoy playing poker, too, Señor Smith. Perhaps one day we can sit down and bluff each other."

A small smile came to Smith's lips. "I would like that," he said. "And perhaps show our hands."

"Tell your people that they will be free to go in a few minutes. I do ask that because you are the spokesperson for the group that you stay in close touch with me."

"Of course. And thank you for your candor."

Smith's stomach churned as he left the room to rejoin his colleagues.

Max Pauling, Jessica Mumford's lover, murdering Price McCullough?

James L. Walden, President of the United States, was nursing a rogue head cold and had retired early to the family wing of the White House when the call came from Paul Draper, his national security advisor.

"He's *dead*?" Walden said, his nasal voice heavy with disbelief.

"Yes, sir."

"Where did it happen?"

"An apartment in Havana. Nothing more on that at this juncture."

"An apartment? What was he doing in an apartment?"

"I don't know, sir."

Walden hesitated before asking, "Did this involve a woman?"

"I don't have an answer for that, sir."

"Do they have any suspects?"

"Not that I know of. Brown—he's chief of section in our Havana Interests Section—told Langley that the Cubans are claiming that a suspect has been identified, but no names, no nationalities."

" 'Nationalities'? He's Cuban, right?"

"We're all assuming that, Mr. President."

"Get the crisis team over here in an hour. Has the press picked up on it yet?"

"CNN has a call in to State about it. They haven't aired anything yet."

Another call, this from the White House press office, ended the Draper conversation.

"Mr. President, we've just received word that—"

"Yeah, I know. Price McCullough."

"CNN wants a statement."

"No statement. We're meeting in an hour."

"They're going on the air right now."

Walden used his remote to turn on the TV and heard the anchor announce a breaking story from Havana and cue CNN's Cuba correspondent, a woman named Perez.

"Is it true, Lolita, that former senator Price McCullough has been shot?" the anchor asked.

Perez: "Yes, Brad, that's what we're being told. Senator McCullough, who came here to Cuba as head of a trade delegation, is reported to have been shot to death somewhere in Havana."

Anchor: "Was he involved in some official function when it happened?"

Perez: "Evidently not. A number of his delegation attended a performance this evening of the Cuban national ballet troupe. Senator McCullough was not part of that group, we're told."

Anchor: "This is a remarkable event considering the attempt on Fidel Castro's life earlier today. Is there any link to that failed assassination attempt?"

Perez: "None that we're able to ascertain so far."

The anchor interrupted the conversation with the correspondent as he listened to something being said through his earpiece. He nodded, made a note, and faced the camera. "I've just been informed that there is an unconfirmed report that the assailant—and I should stress *alleged* assailant—might be an American citizen. Have you heard anything to that effect, Lolita?"

Perez: "No, I haven't, Brad, but we'll continue to monitor this breaking story and report any further developments."

Anchor: "That was Lolita Perez, CNN's correspondent in Havana, Cuba, reporting on what is alleged to have been the shooting death of former five-term U.S. senator from Texas, Price McCullough. Stay tuned. We'll bring you updates throughout the night."

By the time the president met with his crisis team in the Situation Room on the first floor of the White House, the press office was fielding queries from dozens of news organizations. At first, the news people making the calls knew little more than had already been reported on CNN. But fifteen minutes into the meeting, Walden's press secretary interrupted. All eyes at the table turned to him.

"Mr. President," he said, "this just came over the wires, and TV is running it, too."

Walden scowled as he looked at the photograph handed him by his press secretary, a police mug shot.

"Who is he?" Walden asked, sliding the picture down the table for others to see.

"His name is Pauling, Mr. President. Maxwell Pauling."

"Where'd this photo come from?"

"The Cubans released it. They're claiming he's Senator McCullough's killer."

"Isn't that convenient? You don't know anything about this Pauling other than Fidel's claim that he shot McCullough?"

"We're trying to get background on him now, sir."

"Let me know."

"A statement, sir? How do you want this handled with the press?"

"Prepare something for me to give at my press conference in the morning, you know, the loss of my good friend, the nation's loss, and for Christ sake, keep it personal. McCullough is—was—a *former* senator in Cuba on private business. Nothing political about it. Private citizen gets killed by some nut."

Draper said, "Mr. President, I don't think we can go that far."

"About what?"

"About billing the senator's trip as purely personal, private business. The press knows it was set up through government channels. I suggest we—"

"Couch it any way you want, but don't emphasize any political or governmental connection. Play it down. Sheila is calling Price's sons. They already know. Nothing like having CNN notifying the family. Include something about how fortunate it is that the attempt on Castro failed, but keep it matter-of-fact. And get me everything you can on Pauling."

"Yes, sir."

The meeting broke up forty-five minutes later.

"I'll be in my quarters," Walden informed them as they were leaving the Situation Room. "I feel like hell with this cold."

Walden kept switching between channels in the living room until he started dozing in his chair. His wife, Sheila, had already placed calls to McCullough's sons to offer the First Family's condolences. "How dreadful," she said as she prepared to go to the bedroom.

"Worse than that if it turns into a political issue with Castro. Go to bed, hon. I'll be along shortly."

He reached for the remote to turn off the set when

CNN's anchor broke into a prerecorded news feature with a bulletin.

"New developments in the murder of former senator Price McCullough in Havana. CNN has learned that the alleged killer, an American named Maxwell Pauling, formerly worked for the Central Intelligence Agency and the State Department. According to our sources, he left the State Department more than a year ago and has been living in Albuquerque, New Mexico, where he is a private flight instructor. His reason for being in Cuba has not been established, nor has any connection been made between his former employment as a CIA operative and the murder of Price McCullough."

Walden slammed the remote down on a table and cursed under his breath. *The damn media,* he thought, *trying to invent some sinister link between the murder and the CIA.*

Draper called.

"How come, Paul, CNN gets background on this nut before we can?" Walden asked angrily.

"That's what I'm calling about, sir. Sorry to bother you but—"

"What is it?" the president asked, blowing his nose.

"I have a full background report on Pauling, Mr. President."

"Bring it up here."

"Yes, sir."

"Where is Pauling? Is he in custody in Havana?"

"Negative, sir. The Cuban police have put out an all-points on him, and have distributed the photograph everywhere."

"He was CIA?"

"Yes, sir, he was."

"No ties now?"

"Supposedly."

"He's a pilot. What was he doing in Cuba, giving flying lessons to Fidel?"

"That's not in the report, sir."

"Bring it up—now!"

A sleepy Sheila Walden emerged from the bedroom. "What's wrong?" she asked. "Is it about Price?"

"Yes, it is. The crazy who shot him turns out to have worked for the CIA. Fidel will get plenty of mileage out of that."

"You don't think—?"

"That he might have been in Havana and killed Price *for* his former employer? If that's the case, Sheila, somebody over at Langley is going to end up with a lot more than a head cold."

Joe Pitura, the CIA's Cuban section chief, closely monitored events in Havana that night. Like the president, he'd been flipping through TV channels to keep abreast of what the media were reporting. But he had his own independent sources of information that continued to feed him the latest developments, either directly or through intermediaries. One such intermediary communicated with Pitura from Miami.

"What's up?" Pitura asked. It was the third call from Miami. He sat, grimacing against pain in his shoulders. His rheumatoid arthritis had been especially active the past few days; the painkillers were losing the battle.

"They are searching for the American, Pauling," Ramon Gomez responded. The leader of the Miami-based anti-Castro group, the Cuban-American Freedom Alliance, was being kept informed of events in Havana from the back room of the art gallery. The calls came to him at a small satellite CAFA office a block from Café Versailles in Miami's Little Havana. The café had been a gathering place for years for hard-line Cuban ex-pats.

"I know they're looking for him," Pitura growled. "It's on TV. Do you or your people know where he is?"

"They are putting his picture up all over Havana. I'm sure it won't be long before he is apprehended."

Pitura had no sooner hung up on Gomez when Zach Rasmussen, director of covert operations, called. "How are you holding up, buddy?" Rasmussen asked.

"I'd be better if that shooter had gotten the job done. Fidel is one lucky son of a bitch."

"It'll run out on him one of these days. What do you hear on Max Pauling?"

"Nothing you haven't heard."

"I just got off the phone with Vic Gosling."

"Better you than me. What does Mr. Slick have to say?"

"He's concerned about Pauling. He says he can't believe Pauling would have shot McCullough."

"That's sweet, standing up for an old friend like that. Where are you?"

"In my office. I just got here. The president's on the warpath. He wants answers."

"So, give him answers."

"He's giving a statement first thing in the morning. He wants to keep it as nonpolitical as possible. Christ, according to Draper, the president is questioning whether we had anything to do with it, whether Pauling was operating on our behalf."

Pitura grinned and worked his large shoulders against the pain that seemed to have taken up permanent residence there. "You told Draper that's nuts, right?"

"Of course I did. Let's meet in an hour. Bring your people. Only those in the loop."

Jessica Mumford sat transfixed in front of the television set in the condo. She had arrived home a little after eleven. It was her habit to watch the news before going to bed, but on this night she decided to skip TV. It had been a stressful day at the hospital where she worked as an administrator. The chief of surgery and the hospital had been sued for malpractice and a recent audit had uncovered missing funds.

She hadn't bothered to check the answering machine when she arrived. It was in the spare bedroom she and Max used as an office and as a guest room for visitors. Had she gone in there, she would have seen that there were seven messages on the machine. The eighth call came as she was brushing her teeth.

"What?" she exclaimed when her caller, a colleague at the hospital, told her that Max was being accused on TV of having shot McCullough to death in Havana. She thanked her and tuned to CNN. Nothing there. But MSNBC was carrying the story, and Jessica watched in open-mouthed shock at what was being said and what she saw, Max's mug shot a full-screen backdrop for the anchor's report.

She found the itinerary he'd left among a pile of papers in the office and looked for the name of the hotel in Havana at which he was staying. It wasn't included. Only the motels in Pittsburgh and Miami were on the list.

"Damn," she muttered as the phone rang again. "I can't talk now," she said to the caller. "I'll get back to you."

She dialed Annabel Lee-Smith's number in Washington.

"I was about to call you," Annabel said, breathless. "Have you heard from Max?"

"No, and I don't know where he's staying in Havana. I thought you might have found out from Mac. He's still there, isn't he?"

"Yes, but I can't get through to him. There's no answer

in his room. I'm sure they're meeting. It must be chaotic there. I—"

Jessica's tears stopped Annabel.

"I can't believe this," Jessica moaned. "God, Annabel, Max wouldn't kill Price McCullough. He went to Cuba on a private assignment. He was supposed to find out something about McCullough's pharmaceutical company but—"

"He was?"

Jessica's sigh was long and loud. "Yes," she said, realizing that linking Max with McCullough in any regard wasn't very prudent.

"How can I help?" Annabel asked.

"I don't know. Maybe if you get through to Mac you could ask if he knows anything about Max, where he is— *how* he is."

"Of course I will."

"It can't be true, Annabel. Max can be tough, but he isn't a murderer." She remembered Max saying during his only call to her that he'd already been arrested once for murder in Havana, a mistake, and had been roughed up. She didn't mention it to Annabel.

"If you hear anything, Annabel, you'll call? Any hour."

"Sure. Try to get some rest. I'm sure this is all a big mistake."

"I hope you're right, Annabel. I pray you're right."

Getting some rest was the last thing on Jessica's mind as she poured herself a snifter of brandy and went out to the deck. There, she sat in darkness, the millions of white stars against the sky's black scrim only a tease of well-being. She thought of Max and that he could be looking up into that same sky at that very moment. The news reports indicated he was still at large. Where was he? What was he doing? Was he frightened? He was not a man who frightened easily. Still, to be accused of murdering a distinguished visitor and to be hunted down for that crime would rattle even the most fearless of men.

As hard as she tried, she could not push from her consciousness the reality that Max had gone to Cuba to investigate Price McCullough's company and the business it was conducting there. Had McCullough discovered what Max was doing and confronted him? "No," she said aloud, shaking her head.

Her thoughts drifted to her life with Max Pauling. Her former husband had been an FBI undercover agent who was away more than he was home—a blessing for her most of the time—and who, she came to learn later, had killed, initially as part of his job as a special agent, then in a warped attempt to become rich.

Had Max ever killed in the line of duty while with the CIA, or as a special undercover operative for the State Department? She preferred to think not, but how could she be certain? You could never be certain about such a thing with Max and people like him. They lived shadow lives, shielded from sunlight by the very nature of intelligence agencies, wrapped in the flag, confident that what would be misdeeds for most people would, instead, be viewed as admirable and honorable in their case—"Job well done!"

She'd spent enough time in Washington before moving to New Mexico to know that what is said there and in all nations' capitals is often not the truth; it is "disinformation," to be polite. In Max's former life he had to lie, was expected to lie if he was to be successful and survive. Had he lied to her about the nature of his trip to Cuba on the Vic Gosling assignment? Was it purely a private undertaking, as he claimed, or had he signed on for a job with the CIA as an independent contractor, using Gosling and his client as cover?

"No," she repeated, again shaking her head. One of

the troubles with secret work is that you get to believing nothing—or everything. You can only wait for the truth to emerge, if it ever does. The half-full glass slipped from her hand and shattered at her feet. She cried for only a minute before returning to the TV set.

The lights in the U.S. Interests Section at the foot of
Calle L burned bright.

Gene Nichols, the senior CIA operative, watched
Cuban television and its coverage of the McCullough
murder and the failed attempt on Fidel Castro's life.
Nichols, who spoke Spanish, made notes of what the
Cuban commentator said, glancing occasionally across
the room at section chief Bobby Jo Brown, who was on
the phone with the crusty Joe Pitura, head of the Cuban
section at Langley.

"Let me give you over to Nichols," Brown told Pitura
in answer to his question.

"Nichols, here."

"Hey, Gene. How goes it?"

"A laugh a minute. What can I do for you?"

"Where's Pauling?" Pitura's directness was both appreciated at Langley, and troublesome to those without immediate answers.

"Wish I knew, Joe. The Cuban authorities have his picture pasted all over town, and Cuban TV keeps running
it, but he's nowhere."

"What are you doing to find him?" Pitura asked.
Nichols could hear pain in Pitura's voice, knew Joe's
rheumatoid arthritis was especially painful, and that the

increasing number of painkillers he took each day weren't helping much.

"We've got the word out," Nichols replied. "We're also ready for him if he decides to walk through the door."

"I don't really give a damn how he surfaces," Pitura said, "as long as we can get him out of Cuba. Until this McCullough mess, the Cubans weren't claiming that the attack on Castro was a CIA act, were they?"

"No. I got word just an hour ago that the guy who took the shots at Castro was released from a Cuban prison only a few days ago. A mental case. Fidel would really have to stretch it to link this nut with us."

"But now he's got Pauling to make the connection. Castro is attacked, and less than twenty-four hours later an ex-senator is gunned down by a guy with former CIA ties. If Castro gets hold of Pauling, he'll parade him all over Havana as proof that we took a shot at him. The brain trust here doesn't want that to happen." His lowered voice and measured cadence emphasized his words.

"The Cubans say they want Pauling dead or alive," Nichols said.

"Yeah? So do *we*," said Pitura. "Keep in touch."

Brown, who'd been standing at the window during Nichols's conversation with Pitura, turned at the sound of the phone being hung up. "He wants Pauling," he said flatly, stating the obvious.

"Alive, or otherwise," Nichols said.

"He said that?"

"Yeah, he said that."

"You've got everybody possible out there looking for him?"

"The word's out, Bobby. Every CDR on *our* payroll is looking. I put up a hundred bucks."

"A hundred?" Brown smiled. "You're getting generous in your old age."

"For a hundred, they'll be up all night looking in every alley, café, and Dumpster in Havana."

"If the Cubans find him first, do we have anybody inside who might play ball with us?"

"Sure. But this is too big, Bobby. Let's just hope Pauling decides he needs us and walks through the door."

"Think that's likely?"

Nichols shrugged and said, "I haven't the slightest idea." He drew a deep breath and shook his head. "You ever work with Pauling, Bobby?"

"No."

Nichols's laugh was good-natured. "He was good, Bobby. Brilliant. I mean, in the sense of improvising his way out of trouble. And an idealist."

"I thought idealistic agents didn't last long," said Brown.

"Depends on what the ideals are. With Max . . . well, his ideals said that when you put an agent in harm's way, you don't let the suits back in Langley jeopardize the agent or the mission. Politics, bureaucrats . . . they meant nothing to him. That's why he was always on the carpet. But know what?"

"What?"

"They may have put reprimands in his file, but they never pulled him from the field. He was too damn good at what they asked him to do, needed for him to do."

"Why'd he pack it in?"

"Ideals. He had a buddy eliminated in Moscow, and not by the Russians."

Brown's frown asked the question.

"He was convinced our people did it. His buddy was involved with a Russian woman. What rule does that break, number three thousand? I don't know this for a fact, but I've been told that the death of his buddy was what finally pushed him out the door. That, and a beauty named Jessica."

They shared a few moments of silence.

"I hope he makes it," Nichols said softly.

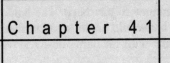

C h a p t e r   4 1

Havana

Entering his hotel was out of the question. Although there did not seem to be any discernible police activity in its vicinity, Pauling knew he couldn't take the chance. He ran through a mental inventory of what he'd left in his room. Nothing of importance. Everything he needed was contained in the twenty-six pockets of his photojournalist's vest.

What the vest didn't offer, however, was a safe place for him to hole up for the night. He needed some sleep to clear his mind and enable him to formulate a further plan of action to carry through to midnight the following night, when he was to meet Nico. But as he thought about that, two problems loomed large.

First, there was the matter of the twenty thousand dollars he'd promised the young Cuban. He had two sources. One was the Cuban office of Cali Forwarding, the Colombian company for whom he'd flown supplies into Cuba, located near José Martí International Airport. Gosling had told him to contact an individual there who would advance him up to twenty thousand after he'd properly identified himself.

The second source of funds was Banco Financiero Internacional. Gosling had said Pauling could use his Canadian MasterCard there to take an advance up to five thousand dollars, only a quarter of what he'd promised Nico.

The choice was simple, provided that he even bothered going after money to pay Nico. The bank was out of the question. What would he do, stroll in there and lay down the credit card with his name on it? It was an invitation to an arrest.

That left Cali Forwarding, providing he could find a way to get there. But that meant trusting the contact at the company—trusting Vic Gosling, for that matter—and he still wasn't of a mind to trust anyone at the moment. He decided to defer that decision until morning. Finding a safe place to sleep was primary.

He left the park and walked away from the hotel, again sticking to back streets. He pulled the candy from a vest pocket and consumed the contents in a few anxious bites. He was hungry and tired.

He reached an intersection that was residential except for a brightly lit café on one corner. He checked the other corners; no kiosks with his picture displayed. No PNR cops either.

He crossed to the café and walked past it, glancing inside as he went. There were a dozen people at the bar and small tables, both men and women. Mambo music and pungent food odors reached his ears and nose as he passed, stopped, turned, and gave the area a final look. Should he chance it, go inside and have something to eat? Given a choice, he would have opted for a steak and salad with Jessica on their deck in Albuquerque, but that wasn't in the cards. Maybe in a couple of days, if his luck held out. Luck! He reached in his pocket, fingered the necklace, the *collar*, sold to him by the street vendor, and entered the café.

As he moved past the bar and through the small, chipped, yellow Formica-topped tables, he remembered how he looked. The bruises on his face had faded somewhat, but it wasn't his face that captured the attention of

other patrons. He now wore a wide-brimmed reed hat—
he had thrown away the bright red hatband—and the
flowing white embroidered guayabera shirt, hardly the
way a yanqui tourist would dress. Nor was it the sort of
place frequented by tourists. Still, it was better than being
bareheaded, he reasoned, pulling the brim of the hat
down even lower over his eyes and taking a chair at a vacant table that positioned him with his back against the
wall and a clear view of the door. He looked to the bartender, an older man with a shiny bald head and tufts of
gray hair at his temples, who was busy serving other customers. Pauling didn't know whether he'd be served at
the table, or was expected to go to the bar and order. Because there was no sign of a waitress, he soon decided to
get up and approach the bartender. But before he could,
a woman who'd been sitting at the bar slowly swung
around on the stool, sent a wide, inviting smile in his direction, stood, and sauntered to his table. She was light
skinned, a mestizo, one of eleven million Cubans of European, African, and indigenous ancestry, although Pauling thought he detected a faint Oriental cast to her
features. She was ripe bodied and walked with a slow, deliberate sway to her hips, causing her red miniskirt to
provocatively follow her movements. Her blouse was
black and low cut. In the time it took for her to cover the
distance between the bar and his table, Pauling pegged
her to be anywhere between twenty-five and thirty-five,
older than most prostitutes he'd been approached by. She
had a round, pleasant face; her makeup was more subtle
than that of the *jineteras,* the teenage sex jockeys working the streets.

She didn't ask whether she could join him, simply
pulled out a chair and sat down next to him.

"Hello," she said.

"Hello," he said.

"American?"

"Yes. How do I get a drink and something to eat?"

She caught the bartender's eye and waved him to the table.

"What do you have?" Pauling asked.

The bartender shrugged: *"No hablo inglés,"* he said.

The woman said to Pauling, "They have *ajiaco*. It is a stew with meat and vegetables."

"Nothing else?"

"No. People do not come here to eat. It is a place to drink."

Pauling nodded at the bartender. "All right," he said, "give me some of the stew."

"Ajiaco," the woman said. To Pauling: "You would like a drink?"

"Sure, a beer, any beer."

"You will buy me a drink?"

"All right."

She moved in her chair so that her hip touched his. Her perfume was delicate, another difference from those Cuban women who seemed fond of dousing themselves with heavy scents.

"I like what you wear," she said.

Pauling looked down at his shirt, and up at the brim of his hat. "This?" he said. "I like to blend in."

"Blend in?"

"Look like a Cuban."

She laughed. "You do not look like a Cuban."

"I try. What's your name?" he asked, his eyes on the door.

"Isabella. Who are you?"

"Smith. Joe Smith."

"Señor Joe Smith," she said, dropping her hand on top of his thigh. "You are here on business?"

"Yeah, that's right."

"What business?"

"Ah, oil. I'm in oil."

"Oh. You must be very rich."

"Rich? No, I'm—" Flashing lights in the street stopped him. He tensed, and pressed his right hand against the bulge of the Glock in the vest. The police vehicle passed the café and disappeared from view.

He turned to her. "I have some money."

"Would you like to spend the night with me, have some fun?" she asked, her full, red lips an inch from his ear.

He looked into eyes that were a little too close together above a prominent nose, but light blue, which surprised him considering her dusky skin.

"We can go to your hotel. What hotel are you at?"

"I'm not," he said, again turning his attention to the door. "I checked out."

"That is not a problem. My home is close to here."

"Yeah?"

The bartender delivered a small, steaming bowl of stew and placed it in front of Pauling.

"Do you want something to eat?" Pauling asked Isabella.

She shook her head and squeezed his thigh. "Hurry up," she said. "I want to make you happy."

He tasted the stew. It had a heavy, oily, onion taste, but felt good going down. He took a drink of beer and processed the situation. Obviously, he could cut a deal with her to spend the night, which appealed to him, not for what she was selling, but for the four walls she could offer. He wondered why she was in this joint, rather than at one of the fancy hotels catering to foreign businessmen with hefty expense accounts.

"Do you work here all the time?" he asked, indicating the café with his hand.

"I come here after work," she said. Her English was good; she'd obviously been educated. Celia had told him that the literacy rate in Cuba was almost 100 percent, the result of a concerted effort by Castro to raise the educational status of citizens, along with supplying universal health care.

"Where do you work?" he asked, dipping stale bread into the stew.

"I work for the organic farming association," she said.

"What do you do there?"

"I am a secretary."

He paused before asking, "But then you do this."

"This?"

"Offer to make a man happy—for money."

"Does that bother you?"

"Not if it doesn't bother you."

"Perhaps you do not want to be with me tonight."

"No, no, I didn't mean anything like that."

"We are a poor country."

"I know."

"Do you still wish to come home with me?"

"Yeah, I do. How much?"

"It depends on how long you wish to stay with me."

"All night?"

She nodded. "Fifty American."

It was shockingly low compared to what he'd expected. He'd have given her a hundred.

"All right," he said.

"Leave money on the table," she said, pulling a small mirror from her purse and checking her hair and makeup.

Pauling laid dollars on the table. She looked at the

money and said, "More. Leave more or he might make trouble." She nodded in the bartender's direction.

Pauling left another five dollars on the table, which satisfied her. He followed her out the door and to the street.

"This way," she said, slipping her arm into his as though they were man and wife, leading him away from the café and around a corner onto a quiet street lined with ceiba trees. Their graceful, wide-spreading boughs formed a comforting canopy above.

She lived on the first floor of a pleasant, narrow, three-story building that had been freshly painted. She took a key from her purse, opened the door, and allowed Pauling to precede her inside. Low-wattage bulbs in two floor lamps provided dim, romantic lighting. Classical music was barely heard from unseen speakers. The lady was good at setting the scene, Pauling thought as she closed the door.

"Rum?" she asked.

"All right." He followed her to the kitchen, cramped but functional. There was a small refrigerator and a two-burner gas stove. A door led to the outside.

"Do you live alone here?" he asked.

"Most of the time," she said as she took down two glasses and filled them with light rum. "My sister, she lives here, too, when she is in Havana. She works in a cigar factory in Santiago de Cuba. Do you know it?"

"I've heard of it."

"A nice place, but so hot. It is on the south coast of Cuba, a large city. It has its own airport."

"Uh-huh," Pauling said, leaving the kitchen and going to the living room where he pulled back curtains on a rear-facing window. He could see nothing in the pitch black outside. She came to him and handed him his drink. *"Salud!"* she said. "Cheers, you say."

"Cheers," he repeated, touching his rim to hers.

She tasted her drink, placed it on a table, and pressed herself close to him, kissing his neck and moving her body against his. He stayed pressed to her for a moment, then stepped back. Her expression asked why.

"Look," he said, "I'll pay you as we agreed. More. But there's no need for you to do what you assume you were going to do. What I would like is to stay here for the night."

"You don't find me attractive?"

"I find you very attractive, and I'm sure you've noticed my reaction to you. But I think—"

"You have someone else."

"Yes, I do."

She sighed, picked up her drink again, and sat in a small, stuffed chair, one of a pair. There was no couch. "And you are in trouble," she said without inflection or meaning.

"Me? No, I'm not in trouble."

Pauling took the other chair. "Is it all right that I stay here without making love? If it's not—if it offends you—I'll leave."

"I am not offended. I am disappointed. I like you. You are a handsome man."

"And you're a beautiful woman. Do we have a deal? I'll pay you for being able to stay here."

"How long?"

"Until morning. Maybe later. I'll be gone by tomorrow night." He pulled bills from his pocket, reached, and placed them on her lap.

"Yes. It is all right."

They said little to each other as the evening progressed. She had wanted to turn on the TV but Pauling asked her not to.

"Why?" she asked.

"I don't like television. Besides, I don't speak very much Spanish."

She didn't argue. He stayed in his chair while she busied herself ironing and mending. Later, she took a break and sat next to him.

"I asked you why you worked in that café," he said. "I would think you'd work your other job at some big hotel where you'd find customers."

"I do," she said, "when I leave my work at the association. I work only by appointment. I worked at Hotel Plaza earlier this evening. A Canadian man, very nice, very generous."

"And you figured you might as well have another customer before going home."

"That's right. The café where we met is close to here. My friends go there. I did not expect to meet you, to find another customer. I was not looking for that."

"I understand."

They fell silent again as she went back to her chores. An hour later, she announced she was going to bed.

"Good night," he said. "And thank you."

"I will be in there if you change your mind," she said, indicating one of two doors off the living room. "The other room is used by my sister, but she is not here. You can sleep in there."

"All right."

He sat up in the living room for two hours after she'd left him alone. At first he feigned sleep to see what would happen. He didn't want to fall asleep but realized he was losing that battle. His head kept falling forward, then snapped back to wakefulness. If there had been a couch, he would have stretched out and closed his eyes for a moment. Since there wasn't, he slowly got up and went to the door to Isabella's room, which she'd left open a crack. There was no sound. He went to the sister's room, propped pillows up against the iron headboard, and sat up against them, his eyes on the living room where the lights were still on, and where the soothing music—was it Mozart?—continued to play.

He was asleep in less than two minutes.

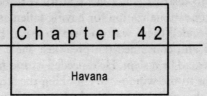

Pauling awoke with a start.

"Isabella?"

He was still propped up against the pillows and headboard, his hat on the bed next to him. He blinked several times to clear his vision, swung his legs over the bed's edge, and focused his hearing. No sound came from the rest of the apartment.

He stood and twisted his neck against tightness. It was early morning; the light coming through the window said dawn.

"Isabella?" he called again when he reached the bedroom door.

The door to her bedroom was open. Her bed was empty, but neatly made.

He went to the kitchen. On the counter was a plate containing two sugar-coated donuts, a glass of orange juice, a carafe half-filled with coffee, and a piece of paper, which he held up to light coming through the window.

Mr. Oil Man—I went to work. These things are for you to eat. Come to see me again.

Isabella

He didn't like having her leave without his knowledge, but it was too late to worry about that now. He had no reason to distrust her, a naïve attitude to be sure, but a necessary rationalization for having fallen asleep.

He decided there was no rush to leave. He sat at the counter and consumed the breakfast she'd left for him. He was glad he'd slept. He'd needed it, and felt refreshed. He went to the window overlooking the street, carefully parted the curtains, and looked out. All was peaceful. Few people passed the house, only a young woman pushing a baby stroller. It was a quiet area of Havana. Stopping in that café had proved to be fortuitous. He'd found a temporary safe haven in which to buy some time and to be able to do some clear thinking. It was almost over. Yes, there were still problems to be overcome—getting the money for Nico, making his way to their rendezvous, and getting out of Cuba. But none seemed insurmountable at that tranquil moment.

He tidied the kitchen—Jessica had trained him well— and decided to take a shower. He stripped off his clothes and stepped into the cramped shower stall, turned on the water, and let out a sigh of contentment as the blessedly hot water poured over him.

As Pauling basked in the pleasure, Isabella stepped into one of the new dollar phone booths that had been established as part of Cuba's massive overhaul of the telephone communications system. She pulled out her *tarjeta,* a dollar phone card she'd purchased at a branch of Photoservice, and consulted a small phone book from her purse. She had a choice of numbers to call—the contact number at Minint, the Ministry of Interior, to which CDRs were to report with information that might be useful to the intelligence agency; or a number at the U.S. Interests Section. She dialed the latter; the Americans would pay money for information; Minint would only praise her loyalty to the republic.

When she was put through to a man's voice, she

identified herself and told him that the American they were seeking was at her house. Gene Nichols thanked her and issued instructions on how and when she could collect her reward.

She hung up and suffered a momentary twinge of guilt. Her overnight guest was a nice man, and she'd briefly debated making the call. But such decisions were always determined by her overriding goal: to one day leave Cuba and live in Miami. The extra money would help her achieve that dream.

She left the booth, leaving behind on the floor the crumpled "Wanted" poster she'd torn from a lamppost on the corner near the café. It had been affixed in the early morning hours, after she and Pauling had left the café and gone to her home. Until seeing it, she'd intended only to call the Interests Section to report an American whose actions had been strange. Now she knew who he was, and that he specifically was being hunted.

She considered for a moment returning to her street to see what happened. But she didn't want to be late for work at the association. It had been a lucrative twenty-four hours—the appointment with the Canadian businessman the previous night, the money from the American named Pauling, plus the big bonus from the American office.

Miami was getting closer all the time.

At precisely 8:00 A.M., President Walden stepped to a podium in the Rose Garden outside the White House. Unlike some previous presidents who only infrequently held press conferences, and who usually preferred that they be conducted when TV viewership was at its lowest, Walden gathered the press on a monthly basis at eight o'clock, forcing the networks' popular early shows to carry the conferences. Some reporters grumbled at the hour, and that the conferences, weather permitting, were held outside. But Walden was an inveterate early riser, as well as a committed outdoorsman. His press conferences would be held where and when he wanted.

He said good morning and gave a brief statement that touched upon a variety of domestic and foreign issues before turning to the real news.

"The death of my friend Senator McCullough in Cuba represents a sad personal loss for the senator's family, me, and my family, and a loss for the American people. Price McCullough proudly served the American people for most of his adult life. His intellect, strength of character, and commitment to the rights of all people regardless of race, creed, or social status set a moral tone for his Senate colleagues that lingers long after his choice to retire from that body to pursue personal business interests. He was in Cuba as head of a delegation whose mission was to explore future trade with the Cuban government. While in Havana, Senator McCullough took advantage of every opportunity to press Cuban officials to improve their record on human rights. He was an American hero. I shall miss his guidance and friendship very much."

A cacophony of voices posed questions to Walden, few having to do with the issues he'd raised at the beginning of the conference.

"Mr. President, the Cubans are reporting that the former senator was killed by an American with ties to the CIA."

"I'm well aware of that," Walden said. "The fact is that this American, who is alleged to have shot Senator McCullough, evidently had worked for the Central Intelligence Agency years ago, and has had no official ties to that agency since then."

"Have you or your people been in close contact with Cuban officials about this?"

"Contact with the Castro government is being conducted through existing diplomatic channels. I hasten to add that the American, whose name is Pauling, has only been *accused* by authorities as Senator McCullough's killer. As I hope you're aware, we view the accused in this country as being innocent until proven guilty."

"If this Pauling is apprehended by Cuban authorities, are negotiations under way to extradite him to this country?"

"That will be discussed."

"Do you really think Castro will cooperate, Mr. President? He's having a ball crowing about how a CIA agent is the murderer and claiming that this same Pauling guy was behind the attempt on his life."

"Speculation on this is premature. Until we have more tangible facts, let's move on to something else."

Questions arose about the failed attempt on Castro's

life. Walden answered them with, "The alleged gunman is, as all reports indicate, a Cuban citizen. This is a Cuban matter. Fortunately—" He paused for effect. "The assassination attempt failed."

Fifteen minutes later, Walden and members of his staff gathered in the Oval Office. Walden tossed his suit jacket on a chair, rolled up his sleeves, sat behind his desk, and addressed the national security advisor. "Any response from Havana?"

"No, sir," Draper said. "Vasquez, President Castro's foreign affairs minister, hasn't responded to my call this morning."

"What about Langley? What the hell are they doing?"

"They dispatched a tracking team to Havana last night. They'll be working through our Interests Section there."

"Who gave authorization for that, damn it? What good they can do? The Cubans are still linking Price's murder with the attack on Castro."

Walden's chief of staff, Charlie Larsen, entered the room and handed the president a communiqué he'd just received from the CIA's Zachary Rasmussen. Walden muttered under his breath as he read it, and gave it to Paul Draper. "Damn!" the national security advisor said.

"Castro now says they'll prosecute Pauling when he's found. So much for extradition," Walden said. "Keep after Vasquez, Paul. Make sure he understands that if Castro grabs this Pauling character and parades him through Havana as a murderer and assassin, he can forget about any easing of the embargo."

"Mr. President, that isn't much of a threat to Castro," said Draper. "Again, he likes the embargo. It's helping him. Canada's foreign minister, Axworthy, got it right yesterday when he said the embargo's the one thing keeping Castro in power."

"Yeah, yeah, I know," Walden said, anger rising in his

voice. "If the embargo ended tomorrow, Cuba would go up like wildfire—Axworthy's words. Well, I don't need him or anybody else giving me a lecture on how to deal with Fidel Castro." He glared at Draper, then turned to Larsen: "When are Price's sons coming?"

"Tomorrow, sir. The press has been alerted."

"Good. I have another meeting." He put on his jacket and checked himself in a mirror. On his way out, he turned and issued a final instruction. "Keep the CIA out of this any way that you can. They've screwed up trying to get rid of Castro a dozen times before, and I don't need another screwup while trying to placate him. Keep working through direct channels with Castro and his people. Christ, if the CIA gets hold of Pauling, they're liable to shoot him by mistake."

As he strode from the room, two unstated but pervasive questions filled his mind.

Had the CIA been behind the latest assassination attempt on Castro?

And had they played a part in Price McCullough's murder?

He fervently hoped not.

But he knew it was entirely possible. *Anything* was possible with the CIA.

Clean and dressed, Pauling went into the kitchen and wrote on the bottom of Isabella's note to him:

Gracias, pretty woman. I hope to see you again.

He'd decided while showering that he would take a chance and flag a taxi in order to get to Cali Forwarding's office near the airport. It was either that or steal a car; hot-wiring cars wasn't in his bag of tricks, and he wasn't about to take one at gunpoint.

He'd checked the night before to see whether Isabella had a phone. She didn't. If she had, he would have tried to reach Jessica that morning to let her know he was all right. He also weighed the pros and cons of trying to reach Mac Smith at Hotel Nacional. Although he barely knew Smith, he was aware of his reputation as an attorney and law professor, but more important, as a straight shooter. Jessica had known him for years, most recently because she'd taught a course at GW on international relations, an extension of her job as an analyst in the State Department's Russian section. But could he trust Smith in this situation? For all he knew, Smith might actually believe he'd killed Price McCullough, who was probably Smith's friend. He decided to play that option by ear.

He'd call him if things got tough and he needed a court of last resort.

He checked the pockets of his vest, slipped the white guayabera over it, put on the hat, and started for the front door. He had touched the knob when someone knocked.

It froze Pauling like a player in a game of statues, leaning forward, his right hand extended.

Another knock, this one louder and more forceful.

Pauling drew the Glock from his pocket, moved to the side of the door, and placed his ear against it. There was no way for him to see the visitor; the single window facing the street was too far away to allow a view of the front steps. He held his breath and waited. Whoever it was—one of Isabella's friends; a former Juan, a "customer"; a neighbor; the Avon lady—would hopefully give up and go away. He anticipated another knock, the last, he hoped.

Instead he heard: "Max?"

The voicing of his name by the unseen man was startling and confusing.

"Max. You in there? I know you're in there. Come on, open up."

Pauling recognized the pinched, nasal voice: Hoctor.

The man confirmed it. "It's Tom Hoctor," he said through the door. "Don't be a jackass, Max. I'm here to help you."

Pauling moved in front of the door and asked through it, "What are you doing here?"

"I said I'm here to help you."

"How did you know I was here?"

"I'll tell you when you let me in. Do you have any of that wonderful, strong Cuban coffee? We can share a cup and talk."

"You want *coffee*? Who's with you?"

"No one, Max. Come on, open the door."

Pauling went to the window and surveyed the street. There didn't seem to be any activity out of the ordinary, which didn't mean, of course, that there weren't a dozen armed men outside. "All right," he said. He flipped a simple lock above the knob and opened the door a few inches. Hoctor was alone. He wore a rumpled blue suit, white shirt, and narrow blue tie. The morning sun shone off his bald pate, and his right eye was at half-mast, as usual. He was smiling.

Pauling opened the door the rest of the way and stepped back. Hoctor entered the house, looked Pauling up and down, and said, "A regular caballero, Max. I'm surprised you're not carrying a lariat and a bull-whip."

"What the hell do *you* want, Hoctor?" He closed and locked the door.

"To see my old friend and to be of service. Please put the gun away. Is there coffee?"

"No. Yes. How did you know I was here? What are you doing in Cuba?"

"Looking for you. As for knowing where you were, a charming lady called the Interests Section this morning and reported that a handsome, dashing gringo by the name of Max had taken up residence in her home. Was she good?"

"Get to the point, Tom. You were there when she called?"

"Yes. I flew in last night with a few of your compatriots."

"Former compatriots. Why did they send *you*?"

"Because I convinced them that because of our close and sustaining relationship, you'd be more likely to listen to me than to them."

"Go ahead, I'm listening."

"Mind if I sit down?"

Pauling shrugged as Hoctor slipped his small frame into one of the matching chairs and sighed. "That feels good," he said. "My back has been acting up recently. And could you take off that ridiculous hat, please? It's very distracting."

Pauling tossed the hat onto the matching chair, went to the front door, and leaned against it, arms folded across his chest, head cocked.

"You have a remarkable talent, Max, for stirring up trouble wherever you go."

"I didn't stir up any trouble, Tom. Like they say, trouble just seems to follow me. I didn't kill Senator McCullough."

"Your Cuban hosts seem to think otherwise. Who did?"

"Who did what? Kill McCullough? I'll tell you who did it. A beautiful Cuban lady who just happens to hire herself out now and then to an agency we know well. Celia Sardiña. Know her?"

"I believe I've heard of her."

"Vic Gosling sure knows her. He put us together. She's done contract work for the agency." *Of course you know her,* Pauling thought. *You've probably hired her yourself.*

"She set me up," Pauling continued. "She got me to her apartment just in time for the police to bust in and find me standing over one dead ex-senator. Her timing stunk. I was gone before they got there."

"Then why did the police go after you?"

"I assume she told them who I am."

Hoctor sighed and examined his fingernails.

"You don't believe me," Pauling said.

A shrug from Hoctor.

"Why would I want to kill McCullough?" Pauling asked. "I didn't even know him."

"But you came here *because* of him," Hoctor countered.

Pauling tossed the hat from the chair and sat. "Why would Isabella—she's the woman who lives here—call the Interests Section?" he asked.

Hoctor's thin smile was knowing. "You've been away from the life too long, Max. You used to recruit nationals to lend their eyes and ears to the cause. Actually, Bobby Jo Brown and Gene Nichols are quite skilled at that exercise here in Havana."

"Nichols," Pauling muttered. "Yeah, he always was good."

"The important thing is that you've found yourself in one hell of a pickle, one with serious political overtones. Mr. Castro is anxious to find you and make you a guest of the state. You have the potential of becoming his most effective propaganda tool since the Bay of Pigs."

"He should give me a medal. I knocked the gun away from the guy who tried to shoot him."

"Yes, I heard scuttlebutt about that, Max. Another enemy made."

"What do you mean?"

"Those who wanted the bearded one dead aren't very fond of you for saving his life."

"Who's that?"

"It really doesn't matter, although I'm willing to share what I know with an old friend. Everyone in President Castro's inner circle isn't an admirer, Max. And, as I'm sure you know, the Cubans in Miami haven't given up on their efforts to send Castro out of Cuba in a box. They aren't very good at it but—"

"You're critical of *them*? The Company has fallen on its face every time it tried."

"That isn't very loyal, Max."

"Loyal? To whom? The agency? Nobody was more loyal than me."

"When you were getting your monthly check. I'm talking about a deeper, more philosophical loyalty, Max."

"Save your breath, Tom. So, who was behind the hit on Castro, his own people, or the Miami gang?"

"I honestly don't know."

Pauling wished Hoctor had not added "honestly" to the lie. "What do you want?" he asked Hoctor. "Why are you here?"

"I'm here to save your disloyal neck. I assured Bobby Jo Brown and Nichols that I would bring you into the Interests Section. You can hole up there until a way is negotiated to get you out of Cuba without angering the beard. Do you know what the Cuban people call him behind his back? They call him El Mulo, the mule, because of his stubbornness."

"I can't do that. I have things to do before I leave Cuba."

"For the dashing Mr. Gosling?"

"That's right. Tell you what. Help me finish up what I came here to do. Then I'll come to the Interests Section with you and we'll all leave Cuba together."

"A wonderful suggestion, Max. You want me, an employee of the federal government, to accompany a fugitive charged with the murder of a distinguished former U.S. senator while he finishes up his assignment for a private security firm. You've been drinking too much rum. Then again, you always did fashion yourself a Hemingway type."

"Thanks for stopping by, Tom. Always a pleasure." Pauling stood, picked up his hat, put it on his head, and went to the door. "You know your way out."

"You won't make it on your own, Max. Your face is on

every telephone pole and billboard in Havana. There are hundreds, maybe thousands, of Cubans out there like your lovely whore, Isabella, who won't call *us* when they spot you. They'll be on the phone with Castro's intelligence service. I give you until lunchtime before you're in a Cuban jail."

"I'm touched by your concern."

In all the years Pauling had known Tom Hoctor, including his tenure at the CIA where Hoctor was his mentor and manager, he'd seen him only occasionally display overt anger. When he did, his voice, naturally high-pitched in his calm moments, became even shriller—like now.

Hoctor got out of his chair and closed the gap between them. His thin, sharply chiseled face was red, his mouth a gash. He spoke like one of those digital voices used to read back credit card numbers over the phone.

"You are a horse's ass, Pauling. As far as Americans are concerned, you're a murderer. TV coverage of Price McCullough's assassination has seen to that. The Cubans want you, too. Ever been in a Cuban jail, Max? I haven't, but I understand they make Attica look like a Four Seasons hotel. Despite your pigheadedness, there are those of us who care about you and want to help you out of this mess you've created. You need us, Max. You need me. Wear that ridiculous hat if you must, but come with me. I'm sure Vic Gosling will understand that events beyond your control prohibited you from completing the assignment for him."

While Hoctor gave his speech, Pauling used the time to review his options. Obviously, Hoctor wasn't about to back down, leave, and wave adios on his way out. Despite the little man's proclamation about wanting to help, Pauling knew there was nothing personal about it. Doing personal favors wasn't in Hoctor's job description.

Pauling remembered when he'd been sent to Russia by the State Department to track down the source of Soviet-made SAM missiles that had been used for attacks on American airliners. While in Moscow, he'd reported to an old and dear friend, Bill Lerner, a CIA veteran, who operated out of the American embassy. Lerner had been involved in a long-term, low-profile affair with a lovely, mature Russian woman, Elena Alekseyevna. Consorting with the enemy, sleeping with the enemy, was frowned upon by agency brass, although those who knew about Lerner's relationship had tended to look the other way—until Lerner was compromised by a Russian banker for whom Elena worked.

The situation didn't involve state secrets; no national security on either side had been compromised. It was money, pure and simple. Hoctor had gone to Moscow to help bail Pauling out of a dangerous situation—yes, trouble did seem to follow him—and succeeded. But as they readied to leave Moscow, Pauling stopped by Lerner's apartment to say good-bye and found his friend dead on the bathroom floor. Hoctor, who was at the apartment when Pauling arrived, claimed he'd found Lerner dead, apparently of a heart attack. Pauling had no choice but to believe it; their departure was scheduled for only hours later. But he had never forgotten Hoctor's words when asked whether Lerner had been eliminated. "We make our choices in this world, Max, and live with the consequences. The only choice you have now is to come with me. The plane is waiting."

The only choice you have now is to come with me.

If, in Hoctor's opinion—which would reflect those of many others—he, Pauling, posed a serious risk to America's interests should he be incarcerated and used as a propaganda tool by Castro, Hoctor and the agency he represented would ensure that this didn't happen.

We make our choices in this world, Max, and live with the consequences.

"Okay," Pauling said. "Let's go."

Normal color returned to Hoctor's face, and he smiled. "You still have some reasoning powers left, Max," he said.

They went through the front door and to the sidewalk. Pauling didn't turn his head, but allowed his eyes to pivot left and right. He saw a shiny new black sedan at one corner, its front end protruding beyond the intersection. At the other end of the street was a similar vehicle.

"Damn!" Pauling said.

"What's the matter?" Hoctor asked.

"I forgot to lock Isabella's door. I told her I'd do it when I left."

Hoctor started to tell him to forget the lock, but Pauling bounded back up the steps, went through the front door and left it open, headed straight for the kitchen, opened the back door in that room, and saw, for the first time, the layout behind the building, a postage stamp–sized yard littered with discarded tires, fenders, and other automotive parts from the scrap heap. There was no fence. He jumped over a pile of tires and ran into a neighboring yard as Hoctor came to the open kitchen door and shouted, "Max!"

Pauling didn't pause to respond. *You can't trust anybody,* he thought as he kept running, never looking back. The sobering realization was that at that moment, he trusted Fidel Castro more than his own CIA.

Chapter 45

Havana

Dr. Caldoza called his office first thing that morning to inform them he would be coming in late, probably not until midafternoon. He hadn't slept all night. He and his wife, Maria, had sat in their kitchen in the house in Vedado that had been their home for many years, drinking coffee and talking, their voices low and urgent, sadness in their eyes as they sought to come to grips with the dramatic change that was about to occur in their lives.

"The choice is not ours," he said to her, his voice heavy with fatigue. "The forces have been unleashed, Maria. Our only option is to leave."

Silent tears filled her eyes, and he covered her hand on the table with his. "I have lived all my adult life, Maria, as a loyal Cuban. No one loves his country more than me. But my loyalty also extends to my work. I am a physician, someone who is expected to put the health and well-being of my patients, *all* patients, before any other consideration. I have been blessed in my life and work. I believe that all the years I have spent attempting to find one or another of the cures for cancer will one day be fruitful." He squeezed her hand, and his voice took on added urgency. "Think of it, Maria. Think of millions of people suffering from this disease who might find new hope as a result of what we have been able to accomplish."

"I know," she said, dabbing at her cheek with a

napkin. "But isn't there another way to make it right without having to leave?"

"I don't see another way, Maria." He sat back and rubbed his eyes. "It is such a disappointment, what has happened. I do not believe we, as a people, are better because of the Revolution and the Socialist society we have lived in for more than forty years. But I admired President Castro for his commitment to the health of our citizens. He promised to eradicate cancer in his lifetime, and supported that promise with the money that enabled us to build the laboratories and conduct our research."

"It was not his fault that the Soviets left, Manuel. The money was stopped."

"I know, I know, but my disappointment is not because of that. Others have been investing in our work—the Canadians, the French, the Spanish. But they have not made it a condition of their investments that they own the research. They wish to profit as partners. This is different, Maria." He leaned very close to her and spoke slowly and deliberately, in a whisper. "He is willing to sell my years of work to the highest bidder, Maria. Think of it! He is a traitor!"

"Ssssh," she said, placing her fingertip to her lips. "The murder on TV. It was the senator whose company was buying the research? That is what you say?"

"Yes. The man they are looking for was sent here to prove that. Pauling is his name."

"How can you be sure?"

"They told me, Maria. The people here in Havana who plot against—" He stroked his chin. "They are aware of such things. They know such things. They have a tape."

"But the senator is dead, Manuel. Now maybe the research will not be sold to his company. We will not have to leave."

Caldoza slowly shook his head. "If it is not his company, Maria, it will be another. Castro's motives are now clear. He will sell our accomplishments for his personal gain." Another shake of his head. "The die is cast. We must leave. I expect the call from Washington today, here, at the house. The conference will be held in two weeks in Washington. Dr. Mancuso will request my appearance there. Now that I have already attended a medical conference in the United States and returned to Cuba, they will allow me to attend this conference, too. I have spoken with the minister about allowing you to make such trips with me. I told him that all the doctors at the conferences bring their wives with them. It is expected. He has given permission for you to accompany me to future conferences."

Her sigh was sustained and reflective of the inner turmoil she was experiencing.

"We will enjoy a new life in America, Maria, and be closer to our sons. It is the only thing we can do."

He spent the rest of the morning in his study awaiting the call from Barbara Mancuso at NIH. It came at one that afternoon. The official invitation for him and his wife to attend the medical conference in Bethesda would be sent to him overnight.

"And everything else is arranged, Doctor?" he asked.

"Yes, Dr. Caldoza, everything else is arranged."

Upon completion of the call, Caldoza went to a large closet, removed a key from his pocket, and used it to open the doors, moved a pair of two-drawer file cabinets out of the way, and pulled an expanding, brown leather briefcase from beneath light blankets that had been piled on it. He took the briefcase to his desk and used another key to open it. Inside were more than a hundred computer Zip disks, each with the memory capacity to hold volumes of information. He pulled one out, read the label, replaced it in the case, locked it, and returned it to the closet. Years of painstaking research into dozens of potentially effective cancer drugs were contained in that briefcase, the originals methodically backed up on the disks.

Until being informed of the tape recording of the meeting between Castro and McCullough, Caldoza hadn't been sure that something unusual was happening with the labs and the Health Ministry, although he had suspicions. Little things, indiscreet comments, meetings at the Health Ministry attended by the liaison in Havana for the German company, dozens of small, inconclusive events that had led Caldoza to begin questioning the future of his labs. Eventually, he had decided to make a surreptitious second set of backup disks.

His unscheduled meeting with Barbara Mancuso at the American Society of Clinical Oncology meeting in San Francisco had been rushed and decidedly clandestine. If he ever decided to bring his research to NIH, would he be allowed to continue his work with it? "Of course," was her answer.

"And would you and your superiors intercede on behalf of my wife and me to defect to the United States?"

"I will do everything in my power to accomplish that," she'd said. "Are you certain you want to do this?"

At that moment, his honest answer to her was, "No."

But this was a different time. Now there was the tape.

Pauling knew one thing as he ran from yard to yard, ducking clotheslines, zigzagging around obstacles, and hoping the barking of an occasional dog was, indeed, worse than its bite—he had to find a way, and fast, to get as far out of Havana as possible.

A rattletrap Cadillac painted pink and yellow stood at a corner when he emerged from the yards. Its driver, a young Cuban man, appeared to be dozing behind the wheel. Pauling yanked open the rear door and jumped inside, the driver waking with a jolt.

"Taxi, *sí*?" Pauling said.

"*Sí, señor.*"

Pauling gave him the address for Cali Forwarding. The driver focused on Pauling in his rearview mirror but didn't start the car. Pauling leaned over the driver's seatback and immediately saw the problem. A flyer with his photo lay on the front passenger seat, along with a lethal-looking machete. He considered pulling the Glock. Instead, he took a wad of American money from his pocket and held it up in front of the driver, whose eyes widened. "Look, *amigo*, this is a mistake," he said, picking up the flyer. "You speak English?"

"*Sí.* Yes."

"No trouble," Pauling said. "*No problemo*. Here." He

took his wallet from his pants pocket and displayed more dollars to the driver. "Okay?"

Pauling knew that one of four things could happen. One, the driver could agree to take him, but deliver him to the nearest PNR precinct. Two, he could jump out of the Caddy and run, which would leave Pauling with the vehicle, not much help because he didn't know where he was going and would probably be picked up as soon as the driver reported his stolen car to the police. Three, the driver could pick up the machete and relieve Pauling of his head. Or four, he would succumb to the lure of *mucho* American dollars and take his chances transporting a gringo wanted for murder.

"Okay," the driver said, grabbing the money, shoving it into his shirtfront, and starting the engine.

"What's your name?" Pauling asked.

"David."

"David? Okay, David, don't speed. Don't attract attention."

"You, get down," David said, indicating the backseat.

Pauling nodded and smiled. "Good idea," he said.

He tossed his hat on the floor, reached under his guayabera, and quietly removed the Glock from his vest as he stretched out on the backseat. The Cuban good-luck charm he'd bought from the street vendor, the *collar,* came out of the pocket along with the Glock. He rubbed his thumb over it like a worry stone. He didn't believe in luck, but it couldn't hurt.

The Caddy's springs were shot; it felt as though they were riding over railroad ties as the driver maneuvered through Havana traffic and headed in the direction of the airport. Each time he had to stop for a traffic light or an officer directing traffic, Pauling was tempted to raise his head to see what was going on around them. He controlled the urge. He'd made his choice; he was putting faith in David. He wished he'd promised more money. If he could get twenty thousand from Cali Forwarding, there'd be plenty to go around. Nico had been promised ten. Of course, Pauling had also promised Nico a flight to Miami in Pauling's twin-engine plane. That was out of the question now. Going near that aircraft would be like hoisting a white flag and surrendering. It ran through his mind as David continued the journey that the airplane Vic Gosling had provided was rented. Gosling had asked him to not damage it. Damage it? Try having it become part of Castro's air force. Funny, he thought, how such irrelevant thoughts run through your mind when the only thing that should be on it is how to save your skin.

He sensed they'd left Havana's bustle and were now into a less congested area. He brought up his head and looked around. David noticed him and laughed. "Hey, amigo, everything okay?" he asked.

"Yeah, everything's okay," Pauling replied, feeling suddenly relieved that he'd picked the right cabdriver. "Do you want to stay with me all day?"

David frowned as he pondered the question.

"Stay with me all day," Pauling repeated. "Plenty more money for you. *Mucho dinero.*"

"Okay, I be with you all day."

"Great!"

David made a series of wrong turns before finally locating Cali Forwarding. He announced that he had to get oil for the Cadillac. Pauling told the cabby to drop him a hundred yards from the building, get the oil, then return and wait until he'd completed the business inside.

"Okay," David said, flashing another grin, wider this time. He seemed to be enjoying the excursion quite aside from the payday that promised to be the biggest in his young life.

Pauling got out of the car and watched David drive off,

black, noxious smoke billowing from the Caddy's tailpipe. *He may be someone I can trust,* Pauling thought, *but maybe the car isn't so trustworthy.* Would it get him to the seaside village where Nico promised to be waiting? Would Nico be there alone, or bring the police with him?

One step, one worry, at a time.

He'd been told by Gosling that if he needed money, he was to go to Cali Forwarding, ask for Dominique, and say that Chico had sent him. Hopefully, this Dominique still worked for the company and was on duty that morning, not off on holiday.

The building was low and squat, gray and plain, with only a small sign to the right of the door to indicate the place where Cali Forwarding conducted business. Pauling was relieved there were no police in the area. Either they hadn't yet learned of his connection with the company, or had already been there and left.

He approached the building and stepped through the door, causing a bell above it to sound his arrival. Dozens of small boxes were piled behind and on the counter. A large poster of Fidel hung high on the wall. Pauling detected the odor of marijuana.

There was a door behind the counter that opened to a large staging area where pallets piled with boxes sat awaiting disposition.

"Hello?" Pauling shouted. "Anybody home?"

He heard sounds beyond the door, but no one appeared. He circumvented the counter and was about to go through the door when a short, wiry man wearing blue coveralls came from behind a pallet and stared at him.

"Buenos días," Pauling said.

The man said nothing.

"Dominique. I'm looking for Dominique."

Still no response from the employee, and Pauling

wondered whether he was hearing impaired. The man came to the counter, stood as though wanting to activate an inactive vocabulary. Pauling looked at the small yellow nameplate over the breast pocket of his coveralls: DOMINIQUE.

"Chico sent me," Pauling said.

Dominique continued to stare at Pauling. Pauling removed his reed hat. "You *habla inglés*?"

A nod before replying, "I speak English. Chico sent you?"

"That's right."

"One minute."

He turned and started through the door. Pauling came around the counter again and said, "I'll come with you." For all he knew, Dominique was on his way to call the police from a phone in the back. He followed the Cuban through a large storage area to an unoccupied loading dock where the corrugated metal door was rolled up. When they were outside, Dominique said, "You should not be here. There is trouble."

"Yeah, I know there's trouble. Have the police been here?"

"*Sí.* Last night. This morning. They told me to look for you. I have the picture."

"Forget about that. I need money. They said you'd give me money."

"You should not be here," he repeated. "Leave now." He waved his hand for emphasis. "Go away. Too much trouble."

"Look, I am here and I need money. Twenty thousand. Give me twenty thousand and I won't be here—ever again."

Pauling didn't know whether the Cuban knew he was working for a CIA front organization, or thought that passing out thousands of dollars to some American claiming that Chico sent him was the forwarding company's normal way of doing business. It didn't matter who or what he was, however. Pauling just wanted the money, and to be gone before the police decided to make another visit.

He didn't have time for games.

"Look, damn it," he said, "I need the money and I need it now."

Dominique started to urge him to leave when the sight of Pauling's Glock stopped him. Pauling held the weapon at his side, but pointed it directly at the Cuban's midsection. "Let's not have any trouble, Dominique. You have the money, I said the magic word, and now you give it to me or—"

"Not here," Dominique said.

"What do you mean 'not here'?"

"The money, it is in another place. Not far."

"Now we're getting somewhere. Let's go get it."

He led Pauling down a short set of steps to his car, a battered Russian Lada. Pauling kept the Glock pointed at Dominique during a ride of no more than two miles to a dilapidated shack, one of a dozen in a clearing cut from what had once been a forest. Inside was one room chockablock with ripped furniture, empty cartons, and two bicycles. Pauling watched with a combination of amusement and disbelief as the Cuban shoved aside some of the furniture and pulled a cardboard box from a hiding place covered by packing blankets. He tore masking tape off the box, opened the flaps, and began pulling out wrapped packages of American money, hundred-dollar bills. He handed Pauling four of the packages. "Twenty thousand American," he said, nervously eyeing the weapon in Pauling's hand.

"See?" Pauling said. "It was easy. No need for this," he

added, indicating the Glock. "I know. You were afraid. Nothing to worry about."

Dominique smiled and nodded, his attention now on the packages of hundreds.

Pauling smiled, too. "Sure," he said, opening one of the packages and handing Dominique two bills. "For your trouble," he said as he created some room between himself and the Cuban, laid the Glock on a carton, pulled up his guayabera, and shoved the wads of bills into various pockets of the vest. If he hadn't spent years of his life picking up CIA cash from unlikely places, he would have found the scene mind-boggling, tens of thousands of dollars stashed in a cardboard box in a shack, handed out by a working-class guy on the CIA's payroll who, if he wanted to, could walk away a rich Cuban—and hope the person who'd "turned" him never found him again.

Years ago, he'd been introduced to Tony Ulasewicz, the ex-cop who became the bagman for Nixon and his "plumbers" during the Watergate fiasco. The big, affable Ulasewicz told Pauling that he'd routinely carried satchels containing as much as thirty thousand dollars in cash around the country, and was instructed that if he ever was faced with having to display a satchel's contents to airport security, he was to dump the bag and money into the nearest trash bin. Always plenty of money around when you were operating in the shadows.

"*Gracias,*" Pauling told Dominique. "Come on, take me back before you're missed. And keep up the good work. One of these days . . ." He stroked an imaginary beard and sliced his index finger across his throat. Dominique grinned and nodded enthusiastically.

Minutes later, Pauling left Cali Forwarding's building and looked for David, who was parked where he'd originally deposited Pauling. *Maybe there is something to luck,* Pauling thought, relieved that the young Cuban driver had kept his word. He got in the backseat of the two-tone Caddy and asked, "You got oil?"

"*Sí,* three quarts."

"So we're good for another hour."

"*Como?*"

"Nothing. Just thinking out loud."

"Where do we go now?"

"Do you know a town called Cojímar?"

"*Sí.* It is on the water. I have a friend who lives there."

"There's a motel, Casa something or other. Casa Marisol?"

David laughed. "Casa de Mar y Sol. House of the Sea and Sun. You want to see Hemingway?"

"Hemingway?"

"*Sí.* It is where he kept his fishing boat and wrote his great book *The Old Man and the Sea*. There is a monument of him in Cojímar. All brass, very shiny, very beautiful. The fishermen gave brass pieces from their boats. It was melted down to make the monument. You want to go there?"

"Right, but I don't care about Hemingway or any monument. I don't have to be there until tonight. Twelve midnight."

"What do we do until then?"

"I don't know, but let's get out of here. Oh." Pauling extracted one of the packages of money given him by Dominique, peeled off three hundred-dollar bills, and handed them to David. The young man seemed almost embarrassed to be taking more money.

"Go on," Pauling said. "You're earning it."

David put the money in his shirtfront along with the previous cash that Pauling had given him, and started the engine. Before slipping the gearshift into DRIVE, he turned and asked, "You want him gone, *sí*?"

"Want *who* gone?"

David stroked a beard that wasn't there.

Pauling smiled. "Yeah, I want him gone."

"Good," David said. "Me, too. If he"—another stroke of the chin—"wants to find you, you must be a good guy. Okay, we go to Cojímar."

Jessica Mumford felt utterly helpless.

There was no one to call to find out about Max. Victor Gosling said he lived in San Jose, California, she remembered, and tried to get a number for him there. No listing. She did come up with the phone number at the firm for which he worked, Cell-One, and called the New York office.

"I have no record of any Victor Gosling, ma'am," said the woman who answered. Jessica pressed, but to no avail. The voice in New York said she'd checked the employee roster for the company's offices not only in New York, but also in London and San Francisco. No Gosling.

Jessica knew the number in Pittsburgh of Max's former wife, Doris, but there was nothing to be gained by calling her. She would know no more than Jessica was learning from TV news and the papers.

That left Annabel Reed-Smith in Washington.

"Annabel, it's Jessica."

"Hi. You must be frantic. Have you heard anything from Max?"

"No. I'm so worried. Have you talked to Mac?"

"I got off the phone with him just a little bit ago. The delegation was sequestered and everyone has been confined to rooms in the hotel. The Cubans are concerned for their safety."

"Concerned that Max might try and kill them, too," Jessica said glumly.

"We know Max didn't kill anyone," Annabel said. That, she knew, was her own assumption, the one she preferred to the alternative.

"I thought Max might have contacted Mac. He knows where he's staying."

"He hasn't, Jess. I asked Mac about that. He hasn't heard from him. He did tell me that Cuban television is running the story and Max's picture every half hour, it seems."

"Has Mac told anyone there that he knows Max, Annabel?"

"He didn't say, and I didn't think to ask. I would doubt it. Why?"

"I just thought that because of Mac's stature—I mean, he's part of the delegation, and he's friends with President Walden—that he might have some clout with the Cubans."

"I doubt anyone has clout with the Cubans at the moment, Jess. Mac says this is a political issue, that Castro is making propaganda points because of Max's former involvement with the CIA. Price McCullough's murder came right on the heels of the attempt on Castro's life. He's making political hay by linking the two events. Mention the CIA, Jess, and it sends Castro off and running."

"Frothing, you mean. I wish Max would call. I'm surprised he hasn't. I know he's on the run, but he could get to a phone, if only for a minute, unless—"

"Unless he's—I'm sure he wants to call, Jess, and will do so the minute he gets a chance. Look, I'll be in touch with Mac on a regular basis. He can't leave his room so he's a captive audience for my calls. I'll keep in touch with you."

"Thanks, Annabel. I appreciate it."

Jessica hung up, went to the deck, and looked out over Albuquerque and the surrounding mountains that never failed to inspire. She was going to ask Annabel whether the friendship that she and her husband enjoyed with the president could be put to some use on Max's behalf, but it seemed inappropriate.

Just talking with Annabel had been therapeutic for Jessica. She'd calmed down, and felt her heart and pulse rates lower. In this more tranquil state, she was able to better focus on Max's survival skills, rather than succumb to macabre visions of him lying in some Havana gutter, shot down by the authorities. The truth was, if there was anyone she'd ever known who had the ability to handle such a situation, it was Max Pauling.

And she'd say a little prayer now and then, assuming God listened to prayers offered for former CIA agents.

James Walden conferred in the Oval Office with his national security advisor and his chief of staff, Charlie Larsen. Paul Draper had just gotten off the phone with the Cuban foreign affairs minister Diego Vasquez, and had reported the gist of the conversation to the president, concluding with, "He wouldn't confirm that Castro met with Senator McCullough before his death, although he did allude to some assurances McCullough had given on your behalf."

"Did he get specific?"

"No, sir."

"What about Pauling?"

"Still on the loose, sir, if he's alive. Vasquez says they're intensifying the search. According to him, the Castro government is fully convinced that the CIA, using Pauling, was behind the attack on Castro. They're planning a big rally when Pauling is apprehended."

"This is outrageous," Walden said. "Pauling is supposed to have saved Castro's ass when he knocked the assassin's gun away. Isn't that what our sources say?"

"It doesn't matter what actually happened, Mr. President. You know that. Castro will twist the truth to suit his own purposes. He'll hold Pauling up as another symbol of the big, bad United States and the CIA trying to destroy his regime."

Walden swung around in his chair and faced the window. He said without looking back at them, "Get Director Brown on the phone for me." George Brown had been nominated to be director of the CIA by Walden early in his administration and, after undergoing a rough Senate hearing, was confirmed. "And cut me some slack today. I need think time."

"Yes, sir."

Chapter 48

Havana

"How far is Cojímar?" Pauling asked David as they drove away from Cali Forwarding.

"Not so far, only twenty, twenty-five miles."

"That's if we go back through Havana," Pauling said. They'd driven southwest to reach the airport. Cojímar was east of Havana, on the northern coast. The most direct route was through the city.

"We have time," Pauling said. "Go a different way, not through the city."

"The roads are bad," David said.

"That's okay. Will this wreck make it?"

"Wreck?"

"This car. Will it get us to Cojímar?"

"If we buy oil."

"I'll leave that up to you, David. I'm in your hands."

Pauling's luck was holding. The hands into which he'd placed himself were good hands, indeed. As it developed, David hated Castro and the situation in Cuba. He'd had an uncle who'd been arrested for subversive activities, jailed, and never heard from again. A cousin with whom David was especially close had been raped by a member of Castro's military police. David had told friends harboring similar feelings that if given the chance to shoot the dictator, he would gladly do it.

There was also the matter of his sexuality. David was

gay, although he maintained what appeared to be heterosexual relations with young women in order to avoid public discrimination. His discreet homosexuality branded him a *maricón,* a "queer," as opposed to overtly gay men known in Cuban society as *bujarrones,* or "butch." He'd seen the early 1990s film *Strawberry and Chocolate,* many times. It depicted a homosexual love affair between a gay intellectual and a heterosexual Communist Party militant. It played to packed houses in Havana; why Castro had allowed its public showing puzzled many. Despite the movie's success, homosexuals were still banned from Communist Party membership. Not that this bothered David. His only political leaning was to see Castro dead and gone.

They drove south on Avenida de la Independencia, a heavily traveled major road, until reaching the town of Santiago de las Vegas, where David turned east onto a lesser road leading to Managua. From there, he continued east until heading north at Cuatro Caminos, staying off the busy Via Monumental by following narrow, rutted dirt roads winding through rich farmland. In need of gas and oil, they joined a line of cars at a Servi-Cupet station. Pauling, who spent much of the trek crouched in the backseat, stayed in that position while David inched forward in the line. It took almost forty-five minutes to reach the pumps, to fill up, and add another three quarts of oil to an engine that increasingly sounded as though it was about to give a last gasp and die at any moment.

"Get some extra oil," Max ordered. "I don't want to stop at a station again."

With the Caddy serviced and four cans of oil in the trunk, David returned to rural roads where he dared not exceed ten miles an hour for fear of collapsing the car's suspension. Eventually—it had been six hours since leaving Cali's building at Aéropuerto José Martí—they arrived at the coast just west of the fishing village and seaside resort of Cojímar. There, in 1994, thousands of Cuban *balseros,* rafters, launched their makeshift craft into the warm waters of the Florida Straits in the hope of catching the Gulf Stream—destination, Miami. Forty thousand Cubans set sail for the United States that year, more than twenty thousand of them rescued at sea and shipped to Guantánamo naval base. Thousands died at sea.

Casa de Mar y Sol was a small, one-story motel directly on the beach, across the road from a cluster of ramshackle, five-story walk-up apartment houses, home to more than a hundred thousand Cubans. "Siberia," David said, laughing and pointing to the apartments. They continued past a long row of red-tile-roofed cottages, their façades stripped of paint by the salty sea spray blowing against them with regularity. Above them rose a hill on which a stone fortress, the Cuban flag waving in the breeze atop it, stood silent sentry over the town and shoreline. Pauling asked about it.

"El Torreon," David explained. "Built to guard this coast many years ago."

"Is it empty?" Pauling asked.

"Oh, no. The military is still there."

A good place to avoid, Pauling thought.

David pulled up in front of the motel.

"Go around to the side," Pauling said.

David did as instructed and turned off the ignition, the engine shuddering like a death rattle before going blessedly silent.

"Okay," Pauling said, "here's what I want you to do. Go inside the motel and book a room. Get one that opens onto the beach, not in the front. Book it in your name. *Comprende?*"

"I understand."

"Go to the room and stay there a few minutes. I'll be here in the car. Open a door or window on the beach side, come back out, and tell me where to go."

"Okay."

Pauling lay on the backseat and waited. So far, so good. He'd made it to Cojímar, and had the money he needed. He could hole up in the room until midnight when he was to meet Nico—provided he showed. It occurred to him that with his picture splashed all over Havana, and the charge that he'd killed Senator McCullough, Nico might get cold feet and decide that meeting up with a wanted killer might not further his career. But he couldn't worry about that. He either showed or he didn't.

Pauling was thinking of Celia, a mixture of thoughts, when David opened the driver's door. Pauling sat up. "All set?" he asked.

"All set."

"What's it like inside? Busy?"

"No, not busy. Nobody there."

"Nobody asked you questions?"

"No questions."

"Good. There's a door?"

"*Sí.*"

"Go back inside and stand by the door. I'll be there."

The room was surprisingly large; the few pieces of furniture made it seem even larger. There were two cot-sized beds, a white Formica dresser, two straight-back chairs, and a television set with a twelve-inch screen. Pauling looked for an air conditioner that wasn't there.

He removed his wide-brimmed hat, pulled off the shirt, and sat on one of the beds. David stood by the door opening to the beach. Pauling realized he had to decide what to do about the cabby, send him on his way or keep him around.

"You want to stay with me?" he asked.

"If that is what you want me to do."

"Yeah, I think so," Pauling said, reasoning that if Nico showed, they'd need some way to get to—get to *what*? How to leave Cuba now loomed as his biggest challenge.

"David, you said you have a friend here in—what's this town?—Cojímar."

"Yes."

"What does he do?"

"It is a girl."

Pauling raised his eyebrows. "A girlfriend?"

"Sometimes," David said, grinning.

"I've got a problem," Pauling said.

"I know," said David.

"No, no, another problem. I'm a pilot. I flew to Cuba in a twin-engine plane, but I can't use it to leave. It's back at the big airport."

"The *policía* will be there."

"That's my problem. I need a way to leave Cuba tonight, after I meet someone here. Got any ideas?"

"You need a boat."

"Yeah, a boat. A good boat. A big boat."

David sat on the second cot, his brow creased in thought. "My girlfriend," he said to himself.

"What about her?"

"Her brother has boats."

"Here? In Cojímar?"

"No. In Santa Maria del Mar. It is not far from here, maybe ten miles."

"What kind of boats does he have?"

"Fishing boats. Very good boats."

"Would he sell one to me?"

David shrugged. "Maybe if there is enough money for him to buy another."

"There's plenty of money."

"There is a plane there, too."

Pauling straightened. "A plane? There's an airport there?"

"No. No airport."

"What kind of plane?"

"A water plane."

"A seaplane? With pontoons?" He illustrated with his hands.

"*Sí.*"

"Who owns it, your girlfriend's brother?"

"No. His friend."

"Does it work?"

"Yes. I have seen it fly. It is very old but—"

"But you've seen it fly. How long ago?"

"I don't know. Two months maybe. Maybe four months."

"Can you go talk to your 'sometimes' girlfriend, ask if her brother's friend would like to lend it to me?"

"Lend it?"

"I'll rent it from him."

"How would you get it back? You are coming back to Cuba in it?"

"I'll buy it from him. Ask how much."

"All right. I will do it."

"Will you get me something to eat first?"

"What do you want?"

"Anything. Are there restaurants here?"

"*Sí.* A good one. La Terraza. Hemingway ate there many times. There is a statue there for him."

A statue of Papa everywhere, huh? Fidel's rival. "Bring me something. Then go find your girlfriend."

David returned a half hour later carrying a small basket made of reeds. In it was a bowl of paella and a loaf of bread.

"Great," Pauling said, using one of the chairs as a table. "Go on, to your girlfriend. I'll be here."

Pauling watched television after eating. The Cuban channel reported on the search for him, the announcer pointing out that every conceivable way of leaving Cuba had been blocked by authorities, including the airports and docks. There appeared footage of Cuban military boats patrolling shorelines in and around Havana, and of Pauling's plane at Aéropuerto José Martí. *Let's see if your expense account covers* that, *Gosling,* he thought.

He fell asleep. When he awoke, it was dark outside and in the room. He turned on the only lamp and checked his watch. Ten o'clock. Two hours until Nico was to arrive. Where was David? Pauling wasn't putting much stock in the floatplane he'd mentioned. Chances were the owner wouldn't want to sell it, not if he used it to make money. Of course, Pauling could always commandeer it at gunpoint, but that didn't appeal. More than anything, he wanted a quick, smooth, nonconfrontational way out of Cuba, with nobody shooting at his back.

By eleven, he'd become jumpy. He paced the room, stopping frequently to open the curtains a crack to peer outside to the beach. Nico hadn't said how they would meet up at the motel. What was he supposed to do, sit in the lobby? Probably. When Nico had told him where they would meet, Pauling hadn't yet been the subject of a manhunt. Now that he was, putting himself in one more public place was risky.

At eleven-thirty, he'd decided he didn't have a choice. He'd go to the lobby to allow Nico to spot him. He got up to leave. Someone knocked. Pauling drew the gun from his vest and went to the door. "Who is it?"

"David."

He opened the door to see David standing next to a petite, pretty young girl, no older than sixteen, in jeans and a blue denim shirt. A sturdy young man wearing white shorts, a yellow T-shirt, and sandals waited in the doorway with them.

"These are my friends," David said. He introduced the girl as Ernestine and the young man, her brother, as Joe. Pauling stepped back to allow them to enter, and closed the door behind them.

"Joe says he will sell you one of his boats," David said, sounding excited that he'd successfully brokered the deal.

"Good," Pauling said. "It will get me to Miami?"

Joe, who was one of those perpetually brooding young men, hunched his shoulders and conversed with David in Spanish. David said to Pauling in English, "He says he will not guarantee it. He says you pay the money and take the boat. If it doesn't go all the way to Miami, he will not give back the money."

Pauling laughed and said to David, "Tell him I won't need the money back if I don't make it to Miami."

David motioned Pauling aside and whispered, "You said you were meeting someone here."

"Right."

"There is a man and woman in the lobby, sitting there."

"Man *and* woman?"

"*Sí.* I thought—"

"You and your friends stay here. Is there anyone else?"

"Just the clerk at the desk."

"I'll be back."

He stepped into the hallway and listened for sounds. All was quiet. He slowly approached the lobby, pausing at each door before moving past. He reached the break in the wall and took a few steps to his right, giving him a view of the small lobby. Seated in adjacent chairs, and looking every bit like a couple in a doctor's waiting room, was Nico—and Celia Sardiña.

Pauling was stunned. Although she'd been on his mind almost constantly, coming and going in flashes of anger or confusion, the last thing he expected was to see her again. He stared, incapable of saying or doing anything. Although he was partially concealed by the wall, she spotted him, told Nico, stood, straightened her skirt, and crossed the lobby to him.

"Hello, Max," she said.

"What are you doing here?"

"I came with Nico. He told me he was meeting you."

"You've got one hell of a nerve."

"I take that as a compliment. You're ready to go?"

Pauling glanced behind the desk at the clerk, who seemed disinterested in their conversation.

"Hello," Nico said.

Pauling ignored him. He lowered his voice and snarled at Celia, "Why did you set me up like that?"

"I don't have time to discuss it, Max. The important thing is for you and Nico to go. He has everything you need." She turned and nodded at a briefcase Nico held in his hand. "How are you leaving?"

"We would have been leaving in the plane I flew in on, but thanks to you, it now belongs to Cuba. I think I have a boat."

"No good. They're patrolling the coast with boats and helicopters."

"Then you tell me. You seem to have all the answers."

"You need another plane. Let's go to your room."

"How do you know I have a room?"

She looked at the clerk, then back at Pauling. "He's one of us. Please stop asking questions. You and Nico don't have time."

Pauling took them to his room where David, Ernestine, and Joe waited.

"Who are they?" Celia asked.

"Friends. After you, I needed some." He said to David, "The boat's out of the question. I need a plane. Where's the guy who owns the floatplane?"

David spoke in Spanish to Joe.

"He lives in Santa Maria del Mar, where the plane is."

"Tell Joe I have plenty of money if he'll help me get that plane. Plenty of money for all of you."

David's translation didn't bring a smile to Joe's sour expression, but he did nod.

"Then let's go," Pauling said.

They all left through the back door and went to David's Cadillac. Joe and Ernestine got in the backseat and David climbed in behind the wheel.

"You have the money for Nico?" Celia asked Pauling.

Pauling could no longer corral the anger that welled up in him. He grabbed the front of her blouse and pushed her against the wall. Nico put his hand on Pauling's shoulder but it was shaken off. "Get in the car," Pauling ordered. Nico backed off, and Pauling, his face inches from Celia's, said, "I'd have no problem killing you right now."

The smirk on her face only further infuriated him. He shook her by the blouse but the grin remained. "Why?" he asked. "You killed McCullough and set me up to take the fall. *Why?*"

"Get your hands off me, Max." The smirk was gone, replaced by a venomous stare. "I did what I had to do. Sorry if it caused you any inconvenience. We are at war against Castro, Max. There are no rules, no allegiances if they get in the way of winning. You got what you wanted. You can leave here and forget it ever happened. Unfortunately, we can't do that."

He released his grip on her and drew a deep breath, which carried the sweet scent of her up to him. He shook his head. "Why McCullough, Celia. For who? Who?"

"Does it matter? He couldn't be allowed to steal from the Cuban people and line Castro's pockets."

"Christ, what about the information I'm taking back to Gosling? That would have been enough to kill McCullough's deal without killing *him*."

She looked into his eyes for what seemed a very long time, and although no words were said, he knew what she was thinking, that she was living in a different world, a world he once occupied but one that no longer consumed him. For him, there were no causes left. For him, the challenge to which she responded had faded from his life.

"The money for Nico. You have it?" she asked.

"Yes, I have it."

"One day, when this is over, perhaps we can sit down together and discuss it. Have you forgotten? Have you been away from it so long that you have forgotten expediency and the need for it, urgency that breaks all the rules between people? I didn't want to hurt you, Max, but I'm not sorry that I did. Enough of this. For now, concentrate on leaving Cuba."

She walked away, disappearing into fog that had rolled in off the water. Pauling almost went after her. He wanted that discussion with her now. He wanted answers, didn't want to leave Cuba without them. But he knew that wasn't about to happen.

Nico stood next to the open rear door of the Cadillac.

"Get in," Pauling said, and joined David in the front seat. "Santa Maria del Mar," he said. "And don't talk to me."

It took David ten minutes to get the Caddy started: "We need oil," he said.

"Just get us there," Pauling said. "You can junk this thing after we're gone and buy something else."

They chugged along the coastal road, loud, constant

backfires startling everyone in the car, the engine hacking like a sumo wrestler with bronchitis. Police vehicles passed in the opposite direction but paid them no attention. Pauling didn't bother scrunching down in his seat. He wore his hat low over his eyes, holding the Glock on his lap. No one spoke; only the engine's grumble intruded on his thoughts.

When they reached their destination, Joe instructed David to turn down a narrow residential street to a house at the end of a row of cottages. David didn't turn off the engine as Joe got out and disappeared into the cottage. A few minutes later he emerged with a tall, rangy young Cuban who spoke to David in Spanish. He, in turn, said to Pauling, "He will sell you the airplane for ten thousand, American."

"I don't . . . I want to see it first."

They piled into the car with David following verbal directions to a floating dock a thousand yards from what appeared to Pauling to be a string of seafront hotels. The fog had thickened, but he could see the vague outline of an aircraft bobbing in the water at the end of the dock. They got out of the Caddy and walked to where the plane was secured to the dock by mooring lines.

Pauling pulled on the lines and brought the plane against the dock. He handed the lines to David and said, "Keep it close. Does he have the keys?"

The lanky Cuban handed a set to Pauling, who opened the door on the left side of the plane and slipped into the seat. He fumbled in his vest, found a small penlight, and played it over the instrument panel. The plane was a very old Cessna Stationair. The panel was crusted with dirt and nicotine; he moistened his fingertips and cleaned the glass on some of the gauges. He trained the light on the front passenger seat. The gray fabric was ripped as though a large cat had run its claws over it. The way an aircraft looked cosmetically was a clear tip-off as to how it had been maintained mechanically, he knew. But he wasn't there looking to buy the best used airplane on the lot. All he could do was hope that the engine turned over and the plane didn't, and that it had enough left in it to travel the ninety miles to Miami.

He inserted the key and turned it. The engine seemed to think about it, made a few false starts, then coughed to life, turning the prop in fits and starts before smoothing out and sending it into a continuous circle, shaking the craft and causing its ancient fittings to creak and whine in protest. He checked the fuel gauge; half a tank in each wing, enough for the trip unless they were forced to make a wide detour. Or, if the fuel had been sitting in the tanks for months and had become diluted from condensation . . . He asked about it when he got out, the engine idling, and joined the others on the deck.

"Not so old," the plane's owner said of the fuel. "New. Last week."

And I'm Fidel Castro, Pauling thought. It didn't matter. The plane, and its questionable fuel, was the only game in town. "Ten thousand is too much," he told David, who passed it on to the plane's owner. "It's old, probably doesn't have a hundred hours left on the engine. Two thousand."

They bickered back and forth, with David in the middle as occasional translator. Finally, the owner suggested four thousand, and Pauling agreed. It was still an outrageous price for the plane, but every minute spent haggling was a minute longer in Cuba.

"Ready, Nico?" he asked.

"Yes. I am ready."

"I have the money for you. I'm trusting that what you have in that briefcase is worth it."

"It is, Señor Pauling. Trust me."

Pauling didn't express his feelings about trust at that moment. He handed David one of the four bundles of bills he carried and told him to take care of his friends with it. "I got lucky getting in your taxi, David," he said. "You're a good man. Hang in there. This place will be free one of these days and—" He grinned and stroked his chin. "And he'll be gone."

"Good luck, buddy," David said, gripping Pauling's hand and shaking it vigorously.

"You, too."

Nico and Pauling climbed into the Cessna. Nico's seat belt had been severed, and Pauling's wouldn't extend far enough to buckle. Pauling reached to turn on the running lights, assuming they worked, but decided not to. There was no telling whether police boats might be out there in the fog. Of course, that same fog posed another problem. Pauling had no idea what was beyond his hundred-foot field of vision. Were there buoys out there with boats tethered to them, or floating debris? He reached into his vest, pulled out the *collar,* rubbed it, and hung it on a knob on the instrument panel. Not smashing into something during takeoff would be pure luck.

The owner of the plane, anticipating Pauling's need, untied the two ropes from the aircraft and pushed it away from the dock. It floated freely out into the water. There hadn't been the time or opportunity to conduct an external inspection of the plane, nor to run down a preflight checklist, things about which Pauling had always been meticulous. But that wasn't his biggest concern at the moment. He ran through a mental recounting of the few hours of floatplane instruction he'd received years ago while on assignment for the CIA in Florida. It wasn't totally unlike flying a land-based plane, but there were some differences. The floats on which the plane rested had water rudders at the rear to help control taxiing while in the water. The elevator trim on a seaplane had to be set to give the control yoke neutral pressure, and unlike on a runway where the aircraft remains fixed until power is applied, the water currents continually keep a floatplane moving, often in a direction away from the one intended by the pilot. He knew that the key to taking off was to get the aircraft up on its floats in the proper planing position to minimize resistance from the water.

This night, he realized, had certain advantages. The wind was calm, as was the water. With any luck—he touched the *collar* again—they'd make it into the air. The craft didn't have navigation instruments except for a simple compass, which would have to suffice. He looked at Nico, whose expression was one of extreme discomfort. "All set?" he asked.

"I think so," the Cuban replied.

Pauling slowly advanced the throttle. The plane trembled like a corrugated tin house in an earthquake, but began its taxi into open water. Pauling looked back at the dock where David and the two others watched. "Thanks," he muttered as he advanced the throttle and made a determination as to which direction to take off. It made almost no difference because of the lack of wind. Had there been a breeze, he would have taken off into it to increase lift on the wings.

"We will be okay?" Nico asked.

Pauling flashed him a reassuring smile. "Nothing to it, Nico. Piece o' cake, as we Americans say."

He pushed the throttle to the firewall and the plane began to move, slowly and laboriously. The floats attached to the belly of the plane in place of wheels fought to gain speed against the water's resistance. Pauling felt the plane lift a little, and soon it had achieved the requisite planing attitude to allow gathering speed. "Come on, come on," he exhorted the craft, raising himself slightly off the seat as though to add buoyancy to the process. The water was less calm farther from the shore, and small swells slapped against the floats. Pauling peered into the fog. "Almost there, baby," he said over the engine's roar. "Come on, come on, get up, get up."

The aircraft's floats lifted clear of the water. As they did, lights appeared in the distance. It was a boat, a sizable one, and it was heading straight for the plane, which was only five feet off the water. Pauling pulled the yoke back into his crotch and held it there as the approaching lights raced closer. Pauling could now see that it was a military boat. A searchlight swung around and flooded the cockpit with a blinding glare. Pauling closed his eyes against it, filled his lungs with air, and waited for the collision.

It didn't happen. The plane's floats missed the patrol boat's cabin by a foot, spraying water over the deck and sending the Cuban sailors sprawling.

Pauling exhaled, and turned to Nico, who forced a smile.

"Like you said, Max—a piece o' cake."

Walden was in the Oval Office. On the desk in front of him were two photographs and a typewritten series of "talking points" provided for him earlier in the day after a lengthy meeting with CIA director George Brown. Paul Draper sat across the room at a table on which rested one of two extensions of the president's secure line. The phone rang. National Security Advisor Draper picked it up, listened, placed his hand over the mouthpiece, and said, "Mr. President, President Castro is on the line."

Walden picked up the phone on his desk. "This is President Walden, Prime Minister Castro."

A translator said in English, "Prime Minister Castro is ready to speak with you, Mr. President."

"Good. I appreciate this opportunity to communicate directly with you," Walden said. "You are well, I assume."

Translator: "Yes, I am extremely well, Mr. President. And you?"

Walden: "Quite well, thank you. I asked for this conversation because of the serious situation that exists regarding the unfortunate attempt on your life, and the death of my very good friend Senator McCullough. To get right to the point, Mr. Prime Minister, I have before me irrefutable proof that the American you've been looking for, Maxwell Pauling, did not have any role in the attempt on your life. In fact, he was the one who saw the gunman pull the weapon and knocked it from his hand. I have been given by our intelligence officials photographs of Mr. Pauling performing that act."

Walden's words were translated for Castro, and the Cuban dictator responded.

Translator: "Your Mr. Pauling is a CIA operative sent here to disrupt my government and to attempt to take my life. In addition, he took the life of your friend and former senator."

Walden: "That is not true, Mr. Prime Minister. I have been assured by the highest echelons of our intelligence community that Pauling had nothing to do with either event." He consulted the notes on his desk. "His connection with that agency ended years ago. Until retiring from government service, Mr. Pauling was with our State Department as an analyst, not the CIA. He is a private citizen who teaches flying in New Mexico. Mr. President, we will get nowhere making claims and counterclaims. I am fully aware that you and Senator McCullough met, and during that meeting, Senator McCullough expressed certain views of mine."

The translator repeated in Spanish.

Walden: "I am also aware that during that meeting, Senator McCullough entered into a private business arrangement with you. His untimely death obviously affects that arrangement, but does not necessarily mean it must be canceled. Once the shock of his death is eased, I believe those now in leadership positions at his company will be able to resurrect your agreement with him. That is not my concern, however. That represents a private business agreement. But as president of the United States, I wish to inform you that should you go through with what I'm told are plans to exploit the capture of Pauling,

any progress that's been made to date regarding the embargo, as well as other elements of the relationship between Cuba and the United States, will necessarily be
abandoned. In short, Mr. Prime Minister, unless you
withdraw your charges against Mr. Pauling and the CIA,
acknowledge that Senator McCullough was murdered by
one of your citizens—perhaps someone as demented as
the man who tried to shoot you—and drop your plans to
make a political statement over this, the direction that
our administration will be forced to take will not be to
your benefit or to the benefit of the Cuban people."

Walden and Draper listened impassively as Castro
launched into a lengthy sermon on the moral bankruptcy
of the United States, grandiose plans for Cuba's future,
and myriad other issues, some of which caused Walden
and Draper to glance at each other and smile. When the
Cuban dictator had finished the tirade, the translator
asked whether Walden had anything else to say.

Walden: "No, I'm quite finished. We'll be awaiting the
Prime Minister's official response to what I've proposed."

With the conversation completed, Walden asked his
national security advisor, "What do you think, Paul?"

"Castro is volatile and unreasonable. We all know
that. But he's not insane. He's also a savvy politician. I
think he'll weigh using Pauling as a propaganda tool ver-
sus not derailing his deal with Senator McCullough and
BTK Industries, or your efforts to bring us closer to some
sort of rapprochement. The Pauling thing will come and
go, like the downing of our U-2, the Bay of Pigs, and all
the other tensions we've experienced with Castro over
forty years. No, Mr. President, I think he'll come
around."

"I think so, too. I'm putting my faith in George Brown
and his assurances that this Pauling didn't kill Price. He
wouldn't be specific with me about how he knows, but he

said without hesitation or qualification that it wasn't Pauling who pulled the trigger."

"Did he indicate who might have?"

"No, although I haven't the slightest doubt that he knows. My money is on one of the Cuban-Americans from Miami."

"That doesn't rule out the CIA, Mr. President. We know they provide all sorts of support to those anti-Castro groups."

"Yes. And, Paul, you know the importance of keeping the McCullough business deal in this room. The Republicans, and the public, might misconstrue my support of it."

"Of course, Mr. President."

"Ironic, isn't it?"

"What is, sir?"

"I backed Price's attempt to buy Cuba's cancer research because it would bring to this country the latest advances against the disease. Better to have the United States come up with hope for cancer patients than Castro and his dictatorship."

"Without a doubt, sir."

"The defection of Dr. Caldoza will accomplish the same thing, won't it? If I'd known that was a possibility, I would have dissuaded Price from trying to make his deal. The NIH is the logical place for Caldoza to continue his work, more logical than Price's private company. I wish he hadn't lost his life over it, but it turns out better for America."

"Yes, sir."

"No hitch in the plan for Caldoza to come here with his wife and seek asylum?"

"None, sir. Your wishes have been made known to all appropriate authorities."

"Good. Wait'll Castro hears that." The president

laughed. "As much as I'd like to get something good and solid nailed down with Castro before leaving office, there is a certain pleasure in sticking it to Fidel. Let me know the minute you hear the next howl from Havana."

"Yes, sir."

The call came to Draper two hours later from the Cuban foreign affairs minister, Diego Vasquez.

"I am calling to inform you," Vasquez said in measured tones, reading from a prepared statement, "that we have apprehended the person who murdered Senator Price McCullough. The perpetrator is a Cuban citizen, a known enemy of our Socialist government, who has been wanted for crimes against the state for some time. He has been taken into custody and will face indictment by the People's Supreme Court of the Independent Socialist Republic of Cuba. Prime Minister Fidel Castro has been personally involved in resolving this tragic matter, and is to be commended for his efforts. A statement of appreciation from the most senior possible representative of your government will be highly appropriate."

Draper hung up and smiled. *The president will be pleased,* he thought. A less pleasant contemplation was the fate of whomever the Castro government had decided to charge with Price McCullough's murder. He would be found guilty, of course, and shot.

He dialed the president's private number in the First Family's quarters.

Chapter 50

New Mexico

Jessica Mumford joined Max Pauling on the deck.

"Who was that?" he asked, referring to a phone call she'd taken inside some ten minutes ago.

"Annabel."

"How is she?"

"She and Mac are fine. She asked for you."

"What did you tell her, that the fugitive is resting comfortably?"

She sat next to him and placed her hand on his arm. "You're not a fugitive any longer, Max."

"I wonder why. One minute the whole Cuban government is after me for killing McCullough, the next minute they're crowing about having caught the real killer, some poor Cuban slob who's taking the rap."

He'd decided upon returning to New Mexico to tell Jessica everything, including his belief that Celia Sardiña had murdered McCullough. In his former incarnations with the CIA and State, he returned from assignments tight-lipped, offering nothing to any woman in his life of the moment, no details, just, "The assignment went okay. Glad it's over."

But he no longer felt the obligation to remain silent. And so he'd filled her in on every step of his adventure in Cuba. He began with the flight to Pittsburgh and time

spent with Doris and her new husband; the trip to
Miami; meetings there with Vic Gosling; the twin-engine
plane and his flight to Cuba via Colombia; Blondie and
Grünewald; his arrest; the attack on him at the hotel;
finding McCullough's body; evading authorities; the visit
to the part-time prostitute's apartment; lucking out with
the taxi driver, David; Nico and what he'd dug up for Signal Labs; the harrowing flight in the battered floatplane
to Miami with Nico; and, of course, Celia.

"But you don't know with certainty that Celia killed
McCullough," Jessica offered.

"You mean I didn't watch her pull the trigger? She
killed him, Jess. I don't know who ordered the hit—CIA,
anti-Castro groups in Miami—I don't know that. But she
acted on somebody's orders and murdered him."

"And tried to frame you."

"Yeah."

"Why?"

"Because I was there."

"On her own? Or on someone's order?"

He shrugged.

"She didn't need to set someone up, did she?" Jessica
asked.

"McCullough was shot in the apartment she was
using, Jess. She probably promised sex to entice him there
and killed him. The apartment's an agency safe house,
I'm sure. No record of tenants or owners. That's the way
they work. I think back on it and realize she didn't seem
to know anyone in her building or even the neighborhood. But they could have I.D.'d her. She knew I was a
known entity with the Cuban police. Made sense to her,
I suppose, to shine the light on someone else. I was an
easy target."

"You."

"Yeah. Me. I just don't know."

He didn't continue to share his musings with her. The possibility that someone at Langley had ordered Celia to arrange for Max Pauling to take the fall wasn't far-fetched. He'd seen that scenario before, when he was one of them, when an *individual* within the CIA—not the agency itself—had concocted a plan to frame him. That was the problem with the CIA, he knew, so many secretive cells with separate agendas, so many rogue characters operating in the shadows—to explain it to her would only create apprehension, even fear.

She sensed and respected his further silence on the subject, and changed it. "You were telling me about this young man Nico," she said. "Was he—?" The ringing phone sent her inside again.

He'd managed to navigate the elderly Cessna Stationair to Miami despite a series of mechanical problems that promised to land them in the drink a half-dozen times, and put down at a private floatplane marina near Fort Lauderdale. Nico knew precisely where he was to go in Florida and wasted little time thanking his pilot for the flight and the money, and wishing him well. He handed over the briefcase, got in a cab, and was gone. Pauling had wanted to pump him about Celia, but the opportunity never materialized, not while having to virtually force the plane to remain in the air for the entire flight to Miami, and then experiencing Nico's quick getaway once they'd arrived.

He had called a number given him by Gosling, which connected him with the Cell-One London office.

"I'm calling Victor Gosling. Please tell him that his pilot is back in Miami and that I'll try him again."

Aware that he was an accused murderer in the States, too, he took a taxi to the closest motel, checked in under an assumed name, and called Jessica.

"God, I was so worried about you," she said. "Where are you?"

"Florida. I just got here. I need some sleep. I'll fly back first thing in the morning."

"You're all right?"

"Yeah, I'm all right."

"They're still saying you're wanted for Senator Mc-Cullough's murder," she said, lowering her voice as though that might keep anyone from hearing it over the line.

"I know," he said. "I'll be careful. I didn't kill him, Jess. You know that."

"Of course I know that. I love you, Max."

"You're probably the only person in the world who does right now," he said.

He lifted off in his Cessna 182S before daybreak and set a course directly for New Mexico, stopping only to refuel at small airports where the authorities weren't likely to be waiting. As he neared the airstrip where he taught flying, he decided to forego it and use a field thirty miles away, reasoning that those who knew him at his home base nearest the condo would have been contacted by the FBI. He called Jessica from the alternate airport, gave her the location of a pay phone from which to call him back in the event their home phone had been tapped, told her his location on the second call, and she picked him up there. The FBI and local police had indeed visited the condo, but seemed to be operating on the belief that he was still in Cuba. In a sense, the Cuban broadcasts about him had perpetuated that faulty assumption on the part of U.S. law enforcement.

"You didn't have to divert to this field, Max," she said the minute he got in the car. "You're cleared. No one is after you. The Cubans announced they've caught Senator

McCullough's killer. He's a Cuban, a fugitive from Castro's cops for other crimes."

Just like that, he thought. Another patsy, this one Cuban, a deal struck somewhere, with someone. He didn't even try to understand the forces at play. He was just glad to be home.

Jessica had received many phone calls while Max was flying from Miami to New Mexico. Victor Gosling phoned and left a number where he could be reached, day or night. Tom Hoctor called and asked that Max return his call. And there had been dozens of messages from media wanting an interview regarding McCullough's murder. Mainly, the reporters wanted to know how he'd ended up being accused of assassination and forced to flee Fidel Castro. Once at home, Max ignored the media calls. But, after a slow drink, he did phone Gosling. They agreed that Gosling would fly to Albuquerque, and that Max would meet his flight. Gosling had suggested that he visit the condo to pick up the briefcase, but Pauling declined. "I'll meet you at the airport, Vic," he'd said, "and give you the bag. Then you take the next flight out of here, to anywhere."

Gosling arrived the next day on a flight from Washington, D.C., and was met by Pauling. He handed over the briefcase.

"The documents aren't that important now that McCullough is dead," Gosling said, "but we'd still like to have them in case his successor decides to resurrect things. You gave me quite a scare, being accused of killing him and all that. I'm glad you're home safe. Nice job, Max. The balance of the money is on its way to your bank."

"Do you know why McCullough was killed?" Pauling asked as they stood at the arrival gate. "Who ordered it?"

Gosling feigned being offended. His hand went to his

heart and his brow was deeply creased. "How would I know something like that, Max?"

"Who gave Celia Sardiña the order?"

Gosling's sigh was equally disingenuous. "Max, I suggest you check in at some posh spa and get some rest."

Pauling ignored the comment. "Celia killed McCullough, Vic. She was working for you, and for Langley."

"Then it must have been our former employer, Max. As we both know, you simply can't trust anything they say or do. Are you sure I can't spend a few hours with you and your lovely lady friend? I almost feel as though you're angry with me. Don't be. We've shared too many experiences for that to happen."

"Do you know why she tried to set me up for the murder, Vic?"

"She must have been angry with you, Max." Gosling smiled.

The Brit's flippancy came close to earning him a fist in the face. There were many things Pauling wanted to say, few of them complimentary. He settled for, "So long."

His phone conversation with Hoctor was equally brief.

"I should be furious with you, Max," Hoctor said, his small, nasal voice penetrating Pauling's ear. "You sullied my reputation with our Interests Section in Havana. I convinced them to let me come get you myself. I told them we went back a long way, and that you'd happily leave with me."

"To lead me to one of those cars parked at the corner," Pauling said.

"I suppose you're feeling pretty good about yourself, getting out of Cuba on your own, and being cleared by Castro of the murder."

"I always feel good about myself, Tom. That's why I'm such good company."

He almost asked Hoctor the same questions he'd asked Gosling about McCullough's murder, who'd ordered it, and why he'd been framed, but knew it would be wasted breath.

"I have to get off, Tom. This is a busy day for me. I have to nap."

"Yes, I'm sure it is. By the way, in case you've been worrying about whether your lady friend's door was left open after you ran out the back, I closed it."

Pauling said, smiling, "I appreciate that, Tom. You're a hell of a guy."

"Keep in touch, Max. You never know when we'll need each other again. To close a door—or open one."

"Who was that?" Pauling asked when Jessica rejoined him on the deck.

"Roberta. From my bird-watching group. She wondered whether I'd like to go on a watch next weekend."

"And?"

"I said no. I want to spend all my time watching you."

"Go ahead," he said. "I know how much you love it."

"Not as much as I love this bigger-than-life character named Max Pauling. You've taken years off my life—but made it sweeter." She wondered what he was thinking but didn't intrude. He'd been so open after arriving home, more than she'd ever experienced with him before. But once he'd spun his tale about having been in Cuba and everything that had ensued, he'd fallen silent again, not sullen, never unpleasant, but closed, guarded, insular.

"Sure you wouldn't mind if I go with Roberta?"

"Not at all, sweetheart."

What he'd been thinking at that moment was what he'd been thinking ever since leaving Cuba. *Celia Sardiña*. Would he ever have that chance to sit with her and learn the truth? He doubted it. All he knew was that she would enter his thoughts every day, at odd moments, and probably for the rest of his life. He wondered where she was, what she was doing, and who she was doing it to. Would she affect other men as she did him? Of course. He hadn't the slightest doubt that she'd murdered Price McCullough, and had set him up to take the fall.

Would she be willing to kill again for the Cuban cause? Or for some other cause?

Could she live comfortably with herself for the rest of *her* life as someone who killed strangers for causes, looked them in the eye and pulled the trigger, a smile on her lovely lips, a hot temperament but blood so cold that ice wouldn't melt in her mouth?

He knew the answer. Chances are she would marry, have children, and assign the murderous portion of her life to that segment of the brain in which youthful indiscretions, faddish teen behavior, and hurtful lies are relegated.

Like himself.

How did you feel when you killed him?"

"How did I *feel*?"

"Yes."

"I—I didn't especially feel anything."

"Nothing? Not a moment of doubt? Of guilt?"

"No."

"Did you know him?"

"I knew of him."

"Meaning?"

"I knew who he was. I knew *what* he was."

"What was his reaction?"

A bemused raised eyebrow preceded, "He didn't have time to react. It's the best way."

"I see." He added to notes he'd been making. "How do you feel now?"

"Fine."

"Trouble sleeping? Nightmares?"

"Of course not."

The sound of a window air conditioner gently bridged the lull.

"You'll be gone for two months," he said. "On leave."

"Yes."

"Where will you go?" he asked, knowing it was a question that would not be answered. His was not a need-to-know.

Silence.

He made another note and closed the black leather portfolio resting on his lap. "Thank you for coming in."

After watching her departing figure, great legs and all, he opened the portfolio and stared for a moment at the name on the file. Celia Sardiña. He wrote CLEARED, which reflected his psychiatric judgment, closed it, went to a safe in a corner of the austere room, opened it, placed the folio inside, closed the door, spun the wheel, checked the door, then returned to his desk and dialed a number.

"I'm leaving," he said. "See you at home."

He left the building and got behind the wheel of his black Jeep Cherokee. If the traffic cooperated, he'd be in time to catch the final few innings of his son's Little League game. Usually, as a psychiatrist cleared by the Central Intelligence Agency to treat that agency's operatives and to do an assessment following any assignment in which the operative had been called upon to kill, he had trained himself to immediately forget about the interview and the person. But this woman was different. She was terrifically appealing, bewitchingly beautiful, and smart—a degree in biochemistry—analytical, and in control of her emotions.

Who had she killed on behalf of the agency? Where? Why? What had the victim done to prompt it? Where would Ms. Sardiña go on her two-month mandatory leave? And after that, would she ever be called upon to kill again, and do so without hesitation?

Strange people, those who work undercover, he thought as he pulled into a parking space next to the ball field. His son's team, in their green shirts and baseball hats, was at bat. The boy stepped into the batter's cage as his father reached the long wooden bench on which other parents sat.

"Come on, Joey!" he shouted, hands cupped around his mouth. "Good eyes, son. Take a good cut."

His eyes followed the ball as it left Joey's bat, shot between the third baseman and shortstop, and rolled to the outfield fence.

Travel guides claim that the average high temperature in
Washington, D.C., in September is seventy-nine degrees
Fahrenheit. But on this particular Tuesday, the day after a
long Labor Day weekend, the thermometer read eighty-one
at seven in the morning, which meant ninety was a possibility by noon, a hell of a time for Johnny Wales's air conditioner to decide to crash. It had ground to a halt
sometime during the night; it had to have been between two
in the morning when Wales returned from a night of drinking with his buddies, and five A.M. when he was awakened
by the sound of the vintage window unit seizing up.

He rolled his sticky body out of bed at seven and stood
in front of an oscillating table fan, raising his arms to
allow the moving air to wash over his nakedness. Under-
standably, his mood was palpably foul; his mutterings
were mostly four-lettered as he poured orange juice,
washed down a handful of vitamins, and entered the
shower. The weather was bad enough, and you couldn't do
anything about that. But Bancroft's early crew call at
Ford's was arbitrary. What was the big deal? he wondered
as he readjusted the faucets to add cooler water to the mix.
It was only a teenage drama workshop production.

As he moved about getting ready in his room above an
army-navy store on Ninth Street, not far from the Capitol
City Brewing Company, the final stop on last night's toot,
and only a few blocks from Ford's Theatre, where he'd

been employed as a stagehand for the past two years, his size—six feet four inches tall and 220 pounds—made the cramped studio apartment seem smaller. He pulled on a faded pair of blue jeans, Washington Redskins T-shirt, slipped tan deck shoes over bare feet, attached a black fanny pack to his waist, and checked himself in the mirror. Building and erecting stage sets hadn't been his ambition when graduating from the University of Wisconsin seven years ago. He'd been a leading man in university productions, a big, handsome guy who might make it in Hollywood one day if the chips fell right. He'd tried that for a year, but left Tinsel Town weary of failure and wary of tinsel and followed a girlfriend to Washington, where his stagecraft courses at Wisconsin landed him after a while membership in the union and a job at the theatre. It wasn't acting, but at least it was showbiz: No jokes about following circus elephants with shovels, thank you.

He stopped at a Starbucks, eschewing an effete latte at scandalous prices for a large coffee light and sweet, and walked through the stage entrance of Ford's Theatre at precisely eight. His pique at having to be there early was eased by the welcome blast of AC. A uniformed park ranger stood backstage with some of Wales's fellow stagehands, drinking coffee and laughing about something. The ranger in the drab brown uniform was one of many who would conduct hourly, fifteen-minute lectures for tourists later that day as they wandered into America's most infamous theatre, the place where, not playacting, Abe Lincoln had been shot to death by the actor John Wilkes Booth.

"Hey, big guy, good weekend?"

"Yeah," Wales said, leaning against a piece of stage furniture and sipping his coffee. "Over too soon." A pulsating headache had developed between leaving the apartment and arriving at the theatre. No sense mentioning it; he wouldn't get any sympathy anyway. "Where's Sydney?"

"Who cares?"

"I care," said Wales. "He called this stupid meeting."

"Don't speak ill of the famous Bancroft," someone said.

"Screw the famous Sydney Bancroft," Wales said, pressing fingertips to his temple. "Besides, he's not famous anymore. He *was* famous."

"I sense a hangover, Johnny."

Wales laughed. "You sense it, I feel it."

"Snap to. Our leader has arrived."

Attention turned to an open yellow door linking the theatre to the adjacent attached building in which the Ford's Theatre Society offices were housed. While the National Park Service maintained the theatre as an historic site, it was the nongovernmental Ford's Theatre Society that used the venue to mount its ambitious schedule of theatrical productions. Heading that society, and coming through the door, was the theatre's producing director, Clarise Emerson, a former Hollywood TV producer who'd been recruited three years earlier to replace the departing Frankie Hewitt. Hewitt had been brought in almost thirty-five years before by then Secretary of the Interior Stewart Udall to help develop a plan for the theatre following its most recent renovations, and to choreograph fund-raising efforts. Hewitt was a tough act to follow. The former wife of *60 Minutes* producer Don Hewitt, Frankie had guided Ford's Theatre from being solely a government museum chronicling the Lincoln assassination to one of America's preeminent resident theatres, a living tribute to Lincoln's well-known love of the performing arts. More than twenty musicals had received their world premieres there since the beautifully restored theatre opened in January 1968, many moving on to Broadway. And hundreds of plays had been performed, all adhering to Ford's stated mission: "To produce musicals and plays that embody family values, underscore multiculturalism, and illuminate the eclectic character of American life."

"*Dull* theatre!" some critics said.

Certainly noncontroversial. Avant-garde playwrights need not apply. Nothing to ruffle the feathers of members of Congress who decided how much to include for the theatre in the yearly congressional budget, particularly eighty-six-year-old Alabama Senator Topper Sybers, chairman of the Senate Committee on Labor and Human Resources. Unlike some "reviewers" who never saw a play or painting or book they didn't like, Sybers had never seen a play or piece of art that wasn't lubricious. But Clarise had more than financial reasons these days for not wanting to provoke the elderly, feisty senator from Alabama. The president, Lewis Nash, Clarise's lifelong friend, had recently nominated her to chair the National Endowment for the Arts (NEA). Sybers's Labor and Human Resources Committee would conduct her confirmation hearing.

Clarise's appearance that morning was surprising to the assembled. She seldom set foot inside the theatre, delegating virtually every creative aspect to others. Her time was better spent, she often said, squeezing money out of wealthy patrons, individuals and corporations alike.

"Good morning," she said brightly to the half-dozen stagehands marking time.

" 'Morning, Clarise," they responded.

Because of her status on the Washington scene—not only was she a personal friend of the president and headed for the NEA, she'd once been married to Bruce Lerner, senior senator from Virginia, a handsome, sixty-year-old bachelor often seen on the arm of beautiful, high profile women—there was the natural tendency for younger people at Ford's to address her as Ms. Emerson. But she'd put an end to that shortly after taking up her post there, and everyone called her Clarise.

That she was youthful in appearance and manner helped. People took her to be considerably younger than fifty-four. Good genes had given her not only beauty but boundless energy. Clarise didn't walk, she moved at an almost constant trot, up on the balls of her feet, looking as though she might suddenly decide to become airborne. She stood military erect, like her father, who'd served twenty years in the air force, retiring to their small farm in Ohio to die of a coronary three years after exchanging his blue uniform for coveralls. She was in fact like her father, Luke Emerson, in almost all ways, physically and philosophically, except for her sense of humor, which was decidedly her mother's, a short, plump woman better suited to the role of farmer's wife than military spouse, subservient to her dour husband when in his presence, but wickedly prankish about him when chatting with women friends.

"Early start," Clarise said. "What's the occasion?"

"Sydney called a meeting," a stagehand said.

"Oh?"

"The teenage show," Wales said.

"Is there a problem with it?"

"Not that we know of, Clarise."

"Sydney's not even in town," she said.

"That's just terrific," Wales said, dropping his empty cup into a trash can. "Anybody got an aspirin?"

"Do you know why Sydney wanted a meeting?" Clarise asked.

Shrugs all around.

"Well, sorry you're here so early for nothing. I'll speak with Sydney when I see him."

Clarise turned and retraced her steps to the door connecting the buildings. The four men and one female apprentice watched her retreat from where they stood backstage, the men appreciating the attractive sway of her tall, lithe figure, a gazelle in an expensive, tailored gray pantsuit, neck-length reddish blond hair bobbing, hips moving in perfect rhythm with her long strides.

"That is one good-looking woman," the oldest of the stagehands said quietly. He'd been at Ford's for twenty-two years.

"Yeah, I've noticed," Wales offered.

"Hate to see her go," the older man said.

"Better Sydney should go," Wales said. "We going to hang around?"

"Might as well."

"I'm going out for a cigarette," Wales said. He'd cut back on his smoking, limiting himself to ten cigarettes a day, except when he was out drinking. He didn't keep count those occasions.

"I'll go with you," said the young female apprentice.

As Wales and the girl headed for a door at the rear of the stage leading to a narrow area behind the theatre called Baptist Alley, the older stagehand laughed and said to the others, "She hangs around Johnny like a puppy dog. Really got the hots for him."

"He could do worse. She's a fox."

"I'll take Clarise," the older man said. "Women aren't any good until they've got a little wear and tear on them."

"You'll 'take' Clarise'? Fat chance. She's strictly money and power."

"You never know," the older guy said, chuckling. "My wife's too good at homicide anyway. Let's put this furniture in place as long as we're here."

Wales and the girl, Mary, had paused at the door to the alley while he fumbled in the fanny pack for his cigarettes. "Just got ten," he said. "You owe me one."

She punched his arm and turned the security lock on the door.

"Got 'em," Wales said, retrieving the crumpled half pack and pulling two cigarettes from it.

"Every time I go through this door," she said, "I think of Booth."

"John Wilkes? Crazy bastard. Got his fifteen minutes of fame."

"He escaped through this door. He had his horse tied out in the alley."

"I know, I know. I've heard the tourist pitch a thousand times."

Wales grasped the doorknob and pushed on the door. It opened only a few inches. Something was blocking its way. He pushed harder, resulting in another inch or so.

"What the hell?" he muttered.

He leaned his body against the door and exhaled a rush of air as he tried again. This time the opening was wide enough through which to poke his head.

"What is it?" Mary asked.

He'd been looking straight ahead, up the long alley that forked left and exited onto F Street. He wedged his shoulder into the gap and twisted his head to look down at whatever was preventing the door from swinging open.

"What is it?" Mary repeated, envisioning some drunk sleeping it off against the door. Baptist Alley had become a downtown lovers' lane for couples looking for smooch time, drug addicts shooting up, or alcoholics deciding to nap.

"Jesus!"

"What is it?" she repeated.

"Jesus!"

"Johnny."

"It's Nadia," he managed, his voice raspy and higher than normal as though the horror on the dead girl's face had reached up and gripped his throat.